# ALL MY RELATIONS

To Geneva
Meeting you at Warren's party in New York was a pleasure. I hope we meet again — perhaps when I travel south. In the meantime, I hope you enjoy my first book
Fondly,
"Rhea"

# ALL MY RELATIONS

*Rhea Aquillo*

iUniverse, Inc.
New York Lincoln Shanghai

# All My Relations

All Rights Reserved © 2003 by Rhea Aquillo

No part of this book may be reproduced or transmitted in any form or by any means, graphic, electronic, or mechanical, including photocopying, recording, taping, or by any information storage retrieval system, without the written permission of the publisher.

iUniverse, Inc.

For information address:
iUniverse, Inc.
2021 Pine Lake Road, Suite 100
Lincoln, NE 68512
www.iuniverse.com

This is a work of fiction. Although it is set in actual towns in New York City and Long Island, all characters, relationships, and events portrayed are entirely imaginary.

Oh, Sister. Words by Bob Dylan and Jacques Levy. Music by Bob Dylan. Copyright © 1975 by Ram's Horn Music. All rights reserved. International copyright secured. Reprinted by permission.

ISBN: 0-595-28257-1

Printed in the United States of America

For Joan

# *Acknowledgements*

Many people have supported me in the writing of this book. In particular, I'd like to thank Leanne Staples for her enthusiasm, reading the manuscript so carefully, and pushing me to the final steps of publication. Thanks also to Owen Waite for taking the cover photos, and particularly for making the one I was having so much trouble with, the author photo, such a fun session. Thanks to Mary Yost for reading the manuscript and giving it cohesiveness and direction. And I'd like to thank my spunky, real-life sister Dominique, whose irrepressible personality provided such a rich character for me to put through paces that her real-life model would never have the time or inclination to even dream about. Finally, I'd like to thank Joannie who has continued to call me a writer and has given me the space to write.

# CHAPTER 1

Wispy white fingers of fog searched silently around the skeletal remnants of the cattails that protruded from the melting ice, seemingly grasping at straws, looking for signs of life. On that January afternoon, anyone who happened to be standing on Rivera Drive looking north toward the Long Island Sound would have seen the ghostly grey cloud floating toward the shore, covering everything in its wake with an impenetrable veil. The winding road, that followed the contours of the bay at sea level, was deserted.

Irene Adriatico often stood at the picture window of her clapboard, ranch-style house at dusk, specifically to watch the fog come in. She loved the fog. It was such a mystery; it never came in quite the same way. Some days it came in slowly, hesitating. Other days it came in quickly, like a bulldozer. As soon as it covered her front lawn and ensconced her house in its blanket of condensation, nothing, not even the road, which was less than ten yards away, could be seen from that picture window. On crisp, windy days, the fog did not come in at all. But on these winter evenings, when warmer air came in on the Gulf Stream and snow was still on the ground, the fog obliterated everything around her, and she felt like she was the only person in the comfort of a private and silent world.

But on this particular afternoon, Irene was not at her post. She had been working at her potter's wheel earlier in the afternoon when the doorbell rang. Wiping her hands on her loose smock-shirt, she tried not to get any clay in her short, jet-black hair as she picked her way to the front door from her studio. Passing through the dimly lit living room on that sunless afternoon, she avoided a stray sneaker in the doorway, a Hot Wheels track attached to the coffee table and a football lying in the middle of the living room. But as she passed the big bay window, she noticed that there was no car parked in the driveway or on the street.

"Joe." Her voice was indefinable as she opened the door to admit a man dressed all in black: black pants, black hiking boots, black scarf, black baseball jacket and black baseball cap. With intense, blue eyes, he took her into his gaze as he quickly stepped inside, and she closed the door behind him. With one arm, he grabbed her and kissed her. With his free hand, he removed his cap to reveal a head of shockingly bright blonde hair, which instantly fell forward over his left eye. He shoved the cap into his jacket pocket, and with a characteristic movement, pushed his hair back off his face. Because the back of his hair was short, this splash of color had been entirely hidden by the cap.

"God forgive me. I couldn't stay away. I…" Looking directly into his cobalt-blue eyes with her almost-black ones, she stopped his words with another kiss, deeper and more passionate than the first, and then wordlessly led him down the hallway to the master bedroom. At the door, he hesitated again, about to speak, but she stopped him, taking his hands and bringing them up under her smock. Whatever he was about to say was, for the moment, forgotten.

She pushed his jacket off his shoulders, and he pulled out his left arm first, and then the right, letting the jacket fall. He was still kissing her as she took off his scarf, revealing a cotton shirt with a Roman collar—the only part of his attire that was not black. She left the white square intact at his throat as she undid the buttons below it, revealing the light blonde hair on his chest.

Again, he took a breath, trying to say something between kisses. But she untied her wraparound skirt with nothing underneath. His body reacted and his words deserted him as they abandoned themselves to each other. In that moment the full wolf moon broke through the fog.

Later, in the darkness of twilight, as they sat at the edge of the bed, wordlessly reclaiming their clothes, they heard a car in the driveway, and then the sound of the garage door.

"Oh my god! He's not supposed to be home with the kids until nine," Irene's voice shook. Joe pulled on his pants, stepped into his shoes, and grabbed the rest of his clothes while Irene opened the storm window and screen on the back window. She helped him climb into the murky darkness that matched his work clothes. By the time she had closed the window, he was consumed in fog and darkness.

She lit two candles in the bedroom, and had the shower running when her husband walked in. As the former college linebacker crowded into the doorway, he loosened the knot in his tie. "Why the hell don't you ever turn on any lights?" Not turning any on himself, he threw his tie on the bed, and hung his suit jacket on the valet in the corner.

Irene smoothed the down comforter on the bed and then headed toward the door. "You're home early. I'm taking a shower."

"Your mother said she'd keep the kids until tomorrow," he called after her. "I'll pick them up on my way home from work. Hurry up with that shower."

He attacked her ravenously when she stepped out of the master bathroom in her black silk robe.

"Pino, wait," she protested.

Unheeding, he carried her to the bed. He did not notice her lack of response. He approached sex like he approached all the other aspects of his life—intensely, single-mindedly, with a goal in sight.

After it was over, he fell asleep, and Irene rolled over to her side of the bed. When she slipped her hand underneath the pillow, she felt something rough and unfamiliar. Pulling the object out, she could see it even without any lights. Its eerie whiteness was visible even on that moonless, foggy night.

She clutched the Roman collar while its owner, who had moved sure-footedly down the nature path through the woods, sat in his Dodge, which he had left at the far corner of the Old Dock Inn parking lot. His face was in his hands.

# CHAPTER 2

❀

"How ya doin'? My name is Veronique Adriatico. My friends call me Veronique. Rhymes with 'I'm unique.' Anyone who's known me since before I was ten calls me Ronnie. It's Ms. Adriatico to the rest of you. Only kidding. Not. If you don't fit into either of the other categories, you shouldn't be here.

"I told everyone I know that if they really loved me they would NOT give me a wedding shower. So my sister rents the fuckin' Old Dock Inn—sorry, Mom and Father—the *friggin'* Old Dock, and does a *This is Your Life.*"

Veronique was clearly delighted. She was in the spotlight, wearing a straight-cut, floor length, shimmering silver gown, slit up to the hip on the left side. Three-and-a-half-inch spike-heel shoes completed the outfit. Her raven hair was shining under the spotlight. Seated at round tables before the small stage, her friends and siblings enjoyed her delight.

At one table near the middle of the room the older generation was seated. Ronnie looked at "the happy trio"—Mom, Father and the priest. Seated next to them were her mother's mother and her father's brother and his wife. Unlike the others in the room, the occupants of this table did not laugh at the use of the obscenity. But Ronnie didn't care. This was her night, and she was not going to clean up her act, at least not too much, for anyone.

The room was decorated with balloons and birds of paradise. As she looked out the window opposite her, she could see the remnant of sunset—a deep red line on the horizon. And below it, she could see the lights of Connecticut across the Long Island Sound. She looked at the people sitting in clusters around the tables: her fiancé and her siblings at one table near the front, and several of her cousins at another table. Groups of friends, old and new, filled the rest of the seats in the banquet hall.

"Well, thanks for the recap of my life." Veronique continued. "Who would have believed so much could have gone on in twenty-five years? Yes, I must admit, I'm a quarter of a century old." There were groans and jeers from the audience. "I promised myself that I'd get married before the millennium, and, well, I just made it—New Year's Eve afternoon…Anyway, thanks to everyone who got up here and sang or talked or performed in some other way. I felt like my life was passing before me. Isn't that how you're supposed to feel when you're gonna die? Well, I promise, I'm not. But this wedding will be to die for." She smiled at the groom-to-be. "I can't wait. I want to thank everyone for showing up, and thanks especially to big sis Delfina and big bro Jon for setting the whole thing up…Okay, where's the deejay? Let's dance. Practice for the big day. It's tomorrow! I can't believe it." With a final whoop, to the applause of her friends, she abandoned the microphone for the dance floor, stepping off the stage, grabbing her future husband's hand, and leading him to the dance.

# CHAPTER 3

Organ music blared as Irene Adriatico ushered her small tribe down the aisle to the first pew in Saint Joseph's Roman Catholic Church. It was Easter Sunday, and Irene wanted to make sure they all got a seat together. All the twice-a-year Catholics would be in the church for High Mass, she knew, and she did not want to stand with three fidgety children for an hour and a half.

The huge wooden crucifix hung behind the white marble altar, which was decorated with hundreds of Easter lilies. Even the two side altars, one for The Virgin Mary on the left, and the other for Saint Joseph, patron saint of the parish, on the right, were covered with the fragrant white lilies. A row of the same lilies also lined the altar rail.

As ten-year-old Delfina Adriatico followed her mother up the aisle, she looked at Jesus on the cross, and thought again about having a moveable Jesus, since on Good Friday, Jesus was on the cross, and dying. But today was Easter Sunday, and by Easter, Jesus was supposed to be off the cross and alive again. So having him still on the cross was disconcerting. It had been disconcerting to her ever since she was old enough to realize that Easter meant that Jesus was no longer on the cross. Delfina had always hated the idea of nails in a person's hands and feet.

How could they make a moving Jesus, she wondered, one that was on the cross one day a year, but walking around on water, or preaching, or waving palm fronds, or all the other things Jesus did in his lifetime for the rest of the year? She was sure there was a way. Of course, the drawback was that then Jesus would have to go through the whole ordeal with the nails every year, whereas now he was permanently nailed. Either way, it was a problem.

Delfina, Irene's eldest child, had many thoughts like this. All of them went unspoken, but they flowed freely and unedited in her imagination almost constantly. Sometimes multiple thoughts simultaneously ran through her head. As she walked down the aisle thinking about Jesus and the cross problem, she also scanned the crowd at church, looking for redheaded Mrs. James, one of her favorite people in the whole wide world.

Delfina went first into the natural pine wood pew that had been selected by her mother. She immediately picked up the church bulletin, which declared on the front page, "Easter 1973—Welcome back to the flock." Absent-mindedly, she started to peruse the bulletin, thinking about welcome mats for sheep. Jonathan, three years younger than his sister, went into the pew next, and Irene followed, dragging four-year-old Marc behind her. Irene looked proudly at her offspring all dressed up in their Sunday best. The two older children had her jet black hair and eyes. Marc, the youngest, had his father's Northern Italian blue-eyed blonde looks, complete with dimpled cheeks. Delfina wore a print skirt and a white blouse that Irene had made for her. The boys wore suits and ties—little replicas of their father—who was walking regally down the aisle to join his family.

Delfina quickly lost interest in the bulletin, which Jonathan then grabbed from her. She observed the showy entrance of her father, Pino Adriatico, and wondered who needed to see him at church this week. Delfina knew that her father was definitely on display today. She could tell by the way he moved toward their pew.

A politician or a reporter, Delfina decided, as her father flashed his most congenial friend-to-everyone-in-the-community smile to someone in the pew behind them. Pino's wavy blonde hair, ocean blue eyes, dimpled cheeks and muscular, six-foot-four-inch athlete's body made everyone including Delfina's friends, say, "He's soooo cute."

She shrugged to herself. Delfina was not interested in her father's reasons for coming to church. She had her own reason. As the organ stopped, and the folk choir started playing, she slowly turned to look up to the choir loft, ostensibly to see who was playing. In fact, she was again scanning the ever-growing crowd as she had when she first walked in, looking for a particular face. Not seeing it, she turned to face forward, looking at the altar, and thought once more about the Jesus-on-the-cross problem.

But after a while, Delfina turned around again.

"Mrs. James is over there," Jonathan pointed, using a stage whisper, which Delfina felt could be heard to the furthest corner of the choir loft. Her ears burned. She couldn't help looking where he pointed, which was several rows back on the other side of the aisle. Sure enough, Mrs. James, Delfina's third grade teacher, was sitting with her husband. Her flaming red hair was a stark contrast to the white suits and dresses around her. She must have come in while Delfina was occupied with her technical Jesus dilemma. Now that she was in fifth grade, Delfina did not get to see much of Mrs. James, except at church functions. Mrs James' three red-headed children sat in the pew in front of their mother—no chance for Delfina to offer her seat to her former teacher. Much to Delfina's relief, neither Mrs. James nor anyone else seemed to have heard or noticed Jon.

"Shut up, stupid. I don't care who's here." For reasons unknown to her, Delfina was angry, and she was taking it out on Jon. Her brother rolled his eyes, shrugged good-naturedly, and returned to reading the bulletin.

"Do not call your brother names, especially not in Church." Irene had heard Delfina. At that moment, the crowd rose en masse for the entrance procession. As the choir and the faithful started a rollicking version of "Sing of Our God," an altar boy dressed in a red robe covered with a white cassock emerged from the back, carrying a large, dark, wooden cross on a pole. He was followed by another altar boy, also wearing a white cassock over his red robe, carrying a large, unlit, pastoral candle. Two more altar boys, identically clad, walking side by side, came next. Each was carrying two smaller, lit, white candles. The deacon followed them. He was dressed in a black suit, and he carried a Bible, which he held up in front of him, with the front facing the audience, so they could see that, yes, it really was the Good Book from which the celebrants were reading.

Finally, five priests walked slowly toward the altar in single file. They were all dressed in purple robes covered with white chasubles. On each priest's chasuble, the fine gold and white embroidery and tassels were slightly different, indicating their own personal garments.

Delfina turned and pretended to watch the procession, but she was really watching Mrs. James out of the corner of her eye.

Pino stood tall, a picture of intelligent reverence. Next to him, Irene inspected each priest that passed, musing that the Pastor had certainly pulled out the big guns for all the twice-a-year Catholics by having both the traditional choir and the folk choir for High Mass.

Father O'Hara came first, wearing the most simple of vestments. Next was Father Shannon, who worked nearby at the Saint Johnland Nursing Home. The brilliant gold in his robe reflected the rays of light streaming through the stained glass windows as he swayed down the aisle. The third priest was someone Irene had never seen before. Probably a visitor, she mused, making a mental note to find out more about him. His robe was simple, but she could see that it had been hand embroidered. What caught Irene's attention was that his blonde hair almost outshone the gold in Father Shannon's robe. He seemed to glance shyly at the people in the pews, making no eye contact, and pushing a shock of blonde hair off his forehead with his left hand from time to time as it fell forward into his eyes, while leaving his right hand in its vertical, prayerful position. The newcomer was followed by Father Reilly, the Assistant Pastor, whose vestment was almost iridescent in its opulent decorations. Father Patrick McMahon, the Pastor, was the last in the procession. He carried a brass urn of incense on a long, heavy, brass chain which clanged as he swung it to his right and left in a blessing, making his way through the still-growing throng that was beginning to crowd into the center aisle of the church.

The procession passed the pew where the Adriatico family was standing, and approached the altar, distributing itself evenly to the right and left, so that by the time Father Patrick reached the altar rail, the rest of the celebrants were symmetrically arranged in front of the altar, facing the congregation. Father Patrick enshrouded the altar in a cloud of incense, and then handed the long chain and urn to a waiting altar boy.

"In the name of the Father. And of the Son. And of the Holy Spirit," the Pastor intoned. Delfina reluctantly turned to face the altar as all five priests simultaneously karate-chopped the air in slow motion vertically, and then swatted the air horizontally with their right hands, in slow motion to their left and then their right, punctuating the four syllables of the nouns in the sign of the cross. Pino stood straight, and Irene signaled to Marc that he should imitate his father, which the child did to perfection. Irene knew that a well behaved family in church was a benefit to Pino, who had political as well as corporate aspirations. Irene also knew that a well behaved family in church was a credit to her as she was someone who often invited the celebrating priest to Sunday dinner.

When the mass was over, the family filed out the back of the church where the Pastor and other priests were greeting the parishioners. Father Patrick stopped to shake hands with Irene, and he pulled her aside.

"Happy Easter, Father."

"Happy Easter to you, Irene." The old man beamed at her kindly.

"We'll see you at dinner in forty-five minutes or so?"

"Yes. But, Irene, may I ask a favor? The new priest, Father Joe Clementine, he's been working on an Indian reservation out west for the past few years." The priest lowered his voice, "He's a Jesuit, you know." Then, resuming his normal tone, he continued, "Father Joe has been assigned here, um, temporarily. He doesn't have any family, and—"

"Of course, you should bring him to dinner," Irene interjected.

"You're very kind."

"Not at all. The more, the merrier. Please excuse me, Father. I've got to harvest Marc from your flower bed. I'll see you at two-thirty." With three quick strides, she was close enough to pluck Marc deftly from among the flowers, and carry him under her arm to the spot where the rest of the family was standing and talking with some other church goers.

❧    ❧    ❧

"And I have a riddle for you." Father Patrick was sitting at the Adriaticos' dining room table as Irene and Delfina were putting out the dishes for the Easter dessert. Along with the immediate Adriatico family at the long table were seated the two priests from St. Joseph's, Father Patrick McMahon and Father Joe Clementine, Irene's parents, Pino's brother, Otto, Otto's very pregnant wife, Ellie, and their baby, Lou.

"Some archeologists found the grave of the Holy Innocents. How did they tell the boys from the girls?"

"They had name tags," Jonathan guessed.

"Oh, I know," Delfina said suddenly.

"The boys had blue bows and the girls had pink?" Irene said, doubtfully.

"How could that be?" Irene's mother, Grace, asked. "It was an archaeological find. The ribbons would have disintegrated long before they were found."

Grace Lavazza was a petite woman with pure white hair and an imperious manner. She wore a gold wedding band and an engagement ring with a large sapphire on her left hand and a ruby set with diamonds on her right. She often gesticulated when she talked, in typical Italian fashion, flashing her rings to accentuate any point she was trying to make. Enrico, her husband of nearly forty-five years, was a gaunt, dark-complexioned man who spoke so rarely that most people thought of him as part of the backdrop for Grace's flamboyant, colorful life.

"Oh, I give up," Irene said, exasperated.

"What's the answer, Delfina?" Pino asked his daughter.

"There were no girls," Delfina said with finality.

"That's right." Father Patrick was duly impressed.

"That's Delfina's kind of joke," her mother said, starting to dish out the dessert. "Delfina, bring in some more napkins."

When the girl sat down at her place again, Father Joe, the new priest, said, "Had you heard that riddle before?"

She shook her head no as her mouth was full with mocha-filled seven-layer cake.

"Just figured it out logically?"

She gulped down the forkful of cake. "Well, they told us about the Holy Innocents in religious instruction, and so it just made sense."

"But nobody else guessed it."

"It's how you look at it, I guess. It's—I don't know—simple when you can see it right."

"I have a book that I think you'll enjoy. It's different kinds of logical puzzles. I used it when I taught Introduction to Logic a long, long time ago. I think you could do some of them."

"What grade did you teach?" Delfina had been wary of the newcomer at first, but his praise seemed genuine.

"I taught freshmen in college."

"You think I could read a college book?" Delfina was beginning to like this new priest more and more.

"We'll see. I'll—"

"Did you teach fresh women, too?" Delfina asked, trying to determine whether the men were fresh because they were new to college or because they talked back to their teachers.

Father Joe laughed. "Freshmen is a generic term that applies to anyone in his—or her—first year of something, college usually," he explained, confirming Delfina's thought that they were fresh because they were new.

"So freshman is like human. It means everybody?"

"Sort of. And actually," he continued, "a little bit in keeping with the Holy Innocents riddle, there were no women at Fordham College. They all attended Fordham's sister school, Cardinal Spellman."

"That was a waste of time," Delfina observed. "If they were all taught in the same place, the teachers wouldn't have to do their lessons twice."

"I agree," Joe nodded heartily, without explaining that the women often were not taught by the same professors. "Anyway, I'll bring the book over tomorrow, if that's okay with your mother," he added, as Irene came around with a tall, silver coffee pot.

"What was that?"

"I'd like to bring a book for Delfina. I was wondering if I could drop it off tomorrow."

"Dad's dropping us off at Grandma's tomorrow when he goes to work. We get to stay there for Easter vacation."

"I'll be going into the city tomorrow. Perhaps I can leave it for you."

"I'll be around all day," Irene said. "On the Monday after Easter, my mother takes the kids for three days, and I start my herbs and vegetables in the greenhouse."

"Not only does Irene keep this household going while looking after three active children, she also finds time to sew Delfina's clothes and maintain a greenhouse of prize orchids and day lilies. She's a professional potter, too." Father Patrick extolled Irene's virtues to his new associate.

"Irene's little hobbies keep her busy," Pino said offhandedly. "More wine, gentlemen?"

"No. Thank you, Pino," Father Patrick shook his head to himself. He did not like the way Pino shrugged off his wife's accomplishments. Father Patrick thought Irene was very gifted and creative, and Pino was a lucky man to have married such a good woman. Perhaps everyone has a cross to bear, the old priest philosophized. Maybe if he had married a very talented woman instead of entering the priesthood, he would have been threatened by her many gifts while he knew he had few. Maybe, too, part of what made Irene such a good woman was the cross she bore of her husband's disregard for her creativity. Neither of them had ever come to him with marital problems, so Father Patrick surmised that they worked it out somehow. Still, it hurt him to hear her husband belittle her in front of her children.

"Let's go into the drawing room for a drink," Pino interrupted Father Patrick's thoughts as he stood and ushered the priests and his other guests from the dining room.

At the age of forty, Pino Adriatico was on the brink of realizing all the plans he had been putting into place for the past decade. The fledgling computer company he had founded and built from the ground up was about to land its first government contract; he had just purchased a vineyard on the east end of Long Island; and there were rumblings about a political appointment by the Suffolk County Executive after the October elections.

In conservative Suffolk County, Long Island, Archangelo Giuseppino Adriatico, known to everyone as Pino, cultivated all the right contacts. He was a member of the Republican party, dined with the right families, and lived a model life, complete with his attractive and accomplished wife and three smart, well behaved children. Of course, because two of his children were sons, he was justified in being on the three side of having two-point-five children. He enjoyed the companionship of the priests his wife invited to Sunday dinner. They provided intellectual stimulation and peer kinship which he did not find with his associates at the office.

As the boss, at work Pino found that very few of the people were willing to speak their mind to him. At home, his wife merely tolerated him, mostly because of his disdain for her "woman's work," as he thought of it. The sense of companionship had gone out of their marriage with the birth of their third child, which coincided with the beginning of Pino's ascent up the professional and political ladder. The priests were willing to speak frankly to him. Yet Pino, being somewhat disdainful of the priesthood as a life choice, subconsciously felt slightly superior to the clergy who were his guests. This sense was enhanced as he offered them fine food and wine in his well appointed home, which sat at the edge of the Long Island Sound. These things Pino offered freely; the fact that the priests could not reciprocate merely stoked Pino's already well cultivated ego.

The two priests, Grace, Enrico and Pino sat down in the plush chairs of the drawing room, which overlooked the water. This room featured a large bay window with a red velvet-covered window seat. Looking out of the window, one could see that the house was separated from the water by a narrow road and small beach that bordered a marsh leading to an inlet that was not visible from the house. In the drawing room, which also served as the library, one wall was covered with floor-to-ceiling mahogany bookshelves. The span of the shelves was interrupted only by the double entrance doors. The regular bindings of the Encyclopedia Britannica and the Penguin classics were at eye level. The books that were not part of a collection were on lower shelves. Oversized picture books of art, nature, travel and architecture lined the shelves above, which went over the doorway from one wall to the other. Pino's rare book collection was in a glass-fronted case on the opposite side of the room next to the brick fireplace. The central feature of the room was a glossy black baby grand piano, which stood on a plush, deep red, oriental rug. Next to the piano was a music stand that matched the mahogany wood of the shelves.

Opposite the bay window was a sliding glass door that led to the large, grassy back yard with its two greenhouses, above-ground pool and Irene's showcase garden.

"What a beautiful piece," Father Joe exclaimed looking at a large, kiln-baked clay pot that stood next to the sliding glass doors and held several tall cattails.

"Oh, that's one of Irene's creations," Pino told him. "I think it gives the place a homey feeling to have handmade things around."

The priest was about to tell him that the pot was a work of art, not just something that was merely "handmade" as Pino put it, but the conversation was interrupted before it started.

Irene offered the guests some Long Island port wine, and the conversation turned to wine. After enjoying the port, the two priests began to say their goodbyes.

"We'll join you in leaving," Grace told them. "We must go home and get the house ready for the children to visit. You'll bring them by in two hours, Irene?" Her daughter nodded. "What a nice afternoon this has been," Grace said to her son-in-law, not missing a beat, offering her cheek for him to kiss.

"Thank you very much for coming, Grace." Pino kissed her formally and shook Enrico's hand. Because he was so much the shadow of Grace, people rarely spoke directly to Enrico. His son-in-law was no exception.

"Kids, come and say goodbye," Irene called them. Despite the fact that they would be seeing their grandparents in two hours, both Pino and Irene liked the formal ritual of saying goodbye at the end of each visit. Marc came barreling in. He kissed his grandmother and hugged his grandfather's knees. Then he shook hands with the two priests. Jonathan did the same, hugging his grandfather at waist level. Delfina was last. She, too, kissed her grandmother and hugged her grandfather. Then she offered to shake hands with each of the priests, first with Father Patrick and then with Father Joe, who pushed his unruly hair off his forehead as he said, "I'll drop off that book tomorrow."

Delfina smiled at him. "I'll take good care of it, and return it when I'm done."

"No need. You can keep it. I have about five copies. I wrote it."

"You did? Thanks. I've never known an actual author of a book. Would you autograph it?" He smiled at her and nodded, making a mental note to be sure to drop the book off the next morning. He pulled out a green Oakland Athletics baseball cap from his pocket as he turned to his hostess.

Instantly Jonathan and Marc were at his side.

"Look—it's the As." Jonathan's voice was filled with wonder.

"I have a baseball cap collection. One from each team. I also have ump's caps. Now I'm working on the football teams," Joe told them. As the boys touched the cap reverently, Joe turned to his hostess. "Irene, thank you for a lovely dinner. I'll come by tomorrow with the book at, say, eleven. Is that okay?"

"It's fine with me. If I don't answer the door, come around back to the greenhouse." For a quick instant, Father Joe hesitated. Irene, not seeming to notice, gave him a quick handshake and a brush of a kiss on his cheek. He dropped his cap, which Jonathan promptly pounced on and handed back to him. Then the priests left the house with Grace and Enrico.

Irene was amused by Joe's awkwardness in leaving, and she smiled slightly.

"What's so funny?" Pino saw the half smile on his wife's face.

"Not funny, really," she answered. "I was looking at the way the cattails cast a shadow in this half-light. It might make an interesting design for my next piece."

Irene was accustomed to keeping her private thoughts to herself. She had learned by the third month of their marriage that Pino was jealous of her attention to others and that Pino was mostly interested in Pino. Only when something she said could be used against her did her husband even remotely recall anything she told him about herself. Irene was not inclined to divorce, which the Catholic church forbade. And by not sharing her thoughts and feelings with her husband, the number of instances that would lead her to contemplate that possibility were decreased.

Their tacit agreement was that as long as she ran his household as he expected, was the model wife and mother, and made sure his children grew up properly, she could find her outlet in her creativity, the one aspect of herself that she refused to have squelched by his ego. He provided a way of life that enabled her children to live comfortably, and allowed her to do her art and gardening in accordance with a certain standard of living.

The one thing on which both Irene and Pino agreed without argument was that they worked their shared life well together. She turned from the window and went to her studio where she stayed until it was time to prepare dinner.

❦ ❦ ❦

Each morning at precisely 5 o'clock, Father Joseph Paul Clementine woke up to his alarm, which chimed with the bells of the Vatican, got out of bed, and took a five-minute cold shower. Then he dressed in a fresh set of clean, black clothes and donned his Roman collar, which he fastened in place at his Adam's apple with ritual precision. The collar was his symbolic spiritual shield and psychological protection against the pitfalls of the outside world.

At precisely 5:15 each morning, Father Joe could be found kneeling before a simple altar, in meditative prayer to the Holy Family: Jesus, Mary and Joseph, his namesake. He had started the morning ritual when he was a seminarian at Fordham University, and he continued it throughout his schooling and during the various assignments to which he had been sent throughout the world—a series of small and unforgiving towns in South Africa, then Cuzco in Peru, Ottawa in Canada and, most recently, Yumi in Arizona where he had worked among the Cocopah.

Joe considered himself to be a simple man whose daily structure was an indication of a modest, disciplined human being. His world was in order, so that he could offer solace and comfort to those whose lives were in chaos, whether it was chaos due to illness, family situations or innumerable other trials to which human lives were continually subjected. In his moments of self-scrutiny, Joe admitted to himself that he was proud of his discipline. He had lost it once, for a brief time. Without it, he had wreaked havoc on his life and the lives of those around him. He would never lose it again, he promised himself. He considered his discipline a gift that he brought to the people he served. It was one of the things he felt he owed them, and he made sure he delivered it. Another thing Joe felt he owed the people he served was an ongoing pursuit of knowledge. As a Jesuit, his field was philosophy, specifically the philosophy of logic, which he pursued and wrote about with passion.

The third aspect of himself that Joe felt he owed to the people he served was an unflagging sense of faith in God and an unerring knowledge of what is right and wrong in the eyes of God. In accordance with his beliefs, Joe knew that faith and good works together were what constituted the foundations of his religion. From his daily meditation to his pursuit of knowledge and in his counseling of those he served, Joe felt that he was compelled to be a living example of goodness as was defined by the Catholic faith. When he tried to express this to his confessor, he was both praised and warned that even the best of men have bad days. One advisor even went so far as to say it would be hubris for any man, whether a priest or not, to set such a high standard for himself. He reminded Joe that too grand a standard could cause grave problems for Joe, and for those he served. Joe had wanted to storm out of the room that day. But using every morsel of his self-discipline, he did not. He knew intellectually that what he was being told might be true. And as he prayed from his heart each morning, he asked the Lord to make sure that it would never again be true for him.

❦   ❦   ❦

At precisely eleven o'clock the next morning, Father Joe rang the doorbell of the Adriaticos' home. "It's open. Come on in," Irene's voice called from beyond the screen door, from somewhere in the recesses of the house.

Somewhat doubtfully, Joe opened the door and went through the living room, trying to discern where the voice was coming from.

"Through the den, and to the left, past the kitchen."

He found Irene sitting at her potter's wheel, intent upon an intricate design, which she was creating on the rim of a large urn. She did not look up as he entered. He watched her as her full concentration was focused on her task.

"I'll be with you in just a second. I need to finish this," she said. Her voice seemed to come from somewhere other than her body. He looked at the pattern she was creating in the unusually-colored clay. Then his gaze was drawn to her, so high was the degree of her concentration. She had streaks of grey clay in her black hair, and he noticed, for the first time, how long and slender her strong fingers were—perfect for creating such works of art, he observed. From where he stood, the curve of the urn she was working on blended with the curves of her body. Suddenly startled, he realized that he could see her cleavage, and was instantly aware that she was wearing nothing under the loose shirt-smock.

Immediately, he raised his gaze, looking beyond her hunched-up form, behind her to the three sets of glass doors, two of which formed the long part of that wall, and a third which was set perpendicular to it, completing the L-shape, which was the glass wall of her studio. These doors led to the backyard. Two greenhouses stood side by side in the far left corner of the yard. They faced a hedgerow, which separated and protected the glass edifices, the outdoor garden and the pool from what was obviously the children's play area.

"What do you think?" Her wheel was starting to rotate more slowly as she invited him to inspect the piece.

He looked at it, fascinated. He considered the color, the pattern she had created, and the shape. It was unlike anything he had ever seen.

"I don't know how you did it, but it looks like fog."

"Yes." She was clearly pleased. "Fog is one of my greatest inspirations. There's a sense of mystery, of the unseen about it. Maybe I've been reading too many British detective stories. Anyway, I've been trying to create pieces that look like if you touched them, you'd be picking up fog. My last exhibit, this past September in Soho, was ten failed fog vases. I called it something else—I forget what. People loved them, but I wasn't able to achieve the effect I wanted. This one is much closer."

They looked at it in silence for a few moments. Then she said, "I noticed you looking at the backyard. Do you have time to see the greenhouses?"

He looked at his watch. "I should leave in about fifteen minutes."

"That's more than enough time." She opened the sliding glass door, and with a self-assured stride led him to the far side of the left greenhouse. As Joe followed her, he was aware that the way she walked made her seem much taller than her five-foot-four-inch height.

"I've been working in here most of the morning," she told him as she led him past the rows of various crops. "Tomato seeds here, marigolds next, then peas, carrots, sun flowers—the tall ones—more tomatoes, cherry here, beefsteak over there, pumpkins for the kids, summer squash, a few gourds, because the kids like them, and next week, corn. Those trees in the half-barrels near the front are fig trees—three different kinds. The herbs are just in front of the figs. When the weather's right, I'll call someone to remove the panels from the top of this greenhouse so these plants can all get natural sunlight and rain. Pretty neat, huh?"

Without waiting for him to answer, she led him to a door at the opposite side from the one they had entered. Two steps outside, and then she opened a door to the second greenhouse.

"The roof doesn't come off of this one. My orchids are here, to the right. I've got all different kinds. Next to them are ferns from around the world. Birds of paradise are to the left. I love them, but they're hard to keep flowering. And in that empty space over there, I'll begin my hybrid daylilies for the season, probably in three weeks."

As she chatted about the merits and drawbacks of the Long Island climate, Joe listened and nodded politely while musing about how much she was able to accomplish in a day. She also cooked, cleaned and helped with homework for three children. Joe noticed that her vivaciousness carried an energy all its own. He felt perked up, and he was struck anew with the wonder of how one person could affect another in that way. He had gotten an inkling of it while he was at the Arizona reservation, but he had been so anxious to get back to civilization as he knew it that he barely paid attention to that revelation until just before he left. Now he thought of that personal energy again. If it really existed at all, Irene had it. He was interrupted from his musings by the realization that she had asked him a question.

"I'm sorry. What was that?"

She laughed. Whether it was at him or at not being heard, Joe was not sure.

"I said, if you don't leave, now you'll miss your train."

He looked at his watch, noticing that he had not realized how much time had passed. "Thank you. I can't afford to miss this train. They come so infrequently out here."

"Kings Park is almost the boondocks. The town was set up to house—or park—the mental patients from Brooklyn—Kings County. That's why it's called Kings Park. The LIRR—that's the Long Island Rail Road for you newcomers—acts as though we should be grateful to have train service at all. You go into the city often?"

"Every chance I get. I went to school in the Bronx, at Fordham. When I was in Arizona, I think I began suffering from cultural withdrawal. I took the assignment at St. Joseph's with permission to teach, if I could get a job at one of the local colleges. If I get a permanent teaching job in the city, I'll stay at St. Joseph's."

Irene felt that pieces of his story were missing, but she did not venture further. "Speaking of college, I see that's the book for Delfina. You have a real fan now. All you have to do is stroke Del's ego a little, and she'll be in love with you, or at least be your loyal supporter, for life, if only because of your proven discernment and excellent powers of observation when it comes to the most important person in her life, Delfina." The words were spoken like a mother who knows her child and is amused by her foibles. Yet there was a barely perceptible edge to her voice that Joe could not pinpoint.

"Well, she's getting to be a teenager. I don't envy you. I certainly gave my mother a run for her money, especially as a thirteen- and fourteen-year-old." He leafed absent-mindedly through the book as he spoke.

"I'd love to hear about it sometime. You should come by for lunch one day when you're not going into the city." Irene's invitation was genuine. "I assume you're teaching this afternoon."

"You assume correctly. One course in introductory logic at Pace and then up to Fordham Prep for an elective in logic. Then the evening is mine. I'll be going to Lincoln Center to see *Coppelia*."

"I love ballet, almost as much as opera. Pino and I took the kids to see the Nutcracker last year. It was the first time since Jonathan was born that I'd been to see anything in the city. Most people don't like babysitting for two, much less three kids. And now that the kids are getting to be old enough to go, Pino is usually too busy."

"We should go sometime." The words came out in a natural rush.

"That would be lovely. Marc will be in kindergarten three full days a week in the fall, so I might just take you up on that."

They had walked to the front door during their exchange.

"Well, here's the book for Delfina. Some of the information at the beginning is a bit dense. If she has any problems getting started, she can call me." He avoided Irene's eyes, and he avoided making physical contact with her, handing her the book quickly and stepping out of the house.

"You signed it, I see. Thank you. I'll tell her what you said."

He turned and walked to his car. She watched his retreat, amused once again. And she continued to stand at the front door until he drove around the bend and out of sight.

※ ※ ※

Father Joe barely got onto the noon train to Penn Station. Miraculously, he found a parking space close enough to the platform so that he was able to sprint to the train as the bell was ringing and steam was releasing from the brakes. He sat down near the door of the train, glad for the breeze after his run.

He felt exhilarated. From the run, he told himself. From the excitement of almost missing the train, and from the anticipation of the day's classes. He did not allow himself to reflect on it any further. Instead, he tried to fall asleep to the steady rocking of the train.

He did not succeed. A few minutes later, he became aware that he was awake and thinking about Irene, the vase she made, her greenhouses, her vibrancy.

Being somewhat of an anomaly, Joe had very few friends. He had no family, and the close friendships he had formed in the seminary rendered two lasting but long-distance friendships with men he loved like brothers, one now living in New Delhi, the other in Vatican City. He could call or write to these men at any time, he knew, but it was not the same as day-to-day relationships with people.

The priests at his new parish were friendly enough, but they did not engage with him on an intellectual or emotional level. Joe had discovered this when he had tried to find someone to play chess with on the first night he came to Kings Park. Father Reilly could only play checkers. Father McMahon said he was too old to remember how to play, and too tired. The third priest in residence, Father O'Hara, was slowly getting drunk in his room. So much for chess.

The next day, Joe had taken a walk into town where he met some senior citizens who told him about hiking on a nature trail, which started at Sunken Meadow State Park, on the north shore, crossed Long Island, and ended on the south shore at Heckscher State Park. Given the lack of companionship at the rectory, Joe had resolved to explore the trail. In his physical workout, he was able to channel much of his energy, and he enjoyed his walking meditations in the Long Island woods.

He had been assigned to St. Joseph's for a variety of reasons, one of which was his request to be closer to a cosmopolitan area, and closer to the only place he had ever truly considered home—New York City. Arizona had driven him crazy with its lack of culture and void of intellectual stimulation. Finally, after almost nine years away from the city, he had been reassigned to Kings Park. It certainly was not Lincoln Center, but it was close enough, and he was satisfied. His request to the archdiocese for permission to teach had finally been granted, and his one indulgence was attending a cultural event each week. On the train that afternoon, he redirected his mind to the performance he was going to see that evening.

His thoughts wandered again to Irene. Why had he suggested that she accompany him to the ballet? Why was he thinking about her again? He tried to meditate by saying the Act of Contrition ten times. When he lost count, he started again. In this way, he finally arrived at Pennsylvania Station, contrite and ready for teaching.

When Joe left the Adriaticos' house, Irene watched him and thought, as she had the day before, about the sheltered lives that priests led, and how even with all their education, especially the Jesuits, they really seemed to know so little about themselves. Father Joe was probably around her age, she thought, but to her he seemed so much younger. He'd probably get along well with her children, she mused maternally.

Irene wondered how long it would take for him to fall in love with her, and subsequently realize that all the passion he was so attracted to in her was manifested in her pottery and plants, rather than toward any human beings, really. Not even her children. And she wondered how long it would take for him to finally fall out of love with her. When he did, it would cause a momentary empty nest-type syndrome in her heart, a feeling that usually lasted approximately fifteen minutes. After that, it would be forgotten, and all would be right with the world again.

Over the years, there were many priests who fell in and out of love with Irene. And she knew that she was safe to fall in love with, she was warm-hearted and motherly. She was also exciting and interesting. She knew too that part of her allure for lonely priests was that her passion was visible in her creations, palpable in her enthusiasm for those creations and the creative process, and safe, so that these men who had taken a vow of celibacy could enjoy her vicariously and stay within the boundaries of their priestly vows.

This arrangement suited Irene just fine. While they were assigned to St. Joseph's parish, the priests provided excellent companionship for her and her husband. They all had interesting stories to tell. Irene's fascination with everything predisposed her to listening to each priest's story and gaining something out of each one that she might incorporate in a kinesthetic way into her art. She also liked the high of men falling in love with her and the convenience of them falling out of love before she had to send them away. And because they fell out of love quickly, they remained faithful friends. Some, like Father Patrick, had been her friend since she first moved to Kings Park, when she was a twenty-four-year-old bride.

By Joe's slightly bumbling presentation, Irene could tell that he was in what she called the "pre-realization stage." He did not yet know that he was falling in love with her.

"Give it two weeks," she said aloud to herself. "Two weeks."

## CHAPTER 4

❀

"Let's take the kids to see the Nutcracker during the Christmas break," Irene suggested to her husband. They were sitting at the round metal table in the backyard, shielded from the early October sun by a white umbrella, reading *The New York Times* in the Indian Summer sunshine. It was Sunday morning. They had gone to church the night before, and the children were with their grandparents.

"We saw that last year. Besides, I'm supposed to be in Washington then."

She looked at the maples which were just beginning to hint at becoming golden. "Well, what about the Christmas show? You know the one they're billing as "Gala 1973," at Rockefeller Center right after Thanksgiving."

"You know I can't stand that stuff. Isn't there anything we can do with them out here?"

"There is, but I like going into the city, and I can't take the three of them in by myself."

"Well, why don't you go in one day during the week when they're in school? You can ask Sally or Lisa to babysit after school, and you can take in a matinee."

"Actually, Patrick and Joe are going in to see the new exhibit at the Met next Wednesday. They wanted to know if we'd join them and have dinner at the Café des Artistes afterwards."

"I have a board meeting. Why don't you get a babysitter and go?"

"I've been going into the city alone or with friends for almost a full year. I'd like to go with you."

He was engrossed in the Business Section. "I'm sorry, Honey. It's hard for me to get away right now."

She put down the Week in Review and went into the closest greenhouse where she started working in her herb garden. As she worked the rich black earth around the sage and rosemary, she assessed her feelings about her husband's lack of interest in cultural activities. Actually, she thought, he had been uninterested in anything except his business for the last six months or so. She had contented herself with her gardening and art, occasionally going to the city to see shows and exhibits with friends, including Father Joe who, as she had guessed, had progressed from pre in love to full-blown in love like clockwork, including the predictable accompanying shock at his unchaste feelings and chagrin at knowing that she knew it.

He was almost over it, and not a moment too soon for Irene. His inability to articulate cogently when she was around had been amusing for a few weeks. Irene had played with him, enjoying his discomfort, but she soon got bored and began wondering when he would get his wits back, so that she could enjoy some good conversation.

Her reverie was interrupted by the telephone. She picked up the line in the greenhouse.

"Irene." The nasal New York accent came over the phone line. "Darling, is that you? It's Zenobia from the gallery on Spring Street."

"Zenobia. I thought I'd never hear from you again."

"Oh, Irene. You're such a wit. Of course you'd hear from me again. That one sale just fell through, that 's all."

"That was March."

"The summer's a little slow. You know how this business is. Anyway, I've got some news that will make up for all your waiting."

"What? You're giving me my own show."

"Yes."

"At this rate, I'll be old and grey before I get any recognition in the art world."

"I said yes. Yes, you're getting your own show."

Irene was stunned into silence as the information sunk into her awareness.

"Since you're speechless, I'll answer all the questions you'll have ten minutes from now. Yes, it's yours exclusively. Ground floor of the gallery. I'll need at least twenty pieces. I know you can get me twenty. Previews will start in December, right before Christmas, say, around the 20th, because I promised the current artist I'd carry him to the end of the year. I thought we'd hype up your show before the holidays and have a big opening party at the beginning of

January. The timing's not ideal. But, hey, it's a show. I'll carry you through March, and then we'll talk again. You can now say, 'thank you, Zenobia.'"

Irene laughed. "Zenobia, you're an angel. This is the best news I've heard all day—all month, in fact. You'll have twenty pieces, and then some."

"I know it. Sorry to call you on a Sunday, but I wanted to tell you as soon as I was sure."

"Thanks very much."

Irene hung up and let out the hoot that she had been containing during the conversation.

"Who was that?" Pino called from the kitchen where he had gone to get some more coffee.

"Zenobia. You know, from the gallery in SoHo. She's giving me a show in December." Irene did not expect much of a reaction from Pino.

"That's great, Honey. It looks like December's going to be a big month for both of us. I hope your show won't interfere with your entertaining my associates or being the hostess at the company Christmas party."

Something in Irene's spine stiffened and then relaxed. "Of course it won't, Darling," she said, sweetly. "The show's only previewing before the holidays. The opening is going to be around the first week in January. So I'll be able to be at all your parties, and you'll be able to be at my opening."

Pino opened his mouth to say something, thought better of it, and brought the coffee cup to his lips instead. It would work itself out.

Walking on air, Irene went into her studio and began to decide which pieces she wanted to include in the show. She also started to plan some new ones. She wanted to do a few different urns with the new fog motif she had been developing since Easter. She would do at least one more sculpture to add to the collection.

The next morning, after getting Delfina and Jonathan off to school, she went back into her studio, with Marc in tow, to start the sculpture. Irene and Marc worked well together, and the mornings spent in the studio with her younger son were happy times for Irene.

The first sculpture she had ever sold was of Marc as an infant. He had been in the studio with her one day a few months after he had been born. While he was sleeping peacefully, she was moved to try to recreate him in clay. A week later, she had produced a life-size replica of the tiny infant just waking from sleep, curled in his bassinet, with the beginning of a smile of recognition on his face. She had almost decided not to sell it. But the woman who had bought the sculpture had fallen in love with it, saying it reminded her of her grandson who lived in Germany with her daughter and son-in-law. The woman was willing to pay top dollar for the piece, so Irene parted with it knowing that it was in good hands.

Marc had been around the medium of clay literally his whole, short life. He took his place on the stool across from hers, and she gave him a handful of the pliable, gooey substance. He had his own plastic water container which he used with aplomb.

The studio was set up with Irene's wheel in the corner of the room that was created by the two sliding glass doors, so that she could have maximum natural light when she worked. A large, wooden, work table was in the middle of the room. It was high enough for Irene to stand or sit on a stool while working. The side of the table was fitted with a lazy-susan type, elevated, rotating, round shelf that was custom made to her specifications. This is where she sculpted.

After getting Marc situated, Irene started her own sculpture project. In church that weekend, the day before she got the news about the show, Irene had been looking at the crucifix behind the altar. In the early hours of that following Monday morning, while she was again thinking about the crucifix, an idea for a sculpture had come to her: an androgynous torso—ribs to knees. The Crucified Jesus on the cross at church was so thin that all his ribs could be seen, and, if one looked at it objectively, from ribs to knees, the form of Jesus might have been a boy's or a girl's.

In church, Irene would not have let herself have such a blasphemous thought: Jesus' body could look like a girl's? But here in the studio, Irene was a different person. She wanted to try to capture the androgyny she saw, not quite like a Greek sculpture, and certainly not like the wooden statue of Jesus in Saint Joseph's Church. But that statue would certainly serve as a good point of departure, and inspiration, for her.

Irene started putting clay onto the rotating table. She intended to get the basic size down before the kids came home from school. She worked, engrossed in her project. Marc was equally engrossed in his. She measured, added clay, turned the piece, added more here, took away some there, and eventually decided to make the torso life size.

Meanwhile, Marc pounded his clay into one shape and then another, telling himself a story while he worked, always watching his mother out of the corner of his eye. When she dipped her hands into her water basin, he dipped his hands into his plastic water container. He imitated the kneading motions she made, all the while telling himself a story, a running narrative about the monster from the deep meeting up with the Loch Ness monster in Disneyland.

If Irene had stopped to watch him, she would have been amused, but she was in her own world, feeling the clay, becoming part of it, allowing the sculpture to become part of her. To Irene, there was no material more sensuous than that wet compound, not even the touch of another human. When her fingers began to mold and shape the clay, she felt it begin to mold and shape her. She loved everything about her work—the mounting tension as a project took shape and form, the heightened anxiety at the moment when something—Irene was never quite sure whether it was her or the piece she was working on—made a shift, and another rhythm took over, a rhythm that eventually decided the character and essence beyond definition that made up the finished piece, and the final wonder, when it was all over, that her work was finished, and the piece was ready to be displayed.

All these things were what made Irene continue to sculpt, despite her husband's degradation of her work and her mother's vague hints that it was not becoming for a woman to be a sculptor. She had tried LSD once in college, but she had already been sculpting by then, and not even the psychedelic drug made her feel as good as she felt when she had her hands in clay.

She had been thinking about that when Marc said loudly, "Mommy the doorbell's ringing again." Irene was about to call "just come in" to whomever rang the bell, but she remembered that the front door was closed and she would not be heard.

Wiping her hands on her wrap-around working skirt, she padded in bare feet to the front door. Marc clamored down from his stool and followed closely behind her. "Maybe it's the mail man," he said excitedly. The mail man was a big favorite of Marc's. Not only did Marc sometimes get special things in the mail; but when other people got things in the mail, sometimes there was "popping paper," the plastic bubble wrap that Marc could spend hours popping, much to the chagrin of everyone around him.

"Hi, Father Joe," Marc said, crowding in front of his mother as she opened the door.

"Hi, Marc. Hello, Irene. I was just coming back from my hike to the Old Dock Inn along the nature path, and I thought I'd stop by and see if you two wanted to join me for a bit."

"Why don't you come in for something to drink," Irene invited, opening the screen door. "Marc and I were just working in the studio, and we both have wet clay to get back to. But please, come on in."

"Yeah. Come see what I'm making." Marc grabbed Joe's hand in his small, clay-covered one.

"Well, okay. But I don't want to interrupt you," Joe said to the youngster, looking back at Irene as if to ask, "You're sure this is not an intrusion?"

"It's a nice break," Irene assured him. "Marc's been working hard all morning. It's nice for him to have someone to appreciate his work other than just me. Go ahead, Marc. Bring Father Joe into the studio, and I'll bring some juice in for you. What will you have, Joe?"

"Juice is fine."

The two of them went into the studio, and Irene went into the kitchen. When she came back a few minutes later carrying a tray, Marc was saying, "...and then the Loch Ness Monster and the Monster from the Deep both got in boats and went through the 'It's a Small World' ride. It was the only time there was screaming in the 'Tunnel of Love' ride." Little Marc laughed evilly.

Joe laughed too as he took the yellow plastic glass with a built-in straw for Marc and a regular glass for himself off the tray. Then Joe said, "And what's your mother making?"

"She's making a man-lady," Marc shrugged with boredom. "It's headless because it's like Ichabod Crane."

"How do you know about Ichabod Crane?" Irene asked him.

"Jonathan. He told me the story of the guy with no head riding on a horse. It's for Halloween. Me and my friends are all going to be Ichabod."

"You'd probably be better off being the headless horseman," Joe told him.

"Yeah," Marc rubbed his nose shyly. "That's what I meant. I want to walk around carrying my head."

"Your piece is very interesting, Irene," Joe said cautiously.

Irene could not resist baiting him. In an even voice, not to attract Marc's attention, she said, "Now, Father. You're looking at it from the back. Don't you want to come here and see the other side?"

Joe met her challenge and walked around to the other side of the table. To his relief, and her amusement, he saw that the front was not even started.

"Expecting something more finished, Father?" She teased him.

He laughed a good-natured if slightly embarrassed laugh. "I thought you only did vases and pots and things of that sort," he said, trying to change the subject.

"That's what most people want, but every once in a while I get inspired to do a sculpture. I did one of Marc when he was a newborn. Didn't I, Honey?" The little boy nodded, and knowing the rest of the story, finished it for her. "I was the first sculpture Mommy ever sold." He said it proudly. "And now Mommy's doing a whole show of her clay makings. We're gonna be rich, and she's gonna be famous, like Mi-chael-Angel-o." He pronounced the Renaissance sculptor's name slowly and carefully.

"That's a mouthful, isn't it?" Joe said to him.

"I'm a big boy. And I bet if I ask Mommy, she'll make that man-lady sculpture be you, like she made the baby one be me."

Irene started, and not noticing her reaction, Joe squirmed.

"That couldn't be a sculpture of me," Joe objected. "This body's really skinny. I hope I'm not skinny like that one looks. And I hope I'm not a man-lady."

"No, you don't really look like that," Marc conceded, after looking at the sculpture and at Joe for a minute. "Maybe your butt does a little, but everybody's butt looks the same."

"Butt," he repeated, taking delight in the word.

"Marc has just discovered the power of his vocabulary in the anatomical area. It seems that this is a favorite topic of conversation among preschoolers," Irene told Joe.

"Yeah, butts and—"

"Enough, Marc." Irene commanded, knowing that little boys' conversations could only go downhill from there.

Marc quickly lost interest and turned his attention back to his clay monsters. Irene knew better than to react to what the child said, but she noticed that when he dropped the subject, she let out a breath that she had been holding since he started it.

"I should be letting you two artists get back to your work," Joe said. Irene could tell by the way he pushed his hair off his forehead, even though it was not falling forward, that the priest was feeling uncomfortable. As she moved to walk him to the door, he said, "Go back to your work. I'll let myself out."

"Leaving so soon?" Sometimes Irene did not know what came over her, especially in her studio. Her conscience was telling her to leave well enough alone and let him go. But her conscience was not holding the reins at this moment, and the part of her that was controlling her actions did not intend to let him leave until she was ready.

"You're obviously working. And I need to finish my walk and get back to the rectory."

"You know what I love about clay?" Irene said in that same soft, even voice. "I love how it responds precisely to my touch. It's the perfect servant." With that thought, she was transported to another place, and Joe was forgotten for a minute as she felt like she was beginning to get an idea about the sculpture.

"Just like my monsters. Right, Mommy? Father Joe, Mommy says that I can make anything I'm afraid of out of clay, and then turn it into something else, like magic. Then I don't have to be afraid of it any more. Right, Mommy?" Irene smiled and nodded at him, her thought momentarily interrupted.

"Well, I am not a monster, but I am an imperfect servant of Saint Joseph's, and I really must go," Joe told them, taking a navy blue Yankees cap out of his pocket and hastily retreating from the studio.

"I didn't even get to tell you about my gallery opening."

Joe slowed his pace at her news.

"You're doing a show? That's great, Irene. When's your opening?" His enthusiasm was genuine. Because of his sincerity, she stopped teasing him. She gave him the details as she walked him to the door.

"I hope you'll let me come back and see the finished sculpture as well as the other pieces you'll be exhibiting in the gallery."

"Perhaps you'll come to my opening."

"I'd be delighted. Send me an invitation, okay?" He smiled, put on his cap, and left.

This time, Irene did not watch him go. She went quickly back into the studio to finish her thought, promising Marc that if he would wait just a little bit longer, in half an hour they would eat lunch in front of the television—a real treat for him.

※　　　　※　　　　※

Irene worked diligently on the sculpture for two weeks, and at the end of that time, she felt she had created a fine work of art. She was in love with it, and she could not wait to see it displayed at the gallery.

One night, in early December, as the show was drawing closer, she was sitting in her studio looking at the sculpture when Pino walked in. He had not seen the piece before. Coming upon it from behind, he stopped, circled around it, and then took it in from the front before saying what he had come in to tell her.

"Nice piece." That was high praise coming from Pino. "Listen, Irene. We've been invited to the annual Christmas party of the Long Island Children's Fund Board of Directors. It's next Thursday at the Huntington Towne House. I know it's kind of short notice, but do you think Sally will baby sit? It's really a big night. Some people from the state senate will be there. I've been told it's my best opportunity to meet them. There's also a rumor that the governor might make an appearance."

"Pino, we already have a babysitter for next Thursday. Mrs. Lee from Commack is coming, because we're going to my preview at the gallery, and it's going to be a late night. Remember?"

"No, Irene. Obviously, I did not remember. Look, it's not your opening, is it? It's just a preview, for heaven's sake. I need you with me at this Christmas party."

"Pino, you know better than that. Besides you already agreed that we're going."

"That was before I knew who was going to be at this party. Irene, this is my career we're talking about."

She stood up her full height, faced him, and said levelly, "And, Pino, this is my career we're talking about."

They stood, staring at each other. Her petite, five-foot-four-inch frame faced off against his looming, six-foot-four-inch one. At that moment, Delfina walked in, math book in hand. "Could either of you help me with this math problem?"

Both Irene and Pino dropped their gaze. "I'll do it," Pino offered, taking the book from Delfina and starting to walk out of the studio. All of a sudden, he stopped. "Well, Irene, if you don't want to go, how about if Delfina comes as my guest? She's getting old enough. If she can attend the opera with her mother, she can certainly come to a charity ball with her dad."

Delfina's eyes lit up. "Oh, Mom, can I? That would be great."

"If you think it's okay, being a school night and all, it's fine with me."

"All right!" Delfina's math problem was forgotten. "Can I use the phone to call Antoinette?"

"Finish your homework first. Just because you're going to a grownup party doesn't mean that the rules change. Now go back to your room, and your father will be in to help you with your math problem in two minutes."

After Delfina left, Irene said, "Smart move. Not only do you avoid going to my preview, but now Delfina will be very disappointed if she does not get to go to the proverbial ball. Meanwhile, I'm at the gallery without you."

"Nobody's interested in having me there."

"I am."

"You'll be so busy with your potential buyers that you won't even notice if I'm there or not."

"I looked for you for almost two hours that time when you went to the bar to watch the Super Bowl. I didn't know where you were, because you hadn't told me. You didn't believe the people who told you I spent all my time looking for you, instead of working the room and trying to make some sales, because, according to you, they were my friends and would say whatever I wanted them to say. I depend on you for pricing and sales terms, as well as your ability to intermingle with people and make suggestions."

Pino's ego was being stroked, and he was mollified. "I really need to meet these people, Irene," he said softly. "Having my daughter with me does not look as good as having my wife there. Thank goodness it's the Children's Fund. I'll have to live with it the same way you'll have to live with my not being at the gallery. There's nothing either of us can do about it."

※ ※ ※

The annual Christmas party of the Long Island Children's Fund Board of Directors always took place in the elegantly-appointed Huntington Towne House. Delfina had seen its opulent chandelier from the car many times as she had been driven past, but she had never been so close to it as she would be this night. She was feeling very grown up in her slightly high-heeled, black patent leather shoes. She was also wearing a long, deep red, velvet dress that had a tie in the back and black lace at the collar and cuffs of the puffy, long sleeves.

Delfina liked having a specific job to do. In this case, it was to be her father's date. She stood next to him with perfect posture, drinking a Shirley Temple, while he talked with various members of the Board and other prestigious people who had gathered for the charitable event.

In the car on the way to the Towne House, Pino had talked to her about who was going to be there and the purpose of the function, much in the same way as he would have spoken to Irene. Then he added, "Delfina, this is such a grown-up function that I think you should speak to me like a grown up would. Everyone there will know you're my daughter, so it's not proper that you call me Pino, but I think you should call me Father, not Dad. I think Dad is for little girls. As of tonight, you're officially a young woman."

"Okay, Father," Delfina smiled, trying on the grown-up word for size. They pulled up to the Towne House, and Delfina waited for the valet to open her door. When he did, she got out majestically. That evening, in addition to being Father's date, she was Princess Grace of Monaco.

The Long Island Children's Fund was created by a group of mostly childless senior citizens who thought that in order to make sure their tax dollars went far and remained uncorrupted, they needed to create a fund that they could manage and maintain. The Children's Fund was what they created. And while much of the money raised was earmarked to serving the well-being of under-privileged children, most of the Board members—at least in Delfina's opinion based on the way they treated her—had not ventured near a child for at least a decade. Being tall for her age, Delfina was often taken for a young adult, not a ten-year-old child. However, after ten minutes of being awkwardly greeted by members of the Board, she knew that they would be totally inept with actual children. She wondered why they chose to give their money to something they knew so little about. She resolved to ask her father on the way home about the saying, "Charity begins at home."

As she listened to the adult conversation, she was able to discern the reason that it was so important for her father to be there and to be seen in a good light: the governor of New York was going to make an appearance at some point in the evening.

"Pino, there you are." A short, round man came toward Pino and Delfina. He was sweating, although the room was not warm. From time to time he patted his brow with a large white handkerchief. "Hey, Boss. I've been looking all over for you." He spoke with a heavy Brooklyn accent. "Carol is having a drink at the bar. Where's Irene?"

"Irene has an exhibit this evening that she had to attend," Pino said, letting his voice drop. "She was going to be back too late to attend this function, so Delfina was willing to keep me from feeling lonely. Weren't you Honey? You remember Mr. Laurio?"

"Yes, Father." Delfina nodded. "Hello, Mr. Laurio." She shook his hand. Rocco Laurio was someone Delfina particularly did not like. She could not figure out why she felt that way. He seemed, well, *greasy*, somehow. And that greasiness translated into a vague feeling of discomfort whenever she was with him, which was infrequently. When she was, she made sure she was never too far from her father. Delfina never questioned her response to Mr. Laurio. She just followed her instincts and stayed away from him. In the Huntington Towne House this particular evening, Mr. Laurio did nothing to enhance her opinion of him. Barely acknowledging Delfina's existence, Rocco Laurio turned back to Pino and the business at hand.

"Governor's chopper'll be touching down behind the building in about forty minutes. I want you to meet him personally. I'll bring you to the back room where he's coming in just before he gets there. Maybe the kid can, uh, I don't know, go listen to the orchestra or something until you get back." Delfina was fascinated by Rocco Laurio's accent. She knew he was speaking English, but she had to pay attention to understand what he was saying. Every time he said "the," it came out "da," and he usually skipped the letter "r" altogether.

"No. I want her to stay with me." Pino lowered his voice and said, "It's the Children's Fund, for chrissake, Rocco. I want my child with me when I meet the governor."

Suddenly, Delfina caught sight of a familiar shock of red hair. "Father." She tugged at his hand. "Mrs. James is over there. Can I go and say hello?"

Pino followed Delfina's gaze. "Sure, Honey. Just come right back, okay? We're going to meet the governor."

Delfina left, and Rocco Laurio started giving Pino facts that he should know. In a few minutes, Delfina returned, followed by Mrs. James. "Mr. Adriatico," the teacher started, "I just wanted to wish you a merry Christmas." They shook hands and exchanged pleasantries. Meanwhile, Delfina was listening to Mr. Laurio trying to explain to a Brazilian woman what the Children's Fund was.

"It's a...fund that was, um, set up for...children."

"That's a tautology," Delfina muttered under her breath.

"Did you say something about a tautology, Dear?" Mrs. James turned to her.

"Oh. I didn't think anyone would hear that," Delfina said guiltily.

"What's the tautology, Delfina?" Pino asked her.

"Um, well, that lady asked Mr. Laurio what the Children's Fund is. He said that the Children's Fund is a fund for children. Using the same words to define the word—that's a tautology."

"Whaaat? Did I say something wrong?" Rocco Laurio heard his name spoken.

"Would you like to tell Mr. Laurio what you said?" Pino asked his daughter.

"Go ahead, Delfina. You're right." Mrs. James, angered that Pino was thoughtlessly putting his daughter in an awkward position, encouraged her.

"It's just that what you said is a tautology."

"I didn't say nothing like that."

Emboldened by Mrs. James' hand on her shoulder, Delfina persevered delicately. "Um, to say that the Children's Fund is a fund for children is, it's..." Delfina struggled to find the correct form of the word.

"It's tautological." A man stepped from behind a curtained entranceway. He was tall—as tall as Pino—and he wore a stately grey pinstriped suit with a prominent red tie.

"Jeez. It's the governor," Rocco said, moving Delfina aside and springing into action. "Sir, I'm Rocco Laurio, and..."

"Yes, Mr. Laurio. I know who you are. And Pino Adriatico, I recognize you. Nice to meet you. He offered his hand to Mrs. James.

"Mary James." She introduced herself.

He stepped toward Delfina. "And who is our logician?"

Delfina became Princess Grace again. "Delfina Adriatico," she said regally.

"It's a pleasure to meet you, Miss Adriatico," the governor shook her hand gravely. "Now that we have established the tautology, can you tell me what the Children's Fund is?"

Pino held his breath as Delfina took a deep breath and began.

"The Long Island Children's Fund was founded by a group of senior citizens who wanted to make sure their tax dollars went far, so they created a fund that they could manage and maintain. The Children's Fund's what they created, and the money that's raised goes to serve the well-being of underprivileged children." Without pausing to take a breath, Delfina repeated what Pino had told her in the car.

"That is most impressive, Miss Adriatico," the governor said, smiling at her. He turned to Pino. "She's a credit to you."

By that time, people began to realize that the governor had arrived. Flash bulbs started clicking. Rocco Laurio tried to organize people for pictures with the governor, but he was not finished speaking with Delfina. "I think I should have a picture with this young lady, and one with her and her father." The governor pre-empted Rocco.

As people started to organize according to the governor's direction, he asked Delfina, "And what brings you to this function this evening?"

"Father let me come with him, because my mother has a gallery opening in New York City tonight."

"So, your mother is an artist?"

"Yes, Sir. She works with clay."

"Her work must be good if she has a show in the City."

"Yeah, she's really, really good. Her show's at Ritter's in SoHo. You should go if you're in the City." Delfina could imitate her mother as well.

The governor smiled. "Ritters? I'll try to make it." Cameras flashed as the governor posed with Delfina and then with Delfina and Pino. As the governor shook Pino's hand, he said, "Great idea bringing your child to the Children's Fund event. More people should do that."

Pino beamed as the governor shook his hand.

"Well, I guess I'd better do what I came here to do," the governor said to Delfina. "It was a pleasure meeting you, Miss Adriatico. When you're ready for a job, call me." He shook her hand, and then was consumed in the queue that was waiting to greet him.

❦ ❦ ❦

The gallery on Spring Street was bustling on that Winter Solstice evening. Zenobia was on the telephone constantly while at the same time shouting orders to her workers in the studio. Irene flitted around the gallery nervously. She knew Zenobia was calling the shots, but the gallery owner had invited her to be there when the preview was set up, and Irene needed to be where the action was. So she watched, suffering as she held her tongue, while the show took shape before her eyes.

As Joe Clementine walked into the room, one of the workers came from the back, wheeling a large display stand into the middle of the room. The stand brushed the side of the box containing the torso statue. Irene nearly jumped out of her skin. She had not seen Joe enter.

"Watch where you're going," Irene yelled at the worker, unable to keep silent any longer. "That thing can't be fixed if it's broken." The worker nodded, and continued what he was doing.

Joe walked up behind her and touched her elbow gently.

Irene startled. "Joe, you scared me. What are you doing here?"

"You said your preview was tonight. I'm giving a workshop this evening, so I can't make it here at seven when the show officially opens. I wanted to stop by and see what's going on, and just let you know that you're in my prayers."

"Thanks, Joe. That's a comfort."

"Where's Pino?"

"He had a function in Huntington this evening. Delfina's standing in for me there."

"So you'll be all alone?"

"Not really. I have friends in the city. I'll be spending the night with them and going back home tomorrow. Do you have a few minutes? I'd like to show you around the display room." As they walked through it, Irene explained, "The whole show won't be displayed until the grand opening. This is just to give people a taste of what's to come."

"I see. Where's the famous torso?"

Irene laughed. "It's in that box. You'll have to come to the grand opening to see that one. It's not getting out of its box until it has a specific place to stand and it's not going to be moved. Unless it's broken first."

"I never saw the finished product, you know."

"That's right. Well, you'll just have to come back for the opening."

"I'll be there."

"And right now, Father Clementine, you've got a workshop to teach. Don't be late." They hugged each other familiarly, and, on impulse, she gave him a kiss on the cheek. He smiled, pushed his hair off his forehead, put on his black baseball cap, and was out the door.

Irene smiled as she turned her attention back to the show. It felt good to know that someone close to her was taking her work seriously.

🍁 🍁 🍁

After his show of support at the gallery, Irene and Joe became good friends. In the whirlwind of activities between Christmas and New Year's, Irene barely had enough time to complete all the Christmas activities that were required of her, and her show was relegated to the back of her attention while she performed her holiday duties as a wife and mother. Finally, 1973 had come to an end, and 1974 was in full swing.

Irene's grand opening was scheduled for January 5. On January 4, she dropped off her children at her mother's house with several bags of clothes and a three-page list of instructions.

"I'll see you in two days. Pray for the opening to go well. Okay, Markie?" Her youngest child was trying not to cry. "It's just for two days. I'm sure Grandpop will let you stay up and watch the ball game with him." This cheered up Marc considerably, and everyone waved her off as she drove to the train station.

When Irene got to the gallery at noon, she had a full day's work ahead of her, supervising the placement of her work on the main floor of the gallery. The pieces had all been placed approximately where she had indicated on the floor plan. She would personally direct the lighting and final placement of each piece. That night, she stayed in the borrowed apartment Zenobia had arranged for her, planning to be at the gallery early in the morning to finish the job.

Irene awoke at six in the morning and looked out of her window to see that a blanket of snow had covered the city. It was still snowing at midday, and by five o'clock the snow had shut the city down.

"Well, so much for the opening party," Zenobia said, gloomily. "It's settled. The mayor has officially closed the city. No alternate side parking tomorrow." Then she brightened. "But don't worry, Honey. We'll have a party for you next Saturday. Make it a cocktail party. We'll get the buyers and the critics. Just think of this as the dress rehearsal."

Irene was about to retort that she did not think she could go through the same kind of nerve-wracking preparations one more time when the bell on the door rang, indicating that someone was in the gallery entrance.

A lone figure stood in the entranceway, taking off a heavy black overcoat, which was covered with snow. The visitor was wearing a snow-covered baseball cap. Under the coat, he wore black pants, a black shirt and scarf, and black hiking boots.

"I'm sorry. The opening has been postponed," Zenobia announced, walking through the main gallery toward him.

"Oh, that's really too bad. I guess the weather's got the best of us."

"Joe. I can't believe you're here." Irene was very surprised to see him.

"And I can't believe your opening's today. My classes were cancelled. I didn't hear about it until I got to the school, so I decided to come over here early. I should have known that if the colleges are closed, it makes sense that most other places, like galleries, would be closed too."

"Well, come on in for a minute and warm up." Zenobia invited him.

"Thanks. Irene, maybe you could give me a private tour."

"That I can do. Let's start here, on the left with my failed fog collection." Irene took him around the whole gallery. The last piece she showed him was the centerpiece of her exhibit, the androgynous torso. It stood exactly in the center of the room, its stark lines and curves accentuated by the lighting. The statue's left arm fell to the side, palm curled outward; the right arm crossed in front of the figure, resting exquisitely in front of its crotch, hiding its gender.

Joe had not seen this work since that first day in the studio. He stood in front of it for a long time, looking. When he finally spoke, it was in a hushed tone. "Well, from pile of clay to finished product. I feel privileged to be able to see the alpha and the omega, so to speak."

"Why are you whispering," she said, in the same low tone. "We're the only ones here."

"It feels like this statue is alive in some way. It's uncanny."

"When I sculpt, I feel like the clay makes me as much as I make the clay. Maybe that's the aliveness that everybody says they feel from me. It's my creativity; it's what I put into the clay."

"Maybe so," Joe said, looking at her. "However you do it, it's a real gift."

She smiled at the compliment. Then Zenobia walked in from the office at the back. "Listen you two, I think I'm going to close up shop and call it a day. Irene, are you still going to stay over tonight?"

"Actually, Zenobia, I think I'll be heading home. I'll just leave my things in the apartment, because I'll be back in a few days. The train may take a long time, but I'd like to try to get home to my family tonight."

"No problem. No one's using the apartment this month."

Joe and Irene left the gallery together. Joe had a schedule in his pocket. "The next train is in five minutes. The train after that is two hours and fifteen minutes later."

"We'll never make the earlier one, and the later one is so much later. What will we do in a shut-down city until the train comes?"

"One of my students is screening a film that he wrote, directed and produced. It starts in…fifteen minutes. We can walk there from here. Do you want to go?"

Irene was willing, and they found seats in the darkened theater just as the film began to roll. Ironically, the film was about a woman who took out her frustrations at her potter's wheel. The images of her working in the clay evoked many of the feelings Irene had when she was working in clay. Irene was thoroughly enjoying the story, including the scene when a man who had fallen in love with the woman came into the woman's studio. He stood in front of her, unable to tell her what he was feeling, and she took his hands and guided them up her body, under the canvas smock she was wearing, showing that it was all she was wearing. At that point, Irene suddenly sensed that Joe was uncomfortable. He was a celibate priest. Of course, he would be uncomfortable with all this explicit sexual activity. She, however, was interested in seeing the end of the story, so she ignored his discomfort.

The movie ended five minutes later, with the heroine, given an ultimatum by the man, choosing her art over him. When they emerged from the small theater, they saw that the snow had stopped, at least for the moment. As they trudged through the drifts toward Pennsylvania Station, Irene said, "I guess the last few minutes of the movie made you uncomfortable, huh?"

"Well, I don't like the fact that so little is left to the imagination, for one thing. For another, I think it was a little unrealistic."

"What was unrealistic?"

"Well, for example, the only thing she was wearing was her smock with nothing underneath."

"When I work, I usually don't wear underwear. I sculpt with the whole of me, and clothes are constricting. Besides, when I work, I get clay all over everything. Since I'm the one who does the laundry, I figure the less I wear, the less I have to wash."

He looked at her sideways. His expression was impossible for her to read.

"I do. If you think that makes me a brazen hussy, then you try doing laundry for five some time, and still keep your black outfits perfectly cleaned and ironed."

"I'm not judging you, Irene. It's just…" He did not finish the thought as they reached the front entrance to Penn Station and found their way to the main board that announced the track from which their train would be leaving. Joe checked the departure track and time with the information booth clerk.

"The train will be departing on time, but they think it's going to be arriving in Kings Park about thirty minutes late."

"That's not bad, considering the one to Montauk is ninety minutes late. Let's get a seat."

Three hours later, they were ensconced in fog, scraping the ice off Irene's car, which was parked in the train station parking lot.

"I can't believe all that snow in the city, and it's only an ice storm here," Joe said as he worked. "I wonder if the snow will come out this way tonight?"

"Well, this fog means it's getting warmer. So, either we'll have snow, or it will clear up. One thing's for sure, though: if we haven't had a power failure yet, with all this ice, we're in for one."

"Really?"

"Yep. We're always the first ones to lose it and the last ones to get it back. And ice is more treacherous than snow, because large tree limbs tend to snap and fall down over power lines. You should have seen…" Irene never finished the sentence.

A westbound diesel train was coming out of the fog as a Ford Falcon was crossing the intersection. The crossing gate was not moving—the power was out.

Metal hit metal as, increased by the momentum of the train, the car's own momentum flipped it over and sent it flying into the defunct crossing gate, through the parking lot fence, and into the side of the ticket house where it landed on its hood and roof. Irene and Joe dropped their scrapers and ran toward the car. Joe got there first, with Irene a split second behind him.

"Oh, God. Don't look," he said, putting his arm up to try to shield her, but it was too late. She saw, as he had, that the driver, the lone occupant of the car, had been decapitated as the hood sliced through the windshield.

"I'll keep the people away while you give the last rites," she said after a moment, quickly becoming efficient. He nodded and let her go. As he reached into the inner pocket of his coat and pulled out a small silver box and a small thin piece of fringed cloth, which he put around his neck, Irene walked quickly toward the small crowd that had begun to gather.

To a couple beginning to walk toward the scene, she ordered, "You, over there, call the police. Now." Three big men also approached. "Listen, the man in the car died. Could you keep other people away until the ambulance gets here?"

"How do you know he's dead?" One of the men wanted to know.

"You can tell. He didn't have a chance."

"We'll keep them away."

A woman stepped out of a car that had been stopped at a nearby intersection. "I'm a doctor. Is there anything I can do?" Irene shook her head, and said, "He's been decapitated. I don't know whether there's something official you need to do…"

"Let me go over and talk with the priest," the doctor said. Irene was not about to stop her.

Within minutes the fire department arrived, from the nearby fire house, sirens screaming and lights flashing. Then the police arrived. After a time, Joe and Irene were allowed to leave, having given their names and telephone numbers. The ambulance left slowly, its lights flashing silently, and Joe and Irene finished scraping the car.

They did not speak at all on the short ride from the station to the rectory.

Joe got out of the car. "Are you okay to drive alone?"

"Oh. Yes, I'm a little shaken, but I'll be okay. I just need to be alone for a while, I think. When I called Pino to tell him I'd be coming home, he said he'd be out with the kids until about nine, so that gives me a couple of hours to recoup."

"Okay. Call if you need to."

"Thanks." She drove away.

When she got home, she hung her wet coat and boots in the mud room, donned her sculpting clothes, and headed to her studio through the semi-darkness of the house at dusk. She grabbed some clay, the first that came to her hands, threw it on her wheel, and started pedaling, pounding and beating the clay in a desperate attempt to exorcize the numbness of shock and come back to feeling something—anything—in herself. Her fingers were working the clay desperately when the doorbell rang. She covered the clay with a damp towel and answered the front door like a somnambulist.

She was neither surprised nor elated to see Joe at the door. She felt nothing. Then, slowly, she felt some force, a power outside herself, take over. She reacted to the force with grateful relief that she could feel again. She responded to the feeling with hungry desperation, being pulled along in a whirlpool of something much bigger than herself, and too intense for her to try to control. Anything was better than the numbness she had been feeling up to that point. When he took her in his arms, she realized that she needed the contact of another human being, and he did too. She watched herself being held by him from somewhere else. Her mind was not functioning, and she that knew his was not either. Their bodies had taken over in an instinctual way to erase what they had witnessed at the station.

It had to happen that way.

※　　　　※　　　　※

It had to happen that way.

At the end of March, Irene found out that she was pregnant.

# CHAPTER 5

On October 15, 1974, Marc Adriatico's life changed dramatically. As the youngest of the three Adriatico children, he had to answer to his parents as well as to his older sister when she was "in charge." In the days as his mother's belly swelled to new proportions, his sister was not in charge as much as she had been before; primarily because his mother was going out less frequently. Despite this fact, Marc was not spending as much time with his mother as he had been, because he now went to kindergarten.

Marc hated kindergarten. Although the other kindergartners did not torture him the way his siblings did, he was much more advanced than the others in his class. He was much better at drawing and working with clay, and, thanks to his big brother Jonathan, he was already able to sound out words, tell stories from Greek mythology, and recite psalms from the Bible. For his abilities, he was sometimes teased, more often ignored or avoided, by the other kids, and he was either overpraised or ignored by the kindergarten teacher Miss Diana and her aides. Because he was often bored, he spent a lot of time sitting in the hall or in the corner, often threatened with being sent to the principal's office.

Marc could have lived with these indignities. After all, he was given a book to sit in the hall and read, thereby giving him something that was fun to do, and at the same time, being removed from the classroom for a while.

What Marc really hated about kindergarten was the interruption in his routine with Irene. He missed having the run of the house when his siblings were at school. He missed the special breakfasts and the other rituals that he and Irene had developed together. Most of all, he missed mornings in the studio with his mother. True, he was only in school for two and a half days each week, and Irene made sure that she still spent at least one afternoon a week in the studio with him. Still, Marc was aware of the change.

After a month in school, Marc had discovered that one way to make school more interesting and at the same time to win the respect of his peers was to tell jokes. This did not win him any popularity with his teacher or her aides, except the art teacher Miss West who came to the kindergarten class on Tuesdays. Miss West loved Marc. She laughed at his jokes along with the kids, and she encouraged him to "show the class how to do it" when she could see that he already knew how to perform the skill that she was teaching. During Art, Marc was happy in kindergarten.

On that particular day, October 15, 1974, the art class had been more exhilarating than usual. Miss West left, and Miss Diana took charge of the class. The stocky thirty-year-old kindergarten teacher had mouse-colored hair, thick round glasses that made her eyes look small and, on that day, a serious relationship problem. She had decided that after snack time, because she was drained from dealing with her personal problems, she was going to tell the class a story. Unfortunately for Marc, the story she was going to tell was the story about Perseus and the Medusa.

"Okay everyone, get out your mats, and lie down for a rest while I tell you a story."

Most of the children settled down quickly; story time was a favorite with the five-year-olds. But Marc was restless; he could not stop moving around.

"Marc, it's time to get out your mat and listen to a story. Everyone, we're going to wait for Marc now."

"I don't want to hear a stupid story."

"I'm sorry you feel that way, Marc. You don't even know what the story is yet; you might like it."

"Are we going to have to listen to another baby story like 'Goldilocks' or 'Sleeping Ugly'?"

Some of the boys snickered.

"No, this one is different. It's about a brave man named Perseus and a snake-headed woman—"

It's *Perseus*, not Per*seus*, and he killed Medusa, who had snake *hair*, not a snake head." Under his breath, he added the newest insult he had learned from his older brother. "Ass."

"What did you say, young man?" Miss Diana had already been having a bad day.

Emboldened, Marc stood up to her. "I said ASS. If you're going to tell a good story, don't mess it up."

Miss Diana grabbed Marc by the arm as she went to the intercom by the door. "You are going to the Principal's office this time. Enough is enough." The rest of the class was transfixed into silence. No one was laughing anymore.

A mechanical beep was heard from the intercom, and then a disembodied voice through static, "Yes, Miss Diana?"

"I'm sending Marc Adriatico to the Principal's office."

"Very well. A monitor will meet him at the end of the hall."

Miss Diana turned to Marc. "I'm very disappointed in you, Marc. I was hoping you'd like the story."

"I do. Remember it's *Perseus*." He turned at the door with another tidbit of information that Jonathan had given to him the day before. "By the way, Miss Diana, did you know that Diana was the lesbian-goddess-of-the-hunt?" This was lost on the class, but not on Miss Diana, who shoved Marc out the door roughly.

"Go to the end of the hall, and you'll be taken to the Principal's office."

"Anything's better than here." Marc's voice was heard fading down the hall by the other children in the class.

"What's going to happen to Marc?" A blonde, blue-eyed classmate's pretty face was clouded with worry.

"The Principal is going to talk to him and probably call his mother. And," their teacher added, pausing significantly, "this is going to go on his permanent record. Okay. Now, for the story."

The children looked at each other. This was the first they had heard of the permanent record. They were not sure what it was, but it sounded bad. Followed by the Medusa, it sounded much worse. Miss Diana was evidently in too foul a mood for anyone to attempt further questions, so the idea of the permanent record grew in their imaginations.

Meanwhile, Marc had been met at the end of the hall by Mr. O'Rourke, the Assistant Principal, who placed a heavy hand on his shoulder and guided him, not very gently, to the Principal's office.

Marc squirmed. "Hey, you're hurting my shoulder."

"That's not all I'll hurt, you little coward," the Assistant Principal growled.

"If you hurt my violin shoulder, my father'll be mad at you."

"Your violin shoulder? Don't be a smart aleck with me."

By this time, they had reached the Principal's office. Mrs. James and Miss West, were standing behind the reception counter looking through their mail as the Assistant Principal brought in his prisoner. Miss West heard Marc's comment, and said quietly to the Assistant Principal, "The boy does play the violin." Mrs. James nodded in affirmation.

Mrs. Marchetti, the Principal, was standing in the doorway, waiting for them.

"Come on in here, Marc."

"He was hurting my violin shoulder."

"Well, people aren't always gentle with little boys who get sent to the Principal's office. Come in and sit down here." Mrs. Marchetti was stern.

Marc sat back in the vinyl-upholstered chair, his legs barely reaching the end of the cushion, and waited.

"Now, Marc," said the Principal, having seated herself behind her large green steel desk, "What did you do to make Miss Diana send you to my office?"

"I told her that it's *Per*seus, not Per*seus*."

"Well, it's actually pronounced either way. But I can't imagine Miss Diana sending you here for that. What else happened? Did you get into a fight with any of the other children?"

"No."

"What then?"

A pause. "I guess she got mad because I called her an ass."

Mrs. James, Miss West and Mrs. Marchetti's secretary, Lori, standing near the open door, exchanged half-amused glances. The Assistant Principal, who was standing with them, was not at all amused.

"You know cursing is not allowed." Mrs. Marchetti said to Marc.

"They use ASS in the Bible." Marc emphasized the verboten word.

Mrs. Marchetti opened her mouth to respond, and then closed it again. Her secretary and the two teachers were silently laughing. Marc, whose back was to the door, could not see them. But Mrs. Marchetti could, and she was having a hard time keeping a straight face. She cleared her throat, and focused on the boy in front of her.

"Did you say anything else?"

Although Marc didn't know exactly what it was, he knew something about the history of her name had enraged Miss Diana. So he decided to tell on himself.

"After she called you, I told her that Diana was the lesbian-goddess-of-the-hunt." Marc's deadpan delivery of the information showed that he had no idea what the phrase meant. Miss West could not contain her laughter, and quickly disappeared into an adjoining office before Marc could turn around to see her.

Mrs. James followed her. In the seconds as he turned around and then back, Mrs. Marchetti rubbed her forehead and regained her composure.

"Marc, being disrespectful to your teacher is not acceptable behavior. You have been sent to sit in the hall a few times as punishment for things you've done in your class, but this time you've gone too far. I know that you're aware that calling people names, whether they are in the Bible or not, is wrong. I will have to call your mother, and you will have to apologize to Miss Diana and to the rest of the class." Mrs. Marchetti decided to ignore the rest of what Marc had said to his teacher.

Mrs. Marchetti waited for a minute to see whether Marc would show any signs of remorse. Usually, children who made some effort to redeem themselves at this point were given a reprieve. Marc was not one of those children.

"Is this going on my permanent record?" He asked the question as she reached for the phone.

"Yes, it is," she said sternly.

"Oh." Marc looked around the office, unconcerned, as she dialed the number.

After several rings, she hung up. "Your mother's not home. I guess you'll have to sit outside my office until she comes to pick you up."

"She's not home?" It was the first sign of worry Marc had shown. "She's always home when I'm here."

"Maybe she had to run an errand before coming to pick you up. I'm sure you don't have to worry about your mother; you're in enough trouble yourself. Go and sit in that blue chair out there until she comes for you."

Twenty minutes later, Pino Adriatico called the school office.

"My wife just had a baby. She's supposed to be picking up Marc right about now. I'm out of town. The baby came a few weeks early. Could you ask my daughter Delfina to bring him home? Their grandmother is on her way to our house. As a matter of fact, both Jon and Delfina can walk Marc home, and that way I can talk to all of them.

"Is your wife all right?"

"Yes, she and the baby are both fine. I want to tell all the children at the same time."

"I'll have Delfina bring Jon and Marc home."

❦   ❦   ❦

That morning, after putting Marc on the school bus, Irene had gone back to her studio to work on a sculpture. As she was getting some water, she was almost bowled over by an unexpected contraction. Since the baby was not due for another two weeks, Irene resumed her work, intent on getting a significant amount done before Marc got back from school. She assumed the contraction was the first of many that would be coming in the next few weeks.

The next contraction, a few minutes later, made her stop what she was doing. Pino was in Tokyo on business; he would be returning two days later. As she was leaving a message at his hotel, her water broke. When she hung up, she called her mother.

"Mom, I'm taking a taxi to the hospital. I need you to come over here and watch Marc after he gets back from kindergarten. I'll get one of the neighbors to bring him home. I just left a message for Pino."

Grace promised to come right over.

As soon as Irene hung up, the phone rang. It was Pino.

"My water broke. I'm on my way to the hospital. My mother's coming over. I need you to get someone to bring Marc home from school."

"Irene, I'm in Tokyo. How am I supposed to do that? This is very inconvenient." Pino had just found out that he needed to stay in Tokyo for an extra week.

"I am having a baby. What's inconvenient?" Irene practically screamed into the phone as another contraction wracked her.

"All right. You say your mother's coming over? Can you give me the number of the school? I'll take care of it."

Irene read the number off the refrigerator message pad, while dropping some towels on the floor to absorb the water. Once off the phone with Pino, she called the cab company. After being assured that a car would be there in less than fifteen minutes, she packed a few things in an overnight bag, amid contractions.

The cab arrived quickly. He honked the horn, and when he saw her lumbering out of the house, he got out of the car to take her bag and open the door.

"Hi. I'm Rory. Where to?"

"St. John's Hospital. Quick, or this baby'll be born in the back seat of your cab." The driver, seeing that she was serious, made the ten-minute drive in five. Irene credited the bumpy ride with hastening the delivery. Irene thrust a ten-dollar bill into the hand of a very concerned Rory as she was being wheeled into the hospital. Thirty minutes later, Veronique Adriatico was born.

🍁     🍁     🍁

On October 15, while Irene was giving birth to her fourth child, Joe Clementine was kneeling on the cold stone floor of the monastery near Montreal where he had been sent four months earlier. He was flagellating himself, as he had been three times a day since he had gotten the news that Irene was pregnant.

After he had left Irene's bedroom that icy evening, he had blindly made his way back to his car. He had not fully recovered from the shock of the afternoon's accident, and the shock of his encounter with Irene had added to his burden. As he sat in his car, staring at a wall of fog for several hours, he was unaware that the temperature was dropping precipitously. As the temperature dropped, the fog began to lift, and eventually snow began to fall. His chattering teeth finally brought him to his senses, and he reluctantly started his car and drove uncertainly toward the rectory.

Once inside, he went directly to Father Patrick's office.

"Joe, you look awful. Here. Have a cup of coffee." Without waiting for an answer, the older priest poured a cup from the stainless steel urn on his desk.

"I need to speak with you." Joe spoke through chattering teeth. As he took a sip of the proffered coffee, Patrick closed his office door and waited until Joe was ready.

"Father, forgive me for I have sinned." Patrick, hearing the familiar start to a confession, got up, signaled Joe to wait for a moment, and donned a thin purple stole, which he placed around his neck as he returned to his seat.

"Tell me what happened."

An hour later, Joe had told the whole story, omitting only the name of the parishioner with whom he had been intimate. This detail was one that Patrick did not want to know. His concern right now was for his young associate whose agitation had only increased during his confessional narrative.

"What is your main worry right now—the woman, or is it something else?"

"Father, I feel numb still. I feel lost. I don't know whether to talk with her or let her come to me. What should I do?"

"You've had a shock witnessing that accident. If this woman is someone who will—"

"She's married."

"Then wait to let her approach you. She's probably feeling as badly, if not worse, than you are. I would counsel you to meditate and pray for guidance. Say two rosaries for your penance, and if you need to talk some more, I'm here." Joe nodded, too ashamed to look the other priest in the eye as he got up to leave. He put down the cup of coffee and virtually limped out of the room, head down. Patrick put a hand on his shoulder as he was leaving.

"God bless you, son."

Stifling a sob, Joe left the office and headed straight for his room. Once there, he knelt in front of the altar for three hours, saying the rosary and praying for guidance. During that time he remembered an ancient practice of cloistered monks who practiced self-flagellation to atone for their sins. He vowed to do the same every day for forty days as part of his penance. The next day he had a switch, and he started his ritual of self-punishment. On the second or third morning, Father Patrick was walking by Joe's room when he heard the regular sound of the whoosh, then crack, of the bamboo reed coming from behind the door. He tapped on the door lightly.

"Who is it?"

"It's Patrick. May I come in?"

"Patrick, it's not a good time." Joe's voice was clear behind the door. "I'll be down in about half an hour."

"Come to my office in half an hour then."

As Patrick started to descend the stairs, the rhythm started again.

❦   ❦   ❦

Thirty minutes later, Joe was in Patrick's office.

"Joe, you've had a double trauma. I know I don't need to lecture you, but as your friend, I'd like to remind you that the sacrament of reconciliation is for us to acknowledge our mistakes and move on without letting guilt and self-blame get the better of us. You look like you haven't slept, and you're too valuable a member of this parish, and too valuable an assistant to me, to be less than your best."

"Father Patrick," Joe spoke formally to underscore the seriousness of what he was saying, "I don't believe I'll be of any use to anyone here after what I've done. I would like to request a transfer until I figure out what I need to do."

"You know you are not under my authority. Your order determines where you go and what you do. You came here under unusual conditions, but it's worked well for the parish, and for me personally. I would ask you to consider making your transfer temporary. I know it may be difficult, but removing yourself from the problem is never a good solution. Leave for a time if you must, but I ask that you return. You're very popular here, and you are a great help and companion to me."

"Then I'll consider making it temporary. I wanted to speak to you before I made my request."

"Joe, the punishment you inflict upon yourself—"

"Father, that's between me and God. I will not talk about it. It is true, however, that as long as I'm living the life of an ascetic, I should not be at this parish."

It took the order three months to transfer Joe. It had been decided that he would remain at the parish to finish the academic year. He and Irene avoided each other until late April when Irene had determined that she was pregnant.

Delfina actually gave Joe the news. She had sought him out after mass one Sunday, wanting to ask him a question about something she had read in his book.

"I'm almost at the end of the book, Father Joe, and I think I really get the syllogisms. It's easy when it's 'All S is P' and 'All S is not P.' But I don't always get it right when it's 'Some S is P.'"

Joe drew her a diagram while explaining the concept.

"Thanks, Father Joe. Me and my brothers really need to call all the priests by their names since Dad wants us to call him Father all the time now."

"He does? Why is that?"

"He says that now that he's advisor to the County Executive, it's better if we practice acting formal all the time. That starts with calling him Father and being on our best behavior. Did you know that Mom's having a baby?"

"No, I didn't."

"Yeah, she is. It's coming in October. What's wrong?"

Joe's stunned silence as he did the calculation prompted the girl's question.

"Nothing, Delfina. I guess I was thinking that October is not that far off. Listen, I'm going to be going away for a while. It's temporary," he added, noticing the girl's dismayed look. "I'm going to some exciting places. Africa for a few months, and then to a monastery in Canada. I'll be leaving in two weeks. Next Sunday will be my last day here, but I'd like to give you a copy of the book I'm using now. I'll drop it off one day before I leave."

"What mass are you saying next week? I want to make sure we're at it."

"Seven A.M."

"Early. I'll try to get Mom to go. I think Father'll be in Japan again."

"He's been going there quite a bit." Delfina nodded. Joe continued, "If you don't make it, don't worry. I'll get the book to you."

"Thanks, Father Joe. I think Mom's talking to Father Patrick at the back of the church. Do you want to tell her you're going?"

"Not now, Delfina. I have to get things ready here."

From a gap in the curtain at the side of the altar, he watched the girl go to her mother. She waited patiently until the adults were finished talking, and then he could see her telling Irene the news as Father Patrick nodded his verification. Irene put her arm around Delfina's shoulders, and seemed to lean on her a bit, Joe thought. Then he shook his head. It was just his imagination, he told himself. He went back to readying the church for the afternoon mass, thinking about whether he should drop off the book or mail it.

Half an hour later, he met Irene coming out of the rectory as he was going in.

"Irene—I—"

"Delfina tells me you're leaving."

"It's temporary. Listen, I've got a book for her. I'd like to drop it off tomorrow if that's okay with you."

"I'll be home." Her eyes masked her emotions as she looked at him unblinkingly.

He nodded and continued into the rectory.

The next day he was at her house at noon. He stood outside the door when she answered, ready to hand her the book and leave.

"Here's the book for Delfina."

"Thank you. She tells me you're going to Africa and then to Canada."

"She tells me you're pregnant."

"You should come in. How about a cup of coffee?"

She held the door open for him, and he entered the foyer where he had not been since the afternoon of the train accident. She watched him remove his baseball cap—a Mets cap this time—and noticed that she felt no physical pull to him.

"I've missed our talks." She was sincere.

"I felt it was best under the circumstances. I didn't know what else to do."

She nodded and led him toward the kitchen. "I guess it's been rough for you."

"Hasn't it been for you?"

"Joe, everything I do goes into my art. I went to confession to cleanse my immortal soul, but I worked it out in clay." In response to his blank expression, she added, "I don't expect you to understand. Suffice it to say that in working on my crash series, I worked out what happened between us."

"And now you're pregnant."

"And now you're going to Africa."

"It's a temporary assignment. I'll be back. I need to ask you—" He paused, not knowing how to phrase his question. Irene waited. "You're due in October," he started. She nodded. "That would make the time of conception—"

"January. Yes." Irene waited again.

"Irene, is there any chance that I'm—" Joe could not finish the sentence.

Irene wiped down the counter and put down a cup of coffee in front of him, caught unexpectedly between pity and anger at him. She decided to give him the raw truth.

"I only had sex one day from January to March." Joe raised his eyebrows as if to say *that* day. She nodded, continuing. "Yes, the day of the train wreck. First you, then half an hour later, Pino." He gawked, surprised at the jealousy that arose in him. "It could be either of you," she continued. "Anyway, it's my baby, and the question of who its father is, well, as far as I'm concerned, it doesn't matter."

"It matters to me."

"Why, Father?" Irene was angry now. "What are you going to do? Raise it as your own? Disrupt the lives of my other kids? Or assuage your guilt knowing it's not yours? I notice this is the first time you've tried to talk to me about that day or any possible ramifications. Why is that, Father? Did you want it to just go away? Well, I have news for you, something they probably didn't teach you at the seminary: your actions have consequences. Now you're just going to have to live with the fact that your actions, our actions, had consequences. I'm prepared to live without knowing who the father of this child is, let people assume what they will. I advise you to do the same."

The torrent was over.

Joe did not attempt to defend himself or to reason with her. He simply put the book for Delfina on the counter and left saying, "I'm going to Africa. I'll be there until September. Then I'm going to a monastery near Montreal."

The following Sunday, Delfina was at the early mass by herself. Afterward she went to Joe and said, "Mom was too tired to get up for this mass, but she let me ride my bike here. I wanted to say thanks for the book. You're going to Africa on Friday?" He nodded. "When are you coming back here?"

"I don't know what God has in store for me. I hope I'll be back by Christmas."

"Mom'll have had her baby by then."

Joe nodded, and, not knowing what else to do, gave her a hug and said, "God bless you, Delfina. Be good. I'll see you when I get back."

And so it was that on October 15 when Irene was giving birth, Joe Clementine was kneeling on the cold stone floor of the monastery near Montreal inflicting the type of punishment on himself that he thought he deserved for having upset the lives of many people, not only Irene's and her new baby's, but her whole family's. And his life, too.

※　　　　　※　　　　　※

As Delfina walked her brothers home from school on that October day, she said to Marc, "You got sent to the Principal's office."

Marc made a face, and Jon laughed. "What did you do?" Jon asked.

"Stupid Miss Diana. She says Perseus."

"He called her an ass," Delfina informed him.

Jonathan was really laughing now. "Good for you."

"She is an ass." Marc was still angry. "I also told her what you said about Diana."

"What's that?" Delfina wanted to know.

"I told him that the next time old Diana gave him any trouble, he should tell her that Diana was the lesbian-goddess-of-the-hunt."

"What's so bad about that?" Delfina wasn't sure what a lesbian was.

Jon did not know either, but he knew it was not good. "I think I heard Mr. Laurio call one of his secretaries that before he fired her. Maybe it means that she's not a good worker."

That did not sound right to Delfina, but she let it go, unwilling to admit that she did not know what it meant. She decided to take the short cut through the woods.

"Mommy says we're not allowed to go through the woods," Marc objected.

"Mommy's not here, and we need to get home quickly so that I can get back to school before reading." Delfina loved the part of the day when the class was allowed to read quietly.

"I'm gonna tell we went through the woods," Marc said.

"Go ahead. Mom's not home. She had the baby. That's why I'm stuck taking you home."

"Did she have a boy?" Jonathan wanted to know.

"Nobody knows. We're going home so Father can tell us first." To Marc, she added, "I wasn't going to tell Father about you getting in trouble, but I will now, since you were going to get me in trouble. Besides, Mrs. Marchetti gave me a note about you."

"I don't care." Marc was defiant.

"Let's see the note." Jonathan was curious.

"We can read it after Father throws it out," Delfina said.

"Why do you call him Father all the time?" Jonathan wanted to know.

"He wants to be called that, and besides, you call him Father to his face. What do you call him when you talk about him?"

"I don't call him anything. Except sometimes stupid." Jonathan was honest. "I HATE him now that he's so fake."

"He's your father. It's a sin to hate him." Delfina was loyal. She also did not want to admit that Jon was right about their father's artificial persona.

"Come on, Del. Let's read the note. We can put it back after. Besides, with the new baby, who'll care?"

"The old baby," Delfina indicated Marc, "will tell on us just because he's in trouble."

"I will not."

"Liar." Jonathan and Delfina said it in unison.

"Let's go home. Gran'ma's waiting for us," Jonathan said, signaling to Delfina, over Marc's head, that they could read it later. Delfina nodded and led the way.

"I want to read the note," Marc whined.

"Forget it. I'm just going to give it to Father." Delfina told him. "All you ever do is get me in trouble."

"Let me see it," Marc said.

"No. Gran'ma's waiting for us. Let's go. You're in enough trouble as it is. If I tell on you, you'll really be in trouble."

Marc reluctantly followed his sister home.

Their grandmother was there, waiting for them, with lunch on the table.

"I've got to get back to school, Gran'ma," Delfina told her.

"You have to wait while we call your father," Grace told her. "He wants to tell you about the new baby."

She dialed the long distance number as the children ate their lunch. "Okay. It's ringing. Delfina, go to the phone in the studio. Jonathan, you can take the one in your parents' bedroom. Marc, you stay here with me."

Still chewing her sandwich, Delfina left the table. Jonathan was already in the bedroom. Pino's tired voice came over the crackling line. "Hi everyone. I just finished talking to your mother. She says you now have a new baby sister. Her name is Veronique. Your mother will be in the hospital for two more days. Your grandmother will be staying with you, so be good. Make me proud of you."

"When are you coming home, Father?" Delfina asked.

"I'll be home next Thursday."

"But that's a week from now," Delfina objected. "Weren't you supposed to be home tomorrow?"

"I have some business to take care of. And now that there's another person in our family, I need to make more money, don't I, Honey? Be a big help to your grandmother and your mother when she gets back. Okay? Jonathan, as the oldest boy, you're the man of the family until I get back. Remember that. Marc, are you there?"

"Yes."

"Be a good boy for your grandmother, okay? Make sure she's comfortable while she stays at our house. Can you do that, Marc?"

"Yes. Do I have to go to school until Mommy gets back?"

"Yes, you do, Marc. You need to go to school and learn all you can so that you can teach your new sister everything she needs to know. I have to go now, children. Grace, thank you for everything. Bye." With that, the line went dead.

"Okay, everyone. Come and finish your lunch," Grace called.

Suddenly Delfina did not feel like going back to school. She ate her lunch slowly, and Jonathan did the same. "Gran'ma. It's almost two o'clock. We get out of school at three-thirty. By the time Jon and I walk there, it'll be time to go back home."

Grace considered this. "That's true. Okay. You don't have to go back today. It's been such an event-filled day. Why don't you go outside and play for a while?"

"I think I'll read," Delfina said. Jonathan and Marc went outside, followed by Delfina carrying a book.

Later that evening, Jonathan came into Delfina's room. "Let's read that note."

"I already opened it," she told him. "It doesn't say anything good, just to call Mrs. Marchetti to discuss Marc."

"Oh." Jon was disappointed. "Del, what's a lesbian? I looked it up in the *Encyclopedia Britannica*, and all it says is from the isle of Lesbos, a school for women started by some guy named Sapf-o."

"That's what it is."

"Then why did Miss Diana get so mad at Marc?"

"I think it was because he called her an ass. I'm going to put the note in Father's 'in' box. He probably won't see it until June."

"But then Marc won't get in trouble."

"Who cares? With this new baby around, who'll have time to worry about something stupid like calling that ass Miss Diana an ass." Sister and brother laughed.

Meanwhile, Marc was sitting in his bed, crying as his grandmother tucked him in. "I want my mommy," he sobbed.

"Mommy's in the hospital with the new baby. She needs you to be a big boy now. Just think, when you wake up tomorrow, you'll only have one more night before she comes home." This made Marc cry more.

"I don't want to be a big boy. I want my mommy."

Grace was at her wits' end. "Delfina, can you come in here and make your brother stop crying?"

Delfina sighed and put her book down. Jonathan followed her into Marc's bedroom.

"I want Mommy," the little boy said again. Their grandmother left the room to make some tea for herself.

"Don't be a stupid baby," Jonathan said to him. This made Marc cry harder.

"That's not helping," Delfina told Jonathan severely. "Marc, don't you want to be a big boy now?"

"No. I want Mommy."

"Jon, if Marc says he'll be a big boy, do you think we could take him to the Chamber?" Marc stopped crying at this. The Chamber was a secret place shared by Delfina and Jonathan, a place Marc had never been allowed, because he was a baby.

"Y-y-you'll t-t-take me t-t-to the C-C-Chamber?" Marc was still tearful.

"On two conditions," Delfina told him seriously. "First, that you act like a big boy forever, starting now." Marc nodded.

Jonathan took over. "Second, that you swear on the blood of your ancestors that you'll never ever tell where it is, even under penalty of death."

"Okay. I s-swear."

"We'll have to see if you're really a big boy first," Delfina told him. "So, starting now, put yourself to bed, turn off the lights and go to sleep."

"Can I keep my door open?" Marc wanted to know.

"Well—" Delfina thought for a moment.

"If he's really a big boy, he won't need to keep the door open," Jonathan pointed out to his sister.

"He can start out by keeping it half open. Father told him to make sure Gran'ma's comfortable, so let him keep the door half open for now." Delfina was more interested in getting back to her book than in being mean to Marc. Jonathan shrugged his assent.

And so it was. Three days later when Irene came home from the hospital with eight-pound, three-ounce Veronique, Marc was the picture of big boyishness. The three children crowded around their mother as she introduced their new sister to them. The baby had a head of jet black hair, and when she opened her eyes, they were cobalt blue.

"Ewww. She's all grey and wrinkled," Marc said when Irene took the yellow baby blanket away, revealing Veronique's face.

"That's because she's been floating around in water in my tummy for nine months," Irene told him.

He cautiously ventured a finger toward the baby's head of black hair.

"Be careful of her soft spot," his mother warned.

"What soft spot?"

"Here at the center of her head. The bone hasn't hardened there yet. I don't want you to touch her head, okay?" Marc nodded to his mother, never removing his eyes from the top of his new sister's head.

Later Irene went into her bedroom where a crib had been set up, and found Marc feeling the top of the baby's head.

"Marc, what did I tell you?"

"Mommy, I want to know what it feels like."

Irene sighed. "Okay. I'll show you, but then I don't want you touching her head again. Okay?"

"Okay."

Irene took Marc's hand and let him feel the fontanelle.

"Gross. What happens if you push in on it?"

"You could hurt her. You're her protector, so I don't want you to do that. Okay? Look at how big your hand is next to hers." Marc looked. His hand did seem much bigger in comparison. "Okay, Markie. Now go and play. I need to feed the baby."

Feeding the baby was a mystery to Marc. His mother just seemed to hold the baby near her, but when she did the screaming stopped, and strange gurgling noises started. Before he could ask his mother any questions about it, Delfina walked by.

"Delfina, would you bring Marc to play with you and Jon? I need to feed the baby."

Delfina sighed and said, "Come on, Marc. Jon's in the living room."

"Mommy let me touch the soft spot."

"You did, Mom? I thought you said it would hurt her."

"I held his hand, and he promised not to touch it again."

In the living room, out of earshot of his mother, Marc asked his siblings when they were going to the Chamber.

Delfina said, "Marc, before we take you to the Chamber, we need to know that you're really not a baby. If you do stupid things like touching the baby's soft spot, we're never going to take you to the Chamber."

"I won't. I promise."

"Yeah. You just did," Jonathan pointed out.

"I won't do it again. You'll see."

"Okay. We'll give it a week. If you don't do anything babyish by next Saturday, we'll take you to the Chamber."

# CHAPTER 6

❃

The nature path started on Long Island's North Shore at Sunken Meadow State Park, and made its way to the South Shore ending at one of the area's many state parks. The path was eventually renamed the Green Belt and maintained as a hiking trail. Long before the environmental revolution, the path gave Joe Clementine many hours of solace. The Adriatico children also spent many hours on that nature path, playing in the woods and on the shores of the Long Island Sound.

On one of their adventures in the woods two summers before Veronique was born, Delfina and Jonathan ventured off the path and onto the Kings Park State Hospital grounds. The hospital, which had the only building over five stories tall in the town, was the home for mental patients, including the criminally insane who were kept in the twenty-story brick building with bars on the windows. Unbeknownst to the children, the criminally insane who inhabited this building were treated to some of the best views of the countryside and the Long Island Sound.

On the day that Delfina and Jonathan found themselves on the hospital grounds, they had passed the run-down marina, which was behind a row of office buildings, and they ventured into a thicket to avoid being seen by anyone who might have been at the dock. As they were making their way through the brush looking to pick up the trail, they heard the sound of a siren, which was coming from the vicinity of the tall brick building.

"Sounds like someone escaped," Delfina told Jonathan. "Should we try to run back to the marina?"

"We'll never make it. Quick, hide in here." Jonathan pulled himself behind an ancient cement slab.

"No, they'll see us there." Delfina looked up. A large cherry tree stood on the other side of the cement slab. "Can you reach the bottom branches of that tree?" Jon nodded yes, and the two children ran to the tree. Delfina got there first and pulled herself up. Jonathan followed, nimbly scrambling up the trunk of the tree after his sister. Moments later, they heard the scraping of metal on cement as a round plate at one end of the cement slab started to move. Minutes later a young man dressed in a green jumpsuit emerged from the slab. Looking around furtively, he crouched by the trunk of the tree, just below Jon and Delfina. The children held their breath as the man decided what to do next. Evidently he was listening for any sound of pursuit. Not hearing anything but the rattling of the cicadas, the man lay down on his stomach and elbowed his way through the brush toward the marina. He did not bother to replace the metal plate.

Delfina and Jonathan stayed very still, barely breathing, waiting. Minutes later, they heard the sound of police car sirens near the marina. A voice, shouting the fact that the man was surrounded, came over a bullhorn. Then the sound of one person splashing in the water. A German Shepard was barking furiously. More people splashing in the water. More instructions over the bullhorn. Finally, the sound of several cars pulling away. Then silence. When the cicadas began their rattling song again, the children knew it was safe to come out of hiding.

Sister and brother climbed down from the tree woozily. Jonathan immediately relieved himself in the bushes.

"Gross," Delfina said, crinkling her nose. "Now, how are we going to get back home? If we go back the way we came, we'll have to go by the marina."

"They got the guy. It should be okay."

Delfina considered this. "Yeah, but we should probably just take the main road back. But wait a minute. I want to see where he came from."

"Not now, Del," Jonathan pleaded. "If we take the main road, it'll take a long time, so we should start walking now. Otherwise Mom will be really mad 'cause we'll be late for dinner. We'll come back another day, okay? Let's just get out of here."

"It does stink here, thanks to you."

"Let's go. We can come back after we find out what happened to him."

"Fine. But swear you won't tell anyone we were here. And swear you won't tell any of your friends about this place until I get a chance to explore it. 'Kay?"

"'Kay. Swear."

❦  ❦  ❦

Nothing appeared on the local news about an escapee from the State Hospital. The next morning, Delfina went outside and got the Sunday *Newsday*, which had just been delivered. She was leafing through it when Irene walked in.

"Since when do you read the newspaper?"

"I don't know. I was looking at the comics, and then I thought the rest of the paper might be interesting," Delfina lied. She and Jonathan had talked about the fact that if they said anything to their parents about the incident, they would not be allowed to return there. They were probably not allowed as far as they went anyway, Jonathan reasoned, and so it was better not to say anything. Delfina had agreed. "It's better for Mom and Father if they don't know where we go all the time. That way they don't have to worry, and we won't be disobeying them."

No mention of the escapee was made in any of the media. What the children did not know was that the goings-on at the hospital were never made public, especially incidents that would make the residents in the vicinity feel unsafe. Hospital officials made sure that patients did not escape, and, on the rare occasion that one tried, those same officials made sure that none of the town residents heard about the attempt. If anyone had called to inquire about a purported escape, they were given the official statement: The hospital had an excellent safety record, no one had ever escaped, and the community at large was perfectly safe. If anyone had been at the marina during the incident, what they had witnessed was a trespasser being removed. Nothing more.

One week later, Delfina and Jonathan decided it was safe to go back and explore the cement slab. This time they brought supplies: flashlights, drinks and snacks. They also wore long pants, not shorts. Jonathan complained about this, but Delfina told him that inside it would probably be cool and slimy. If they were crawling around, jeans would be better. If he didn't like it, he didn't have to go.

They were back at the cement slab at about two o'clock that afternoon. Unseen, they slipped through the woods, past the marina where several people were tending to their boats.

Retracing their steps, they approached the place where the man had removed the round plate. The plate was still leaning next to the uncovered escape route. Delfina crouched down and looked into the darkness. The cicadas trilled loudly in the background. She put her head into the darkness. The cement-cooled air inside was a distinct contrast to the humid sun-warmed air of that summer day. Hearing nothing, Delfina was emboldened to crawl inside. Jonathan followed with trepidation.

Delfina shined a flashlight around the area in front of her. They seemed to be inside a tunnel. The walls were rounded and smooth, like a large pipe. Five feet in front of her, the tunnel got bigger.

"Don't go any further," Jonathan begged her. His voice reverberated in the close space.

"I just want to go over there where I can stand up. You stay here and hold the flashlight. Okay?" She kept her voice low.

Without waiting for an answer, she handed her brother the light, and scrambled toward the larger space. Once there, she stood up. The air felt different there. It was cooler, and gave the impression that it was moving somehow. She looked back toward her brother who was shivering by the entrance. His silhouette was etched against the bright sunlight behind him.

"Come back, Del," he called her.

"Shhh. If there's anyone on the other end of this thing, I don't want them to hear us." She moved back toward him. "Jon, this could be a great hideout. There's nothing to be afraid of.

"Nothing except escaping nut cases," her brother grumbled.

"Once one escaped, I'm sure they closed up his escape route so that no one else could use it. Besides, it couldn't have been a big deal. It never even made the papers."

"There was something weird about that, too," Jonathan said. "They put everything in the paper. Remember the time that Mrs. Weed was caught drunk driving? And when Mr. Caprillo stole the Johnsons' weathervane? Any time the cops are called, it gets in the paper. There must have been at least five cop cars here, and there was nothing in the paper."

"Who cares?" Delfina was more interested in exploring. "Look, Jon, if you're afraid, you don't have to come with me."

"I'm not afraid, I just don't want to get in trouble."

"Yeah. Since when are you worried about getting in trouble? Fraidy cat."

"Am not."

Delfina did not bother to answer that. "Nobody knows this is here. We should camouflage it, so that no one finds it. Then we can explore without worrying about being found out. Would that make you feel better?" The truth was, Delfina felt better having her brother exploring with her.

"Okay." Jonathan brightened at that suggestion. He loved camouflage, and he was good at it. The two worked for the rest of the afternoon, gathering branches and leaves to extend the mound of earth and foliage that rose behind the cement slab to cover the cement slab. Once this was done, they brought more branches and constructed two smaller mounds in front of the opening, which hid the opening from view but allowed them to get in and out without making any noise.

The shadows were lengthening dangerously when their job was finished.

"We have to run home now, or Mom will kill us." Jonathan was never late for a meal.

They ran all the way back to their house, getting into the driveway just after their father's car pulled in.

The next day they went back. Delfina had brought a spool of colored yarn with her. "We'll trail the yarn behind us, so that we can follow it back."

"Like Hansel and Gretel should have done, instead of using crumbs?"

"Yeah. No birds or other animals will eat the yarn."

Jonathan liked the idea of having a Hansel and Gretel type of adventure, but being smarter than the original characters.

The camouflage to the entrance was undisturbed. They tied one end of the yarn to a branch near the entrance, and crawled into the tunnel until they reached the part where they could stand. Jonathan was trailing the yarn, and Delfina was leading, carrying the flashlight. The tunnel had a few puddles in places, but for the most part, it was dry. Broken cobwebs hung from the walls, but the tunnel was mostly free of dirt and slimy algae.

After fifteen minutes of walking, mostly in silence, listening for the sound of anyone coming through the tunnel, they came to a crossroads of sorts. They opted to go to the right. "We'll do the other way next time, and then straight the time after," Delfina said.

The tunnel started a slight incline after that juncture. At intervals, the children started running into cobwebs—large, sticky ones that were intact, not broken like they had been before. The cobwebs felt almost like netting.

The first one took them by surprise. "Yuck," Delfina said. "This feels like it's Spiderman's web." She broke through with her flashlight, making a mental note to bring a stick next time.

"I want to do the next one." Jonathan's fear was quickly being replaced with his sense of adventure.

The grade got steeper, and the tunnel began to curve, first one way and then the other as they continued. About a half an hour later, Jonathan said, "I'm taking a drink. Wait for me."

"I'm just going ahead a little bit. I'll be right back."

"Can't you just wait a minute?"

"I think I see a light up there. Look, Jon. The tunnel stopped curving. It's straight and there's a light or something up there."

Jonathan forgot about his drink and scrambled after his sister. The tunnel ended in a large circular chamber. The entrance to the chamber was thick with cobwebs. Jonathan and Delfina pushed them away and walked into the center of the chamber. Their footsteps were marked in the dusty floor. The light came from a grid work that made up the ceiling. The grid work covered grimy glass which allowed the light in but kept the chamber dry. Cobwebs were everywhere. It was evident that no one had been in this place for many years.

At the far end of the circular room, there was a dark wooden door with a heavy, round brass ring for a handle. Next to the door, the wall seemed to be made out of aluminum or light steel; in the dimness and the grime, it was hard to tell. On closer inspection, this section of the wall actually seemed to be an ancient garage-type door. Delfina went over to the dark wooden door and pulled on the ring. The door was heavy, and it creaked on its two heavy metal hinges, but it moved a few inches. With both children pulling at the door, they were able to open it enough to squeeze through. Three steps led to another door, this one was square, about three feet high. It had an odd type of window to it. Delfina, in the lead, looked out.

"Hey, we're by the Old Dock Inn."

"Let me see." Jonathan looked out and saw that they were at the far end of the parking lot, at the edge of the woods. He could see the restaurant, the entire parking lot, which went all the way to the water, and the dock where two fishermen were hauling their boat onto a trailer with a sturdy grey winch.

"Try to open the door." Delfina directed him.

They pulled on the door together, and it creaked open slowly. Beyond the door, vines and decayed leaves formed a thick veil. The imprint of the now opened door was left in the dried foliage at the threshold. Grey bugs that looked like miniature armadillos ran about confused, their sanctuary disturbed.

"Hey, look at that," Jonathan breathed, entranced by the camouflage and the bugs. Both doors were now wide open. Delfina closed the larger door, which creaked heavily on its hinges as it closed.

Jonathan was making plans. "We can have a round table like King Arthur. What'll we call it?"

"Let's call it The Chamber."

The one activity Pino did with his children was read to them. This summer he was reading Sherlock Holmes mysteries to them. Delfina, having a summer of Nancy Drew in addition to Sherlock Holmes, liked the Holmes-flavored suggestion.

"All right, but you can't tell anyone about it. Okay? No one."

"Not even Mommy and Daddy?"

"He wants us to call him Father. No. Especially not them. But none of your little friends either, especially that blabbermouth friend of yours, Robert."

"What about in confession?" Jonathan's first confession was coming up, and he was beginning to get intrigued with the curtained confessional at the back of the church. He wanted to spend as much time there as possible, so he was compiling a list of things to say.

Delfina sighed heavily. "You're supposed to talk about all the bad things you've done. This isn't bad. It's a secret so that nobody else hogs the place. You've done enough bad things to talk about in confession. Don't waste your time with this. Plus it's a secret, so if you tell, I'll never let you come back here."

"You're not the boss of it."

"I'm bigger than you. Besides if you tell, I won't be the one keeping you away. Just remember that."

❧   ❧   ❧

On the sunny Saturday in November when Delfina and Jonathan went to bring Marc to the Chamber for the first time, they found him in their mother's studio making a small figure out of clay.

"What're you making, Marc?" Jonathan wanted to know.

"Looks like a person, right Marc?" Delfina said.

"Yeah, it is." Marc was working furiously.

"Where's Mom?" Delfina asked.

"In there feeding the stupid baby." Suddenly he finished his work: a small scrunched-up human figure with its arms wide. "Now watch this." He started pounding the clay he had just finished. "This is the baby. Mommy said I could always make monsters out of clay and then turn them into something else, like magic. I want to turn that stupid baby into mush." He pounded harder as his brother and sister watched.

"Did you get in trouble, Marc?" Delfina asked.

"No. Yesterday Mommy said she'd do clay with me today, and just now she said that the baby kept her up last night, and she was too tired, and I have to do it by myself. It's not as much fun without her."

"Don't you get to do clay in school with the other kids?" Jonathan wanted to know.

"I—hate—school." Marc punctuated each word by pounding the clay. He continued to pulverize the figurine. "And, I hate this stupid baby. She's a, a," He searched for a word. "She's a poop." It was the worst word he could come up with.

Delfina and Jonathan looked at each other. Then Delfina, almost feeling sorry for him, said, "Well, when you're a big boy, you have to do things like clay by yourself, especially since you're so much better at it than the kids in your school. But you really have been a big boy all week, so put the clay away, and we'll do something else, okay?"

Marc, remembering their deal, perked up. He put the clay away and wiped his hands on the back of his jeans. Delfina decided to overlook this. She led him to Jonathan's room. "You tell him, Jon."

"Okay. Listen Marc. We're taking you to the Chamber. But first you have to swear on the blood of your ancestors that you will never, ever tell anyone about where we're going. If you do, all the ghosts of everyone who ever died in our family will come back and haunt you. So swear."

Marc nodded with wide eyes.

"Say it."

"I swear."

"Okay. Let's mix our blood together as a solemn omen."

"Oath," Delfina corrected Jonathan.

"Oath."

"I don't want to cut my finger."

"Then you're not a big enough boy to go to the Chamber." Jonathan was serious.

Delfina said, "Don't look, and it'll be over in a second."

"No. I want to do it myself. It doesn't have to be from my finger, does it?

"I guess not," Jonathan conceded.

Marc pulled off a scab on the back of his hand. "Here."

Delfina and Jonathan, holding their bleeding fingers, looked at each other and shrugged. They mixed their blood together, and then headed for the door.

"Mom, we're going to play in the woods," Delfina called to Irene. "We're taking Marc with us, and we're going to have a picnic, so you don't have to worry about making us lunch. Okay?"

Irene, dozing next to the baby, was grateful. "That's very nice of you, Delfina. What did you make for lunch?"

"Peanut butter and jelly. I took three bottles of root beer from the 'fridge."

"Okay." Irene was too tired to check up on her. "Remember, you're in charge. Marc, obey Delfina." Marc was already out the door, and did not hear her, but Delfina knew she could use the admonition as extra leverage if needed.

Half an hour later, they arrived in the Chamber. In the two summers since Delfina and Jonathan had discovered the tunnel, they had spent a lot of time there.

They had briefly explored the other passageways of the tunnel. At the crossroads in the tunnel, where they had originally turned right and found the Chamber, the other two paths, one straight ahead and one to the left, had not yielded anything comparable to that round room. The tunnel straight ahead seemed to go on interminably with an occasional locked door, drainage grating, and no end in sight. The door to the left was obviously the one that the escapee had used. This one had several passageways leading from it. Each of those branches ended in an underground entranceway to the various buildings on the State Hospital grounds. Each entranceway had a door that was marked with the number or name of the building to which it led. Delfina and Jonathan were not familiar with the building identification system, so the numbers and words on the doors were meaningless to them.

They found the tunnel that the escapee had used. The cobwebs in this particular passageway had been broken. They ventured all the way to the door used by the man they saw. As Delfina had predicted, it was boarded up, bolted from the inside. Dried cement seeped between the cracks in the boards, and they could see that it had also been sealed shut from the other side.

In one of the other branches of this particular tunnel, Delfina and Jonathan had found another door that had been marked "Main." The entranceway beyond this door had also been blocked, but with wood, not cement. The children could hear the sounds of typewriters and telephones, as well as the sounds of adult voices on the other side of that wooden barrier. Bored, they did not investigate much further. Many other doors, which could have been opened and possibly explored, did not hold as much allure to Jonathan and Delfina as the round room did. This was partly because they did not relish the thought of meeting another escapee.

Jonathan and Delfina did not bother to tell Marc about the escapee. They led him to the round room, which had undergone some major renovations in the two years since they had first discovered it. First, at Delfina's insistence, they had cleaned the Chamber thoroughly. She had even gotten a mop to clean the glass ceiling. Then they had brought in cushions and blankets to make it more comfortable. In Delfina's opinion, a table and chairs for drawing and other craft work was next. Jonathan wanted a "really long" table for his inventions. They had also brought in an old bookshelf to store the blankets and cushions.

"Wow." Marc walked into the center of the room. "What's behind that door?"

"Tell you later. Let's eat." Jonathan had his priorities.

Marc instantly forgot about the door, and he attacked the plastic-wrapped sandwich Jonathan tossed to him.

While the boys ate, Delfina fastened a piece of plywood to the wall. Then she tacked a Salvador Dali poster to the plywood. Ever since she had seen the three-dimensional-looking painting of Jesus crucified in a library book, she had been transfixed by it. She worked diligently to find and order a poster-size copy. Here, at last, was a depiction that was one step closer to the solution to the Jesus-on-the-cross problem. A 3-D flying Jesus, without the gory details. In the painting, Jesus looked crucified, but he also looked like he could get up and walk around at any time. Delfina thought about this as she worked to tack up the poster.

"Is it straight, Jon?" She was also wondering if Salvador Dali was related to the Dalai Lama.

He nodded. "It's gonna sag."

"I know, but I want to look at it when I'm here."

"Put two more tacks in the middle. That'll hold it better."

She did, and stepped down to start eating her sandwich.

"I'm hungry," Marc said, looking around.

Delfina was hungry also, but she decided to give Marc her sandwich. "I need to be on a diet," she said, echoing her parents' recent conversations. "You can have my sandwich."

"Hey, what about me?" Jonathan wanted to know.

"You can each have half."

Because of its depth and the fact that the walls of the Chamber were made of earth, the temperature inside the round room remained at a constant temperature of fifty-five degrees all year around. The three children were dressed warmly, and they remained there comfortably until late in the afternoon. Delfina was looking at the Dali poster while they boys were scaling baseball cards against the far wall, seeing who could make the cards fly further.

Because Delfina and Jonathan were not sure of their little brother's ability to keep a secret, when it was time to leave, they led Marc back through the tunnels without showing him where the door at the far end of the Chamber led.

That night, noticing Marc's healthy appetite, Irene asked, "What did you do today, Markie?"

His siblings held their breath. He looked at his mother solemnly and said, "I played with Jon and Del in the woods, because I'm a big boy now."

"What did you play?"

"Um, baseball cards."

The baby started crying from the other room. "That's nice, Honey. Del and Jon, I'm proud of you for including your brother in your games." She got up to quiet the baby.

Delfina and Jonathan exhaled as she left.

"See? I'm a big boy now."

❦ ❦ ❦

Father Joe Clementine had finished a forty-day, silent retreat, and was walking down the stone, outdoor hallway which led to the Monsignor's office. He now knew what he needed to do next. During his retreat, he had continued his flagellation three times each day, eating only bread and water, and spending the rest of his time in prayer and meditation. In the last ten days of the retreat, he had started meditating on the now-familiar bamboo switch which had lashed so many lines into his back.

He was now able to admit, between the moments of hunger and shame, the ecstatic moments induced by the pain. Surprisingly, that admission brought him a heretofore unknown sense of freedom. Within that freedom, Joe finally relaxed the hold he had on many of the uncompromising attitudes he held for himself in his mind. For the first time since he left Kings Park, he allowed himself to seriously contemplate Irene and the child, which certainly had been born by that time. He thought of the train wreck, and of Pino and Irene's other children. He allowed himself to admit that he missed Irene's companionship, her advice to him, and her creativity, which had brought so much color in the form of spontaneity to his rigidly arranged life.

He thought again of the child. Joe let himself recognize the fact that knowing Irene had had sexual relations with her husband in the same hour that she had been with him had made him feel both jealous and relieved. At last he admitted to himself that he had felt jealous first.

In his next round of self-inflicted punishment, Joe faced bigger questions. They came to him with the rapidity of the lashes. Was he the child's father? Was he not? Would it make a difference in his actions if he were or were not? Should he remove himself from Irene's life forever? He had promised Patrick Reilly that he would return to the parish. No one but Irene would ever know that there was a question concerning the father of this child. No one except God Almighty, not even Irene, would ever know for sure. What should he do? What should he do? The rhythm of the switch's lashing scored the question on his back. What should he do?

At the end of the forty days, he emerged from his chamber, thinner, bearded, and more solemn. He had the answer.

※　　　　※　　　　※

On a snowy Saturday, a week before Christmas, Father Joe presented Veronique Adriatico to the Catholic congregation of St. Joseph's Church. Two days earlier, he had gone to Irene and spoke with her briefly.

"I'm sorry for the hurt I've caused, and for not recognizing the consequences of my actions. You're right. It doesn't matter who the baby's father is. I have decided that I want to be around to watch this child grow up. I miss your friendship, your companionship."

"Joe, I was very angry with you for a long time. How could you just leave? I thought we had more of a relationship than that. I guess you were scared. I was too. But I was more scared once you left. I love having you around. You provide good conversation and an interest in culture that Pino never could." She paused and looked at him tenderly.

"Are you still angry?" He wanted to know.

She smiled softly. "No, not any more. I've got my baby and my art. I'll always be Pino's wife. You'll always be a priest. But I'd like to have you as a very close friend of the family."

And so Joe entered into the Adriaticos' life on the day of Veronique's baptism. He baptized her, and welcomed her into the one true Catholic Church. After the ceremony, the Adriaticos welcomed him to their home once again.

Delfina and Jonathan were the baby's godparents. The baby slept angelically in Delfina's arms through the ceremony, opening her bright blue eyes briefly as water was poured over her head, and placing her tiny hand on Joe's large one as he anointed her chest with holy oil.

Pino and Irene received Joe warmly. Pino was so glad Joe volunteered to do the baptism that he made the party into a double celebration: a baptism and a welcome home party. Irene was too preoccupied with the baby to engage with Joe very much during the festivities, and only Delfina noticed that Joe seemed more quiet and withdrawn.

After the ceremony, the family, joined by Joe and Patrick, had lunch at the Adriatico's house. Delfina did the hostessing with the help of Jonathan. Since the baby's arrival, Irene was tired much of the time. After lunch, the guests retired to the living room for coffee. Delfina served coffee from a silver urn. Jonathan followed with sugar and cream.

"More coffee, Father?"

"No, thank you." Pino, Joe, and Patrick all answered.

Embarrassed laughter followed the momentary silence.

Pino was surprisingly forthcoming in telling Joe how much his absence had been noticed. After saying how much he had missed their discussions, Pino added, "I hope you're back to stay this time—no more long vacations. I know you Jesuits are called to do missionary work and all, but hopefully the missionary work in the boonies of Kings Park will satisfy the people in your order."

Joe smiled quietly as he noticed how little interaction Pino had with the baby, or with any of his children for that matter. In that moment, he resolved to become a significant part of the baby's life, and the lives of Irene and her other children too. "I have been stationed here indefinitely," he informed his host. "My travels have shown me that I have a responsibility to the people of this parish. This is where my work is."

The baby looked at him with eyes that seemed to get bluer by the day. She cooed contentedly in Irene's arms.

# CHAPTER 7

"Ronnie, if you want to come with me, you've got to get up right now." Eighteen-year-old Delfina turned on the light in the room of her sleeping sister.

"It's still night," Veronique complained.

"It's five A.M. You don't have to come if you don't want to."

"I do want to. Carry me to the car."

"You want to go in your pajamas? Look, if you're too tired, maybe you're too young to go. There's always next year. I'll just turn the lights off and—"

"NO." Veronique got herself out of bed with all the energy that a six-going-on-seven-year-old could muster. She tottered on her feet, rubbing her eyes.

"Good." Delfina approved. "Your clothes are on the chair. If you hurry, we can eat breakfast at a rest area Father showed me."

It was October 1981, a week before Veronique's seventh birthday. As her present, Delfina had promised to bring her sister to a workshop in upstate New York. Sleepwalking, Veronique put on jeans, socks, sneakers, a Mets t-shirt and a Mets baseball cap.

Delfina came into the room. "You've got on matching socks, right?"

Veronique pulled up on the legs of her jeans to show that her socks were matching and clean.

"Cheating on your hair under that baseball cap?"

Veronique nodded.

"Bring your brush, and get into the car." Delfina was not going to have a battle over hair at five in the morning. Irene was up when they walked through the kitchen.

"Mom, what are you doing up?" Delfina could not remember the last time she had seen her mother awake at that hour. In the months before her youngest daughter was born, Irene had stopped getting up to see that her eldest daughter was ready for school.

"Where are you taking her, Delfina?"

"We're going to a workshop on Native American spirituality in Putnam County."

"She's told you that about a bazillion times," Veronique interjected.

"Do you know how to get there?"

"Father had his secretary type up the directions, we went over it five times on the map, and Father and I drove there last month with Antoinette."

"I don't know if this is such a good idea."

"You tell that to Ronnie. I'm going one way or another."

Veronique started whimpering, "Mommy, I was good all week. You can't not let me go now."

Delfina waited. Irene was doubtful that Delfina, who had just gotten her unrestricted driver's license, should be allowed to make the three-hour drive unsupervised. Delfina knew this was the way her mother felt, but she had her father's permission, and she was going. Whether Veronique went or not was up to her mother.

"I'm going." Veronique stamped her little foot emphatically, her blue eyes flashing. "It's my birthday present, and I was really good, so you can't take it away from me."

Irene looked from her angry younger daughter to her impassive older daughter and then back to her younger daughter again. "If Mommy will miss you too much, will you stay home with her?"

"No, Mommy, no. It's not fair. I want to go to the nave'merican day with Del. I'll tell you all about it when I get home."

"If we don't leave now, we'll be late," Delfina said, losing her patience. "What's it gonna be, Mom? Let her go, or deprive her of her birthday present?"

"I'm going." Veronique was on her way to the car.

Delfina followed her, waiting for her mother to object. Irene said nothing. She simply stood at the door in her blue flannel robe, watching the car pull out of the driveway and disappear into the mist that would burn off as the sun rose.

When they got onto the next street, out of view of the house, Delfina pulled out her map and directions with all the authority of an eighteen-year-old. She read the directions one more time and put them on the seat next to her, within easy reach. The early October sun was rising behind them as they sped along the Long Island Expressway, Delfina intent on the road, and Veronique asleep in the passenger's seat.

Four hours later, having stopped for breakfast at the diner near the Taconic Parkway that Pino had shown Delfina, the sisters arrived at the workshop site. The grass was glistening with dew as they walked toward the main house from the parking lot.

Once inside, Delfina registered them while Veronique peered curiously into the large room where workshop participants were gathering. When Delfina came back and handed her a name tag, she said, "Where are the Indians?"

"I don't know if there are any actual Indians—Native Americans," Delfina said. This is about their customs, but the guy who teaches it isn't a Native American."

"Oh." Veronique was disappointed. She had expected war paint and headdresses.

"Just do what I do, and it'll be fun. You'll be good at it. You have a great imagination." Veronique nodded, encouraged by her sister's compliment.

They took off their shoes, and went into the room, finding a place in the circle of people sitting on the floor.

A woman sitting next to Veronique admired the girls' hair, Delfina's one long braid down her back and Veronique's matching pony-tail braids, which Delfina had fashioned for her when they stopped for breakfast. The woman said to Delfina, "Is this your daughter?"

Veronique answered for her, "No, this is my sister, Delfina. I'm Veronique. This is my birthday present."

The woman smiled at her. "What pretty names both of you have. I'm Kathleen. My husband Tom and I are taking this workshop together. How old are you, Veronique?"

"I'm gonna be seven next week."

"Well, if you're the youngest member of this circle, you'll get to put the stick in the fire for the generations to come."

"Really?" Veronique was excited now.

Delfina smiled at her. "Oh yeah. I forgot about that. Sometimes it's the oldest person; sometimes it's the youngest. Don't be disappointed if it's the oldest. Okay?"

"I won't," Veronique promised, praying silently that it would be the youngest.

Just then, the man sitting at what appeared to be the front of the room stood up and shook the rattle he was holding to get everybody's attention.

"Welcome, welcome, everyone. Before I start talking, I'd like to call to the four directions. So, everyone, please," he lifted his hands, palms up, indicating that everyone should stand. Veronique and Delfina rose along with Kathleen, Tom and the rest of the fifty or so people who were attending the workshop.

"We call to the winds of the south," the leader began, facing to the south and raising his right hand. Veronique was concentrating on acting like an adult, and at the same time thinking what would happen if the wind was actually a real person. Suddenly, the group turned to the right. Delfina, standing slightly behind Veronique, pointed her in the right direction. Veronique looked up, and noticed that Kathleen, standing next to her now, had her right hand held up, like the "How" sign that she had seen on *F-Troop* reruns on television. She imitated the action. When the group turned to the right again, Veronique was ready. She turned on cue, hearing the group leader start his call to the winds of the north, but then missing the rest of what he said as she pictured three wind-people in the room. Then the group turned again, and this time she was able to watch the group leader as he swayed and called to the winds of the east, the place of the rising sun. Veronique liked that image, thinking of the sunrise as she and her sister had driven away from the house that morning. It was probably the earliest she had ever been awake and outside.

While she was thinking about this, the leader, followed by the rest of the group, crouched down and touched the floor. In her haste to follow, Veronique was unsure which wind they were calling to, but as she started to listen, she heard the leader start to mention animals "…and on your land and in your water…all our relations."

"All our relations," thought Veronique. "Relations, that means relatives, like Mommy and Father, and Del…does it also mean like Father Pat and Father Joe? What about relations like friends, or like Dawn? It definitely means the boys, and the cousins, like Luca…" By now the group was standing, looking up to the sun, the moon and the stars. Veronique was still thinking about her relations.

As the youngest member of the group, Veronique was the center of attention. When they had to choose partners for a guided meditative journey, Kathleen asked Veronique if she wanted to be her partner. Veronique was delighted. At the end of the very long day, there was an outdoor ceremony around the fire where everyone put in a stick for what they had learned that day. Veronique was allowed to put in an extra stick for all the coming generations.

When Veronique knelt in front of the fire to place the stick in it, an old man standing in semi-darkness on the other side of the flames cackled, "Who's your father? Who are all your relations?" Veronique jumped and looked around, but no one else seemed to have heard him. She looked back to the place where the old man had stood, but either he had moved, or she could no longer see him in the darkness. She shook off a vague uneasiness, and then forgot the incident as the group sang "Happy Birthday" to her at the end of the fire ceremony.

After the workshop was over, while Delfina was getting telephone numbers and information about trips out west, the teacher of the workshop came over to Veronique.

"Well, little one, how did you like this day?"

"It was really fun. I liked that my animal is a horse. It was cool actually. It started out as a lizard that was all the colors of the rainbow, but then it turned into a horse. I like horses. I was afraid I was going to get something stupid like a chicken."

The man laughed. "No animal is stupid. But I think I can understand why you'd prefer a horse to a chicken. Well, have a safe trip home." With that, he was gone. Veronique smiled, basking in the attention she had gotten during the day. Then, suddenly, she recalled the question she had about her relations and about the old man. Vainly, she looked for the group leader, but he was nowhere to be seen.

On the drive home, she asked Delfina about it. "Del, why, at the beginning, did he say all those animals and then all our relations? Is it 'cause we were doing spirit animals, or 'cause humans are animals too? And is relations just my family, or can it be friends too like that lady you were making googly eyes at? How can—"

"Whoa. Wait a minute. One question at a time." Delfina protested. "Why didn't you ask the teacher when you got the talking stick at the end? And I wasn't making googly eyes at anybody."

Veronique rolled her eyes at that, not wanting to get into an argument and more interested in her question. "Who are all my relations? And did you hear the old man by the fire? What did he mean?"

"What old man?"

"The one who said, 'Who's your father,' and 'Who are all your relations.'"

"What do you think it means?" Delfina asked her, not remembering an old man.

"I don't *know* what it means. That's why I'm asking you."

"I think it means, like, all our family and friends, and also all the plants and animals. It also means the spirit animals that we did today, like your horse. It probably means everything you relate to, not just living and breathing.

Remember what he said about the stone people, and, like, the nations in the stars? And what he said about father sun and grandmother moon—I would say it means everything. All your relations."

"Even the plants?"

"Everything."

"Even the air?"

"Everything."

"Even that lady?"

"What lady?"

"The one whose phone number you took."

"I took a lot of phone numbers. I want to take a trip out west."

"Del, you ever kiss anyone?"

"Yeah, just like you."

"No, I mean mouth kisses."

"I'll never tell."

"How come? I want to kiss Luca."

"He's your cousin."

"So what? If you can kiss ladies, I can kiss Luca."

"Why do you keep talking about ladies?"

"I don't know. She just looked like she was ready to plant one on you."

"Where did you learn to talk like that?"

"Jonathan."

"Figures. Did he tell you I kiss ladies?"

"No. I saw you with Antoinette."

Delfina kept silent, remembering that lurching feeling in the pit of her stomach when she had kissed her best friend as they sat on the bed in her room.

"Do you think Antoinette would kiss me like that too?"

Delfina let out a sigh. Choosing her words carefully, she said, "Toni and I have known each other since before you were born, Ron. Don't you have a best friend that you'd like to kiss like that?"

"Well, I love Dawn, but she's not pretty like Antoinette."

"Ronnie, after everything that you learned today, do you think it really matters who you kiss in the end?"

"No. That's why I want to kiss Luca."

❧ ❧ ❧

While Delfina and Veronique were at the workshop, Irene was hosting the last pool party of the summer. That spring, Pino's computer company had merged with a North Shore biotechnology company.

Pino and Irene had discussed—argued, really—about the merits of moving from King's Park to the more prestigious Lloyd's Neck.

"This neighborhood is my home, and it's home to the kids. I will not have us uprooted for your skewed sense of propriety," Irene had yelled at Pino one morning in late May, when the children were in school. "You're so seldom home, it doesn't really matter to you where we are. All you care about is how you look—having the children call you father, needing to have the right car, the right clothes, the right friends. But this is where I'm putting my foot down. We are not moving. You have your job and your business associates. My life is here with the children, their school, the church. You can have a fancy limousine drive you to work every morning. That should look good enough."

To any argument that Pino could give her, Irene had an answer. She had decided. She would not move out of the school district or out of the parish. Pino would have to deal with it. In the end, he acquiesced, but he told her that if they were going to stay there he wanted the house renovated. His way.

"I don't mind if the house is renovated, but let me remind you again we are the ones living in it. You're at work most of the time. So I suggest that you consult your family. If you don't, that wouldn't make you look very good." She threw his obsession in his face.

One month later, Pino had bought the property next door, which included a small cottage. "We'll stay there while the bulk of the renovations are being done. Then we'll convert it into a guest house." Things were cramped for a month, but the contractor's crews worked diligently, given an added cash incentive by Pino. By July, the Adriaticos inhabited their enlarged and modernized home.

Pino had also decided that he wanted a built-in, heated pool. He got no argument from Irene, who merely said, "Don't expect to find me floating in it like they found Carol Laurio."

One night the previous summer, Rocco Laurio's wife had fallen into their pool, hit her head and drowned. None of the official reports mentioned the fact that she had just finished an entire bottle of vodka.

Pino nodded. "Carol had problems. Pity about the children. That reminds me, we should have Rocco and his children over for dinner some time." Carol had left a seven-year-old daughter and a five-year-old son.

"Perhaps in the fall, Pino. After all, since we're getting a pool, it might be in bad taste to invite him and the kids to a pool party."

Pino agreed, and promptly forgot about the subject of the Laurios. By the end of July, a beautiful, new pool graced the lot behind the guest house. It was fully appointed, including a heater and two changing rooms. That summer, the Adriatico's house became the neighborhood meeting place for the kids in the area as well as for the priests of the church.

The day Delfina and Veronique went to the workshop, the pool party Irene was having was for the parish priests and the boys who were on the CYO—Catholic Youth Organization—baseball teams with her sons. The combination of Indian summer and heater would enable Irene to use the pool until the end of October. Joe brought the boys from the church. He also brought a new priest, Father Rex Dunlop, from Arizona, who had been assigned to the parish temporarily.

Father Rex seemed nice enough, Irene observed, but there was something odd about him. She could not quite place it. For one thing, Father Rex did not respond to her the way all the other new priests had. True, since her encounter with Joe, she had become more controlled. But Father Rex's inattention was different. That day, during the pool party, she watched him to try to figure out what it was. He was very attentive to all the boys in the pool. That's what had made him such a wonderful addition to the summer staff at the church and such a popular coach. Still, there was something about him that was different, Irene thought.

"Jonathan, would you bring out some more soda and plastic glasses?"

Jonathan was now fifteen. With his curly black hair, dark eyes and lean, muscular body, he was beginning to show signs that he would be a fine looking adult. "Sure, Mom."

"Let me help you," Father Rex, sitting on the steps of the pool, offered.

"That's okay, Father. You're a guest." Jonathan said to him.

"Not at all. You can give me a quick tour of that new house I've heard so much about."

"Just the main area, Jon," Irene told him. "The cleaning lady won't come until Monday."

Irene watched them walk toward the house. Then she turned to Joe, who was also watching them with an obtuse expression on his face.

"Joe, there's something about Father Rex that's different somehow. I know he's not a Jesuit like you, but that's not the difference. I can't place it."

"I don't know anything about him," Joe told her, more curtly than he meant to.

"You know, I think I'd better just make sure Jon doesn't give him the grand tour." Irene got up. Joe did not stop her.

In the kitchen, Rex wrapped his towel around his waist and watched Jonathan prepare the tray of drinks while joking about old balding ballplayers. "Not that you'd have anything to worry about with your head of hair," the priest said. He tugged at Jonathan's forelock playfully. "Got any of that growing down there?" He nodded toward the boy's swimming trunks.

Shocked and confused, Jonathan did not answer as he finished loading the tray.

Irene came into the kitchen. "Now, how about that quick tour?" Rex asked.

"You take the sodas out, Jon. I'll give the tour," Irene told her son.

Jonathan nodded, grabbed the tray and vanished.

"I'm honored to get the tour from the lady of the house," Father Rex said, bowing grandly.

"I'm sorry the living quarters are too much of a mess to show, but now that you've seen the kitchen, here's my studio." Father Rex got the abbreviated tour, and he and Irene were back by the pool within ten minutes.

Jonathan was thoughtful and subdued as he passed around the sodas. He perked up when his Aunt Ellie arrived with his cousins. Once Otto and Ellie started having children, they had one each year, except for the year that they had twins. So Jon's nine cousins ranged in age from ten to almost two. All the cousins were boys, and all of them, especially the five oldest, loved coming to the Adriaticos, because they could play with the "big boys" Jonathan and Marc, and because Aunt Irene lavished each of them with the special attention that their own mother never had time to give.

"Hi, Jonathan." Lou, the oldest, yelled from the entrance. He was already peeling off his t-shirt as he scampered toward the pool. Alec, eight, and Kyle and Gavin, both seven, followed at his heels. The boys cannon-balled into the water without pausing.

"Boys," Ellie called, chaperoning the four youngest. "Come over here, and say hello to your aunt before you start swimming."

Luca, who had just turned seven, folded his towel, and hung it on the chain link fence that surrounded the pool. He went to his aunt, and kissed her cheek. "Hi, Aunt Irene. Where's Veronique?"

Irene smoothed his hair after returning the kiss. "She's spending the day with Delfina. They went to a nature class in Putnam County. They won't be back until late tonight." Luca's face showed his disappointment. "Oh, Sweetie. You miss your cousin. Well, maybe your mom will let you spend the night, and we'll all have Sunday dinner together tomorrow.

"Is that okay with you, Ellie?" she asked her sister-in-law, who was just sitting down in a chaise lounge next to her.

"Otto and I don't have anything planned. You're sure it's not too much trouble?"

"All right!" Luca brightened and dove exuberantly into the pool.

"I love having them. By the way, Ellie, you know Father Joe. And this is Father Rex."

Ellie nodded hello. "I'd shake hands, but both of mine are occupied." Her youngest child had fallen asleep in one of her arms while she held her three-year-old with her other hand. Her five-year-old ran to his aunt, and jumped into her lap.

A while later, Father Rex and Father Joe herded the CYO boys out of the pool. "Okay guys. It's time to get dry clothes on." Joe directed them. "You can take turns dressing in the two changing rooms."

"Some of the boys can use the bathrooms in the house," Irene said. "Just make sure your feet are dry before you go into the kitchen. Marc, show them where the bathrooms are. Some of the boys can change in your room."

"I'll supervise them," Father Rex offered.

"No," Jonathan said, surprising himself, as he was getting out of the pool.

"What was that, Jonathan?" his mother asked, also surprised.

"I mean, didn't you say that it's too messy to go back there?"

"That's true, but I think it'll be okay."

"We'll all go," suggested Father Rex.

"Fine." Instinctually, for he could not have articulated his feeling, Jonathan did not want Father Rex in Marc's bedroom. What Jonathan really wanted was for his mother to go up to the house with them. She had one of his cousins in her lap. Jon knew better than to draw attention to what he perceived to be a developing problem.

Jonathan was like a drill sergeant at the house, moving people in and getting them out, making sure no wet clothes or towels were left around, making sure that no one, especially his brother, was left alone with Father Rex. Eight boys went into the house with Marc and Jonathan. Father Rex took the first four out when they had changed.

"What's wrong with you, Jon?" his brother asked when the first group had left, "You're acting like you don't like Father Rex."

"I don't. There's something weird about him. Don't ever get caught alone with him, okay?"

"Why?"

"He just says weird stuff."

"Anyone who's done changing can have a ride on Father Rex's motorcycle," one of the boys called into the house from outside.

Marc shrugged, forgetting his brother's warning as two more boys quickly finished changing. Marc ran outside with them.

From where he stood in the hallway, Jonathan could look out the window and see the boys lined up for their rides. When Marc's turn came, he noticed that Father Rex brought him up close behind him and had him hug his waist. He took Marc up and down the block an extra time. By the time he had taken the second, trip with Marc in front driving and Rex behind him holding the handle bars, Jonathan was almost beside himself with rage and frustration, but he didn't know exactly why he felt enraged.

The next day, as Jonathan was preparing to serve as an altar boy for Father Joe's mass, he decided to ask the priest about the incident. The two were in the vestibule. "Father Joe, did you know Father Rex when you were in Arizona?"

"No, Jon. I'm in a different order, the Jesuits. I was on a reservation. Father Rex was in a different place in the state."

"Oh." Jonathan was uncertain where to go from there.

"Why do you ask?"

"I—I just wanted to know." Jonathan found that he could not articulate what he wanted to know. He was loath to repeat the previous day's conversation with this priest. What if he had misinterpreted the whole thing? Maybe adults talked to each other that way. On the other hand, what if all priests stuck together? Jonathan was not sure. He felt he had nowhere to turn.

That afternoon, Jonathan was coming around the side of the house as Delfina was walking down the driveway. He waved to her. "Hey, you wanna go to the Chamber?"

"Okay. I haven't been there all summer. Drive?" He nodded and jumped in the car.

Five minutes later, they had parked by the restaurant and were taking a circular route to the small square door. Two minutes later, they were inside. Everything was as they had left it.

"When was the last time you were here?" Delfina wanted to know.

"Just before school started. After The Happy Trio took us to the Old Dock to celebrate the start of another school year. Great reason to celebrate," Jonathan noted wryly.

The Happy Trio was the siblings' shorthand meaning their parents and Joe. In the years since Veronique's birth, Joe had prompted Irene and Pino to initiate many family get-togethers. Joe did it in the name of family unity. Irene told the children that since Joe had no family of his own, he missed that type of family feeling, and they were Joe's family now. Once Veronique had started school, Joe and Irene began frequenting cultural events in the city. Pino was glad that someone was there to escort Irene and support the children when he could not be at a play or ball game. Pino, Irene and Joe were so frequently seen together at events that, among themselves, Delfina, Jonathan and Marc started referring to them as The Happy Trio, a spontaneous takeoff on The Merry Widow.

"Well, speaking of school, after I get my associate's degree from Farmingdale in May, I want to go out west for a few months before I transfer to a four-year college."

"Oh." The thought of his sister leaving home had never occurred to Jonathan before.

"So, what's wrong with you?" She asked directly.

He decided to see how she would react. "There's something weird about Father Rex."

"Tell me about it."

"You saw it too?"

"Yeah. He's the first one who hasn't gone ga-ga over Mom."

"They go ga-ga over Mom?"

"Figures you wouldn't notice. Anyway, he seems more interested in your butt than Mom's."

"Yeah, well, let me tell you about yesterday." Jonathan reiterated the incident to his sister.

She scrunched up her face as he finished. "Do priests really talk like that?"

"I didn't think so, but this one sure does."

"It's weird. It's not like there's anything explicitly wrong with what he said, but it's, like, private or something."

"Maybe he takes his mentoring role really seriously, and he wanted to talk about the birds and the bees." Jonathan was beginning to doubt himself.

"He's a celibate priest. What does he know about the birds and the bees? We could probably teach him some things from those old *National Geographics*." Brother and sister laughed together.

"Did you warn Marc?"

"I tried to, but I don't think he was listening. What made it worse somehow was the bike rides after. I don't know why."

"It's creepy, to say the least. Maybe we should tell Mom."

"You tell Mom. She'll think it's my imagination."

"What about someone like Father Joe?"

"I thought about that. I actually started this morning before Mass, but then I thought, what if all the priests are in league with each other? Nobody'd believe me."

"You wouldn't make that up, because it's too embarrassing to tell."

"Thanks a lot."

"You know what I mean. 'Sides, it's true. I think we should at least warn the cousins about him, and make sure Marc and Ronnie know."

"Yeah. By the way, Ronnie's been bugging me to bring her here."

"We brought Marc here when he was six. Ronnie's almost seven."

"Yeah, but Marc could keep a secret."

"We could bring her in the long way like we did with Marc, then not show her the exit until she kept the secret for a long time, like, say, a year."

"What about Lou and the other cousins? They're older, and they can keep secrets. If you're leaving for college, I'd like someone else to know about this place besides just me and Marc. Also if Luca knows, I think Ronnie will be more likely to keep it a secret."

"Good idea."

"Should we ask Marc what he thinks?"

"No. We found this place. We'll tell him when we're bringing the other kids here, so he can join in if he wants." Delfina was decisive.

"Do you want to bring Ronnie first, by herself?"

"Let's do them all together. If we tell Ronnie it's a secret, and then we tell the cousins right away, it's like we're telling the secret. If they're all brought in together, they all have to keep the secret together."

"All right. We'll tell Marc tonight, and get the kids together next Saturday."

On the appointed day, Delfina drove her cousins to her house. Jonathan, Marc and Veronique waited for them. At precisely ten o'clock all the cousins, each carrying a lunch, traipsed into the woods in single file. After forty-five minutes, Jonathan led them to the old cement slab, still camouflaged as it had been almost a decade earlier when he and Delfina began exploring it. Jonathan kept up the camouflage, every year making sure that more and more leaves and branches covered the entrance. Now it needed almost no maintenance to keep it totally obscured.

"Okay, follow Jonathan in age order," Delfina directed. "Marc, you go after Jon, and carry the searchlight. Lou, you're next. Then Alec, Kyle, Gavin, Luca and Veronique. I'll be behind you, Ron." Entering the dark tunnel temporarily put a damper on the high-spirited children. They filed through silently, each of them unwilling to be the first to voice any fears. Veronique, fearless, was quieted only as her eyes made the transition from bright sunlight to the dim tunnel. As her eyes got accustomed to the darkness and she was able to make out the walls, she got impatient with the fearful, lumbering pace of her cousins.

"Keep moving," she pushed Luca, who fell into Kyle, causing a domino effect.

This happened two more times before Delfina said, "Guys, let Ronnie go up to Marc."

"Hey, she's supposed to keep in age order," Alec huffed.

"Just let her go ahead of you." Delfina was not going to tolerate an argument.

The yarn that Delfina and Jonathan originally used had long since disintegrated. For the cousins' introductory visit, it had been replaced with bright orange plastic surveyor's marking tape.

They turned right at the crossroads, Veronique scrambling nimbly up the incline. She tried to pass Marc.

"Hey, wait a minute," her brother protested.

"I want to carry the spotlight," Veronique said.

"Ronnie, follow Marc." Delfina's authoritative voice came from somewhere in the darkness below.

Veronique flounced back with a huff, but she did not try to cut ahead again.

Partly due to Veronique's eager pace, the group reached the round room in record time.

"Mint," was Veronique's assessment as she entered the bright space. The Salvador Dali poster still hung on its plywood backing at one side of the room. Marc had put a Farrah Fawcett-Majors poster on a piece of plywood on the wall next to the large metal garage door-wall. Jonathan had his long work table, which was rounded to match the contour of the wall on another side of the room. Above the table were three shelves, also cut to match the wall's contour.

"Hey, this is great," said Lou, looking around. "All it needs is some chairs or something. I bet we could get three of those old Chevy back seats in here."

"Where does that door lead?" Kyle wanted to know, pointing to the wooden door.

"Never mind that. Look at this." Alec, the mechanically-minded cousin, was looking at the metal "wall."

"This is like a huge, kind of rounded garage door. The tracks are all rusty, but I bet we could get this thing open if we had some tools and some hardware."

"Before we show you where the door leads, you all have to swear that you'll never tell anyone else about this place," Marc told him.

"That includes drawing attention to it by doing something without thinking, like opening that metal door loudly when people just happen to be on the other side of it." Delfina spoke forcefully, her protectiveness of the Chamber coming through.

"Okay." Lou spoke for his brothers.

"No," said Marc, remembering his oath, "Swear on the blood of your ancestors."

All the children knew what that meant. Veronique, never squeamish, was the first to cut her finger.

After the blood mixing ritual was over, Delfina said, "Alec, I know you can probably get this door to work. Do it if you want, but don't actually open the door until we're all here. It'll probably have to be at night. Agreed?"

Alec nodded. Then Delfina opened the wooden inner door and let the twins go through. "You need to go one at a time and just look out the window. If we all start piling out of here, we'll definitely attract attention."

"Hey, we're by the Old Dock Inn."

"That's right." Jonathan said. "Now remember. Nobody tells anybody—not your friends, parents, anybody—because if anyone does, this place will be taken away from us."

"That means don't tell Mom, Veronique," Delfina said firmly.

"I never tell her anything."

"Right. That's how she knows what she's getting for Christmas each year."

"That's different. She tells me what I'm getting if I tell her."

"A secret's a secret. Don't tell."

"I think we should all make a pact to meet here once a year and have a cousins' meeting. That way we don't lose touch, and we'll know this place is still here," Jonathan suggested.

"Okay," Alec agreed. "It should probably be on a holiday weekend or something so that everybody can make it."

"Fourth of July," Delfina suggested.

"Okay," Jonathan said, "But let's have the first one now. Delfina's the oldest. She can run it."

"Okay. This is the official start of the First Annual Cousin's Meeting. Does anyone have anything they want to say?"

"You start," Jonathan told her.

"Okay. Before anyone starts talking, I want everyone to agree that what gets said here stays here. We don't talk about it with anyone else. That way anyone can say anything, and they don't have to worry about getting in trouble or stuff like that. Okay?" Getting nods of agreement from the others, she continued. "I'm going to be finishing my associate's degree in May. Then I'm taking some time off to go out west before I transfer to a four-year school for my bachelor's degree."

"That's great," said Lou, "What are you studying?"

"Right now, education, to be a teacher. I don't know what I want to do next. I really like Native American culture though, that's why I'm going out West for a few months. That's all about me for now. Jonathan, you're next."

"Well, what I want to talk about is something I told Del yesterday. I had a really weird thing happen with Father Rex. I just wanted to tell you about it and find out what you think." Jonathan reiterated the story.

"That was a really stupid question," Veronique responded first. "Head hair grows on your head." Luca nodded his agreement. The others let it pass.

"He does like playing 'whip the towels' in the locker room." Marc, who was twelve and just beginning to feel teenagerhood upon him, observed. "But lots of guys do that."

"Yeah, lots of kids, not grown-ups," Jonathan told him.

"What's 'whip the towels'?" Veronique wanted to know.

"They just whip each other with towels like Mom doesn't let us do," Delfina told her. "It's just that in the boy's room, the towels are wet and the boys usually aren't wearing any clothes."

"How do you know so much about the boy's locker room?" Lou asked her.

"Let's just say that once Jon's older cousin 'Delbert' visited from Washington state."

"No wonder the guys asked me if I had an older brother that time," Lou remembered. "That was you, I can't believe it. I would have really gotten in trouble if I went into the girl's locker room."

"Well, I'd probably have gotten in trouble too. But remember, nothing leaves this room. And besides, if you're willing to wear a dress, I think you should be allowed into the girl's room," Delfina said to him.

"I'd never wear a dress."

"Then you should never be let in. But back to this thing with Father Rex. Jon and I talked about it. There doesn't seem to be much we can do. I thought about telling Mom, but I don't think she'd believe us. If Mom doesn't believe us, nobody else will."

"I started to tell Father Joe," Jon said. "But then I stopped for that reason. Who'd believe me? And what if I just made a mistake?"

"Who'd make a mistake like that?" Kyle wanted to know.

Marc, silent up to this point, said, "He was in the locker room with one of the kids at the end of the baseball season. I had to go back, because I forgot my lock. I heard some weird sounds, almost like a hurt animal, but I didn't see anything, and there were no kids around. Rex came out of the office and asked me what was wrong. I got my lock and left. A couple of minutes later, Carlo Dell'Alma came out of the locker room. He looked sick or scared or something. He wouldn't talk to me. He just kind of ran into the woods. But he was running funny. He was limping or something. I don't remember. It was, like, two weeks before he got hit by that train."

"What kind of sounds?" Lou wanted to know.

"Like, I don't know. I don't remember." Marc was clearly disturbed by the discussion.

"Well, Father Rex didn't hold him down and make him get hit by that train. He always played by the tracks," Jonathan observed. "Anyway, just don't get caught alone in the locker room, okay? There are enough of us that we can stick together and watch out for the younger ones. If he's a homo, then we don't have to worry about Veronique. But Luca and the twins, keep an eye out for the littler ones, especially Barr who'll be in first grade next year."

"Yeah, but Mom's not letting him do CYO until third grade. She's too busy."

"That's good." Alec observed. "Too bad there's no way to get this guy."

"Just stay out of his way," Delfina advised them. "Know that he's out there and that there's something wrong with him. Just keep as far away as possible. Okay? Now, lunch break while Marc talks."

"Marc, tell us where you got that Farrah poster," Lou said. "Can we put up posters too?"

"As long as they're not offensive," Delfina said. "This one of Farrah is nice. She looks good. I don't want any stupid stuff here. Okay? You have to get approval from everyone else."

"In case of a disagreement, the oldest decides," Jonathan added.

The cousins passed the afternoon in their meeting. When they were ready to leave, they decided that four of them would leave by the door, and the other five would leave by the tunnel.

"I want to go back by the tunnel," Veronique said.

"Me too." Luca wanted to go wherever Veronique went.

"Marc, you want to take three people back by the Old Dock?"

Marc nodded. "I'll take Lou and the twins."

"Good. Alec, you come with me," Jon said to the boy who was preparing to protest. "I need someone to carry the spotlight."

That ended the first cousin's meeting.

## CHAPTER 8

Veronique knew exactly where to find the cement slab in the woods. She had spent many hours with Jonathan in those woods, learning about the plants and animals that lived there. Jonathan, the camouflage aficionado, was of the opinion that his little sister should have a magnificent vocabulary and that she should know how to survive in the woods. He spent many hours teaching her everything he knew, giving her the vocabulary to match.

Because of Jonathan's tutelage, Veronique was vaguely aware as she and her cousins were walking that her brothers and sister were taking them in circles. When she saw where they entered, she knew it. She did not care too much, being happy to walk around with Luca. She had wanted to go out through the tunnel that day, because she wanted to take another look at the crossroads in the tunnel where they had turned. She thought it looked like a crossroads. On the way back, she confirmed that it was a crossroads.

The next weekend was a holiday weekend. She had an extra day to explore the tunnel. She asked her mother if Luca could spend the night, so that they could play in the woods. Irene agreed, and the next day they ran through the woods with their "provisions"—flashlights, snacks and sodas.

"How come it took so long to get here the first time?" Luca wanted to know.

"They went a different way so that we wouldn't be able to find the place."

"You fooled them."

"Yeah, but nobody, not even them, has to know that we've been back."

Luca nodded. They entered carefully, making sure that nothing was disturbed at the entranceway.

"I want to see what's down those other tunnels," Veronique told Luca as they started down the passageway.

When they got to the crossroads, Luca said, "If that one leads to the Old Dock, this one to the left must go into the hospital grounds."

"Let's look."

The two cousins made their way down the tunnel, breaking through cobwebs and stopping at each marked door. "Building 8…Maintenance…Building 10…Main…" Luca read in a low voice as they passed each one.

"Why are you whispering?" Veronique whispered.

"Same reason you are—so in case anyone is on the other side of any of these doors they don't hear us."

"This one, Main, looks different than the others." The door was white while all the others were a dark green. Veronique stopped and pulled at the handle. The door swung open, revealing three steps up and another door that was about half the height of the first door.

"Shhh," Luca warned softly. "I hear someone." On the other side of the door, a man was yelling. The two children froze, listening. The voice continued for several minutes. As they listened, they could make out some of what was being said in a heavy Brooklyn accent.

"How many times have I told you? The files go in alphabetical order. First the As, then the Bs, et cetera, et cetera, et cetera, et cetera. I know you can do it. You did it before. You're just not trying hard enough."

"But, Daddy, I did do it. Just like you said," a small voice, close to the door, whimpered, sounding close to tears.

"Since when does 'closet' come before 'cleaning'? Huh? If you start crying, I'll give you something to cry about," the man yelled.

"I—I'm not c-c-crying."

A smacking sound was followed by a thud, like someone had fallen. Then no sound, except for someone breathing right on the other side of the door. Veronique and Luca were afraid to move for fear of being heard.

When the man's voice spoke again, it was entirely different from the yelling voice they had heard minutes before. Now, it was wheedling, almost sing-song. The only way they could tell it was the same person was by the Brooklyn accent.

"Come here, baby. I know you don't want to make your Daddy mad, but you have to try harder. You know how much it hurts me to have to discipline you, but how else will you learn? Come here. You're Daddy's special girl, right? We'll kiss and make up. That's right. Come here, special girl. Daddy'll do our special game and make you feel good, okay?"

"Okay, Daddy." The voice was faint, and it had moved away from the door.

Luca pulled Veronique's arm, pointing at the larger door behind them. This was a good time to leave. The cousins moved quickly. They did not stop until they were outside the tunnel.

"I wonder who that was," Veronique said when they were back on the nature path. "That man's voice sounded familiar, but I can't place it."

"It was a weird voice. It almost sounded like a gangster," Luca commented. "Maybe you're thinking of a movie."

"I wonder which one the main building is." Veronique was formulating a plan.

"We don't care, because we're going back to your house," Luca said firmly, steering Veronique in the direction of home. They had finished all the snacks, and he was getting hungry.

That night Veronique racked her brains, trying to remember where she had heard the man's thickly-accented voice before. Her efforts were to no avail, though, and she fell asleep as she got the idea that the other voice could be a child her own age.

❧ ❧ ❧

When Veronique entered the first grade, Pino insisted that she attend an exclusive and prestigious finishing academy for girls in Syosset. The back part of the school's campus bordered on the back of Pino's office complex. Now in her second year at the Academy, Veronique stayed late one day a week for piano lessons. After the lesson, she would walk over to Pino's office where she did her homework or sketched until it was time for her father to leave.

Midway through the year, Pino's secretary Miss Brown discovered that Veronique could read at a fifth-grade level. The child had exhausted her whole magazine supply. Miss Brown decided to give Veronique simple office tasks to perform—first photocopying and putting stamps on envelopes; later, alphabetizing folders that would be filed.

One day as Veronique was working diligently on the floor behind Miss Brown's desk, Rocco Laurio, Pino's long-time associate, came into the office.

"He in?" Laurio pointed a thumb toward Pino's closed office door. The years had done nothing to soften Rocco Laurio's heavy Brooklyn accent. If anything, he seemed to have cultivated it in recent years to make himself stand out within the business and political circles in which he traveled with Pino.

"He's on a conference call to Japan," Miss Brown informed him as he headed toward the door. "They should be finished in about fifteen minutes. Have a cup of coffee and wait in the lounge."

"I have an appointment for five."

"It's four-forty-five now, and I don't see you in the book."

"You must have made a mistake." His hand was still on the knob when he caught sight of Veronique behind the desk.

"What have we here? Little Miss Academy Girl, complete with uniform? Pretty little thing. You must be Pino's kid. You probably don't remember me. I met you at the Children's Fund Christmas party last year." Ever since Delfina's initial success at that event, Pino, encouraged by Irene, had brought one of his children to the Christmas party in her stead each year.

"I'm Veronique. I remember you. You're Mister Laurio." Veronique looked at him directly.

"Yeah, I am. You're smart too. You must be, what, seven years old? My daughter, Renee, was born in September, about a month before you. I'm thinking of enrolling her in the Academy. You like it there?"

Veronique nodded, continuing to work.

"They got you working hard here? What're you doing? Filing?"

"Alphabetizing. Yeah, it's fun."

"That's good. You here every day? Maybe I can bring Renee down so you can tell her about the Academy. Ever since her mother died, she's been kinda down. I think she needs a change of scenery."

Veronique's eyes widened at that bit of information. "Her mother *died*?"

"Yeah, my wife. Very sad. Fell into the swimming pool, hit her head and drowned."

"She drowned?"

"In the swimming pool," he repeated himself. "I came home and found her. Luckily the kids were asleep."

Veronique was processing the information, horrified at the scene she imagined.

Rocco Laurio looked at his watch. "I'll be back in a few," he said to Miss Brown. He returned promptly at five, and asked her to let Pino know he was waiting.

"He's still on that call. He should be finishing any minute now."

"I've been waiting long enough—" Rocco Laurio started to make a scene, but then he caught sight of Veronique behind the counter watching him. He stopped, choosing instead to pace in front of Miss Brown's desk.

Moments later, Miss Brown buzzed the inner office. "Mr. Laurio to see you."

"Send him in." Pino's voice, emanating from the speaker at the edge of Miss Brown's desk, sounded like he was in a tin can.

At six o'clock, when Miss Brown rose to go, they were still behind closed doors. "Thank you for all your help today, Veronique. It's such a pleasure to have you around. I'm sorry your father is still working. Here, make yourself comfortable on the couch. You have a book to read?" Veronique nodded her answer. "Good. It's getting a little chilly in here. I'll cover you with your coat. Here's a cup of hot chocolate. You just read until he gets out. Okay?"

Veronique nodded.

Miss Brown buzzed the inner office and, without waiting for an acknowledgement, announced that she was going home for the night and that Veronique was waiting.

When the two men emerged from the office, it was seven o'clock. Veronique had fallen asleep on the couch.

A few weeks later, Rocco Laurio again showed up for a late-afternoon appointment with Pino. He had his daughter Renee and his five-year-old son Fortuno in tow. The little blonde girl cowered in the doorway when they entered. Her brother ran in on his father's heels and promptly pushed all the magazines on the waiting room table onto the floor.

"Renee, stop being so timid, and pick up those magazines," her father scolded her. The girl, startled at the sound of her name, scurried to pick up the magazines. Her brother promptly toppled them again.

As usual, Veronique was working on the floor behind Miss Brown's desk.

"I see it's going to be a short meeting tonight, Mr. Laurio." Miss Brown observed wryly.

"Why do you say that, Miss Brown?"

"Because your son is not going to be allowed to stay in this office if he continues to act like that."

"He's just active. Renee, control your brother."

Veronique, aware of what was going on at the front of Miss Brown's desk, decided to gather up the folders she was working on. As she did, Fortuno ran behind the desk, intent upon attacking whatever was back there.

"Don't you dare come one step closer," Veronique said, kneeling up and pointing a menacing finger at him.

The little boy stopped in his tracks. He looked at Veronique, looked at her finger pointing at him, and ran to his father and started to cry.

"Now, see what you've done. You made him cry," Mr. Laurio admonished Veronique.

"He's faking," Veronique said. "Besides, if that's all it takes to make him cry, he would have had a conniption if he had messed up my work."

"Am not faking."

"No tears," Veronique said to the boy, angrily. "No tears. You're faking."

Fortuno howled.

Pino came out to see what all the noise was about as Rocco said, "Veronique, you're making him cry. Can't you see how sensitive he is? The poor baby has lost his mother. We need to be nice to him."

Veronique remained impassive, but Pino said, "Veronique, Mr. Laurio and I are going to have a meeting. I want you to take these two children—"

"—Fortuno and Renee—" Rocco Laurio interjected helpfully.

"—Fortuno and Renee. Get them each a snack from the lunch room. Then I want you to color with them at a table in the lunch room until Mr. Laurio and I come and get you."

"Am I in charge?" Veronique wanted to know.

"You're the hostess. You have to make sure your guests are happy."

"Yeah, but does he have to do what I say?"

"Veronique, just make sure he's happy. I don't want to hear any more crying. Okay?"

"Yes."

"Yes what?"

"Yes, Father." Veronique spoke the words through gritted teeth, her cobalt blue eyes flashing into Pino's ocean blue ones.

"All right, then." Pino and Rocco disappeared into the office.

Miss Brown came from behind her desk. "Come on, Veronique. I'll help you get the snacks."

The four of them went into the lunchroom. Miss Brown got the children situated with hot chocolate and cookies, and told them that when they finished eating she would bring out some paper and crayons. She left the lunch room and found an intern. She gave him a list of supplies, and sent him running to a nearby stationery store.

Renee ate her snack quietly, almost hiding behind her hot chocolate cup. Fortuno, on the other hand, was boisterous, and he talked constantly. "I been in a jet plane. I went to California. I been in the Statue of Liberty. My daddy owns a Cadillac."

Veronique decided to ignore him, eating in silence the way Renee did.

Fortuno did not want to be ignored. He wanted a response from this new person.

"My daddy can beat up your daddy."

"That's so stupid." Veronique reacted without thinking. From behind her hot chocolate, Renee laughed, the first sound Veronique had heard from her.

"He can too." Fortuno was not going to be deterred.

Jonathan had prepared Veronique for taunts like that one. She was ready. "Only stupid little boys beat each other up. My *father* is a grown up. He doesn't beat people up. If your father beats people up, he's a stupid boy," adding under her breath, "like you."

Fortuno did not hear that last comment, but Renee did, and whispered, "Yeah."

Fortuno heard his sister. "My daddy's not a stupid boy," he pouted.

"Then *he* won't beat anyone up, and what *you* said is a stupid lie."

"He can too."

"Then he's a stupid boy."

Caught, Fortuno started to cry in frustration. Miss Brown walked in, crayons in hand, and said, "Is everyone finished with the snacks?"

"Yes, Miss Brown," Veronique said. "But Renee and I have to go to the girls' room."

"Okay, you know where it is."

"Me too," Fortuno whined.

"It's the girl's room. You can't go." Veronique grabbed Renee by the arm and left Fortuno with Miss Brown.

In the lavatory, Veronique said to Renee, "If that kid were my brother, he'd be dead by now." She choked on her words as soon as she said them, remembering about Renee's mother.

"Please don't fight with him. It just makes it worse later, and I'll get in trouble for letting it happen," Renee pleaded, not reacting to Veronique's talk of death.

"He can't get away with being such a spoiled brat." Veronique was furious.

"My daddy's good to me. He says I'm special. And since I had Mommy longer than Fortuno, I need to give some of the love I got from Mommy to Fortuno. Daddy says when I do, it makes him love me more."

"Oh." For the moment, Veronique was stymied.

"Daddy says you go to the Academy. Do you like it there?"

"It's okay. School's school, I guess. The teachers are really nice, and there are no stupid boys to mess things up. So that makes it better." Veronique hesitated.

Something about Renee was fragile, and Veronique knew that fragile girls did not always fare well at the Academy. "But if I were already in a different school, I think I'd want to stay there with my friends."

"I used to think that way. But since everybody in my school knows that my mom died, they treat me like I have some kind of disease. Even my best friend doesn't really call me or anything any more. If I went to a new school, nobody would know. It would be like starting new. And I'd know you at the Academy."

While the girls were talking in the rest room, Miss Brown had gotten the intern to take Fortuno to the men's room. While he was gone, Miss Brown, who had had enough of the little boy's antics, made him a fresh cup of hot chocolate and slipped a teaspoon of Kahlua into it.

When he came back, he drank the spiked drink, and was coloring lazily when the girls returned. Ten minutes before it was time for her to leave, Miss Brown put Fortuno down for a nap.

When Rocco Laurio and Pino emerged from their meeting around seven o'clock, Fortuno was sleeping peacefully. The girls were talking and coloring together in the lunch room.

"That's amazing. He never takes naps," Mr. Laurio was incredulous. "Hey, Renee. What did you do to Fortuno?"

"Nothing, Daddy. Miss Brown was watching him, so I could ask Ronnie about the Academy. We were coloring when she left. She just said he was napping."

"Who's Ronnie?"

"Veronique. She says it's really good at the Academy. I want to go next year. Okay, Daddy?"

"Okay, Princess. If you're good and help me with your brother, you can go."

❦   ❦   ❦

Rocco Laurio started bringing his children to his once-monthly meetings with Pino. When spring arrived and their pool was open, Veronique asked Irene if she could invite Renee over to swim.

"I don't know if she'll want to go swimming, seeing as how her mother died in a pool."

"She says everybody treats her like she has a disease since her mother died. She wishes nobody knew. That way everybody would treat her normally again."

Irene considered this. "Okay. We'll invite Rocco and the kids for Memorial Day. It will be Delfina's graduation party too."

※ ※ ※

The day of the party dawned warm and muggy. Irene was up at sunrise, preparing for the day's events. She sat in her well-appointed living room with its bay window overlooking the Long Island Sound, and watched the sun rise from behind the house, reflecting off the thick mist that hung over the inlet in front of her house. The ghostly, cotton-like wisps of fog that floated upward in the first light, accompanied by the cicada's song, promised a hazy, hot and humid day. It would be perfect weather for a pool party, Irene thought to herself, finishing her cup of coffee as she watched the last fingers of fog disintegrate from her front lawn.

She went to the kitchen. It was early, and she knew she had an hour before her family started to stir. Marc and Jonathan had been out late the night before, so they would not be up before nine. Veronique would be up in an hour. She was always up by eight. Delfina, who had actually graduated the weekend before, had spent the night camping with Antoinette. Irene was glad it had not rained. She knew the girls had a tent, and they were within walking distance of the house. She worried about them just the same. Why Delfina insisted on camping when she could have a sleep over with her friends in the comfort of her own room was beyond Irene.

Putting thoughts of her daughter's quirkiness aside, Irene started her to-do list for the day. Six hours later, the list was exhausted, and the party was in full swing. Pino had rented an old-fashioned jukebox, which stood on the dance floor under a rented white party tent. Another tent in front of the greenhouses, which had screen sides, protected the catered food and tables from the sun and the yellow jackets.

Pino had said earlier in the week that even though this was an out-door party, he did not want to sit on the ground to eat. Joe had heartily agreed, and Irene had taken Pino at his word, ordering the chairs, tables and caterer. Delfina, who had arrived at noon to shower and change, was dressed in jeans, a t-shirt and cowboy boots.

"Aren't you hot in those," Irene, putting up a sign that read "Congratulations Class of 1981," asked her eldest child.

"No, Mom. I wanted to dress up."

"Antoinette looks very cool and very dressed up," Irene observed, smiling at her daughter's long-time friend. Antoinette was dressed in a flowing white cotton dress, which had a white lace bodice and a puffy short-sleeved, low-cut top. Her petite figure, blue-eyed good looks and short blonde-streaked-with-bleached-white hair were in direct contrast to Delfina's five-foot-eleven-inch height, dark eyes and long, dark hair. The two girls had always been opposite in looks, but similar in temperament and sensibility. They had always said that would keep them friends forever.

Father Patrick and Father Joe arrived at the same time as Ellie, Otto and the nine cousins. Suddenly, the party was in full swing. Irene watched Delfina and Antoinette walk arm-in-arm toward the jukebox. How nice that they're such good friends, she thought, as she watched them make a selection.

Rocco arrived with Fortuno and Renee, and Veronique immediately went to Renee, taking her to meet her cousins Alec, Kyle and especially Luca.

Grace arrived, chauffeured in a white Lincoln Town Car. Enrico had died four years earlier, and Grace had become the quintessential widow. No longer having her husband to drive her, she had hired a chauffeur. Her entourage was now comprised of her chauffeur and her two best friends, Josephine and Lena, who accompanied her everywhere.

Each of Irene's children was allowed to invite a friend. Veronique had invited Renee, and Delfina's guest was Antoinette. Jonathan brought his girlfriend Margaret, and Marc managed to get two of his friends, Paul and Tom, invited.

Delfina had asked Irene not to invite Father Rex, but Rex showed up on his motorcycle with one of his CYO charges in tow.

Irene had decided to use the guest house as a changing room. She announced that, adding, "the room next to the kitchen has a sign that says it's off limits. That's where I put all the breakables, and where I'm putting Delfina's graduation gifts. So you can use any of the other rooms to change in, but stay out of that one. Now, our lifeguard is here. So anyone who wants to swim, feel free." Otto and Ellie's six older boys were already in their swimming trunks. Veronique was also in her suit. Renee went inside to change, and came out wearing a pretty pink suit. Luca and the two girls played in the shallow part of the pool, because Renee could not swim.

Luca, always attentive to Veronique, was courteous to Renee, who instantly fell in love with him. Rocco Laurio drank a Coors and talked to Otto while watching his daughter carefully. "Doesn't that boy have anything better to do than play with the girls?" Rocco asked Otto. Then he yelled, "Hey, Renee, stay on the shallow end."

"Luca and Veronique are very close," Luca's father responded to Rocco, unconcerned.

"Your father talks like a gangster," Luca said to Renee in a quiet voice before submerging himself.

"He's from Brooklyn," Renee explained to Veronique, floating next to her, remembering for an instant another time she and Luca had heard that gangster voice. "All our relatives in Brooklyn say I'm the one who talks with a Long Island accent."

Luca pulled Veronique under the water by her heels, and the gangster voice was forgotten.

Near the dance floor, Delfina and Antoinette were having an intense discussion.

"Girls, put on your bathing suits and come for a swim," Irene called to them.

"In a minute, Mom," Delfina called, frustration in her voice.

Jonathan stood near the life guard's chair, keeping an eye on Father Rex while Margaret lounged beside the pool, yelping whenever she got splashed by someone jumping in near her.

Outside of the big pool, Irene had set up a plastic pool for the toddlers where Fortuno played with Otto and Ellie's three younger children. Renee was free from responsibility for the afternoon. Later, Irene announced that the food would be served soon, so people who wanted to change should do it now.

"Renee, I think you should put on some dry clothes," her father directed her. "I'll get them for you."

"But Daddy, Veronique and Luca aren't getting dressed."

"I want you to put on some dry clothes. This is the first time you've been swimming all year, and I don't want you to overdo it."

"I'll get dressed too, Renee," Veronique offered.

"Okay, Ronnie," Irene said, approvingly. "You can put on the new yellow dress I left on your bed."

"Okay, Mom. To Renee she said, "Come on up to my room, and we can change."

"Actually, Veronique, I left the kids' clothes in the car." Rocco Laurio told her. "You go up and change. I need to talk to Renee for a minute anyway. She can change in the other house, and she'll meet you when you're done.

"See you in a little while," Veronique said, and ran inside to change.

"Come to the car with me," Rocco directed Renee.

"But it's so far."

"Wait here then, and keep an eye on your brother," Rocco huffed, thrusting Renee into a seat by the pool where she waited until he returned from the long trek down the street to where he had parked his car. Despite the heat, Renee shivered, wrapped in a large, fluffy, green towel.

Veronique finished changing quickly. Hanging her suit in the bathroom, she ran out the front door of her house and over to the front door of the guest house. This was her first moment alone since she had heard where her mother had put Delfina's presents.

She had to take advantage of the opportunity to inspect her sister's gifts. Unseen, Veronique silently made her way to the room off the kitchen. She closed the door behind her and looked around. Her mother had stacked all the breakables on a plush rug at the far side of the room. Several wrapped boxes were on a chair near the closet. The closet itself had some of her mother's fall dresses and coats hanging in two neat rows.

Veronique set about inspecting the gifts. Three of them felt like books. Boring. The next was heavy. It was a box wrapped in shimmering silver Mylar paper. When she shook the box, she did not hear anything. She was trying to decide whether to open it when she heard someone at the door. Quickly, she put the box on the floor and scrambled into the closet, pulling the door shut behind her. The box was in the way, so the closet door was only half closed as the door to the room opened.

Veronique shrunk back, invisible behind the lower rack of clothes.

Rocco Laurio led Renee into the room.

"But Daddy, this room's off limits."

"That's for kids. Grownups can come in here. Now, let me get you changed," he said, pulling some clothes out of the bag.

In the closet, Veronique did not dare to breathe. She kept her eyes glued to Rocco Laurio, making sure he did not see her.

But Rocco was intent upon his daughter. "Take those wet clothes off," he ordered. "So, you liked that boy in the pool, did you?"

"He was very nice."

"Well, I don't like him. He was looking at you like you were some kind of whore. And you, smiling back at him like that." Rocco's voice was low and mean.

"I didn't do anything bad, Daddy."

"Imagine how I felt, watching you. Take off those wet things now." As she undressed slowly, he continued to berate her. "It made me so sad, I thought to myself, she can't be my special girl if she's going to act like that. You know, that's what I thought. Here, let me dry you off. Although I don't know why I should even touch you, you hurt me so much, the way you were acting in that pool."

"Please, Daddy, I'm sorry. I didn't mean to hurt you. We were just playing in the pool."

"No. Don't turn around. Don't try to hug me. Let me dry your hair. I don't think you can be my special girl ever again."

Renee, her back to him, was sobbing. "Daddy, I didn't mean to hurt you. I'm sorry. I'll be good. Please let me be your special girl again."

"I don't know. You hurt me so much."

"I'll make you feel better, Daddy."

"Okay. You can give me one of your special girl kisses."

Veronique watched as she turned around, hugged him, and kissed his mouth. He picked her up by her knees and brought her legs up so that she was straddling him. With bewildered horror, Veronique watched his fingers disappear inside Renee. A few minutes later, he let her go, and she got dressed, still crying silently, while, back turned, he did something with the towel.

"That's my girl," Rocco Laurio said a moment later, "Now, you won't be talking to any more boys, will you?"

"No, Daddy." She answered in a sing-song, high-pitched voice. She was standing stiffly, hugging herself. Her back toward him, she was facing the closet, and Veronique could see her face, frozen and doll-like with tears silently flowing from her empty eyes.

"Good. Now take the bag out, and put some dry clothes on your brother."

❦   ❦   ❦

Veronique emerged from the guest house half an hour later, shaken. She sought out Delfina, who was still engrossed in a conversation with Antoinette.

"I want to have one slow dance with you," Delfina was saying insistently.

"I can't. Not in front of your family. I don't want them to hate me."

"I love you. If they love me, they won't hate you. They don't hate you, anyway. My mother adores you."

"She won't if she sees us slow dancing together."

"Del," Ronnie pulled at her sister's hand, "Del, I need to talk to you."

"Not now, Ronnie," Delfina said, pulling her hand away impatiently.

Veronique looked for Jonathan. Father Rex had left, so Jonathan had relaxed. He was sitting on a chaise lounge with Margaret on his lap, kissing her as they laughed together.

Veronique ran over to him. "Jon, I gotta tell you something."

"Can't it wait, Ronnie?" he asked, turning back to Margaret.

At that moment Renee walked up to Veronique. "Daddy says we've got to go now," she said to Veronique, sadly.

"Why do you let him do that to you?" Veronique blurted out.

Renee looked at her, a momentary recognition in her eyes that immediately clouded over into a disconnected glaze. "We always leave parties early," she murmured. "Daddy doesn't like the noise, and all the people and stuff. He says there's too many boys here. It's too rough for me. I just came to say 'bye."

"'Bye." Veronique did not know what else to say. She watched as Renee grabbed Fortuno's hand and trudged back to where her father was saying goodbye to Irene. She felt utterly helpless and frustrated. She knew that if she told Irene what she had seen, she would have to admit she was in the room with the presents in it. She knew if she didn't tell her mother, she would burst.

As she walked toward the tent where the dance floor was set up, she heard Anne Murray singing "Could I Have This Dance" for the third time in a row. She saw Delfina take Antoinette's hand to lead her to the dance floor, and she saw Antoinette pull her hand away and shake her head. Delfina walked away, across the floor.

Veronique knew that walk. Delfina was angry, and she would have kept on walking if Father Joe had not intercepted her on the far side of the tent. Veronique moved closer to the dance floor.

"Delfina, stay here with me. I want to have a toast for you."

Delfina opened her mouth to protest, but then seemed to think better of it.

Joe led her to the center of the floor where he called everyone to attention. "Everyone, I'd like to propose a toast to Delfina, so raise your glasses with me. To Delfina, Class of 1981: Congratulations on graduating. May the years ahead be happy, prosperous and full of love."

"Hear, hear!" Jonathan seconded him from the other side of the tent.

"Speech," Marc called out.

"Do you want to say anything, Delfina?" Joe asked her.

"Yes, I do. First, thanks for all your good wishes. Next, I just want to tell you all that I'm going to be leaving for the southwest soon, maybe even this coming week."

Antoinette, standing next to Veronique, gasped and said "Oh no," under her breath.

Delfina continued, "As some of you know, I went out to Arizona on spring break. They need teachers on the reservation down there. It's actually the same reservation that Father Joe was at before he came to Kings Park, so he knows where I'll be going." She looked toward the place where Antoinette and Veronique were standing. "I don't know how long I'm gonna stay there. I'm really excited about this. So thanks to everyone for being here today. And now I believe it's time to eat."

Jonathan led Marc and the cousins in a rousing rendition of "For She's a Jolly Good Fellow" as Delfina waived and excused herself from the group, saying, "I'll be back in a minute."

"This is the first I've heard of this," Irene said, surprised.

"The first one to leave the nest," Pino, standing beside her, noted.

Antoinette stood rooted to her spot, tears softly falling down her cheeks. Veronique looked up and, seeing the tears, simply took Antoinette's hand and stood there with her. After a few minutes, she said, "I wouldn't hate you if you dance with Del."

Antoinette looked down at her and smiled through her tears. Then she squeezed her hand and said, "Maybe I should go look for her."

"She looked really mad."

"Well, maybe I need to talk to her." With that, Antoinette made her way toward the house.

🍁     🍁     🍁

Later that night, after the party was over, the tents had been removed, and everyone had gone home. Veronique sought out Irene, who was sitting in the music room on the couch, reading.

"Mommy, I know you're gonna be mad, but I went into the off-limits room in the guest house to look at the presents."

Irene looked at her in surprise. Veronique never told on herself.

Veronique continued quickly. "While I was in there, Mr. Laurio came in with Renee. When she had all her clothes off, he put his fingers in her—down there."

Irene looked up at her momentarily, frowning, and then turned the page of her magazine. "Are you sure that's what you saw?"

"Yes, Mommy. I'm sure. And Mommy," Veronique pulled at Irene's arm to get her attention, "She was crying."

Irene looked at Veronique, her eyes suddenly blank. "She probably did something wrong, and he was spanking her as punishment. I can't interfere with a parent disciplining his child."

"He wasn't spanking her," Veronique said firmly.

"Honey, you were hiding in a closet where you were not supposed to be. How can you be sure of what you saw? I don't believe Rocco would do anything bad to his children. He loves them. He always says they're all he's got now that Carol's gone. I think your imagination was playing tricks on you while you were hiding in that closet."

Veronique gritted her teeth as she left the room. "I know what I saw."

❦ ❦ ❦

The next morning Veronique went into Delfina's room and sat on her bed. Her sister was standing in front of her mirror, brushing her long black hair.

"Del, what if you know you saw something, and you know what you saw was bad, but when you tell, nobody believes you?"

Delfina put down the brush and turned around to look Veronique in the eye. She pulled her hair in place and fastened it with a clip.

"Don't touch my brush," she said as she saw Veronique look at it. "What did you see?"

Veronique opened her mouth to say it was just a "what if" question, but she could not lie to her sister. She told Delfina what she had seen the day before, ending with, "I told Mommy, but she says Renee was probably just getting spanked, and we can't interfere with how Mr. Laurio disciplines his children. But I know he wasn't spanking her."

"It doesn't sound like he was punishing her. In fact, it sounds like she was inviting him. You said she said she'd make him feel better, and then she turned around and kissed him?"

"Yeah. That's what I don't get. She acted sort of like she wanted to do it, but she was crying too."

"Maybe you should talk to her. Be honest. Tell her you were there, and ask her about it."

"She'd hate me."

"If your friendship can't stand being honest, then it's not a friendship that'll last. Talk to Renee. See what she has to say. Talking about honesty, I'm leaving for Arizona on Friday."

"When are you coming back?"

"I don't know."

"Christmas?"

"I don't know. It depends."

"On what?"

"On a lot of things."

"Are you going because Antoinette wouldn't dance with you?"

Delfina sighed. "Speaking of honesty, huh? Well, yes and no. I was going anyway, but let's just say that I wanted to be more honest about some things than Toni did, and because of that, I'm leaving sooner than I might have."

"I wish you weren't going. I want you to be here when I talk to Renee."

Delfina laughed. "Suddenly you want me around? Jonathan's the one you always go to. What's wrong with going to him now?"

"Well, for one thing, he has a girlfriend, so he doesn't pay attention to me. Plus, I haven't told him about this."

"You haven't?" Delfina was genuinely surprised. "I thought you tell him everything."

"I don't know why I didn't tell him this."

"You'll always be able to call me, and we can still talk."

"Yeah, but it's different on the phone. And Mommy's always in the background listening or telling me to hurry and get off the phone."

"Well, we'll just have to tell her it's our private time."

Veronique liked that.

❦   ❦   ❦

Five days later, Delfina left for Arizona. She had spent most of the week in her room, cleaning it out, and putting clothes and other assorted items in bags and taking them to the Catholic Charities drop-off bin. On the evening before Delfina's departure, right before Veronique had to go to bed, she came in and sat on her older sister's bed, watching her pack the rest of her belongings in a large duffle bag.

"You have to go?"

"Yes, Ronnie. How many times are you going to ask me that?" Looking at her sister's downcast face, she added, "No matter how many times you ask, I'm not gonna change my mind. I want to go. It's beautiful out there. I'll send you post cards."

"You said that last time you went out there."

"I was only there for a week that time. I brought the post cards back with me. Remember?"

"Yeah."

Delfina sat back on her heels. "Besides, Jonathan's still here. You spend a lot more time with him than you do with me." Almost to herself, she added, "That's probably a good thing." Then she smiled at Veronique. "Look at how good it is that you and Jonathan hang around together. With all the stuff he taught you, you get to skip third grade and go directly into fourth. At this rate, you'll be finished with school in no time. Then you can come and join me in Arizona if you want."

Veronique brightened at this.

"Here. Take my brush," Delfina said, pulling it out of her bag. Veronique had always coveted her older sister's hair brush, because it seemed that her sister's long black hair never got tangled while her mother always struggled to pull the knots out of Veronique's equally long but thicker black hair. "You can bring it to me if you decide to come to Arizona after you graduate from high school." Veronique took the brush reverently. "Okay, it's time you go to bed," Delfina told her, getting ready to return to her packing.

"What time are you leaving?"

"Really early. The car is coming to take me to the airport at five."

"Wake me up. Okay?"

"I'll try. But it's really late now, so don't blame me if you go right back to sleep."

"You'll wake me up, right?"

"I said I'll try. Now good night." Veronique gave her sister a good night kiss and went down the hallway to her room.

The next morning at quarter to five, Delfina was sitting alone in the kitchen drinking a cup of coffee. She took the cup, and wandered through the house, stopping in the music room, the formal living room, and her mother's studio before putting the cup in the sink and walking down the hall to her parents' bedroom. She knocked on the partly open door and then walked in.

"'Bye, Mom," she said softly, kissing her mother on the cheek. Irene sat up quickly. "What time is it?"

"It's five, Mom. The car's probably outside. It's okay. Go back to sleep. I'm just going to say goodbye to Ronnie, and then I'll go out to the car. I'll call to tell you my phone number." Irene hugged her daughter as Pino rolled over and sat up.

"Bye, Father," Delfina said, going over to his side of the bed and kissing him. "You have everything you need?" he asked her groggily. "Yes, Father. Thanks for the extra money. It'll come in handy." He nodded and stroked her hair as she stood up. She thought about saying thanks for not making a big deal of her leaving, but didn't. Having said her goodbyes to her brothers the night before, she did not wake them. She went into Veronique's room.

"Ronnie, I'm leaving. Wake up." She shook her sleeping sister's shoulder. "Bye, Ronnie," Delfina said, a little bit louder.

"It's still night. You can't go."

"My car's waiting outside. I'll write to you. Bye, Ronnie." She kissed her sister goodbye, picked up her duffle bag by the door, and left.

Later, when Veronique woke up, she found the statuette of a Lipizzan stallion, posed on its hind legs, tucked under her hand on the pillow next to her. It was the one possession of Delfina's that Veronique had always wanted. As Delfina had cleaned out her room, she had given her collection of horse paraphernalia to Veronique, but she had kept this one statuette, saying it was the most special one of the collection, and she wanted to take it with her. Under the stallion, Delfina had left note with a phone number and a message: "Here's a statue of your spirit animal to keep you strong. If you need me, you can always reach me at this phone number. Call collect."

That night before she went to bed, Irene stopped to look into Delfina's empty room. She found Veronique asleep on the stripped bed, wrapped in her favorite blanket, hugging a hair brush and a statuette of a horse.

# CHAPTER 9

Veronique did not get an opportunity to talk to Renee about what she had seen until one day after school in the fall. She had tried a few times over the summer, but her friend had gone to visit relatives in Maine for July and August, so Veronique never got around to that particular conversation. Renee was attending the Academy that year. Although they were the same age, they rarely saw each other at school, because Veronique had skipped a grade.

After school, the two girls often got a ride home from Pino. One afternoon, as they trudged toward the office, Renee said, "It's really nice of you to help me with my homework, Ronnie. I don't know why I'm such an idiot about math."

"You're not really, but it's like you're somewhere else most of the time."

"Oh." Renee fell silent.

As they approached the front door of Pino's office building, Veronique took a deep breath, knowing this was her chance. She hesitated. She had been over the scenario hundreds of times in her mind. Still, when she was actually in the situation, she wondered if she should just leave well enough alone. She put her hand on the handle of the big glass door that led into the office building and stopped.

"Renee, I know this is going to sound awful…" Her voice petered off.

Renee stopped and looked at her questioningly.

"Um," Veronique started again. "Renee, is there anything that could happen that would make you so mad that you would never speak to me again?"

Renee was looking at her with increasing fear. "I don't think so. Why?"

Veronique faltered again. "I don't know. My father can be such a jerk. He doesn't ever listen to me. Sometimes I wonder…" She stopped there and changed the subject. "Renee, is your father mean to you?"

Renee's expression was vapid. "No. He's really good to us."

"You're his special girl?"

Renee startled and then looked troubled. "He says that if I'm good, it helps him not be so sad that he lost Mommy. Let's go in now. They're probably waiting." Her voice was high and thin, and although the two girls were facing each other, Veronique could not tell what Renee was looking at.

She felt she could not reach her friend's eyes, she told Jonathan later.

"Look, Ronnie, you did the best you could," her brother told her. "Now, just concentrate on your own stuff, like maybe skipping another grade or this year's NYSSMA competition, or something." NYSSMA, the state-wide musical competition, was foremost on Jonathan's mind. Veronique played the cello and the piano. This was her first year to enter the NYSSMA event. Jonathan wanted his sister to come away with awards every year of her grade school career. Veronique sighed, and Jonathan patted her shoulder. "You can't help her if she doesn't want to be helped. Maybe one of the reasons you fizzed instead of talking to her is because you knew she wants to keep things as they are."

Veronique was unsatisfied with that explanation, but she did not have another solution, so she applied herself to the task of selecting music for the competition with Jonathan's help.

❋   ❋   ❋

A few weeks later, Veronique was sitting alone in the lunch room at Pino's office waiting for her father to take her home. Miss Brown had left for the day, and Veronique knew Pino would be ready to leave within the hour. The office was very quiet; with the holidays coming, most employees did not work late. She was reading a Nancy Drew book, her back to the door, when the presence of someone in the doorway startled her. She jumped and turned around.

Rocco Laurio stood in the doorway, watching her. "Jumpy, are ya, little miss smarty pants?" His voice was low, snarling.

Veronique returned to her book, her back to the man in the doorway. Her mind was racing. Her instinct was to run to her father's office, but that would mean having to get by Rocco Laurio. She knew no one was close enough to hear her if she yelled.

"Your parents ever teach you any manners, like not turning your back on a grownup, or answering a question when it's asked of you?" His voice was still low and threatening.

She remembered what Jonathan had told her about being in difficult situations: first try outsmarting them. In this case that would be easy, she thought to herself.

Without looking up from her book, she said, "Obviously, my parents never intended for me to reduce myself to responding to being called names."

"Obviously," he imitated her, his voice dripping with sarcasm. "Well, listen to me, girlie," he said, coming around to stand in front of her, his hands in his pockets. "You may know enough to be a tutor to my daughter in math and science, et cetera, et cetera, et cetera, et cetera."

Veronique looked up quickly. This was the voice she and Luca had heard in the tunnel of the Chamber that day. Her mind was racing as Rocco leered at her, his voice a sinister growl.

"You're not as smart as you think in that pretty little uniform of yours." He slammed his hand on the table, and Veronique jumped. "That's right. Now put your book down and listen to me." Her eyes on him, Veronique did not move. "That's better. I don't want you fucking with Renee's head. Do you understand me?" He had stepped closer as he was talking, and shook a finger at her, close to her face.

Veronique was getting angry, but she did not move.

"I said, do you understand me?"

Veronique stared at him unblinking.

"You little bitch." He straightened himself up to his full height, and thrust his hands in his pockets. His voice got lower. "Thinking you're better than me, are you? How full of yourself would you be with my dick stuck down your throat? Yeah, that makes you react, doesn't it? You'd probably like it, you little hussy. Trying to turn my daughter against me, are you? Well, don't think you're so smart in those short skirts." His lip curled. The door to Pino's office opened. Rocco's voice was even lower, and it was menacing as he paused next to her chair, on his way out. "Watch out, little girl. Someone's gonna get you good. Ram a dick down your throat, and we'll see how full of yourself you are then."

Pino appeared in the lunch room door. Veronique got up and ran past Rocco to him. "Father, what's a dick? Mister Laurio said…"

❦ ❦ ❦

Rocco Laurio was never again in Pino's office when Veronique came in after school. This was fine with her. The upsetting thing was that the following day, Veronique found out that Renee was no longer attending the Academy.

No one would elaborate on Renee's abrupt departure. Pino did not discuss what happened with Rocco Laurio. Veronique felt like she had imagined the whole upsetting incident.

Jonathan noticed that she was listless. She had told him what had happened, and how frustrated she was about not getting any answers about it.

"You can't let it get to you. Concentrate on your music now. Renee's probably better off if she's not at the Academy. She wasn't going to make it. The Academy was too much for her. And you're definitely better off if you're not around that psycho Laurio. Trust me, Ronnie. Forget it. Do not let it get to you. You're not afraid of his stupid threat, are you?"

She shook her head, but looked down.

"Are you?" Jonathan lifted her chin. His dark brown eyes looked directly into her cobalt blue ones. "I can't remember you ever being afraid of anything." He paused. "We won't let anybody mess with you. I promise."

She looked at him and nodded, believing what he told her.

# CHAPTER 10

"Richie and I are going to the movies, Mom. I'll be home around eleven." It was April 1989. Fifteen-year old Veronique called to her mother as she left the house. Irene, in her studio, did not answer.

She returned an hour later, fuming. "Richie is such an *idiot*," she seethed, stomping down the hall to her room. Seconds later, music was blasting from behind the closed door. An hour later, when it still had not abated, Jonathan, who lived in the guest house now and taught at the local school, went in to find out what had happened.

"He is such a jerk," Veronique spat through gritted teeth, after she turned down the stereo. "He wanted to start heavy petting—"

"—Heavy petting? Since when—" Jonathan's left eyebrow shot up.

"—SINCE NEVER. Don't you turn into a jerk too." Veronique was very frustrated. "Anyway, I said no, I didn't feel like it.—Happy?—And he said I was his woman, and I would do what he said. I told him to shove it, and got out of the car and walked to the truck stop. Some people were there from school, and they drove me home. I am so *mad* that he thought he could talk to me that way. As soon as I get my license, I'm getting my own car. That way guys have to ride with *me*."

"Oh really? And how are you going to get your own car?"

"Well, I thought I'd get a job now and start saving for it. Father would never just give me a car, and Mom will never think I'm ready to drive. Like she's the best driver in the world."

Jonathan had to laugh. Their mother's little driving peccadillos were part of the family lore. Irene never had accidents with other cars, she had fender benders with mailboxes, ornate iron birds and decorative driveway pillars, usually when driving in reverse.

"I saw a sign at the Lincoln-Mercury dealer's showroom. They're looking for office help. I figure by the time I've got my driver's license, which should be next year with your help, I will be able to afford a second hand car. Not a Porsche, or even a Lincoln, but something that runs and looks good. I'm getting my working papers from the guidance office tomorrow."

꧁ ꧁ ꧁

A week later, Veronique was working two days per week for the Lincoln Mercury dealer on Main Street. She ran errands, made copies and filed, much as she had for Miss Brown in her father's office.

One evening, several months after she started working there, she was late leaving the office. She had been trying to make photocopies, and the machine kept on jamming.

"You sure you don't want to just leave that 'till tomorrow, Veronique?" Laura Mason, her supervisor, asked her.

"I'm only here two days a week, Laura. I think I should just get it done before I leave. Don't worry. I'll be out of here in half an hour."

Laura shrugged. "Okay. The boys are in the showroom until eight. They'll lock up."

Veronique was engrossed in her work, and almost two hours had passed before she had finally finished making the copies and organizing them for the meeting the next day. As she was leaving, she passed the front office. The door was open, and the light was on.

"Goodnight, Bob," she said to the dealership's owner as she walked past the office.

"Whaa—who's there?" Bob always sounded like his tongue was recovering from a dose of Novocain when he talked.

Veronique took two steps backward to stand in the doorway so that Bob could see her. "It's Veronique."

"Oh, uh-huh. What're you doing here so late?"

"I was getting all the papers for tomorrow's meeting copied, and the copy machine kept jamming, so it took a really long time."

"Damned machine. It never works well on big jobs. What time's that meeting tomorrow?"

"Um, I'm not sure. One, I think."

"Yeah, one sounds right. Hey, you want a smoke?"

Veronique just shrugged.

"No, huh? Well, I'm gonna do a line. You want?" She had stepped further into the room, and she could see that he had white powder on a square mirror which was lying on his desk. He took a tube and sniffed the powder into his nose. Veronique watched curiously. She had smoked pot with Jonathan once or twice. She had seen people doing drugs in a movie, but she had never actually witnessed someone snorting cocaine before.

"You sure you don't want?" Bob proffered her the tube as he came up for a breath.

"Nah, I've got some people waiting for me. I'd better be going."

"Yeah, you do that. If you're ever working late again, I'll take you out for a drink or something."

Realizing that he thought she was older than her fifteen years, Veronique left without answering. She felt a surge of power at the idea that he thought she was old enough to go out with him. She wondered to herself if she would go out with him if he asked. No. Bad idea. He was married or divorced or something. Anyway Laura Mason had her eye on Bob, Veronique knew. Veronique was interested in a car, not in Bob. Still, she liked the surge of power that she felt as she walked into the darkening evening air.

❦   ❦   ❦

"No, Richie. I'm not going to the prom with you…I don't care if you go with Geena. I'm not going to be caught dead with you…I don't know if I really want to go to something as childish as the Junior Prom…Since I don't know when…I don't care if you have a car…If I go to the prom, you can bet my date will have a car…You really are an idiot." Veronique hung up the phone quietly, as Richie was answering. She amused herself by imagining how long it would take Richie to realize that no one was at the other end of the line, and then she laughed to herself at how angry he would be.

The phone rang. Richie could not have realized no one was at the other end already.

"Hello?"

"May I speak to Veronique?" A man's voice came fuzzily over the line.

"I'm Veronique."

"Oh. Hi. It's Bob Voldaris. You know, from Voldaris' Lincoln Mercury."

"Oh, yeah. My boss. How ya doin'?"

"You wanna go out this Friday?"

"I don't know. It's prom night. I was thinking of going."

"Prom night? You mean like for school or somethin'?" Not waiting for a reply, he continued, "You got a date?"

"I did until about fifteen minutes ago," Veronique lied.

"Oh." Silence on the other end of the line. Bob was either thinking or snorting. Veronique was still trying to determine whether Bob's slow tongue fronted a slow mind. He interrupted her thoughts. "I'll pick you up at seven-thirty. We can check out the prom, and if it gets boring, we'll go to a real party."

"Okay, but you've gotta wear a tux, Bob."

"No problem. The party that we're going to after your prom is black tie."

❦   ❦   ❦

"Jon, you've got to help me. I'm going to the prom with Bob, the guy from work, but I don't want Mom or Father to mess me up and not let me go with him."

"Actually, you don't have to worry about it. Mom and Father Joe are going to be in the city for her opening on Friday. Father's not getting back from London until Monday."

"Yesssss." Veronique felt victorious. The prom had gotten under the radar of her mother and the even more watchful eye of Joe.

"I want to meet this guy." Jonathan interrupted her mini reverie.

"You'll like him. He's, um, mature."

"Hmmmmm." Jonathan was skeptical.

❦   ❦   ❦

"Ronnie, I thought you weren't going to your junior prom." Irene and Veronique were having breakfast in the atrium that Irene had installed during the last renovation of her kitchen.

"I wasn't, Mom. But then this guy from work, Bob, asked me out, and I thought, for a first date, I'd be better off going a place where I know a lot of people."

"That's probably true. How old is he?"

"I'm not sure. Old enough to drive in Nassau." The minimum driving age in the county to the west of Suffolk county, where the Adriaticos lived, was eighteen. "Actually, he's out of high school." Veronique did not say how far out of high school. "Don't worry, Mom. Jonathan will be here to meet him, and it's only the junior prom, not the senior, so it's not a big deal. I'm even borrowing a dress from Dawn."

"Okay, Honey. If you say it's not a big deal, then I won't worry about it. Father Joe and I will be leaving at noon, and the show starts at five. You're sure it's okay if I'm not here when you leave for the prom?"

"I'm really sure, Mom. Your opening's much more important. Besides, what are you going to do, watch me leave? It's not like you'll *be* at the prom or anything. It doesn't make any sense for you to stay here just to watch me go."

Irene nodded absently, lost in thoughts of her opening. "I was thinking I should include this piece in the show," she said, showing a picture of one of her older works to her daughter.

Veronique observed that her mother had changed the subject and let out a silent sigh of relief.

❦   ❦   ❦

Bob arrived at the Adriatico's front door at precisely seven-thirty. He drove a black Lincoln Town Car, and he wore a matching tuxedo, complete with diamond pinkie ring. Jonathan, his dark curly hair in a neat pony tail, was present to inspect him. The two men shook hands, and Jonathan, who had taken an instant dislike to his sister's date, asked them to pose for a picture.

"I'd, ah, rather not," Bob said. "I really don't have pictures taken of me. It's against my, uh, beliefs."

"No problem, Bob," Veronique said brightly, glaring at Jonathan. "I told everyone not to make a big deal of this prom. We're just going out."

"Don't forget, Bob," Jonathan said over his sister's head, "Veronique is under age for drinking and everything." Veronique looked daggers at Jonathan.

"Don't worry. I'll take good care of her. Shall we, Veronique?" He indicated the way to the car, pinkie ring glistening.

"Yes, Bob. Let's go."

"Be home by midnight, Veronique. Bob, I'm sure you'll see that she is."

"It's prom night, Jon," Veronique protested. "Everyone stays out all night on prom night. My friends will be going to the beach."

"Call me at midnight, then. I'll ask Mom if it's okay. Make sure that she does, okay Bob?"

"Will do, big brother." Bob flashed a false smile at Jonathan, and then escorted Veronique to the car.

※　　　　　※　　　　　※

Veronique and her cousins all attended the same school. And despite the last-minute change of dates, Veronique had managed to call in some favors owed to her by students who were on the prom committee. She got two seats at the same table as her four cousins who were attending the prom that night. She had also managed to get Richie, who was no longer her date, moved to a different table.

Luca, looking tall and handsome, was at the table with his date, the sister of the girl that his brother Gavin, one of the twins, had brought to the prom. Luca was actually doing Gavin a favor. The girls' father said that if one of his daughters did not go to the prom, neither was going. Kyle, Gavin's twin, was also seated with them. Kyle was dating the captain of the cheerleading squad. Alec, a senior, was dating Veronique's friend Dawn, a junior, and that couple completed the table.

Luca danced with Veronique when Bob went outside to smoke. "I don't like that guy, Ronnie," her cousin told her. There's something gross about him, and not just that he's about a hundred years old."

"Luca, he's not a hundred, and he's just a prom date. Don't worry, it's more to say 'screw you' to that jerk Richie over there. He really tried treating me like a piece of meat last time I went out with him, which was the final time ever." Luca looked over to see Richie glaring at Veronique's back as they moved around the dance floor. "You're coming to the beach with us, right?" Luca asked her.

"Bob wants to go to a party with some of his friends, but we can meet you there later."

The song ended. "We'll make plans before we leave."

Luca and Veronique went back to the table as Bob and Alec, who had gone outside with him, were seating themselves again.

The music started again, and Alec invited Veronique to dance. "I hope you don't mind, Bob," Alec said with more-formal-than-usual courtesy.

"Not at all. Veronique's such a vision of loveliness. I don't mind watching her dance with any of her cousins."

As Alec and Veronique danced to the music of Billy Joel, a Long Islander whose love songs were always popular at proms, Alec looked at his cousin with concerned eyes.

"What? What, Alec?"

"I just went out to get some air with Bob who went out to smoke, you know?"

Veronique nodded.

"He's a drug dealer, Ronnie. He's got a stash of—of every drug you can think of in that Lincoln of his. He offered me some cocaine. When I said no, he asked me if I wanted to smoke a joint with him. I didn't, so he smoked it himself."

"Just because he smokes a little pot doesn't make him a drug dealer."

"He *told* me he's a drug dealer. He's got a shitload of cocaine in his trunk."

"He came right out and said, uh, Alec, my new best friend, I just want to let you know I'm a drug dealer?"

"No. I asked him how the car sales industry is doing, and he said it's okay, but the entertainment industry is much better, if I know what he means, complete with a wink."

"Alec, don't worry. He's not going to sell any with me around."

"How do you know?"

Veronique didn't. She shrugged carelessly. "I just do, that's all."

The music ended, and Bob stepped up to have the next dance with Veronique.

"You having a good time, Princess?"

"I am. My cousins want us to meet them at the beach. I told them you have another party for us to go to first, but that we'd meet them later."

"Sounds good, baby. You think you're about ready to go?"

"Give me another half an hour."

"How 'bout twenty minutes?"

"All right."

When they returned to the table, Veronique told her cousins that she and Bob were getting ready to leave.

"Where are you gonna go at the beach?"

"We'll be east of the board walk, near the driftwood."

Veronique knew the place. The driftwood was the bleached remains of a huge oak tree that had been washed ashore about five years earlier during a hurricane.

"If you're not there by three, we're sending a search party for you," Alec told them, unsmilingly.

❦   ❦   ❦

Bob's black Lincoln pulled up to a formidable looking iron gate. The columns on either side of it were lit with white spotlights, which were recessed somewhere in the grass and hedges in front of them. Behind the gate, a fountain, also lit with white light from somewhere within its recesses, surprised the velvet night around it.

Once they left the prom, Bob had headed west. Veronique could see that he had taken the Brookville exit of the Long Island Expressway. But once they had turned off the main street and started weaving through the back roads, she had not been able to discern whether they were in posh Brookville or the even more exclusive Old Brookville.

A man in a dark suit stepped out from behind the door in the column on the driver's side of the car.

"Robert Voldaris." Bob announced himself.

"Mr. Voldaris. Mr. and Mrs. Kent have been expecting you. Please drive through to the house." The heavy iron gates silently opened inward. Although Veronique could not see a house, Bob had only one way to drive: directly forward into the darkness. As the car rounded what seemed to be a hairpin curve around a grove of tall trees, the house, which seemed to be more like a castle to Veronique, loomed unexpectedly before them. The structure seemed to be lit with thousands of candles, and a white canopy extended from the front awning over the three marble steps to the front entrance. A fountain, which was even larger than the one that had been at the gate, graced the center of the circular drive in front of the house.

"Mr. and Mrs. Kent?" Veronique repeated after Bob closed his window. "Would that be Clark and Lois?"

"Uh, no. I don't know them." Bob, oblivious to the Superman reference, drove the car counterclockwise around the circle, stopping when Veronique's door was at the entrance. A man in a pristine white suit, including white cap and gloves, stepped from the shadows to open Veronique's door. He helped her out of the car. Bob, carrying a briefcase, came around the front of the car and extended his arm to her.

"From prom to gala, huh? My friends, the Kents—Jim and Lady—are expecting us. Everybody's probably in the back by the pool. They're waiting for us."

"Really? Why?"

"The party doesn't start until I get here." Bob winked at her and shook the briefcase. Briefly Veronique thought of Alec's warning. She shrugged slightly. She could handle anything.

They walked around the house on a brick path that was lit by candles. Veronique wondered whose job it had been to light them all. She smirked to herself as she mused that whoever it was probably was glad that it was not a windy night.

When they reached the back of the house, the setting Veronique saw entranced her.

"Wow." She exhaled the word quietly.

"Beautiful, huh?" Bob nodded in agreement.

The back of the house was more dimly lit than the front. A pool of indeterminable shape and length was the most stunning feature of the yard. There was also a waterfall that was backlit in salmon colored lights tucked tastefully behind the opulent bar. Veronique could make out approximately fifteen couples in various stages of repose on velvet chaise lounges and pillows on the deck, and in the pool. Soft music played from unseen speakers, which were strategically placed around the sitting area.

"Bob. You've finally arrived." A deep female voice came from somewhere in the shadows near the bar.

"Lady. I'm sorry I'm late. As I told Jim, we had another party to go to first. Lady, I'd like you to meet Veronique. Veronique, Lady." A thin white arm extended itself from the side of the bar toward Veronique.

"Pleased to meet you, my dear. She's a vision in loveliness, Bob. Jim went down to the cellar to get a few more bottles of wine. He was muttering something about sending the Marines to find you."

Bob laughed. "Well, no need. Santa has arrived, magic bag of gifts and all."

"Bob." A man's voice with a southern accent came from the candle-lit veranda. "Where the hell have you been?"

"My date and I were at a dance. Veronique, this is my old friend Jim."

"Pleased to meet you, Ma'am. I'd shake hands, but they're a bit tied up at the moment." He carried four green-glassed bottles of wine, two in each hand. Veronique returned his nod with a smile. "Well, Bob, I can see how a purty little filly like that could make you a bit late for our tired ole party. Hey folks," he called to the people around the pool, "the candy man's here."

As the people started milling around the bar, Veronique leaned over to Lady Kent, whose face she still could not see. "Where's the restroom?"

"I'll get Millie to show you." The white arm floated eerily out of the shadows and rang a small brass bell that was sitting on the bar. Almost instantly, a blonde girl who was not much older than Veronique appeared on the veranda, and walked toward Lady and Veronique. "Millie, bring this young lady to the powder room."

"Yes, Ma'am. Right this way, Miss." Veronique followed Millie into the mansion.

"Wow, cool," she said, looking at the many statues and paintings in the marble-floored hallway down which she was being led.

"Here it is, Miss," Millie indicated a bright room at the end of the hallway. "Towels are on the left. To get back to the party, just walk straight down the hall, back the way we came. It's easy, but I can wait for you if you want."

"No, thanks. I'll find it." Veronique wondered if she should tip her. The question answered itself as Millie bowed very slightly and returned to the gathering.

Veronique closed the mahogany door, and found herself in a salon in front of a full-length mirror, complete with vanity table, red velvet cushioned seat and angled spotlights. She surveyed herself critically, and decided that her lipstick needed touching up. Finishing that, she pulled a brush back through her dark hair, which glistened under the lights.

The plumbing was in a different section of the salon, partitioned off by a half-wall that was covered in mirrors. Toilet, bidet and, on the opposite wall, a sink complete with an elegant fountain-like faucet, all looked like they were covered in liquid mirrors. The room was completely silent. Almost too silent, Veronique noticed as she finished touching up her makeup. Quickly, she rejoined the party.

The music seemed louder, and it had changed to a more techno-electrical guitar sound when she returned to the garden.

"There you are, Baby. I wondered whether you'd gotten lost." Bob's voice came out of the shadows between the bar and the pool.

"No, I needed to touch up my makeup. See?" She smiled at him in the darkness, sure he could not see her.

"Looks great, Baby," Bob's already-sluggish tongue was getting slower. "Come'ere. Sit with me."

"What've you been doing while I was gone, Bob?" Veronique asked slightly teasing, slightly cautious.

"Oh, not much. One little joint, that's all. Not even a line. I been giving it out, 'sall. C'm'ere. Sit on my lap, Baby."

"I don't want you to fall through the chair," Veronique said in the same teasing tone.

"Don't worry. These guys can afford to buy another one if we do." He grabbed her hand and pulled her toward him. "You want a beer or something."

"Sure. A beer would be good. Amstel Light."

He signaled for one of the ubiquitous waiters. Millie materialized from the shadows. "Amstel Light, okay?"

"Yes, Sir." She receded back into the darkness, appearing a few moments later with an icy mug. Veronique started to sip it while Bob prepared to roll another joint. When it was lit, he pulled her close to him and used his free hand to stroke her hair as she drank her beer.

"How old are you, Veronique?" Bob asked, almost half asleep.

"Fifteen."

"No, really, I'm not kidding." Bob was talking through molasses.

"I'm not kidding," Veronique murmured, sipping her beer.

"Shit," Bob took a long drag on his hand made joint. "I guess that means if I even kiss you I'm screwed." He leaned his head back, and his hand dropped down her arm until it rested on her elbow. As he dozed, she looked around. By the dim lights in the yard, she could make out a couple nearby. As she watched, the woman unzipped the man's pants, revealing his unfettered erection silhouetted in the candle light. Having never before seen an adult male in this stage of repose, she watched curiously as the woman massaged and teased her partner before finally moving to kneel by his waist and take him in her mouth. At that, the beginnings of arousal that Veronique had been feeling dissipated immediately, and she gagged.

She put her beer down. "Bob, wake up." She tugged at his arm. He did not budge. He had dropped the end of his joint on the flagstone beneath their chair, and it had gone out. She stood up, shakily, and patted his cheek. "Wake up," she said, her face near his ear.

"Mmmm. Not right now." He mumbled before slipping out of consciousness again.

"Shit. You retard. This is a great party?" Veronique's anger energized her. She grabbed her bag and headed toward the house. Millie met her at the front porch.

"Can I help you, Miss?"

"Yeah, Millie. Can I use the phone?"

"Certainly. Follow me." She led Veronique to a small phone booth underneath the grand staircase at the center of the foyer. "Here you are, Miss."

"Uh, Millie, I'm calling someone to pick me up. Where do I tell them to come?"

Millie seemed to hesitate for a moment, but then gave her the address.

"Would you mind staying here and giving me some directions? I'd never remember them if you told me."

"Here." Millie handed Veronique a piece of notebook paper with something written on it with a pink ball-point pen. "Directions. Give them back when you're done, okay?" She started walking away, and then paused and turned around to add, "When they get to the gate, tell them to say they're here for Rosebud."

"Rosebud?" Veronique repeated, looking at her sideways.

"Rosebud." Millie repeated, expressionless, before continuing down the hall.

Veronique nodded and called Jonathan. During the time that Veronique waited for her brother, Bob did not move once. Jonathan arrived in half an hour, and he was livid. Alec was with him.

"What are you doing here?" Veronique asked Alec as she got into Jonathan's car. Tight lipped, Jonathan drove down the long driveway and out of the gates.

"Just taking a ride with Jon. I was at your house when you called. Well, at least Bob didn't lie about the fancy party."

"Yeah. At least it looks fancy. Everything was very nice. But it was really boring."

"Where's Mr. Personality?" Alec asked.

"Who?" Veronique feigned confusion.

"You know, Bob."

"He fell asleep by the pool." Veronique confessed, more angry at Bob than upset that the party was not all that Bob had said it would be.

"Well, after you left, Richie started hassling Gavin about who your date for the prom was," Alec told her. "He followed the twins out to the parking lot after the dance, and he was really harassing them. He almost hit Gavin. They left, but not before Richie said some really ugly things. He made threats against you as Gavin and Kyle drove away."

"I always knew Richie was a real jerk. But I don't care about him. What could he possibly do to me?"

"Richie has a big mouth, and it got bigger when the twins didn't tell him anything—not that they knew anything to tell him—but I guess you're right. What could he possibly do?"

Jonathan, who had been silent up to this point, finally spoke. "Ronnie, I've got to tell you that your taste in men these past two times really sucks."

Veronique rolled her eyes. "Oh, come on, Jonathan. I wasn't serious about either one of these guys, and I can't do anything about the way they act."

"Well, judging from the fact that there aren't many houses on this street, it looks like you got out of there in the nick of time," Jonathan said.

Veronique looked out of the window, uncomprehending. They were five miles away from the house, just turning onto the main road. Five oncoming police cars, lights flashing, silently sped past them.

"I hope they know to say Rosebud," Veronique said, watching them speed by. "Original, huh?"

Jonathan laughed, finally letting go of his anger. Alec helped Veronique to convince Jonathan to let her go to meet her cousins at the beach. Her brother relented with a minimum of objection. Alec and Veronique joined the rest of the people who had been at their prom table down by the Long Island Sound. The cousins had built a small fire, and they were sitting around it talking about Richie when Alec and Veronique joined them.

"If he's stupid enough to try anything, we'll be ready for him." Gavin was saying.

"He's got a mouth, but no balls," his twin added, and the others nodded.

After a while, their conversation turned to other things. But before another hour passed, a light mist had formed, which turned into a steady drizzle. As the group was hurriedly making its way toward the cars, the rain started.

There was a short discussion about whether to go to the Chamber or not. Everyone was hungry, so Veronique and her cousins ended prom night by watching the sun rise through the rain clouds at an all-night diner.

Veronique called the dealership the next day to quit her job. Laura said that Bob had not come in yet.

"I don't know what's wrong. He's usually here by eleven on Mondays." Laura mused, puzzled. Veronique did not comment. Two days later, she had found a new job working in the Smithhaven Mall. She did not return Bob's telephone calls, which started the next day. She did not see or hear from Richie for the next week. She had almost forgotten about the prom and everything that had gone on.

❦   ❦   ❦

Wendell Clay, age eight, arrived on Jonathan's doorstep at precisely two-thirty in the afternoon. The Fresh Air Fund child was Jonathan's guest for the summer. A small, dark-skinned boy with huge brown eyes, Wendell had a self-conscious, retiring manner. Jonathan settled the child into a bedroom in the guest house, just down the hall from Jonathan's room. Then he took him to the main house to meet the rest of the Adriaticos.

Irene and Pino were not at home, and Veronique was due home from work at five. Jonathan and Wendell knocked on Marc's studio door, and stopped to chat briefly. Marc was working on a new sculpture, and was not able to spend much time talking with them.

"Well, Wendell," Jonathan said, ruefully, "I guess it's just you and me in the pool today."

"You have a whole pool to yourself?" It was the first full sentence the little boy had said since he arrived.

"Yes, when my family isn't around."

"I never been in a pool without tons of people in it."

"Well, here's your chance. Get your suit, and let's go."

While Jonathan and Wendell were in the pool, a black Lincoln pulled into the Adriaticos' driveway. In the pool, Jonathan and Wendell could not hear the insistent ringing of the doorbell in the main house. When Marc, who had been unable to ignore the ringing any longer, answered the door, his hands and muscular arms were covered in clay. He was annoyed.

"What took you so long?" Bob was unaccustomed to waiting for many things.

"Who the hell are you?"

"I'm here to see Veronique."

"She's not here." Marc started to slam the door, but Bob stopped him.

"When will she be back?"

"I don't know. Besides, if you don't know, I don't believe it's any of your damned business. Get lost, I'm busy."

"Can I come in and wait for her?"

Marc looked at him like he had two heads. "Of course not. Now, if you don't get out of here I'm calling the police."

Bob realized that he had taken the wrong tack. He tried a different one. "Uh, look, I'm sorry. I'm, um, kinda upset. You see, I've been trying to call Veronique for a week now, and she doesn't call back."

"And it's not at all obvious to you why she might not be inclined to call you back?"

"I know I'm a little rough around the edges, but I really enjoy her company."

"Why don't you hang around people your own age? Look, I've got uncovered clay to get back to, and I've wasted enough time here. So get out or meet the cops."

"Okay. I'll just wait for her in my car."

Marc shrugged. "Suit yourself." Bob stepped back, and Marc slammed the door.

❦   ❦   ❦

Ever since the prom, Richie Dell'Alma had anger to vent. It was the anger of a seventeen-year-old with pride to protect and hormones that were out of control. He vented it at home where his father, a first-generation Italian American dock worker, vented right back at him. He vented it at school and, for the last week of the year, was given early morning detention, because he had a job after school. He vented it at work in his uncle's garage where he served as a junior mechanic, causing even more damage to the already-damaged vehicle he was trying to fix.

"Hey, Richie," his uncle Leo, his mother's brother and owner of the garage, called him into the office one day. "Come in 'ere and siddown." Leo was more communicative than Richie's father, but he expected to talk to his nephew without interruption. "Look, Richie. You got woman problems. You can't bring them into the shop. Machines and women, they don't mix. When you're here, you gotta take care of the machines. When you're out there, you gotta take care of the rest of your life. This girl, who's got you so upset, she's messing up your work here. Now listen. You're a good boy, and you're gonna be a good mechanic. You got the hands for it. You got the brain for it. But when your heart's not in it or you're distracted, like you are now, you're the biggest fuckup in the shop."

Richie opened his mouth to object, but his uncle raised a big greasy hand to silence him.

"Now, you listen to me. It's Thursday. You're gonna take the rest of today off. You're gonna take tomorrow off. You're gonna take care of your problems outside, and come back into this shop on Monday ready to work. Do you understand me?"

Richie nodded.

"Now go. Here's your pay." Leo handed his nephew a check. It was for a full week's work. Richie at his uncle, surprised that he was being paid for the days off. "Consider it a loan," his uncle answered his look. "I may need your help with something later. Right now, get outta here, and get your shit together."

Richie nodded, speechless. Then he rounded out of his seat and left the office.

"And stay outta trouble," Leo called behind him.

Richie jumped into his green rebuilt Mustang and revved the engine. He pulled out of the shop parking lot carefully. As soon as he was out of his uncle's sight, he careened down the street and skidded to a screeching stop at the corner. He did this for a few blocks and began to feel better even as he started to smell the heated protest of the engine. He started driving more regularly and two blocks later passed a parked police car. He smiled to himself. This might be his lucky day. Time to take care of Veronique.

He cruised past the Adriatico's house as Jonathan, a small black boy and a matronly looking white woman were standing and talking in the driveway. Richie liked Jonathan who, with kindness and humor, had helped him pass eleventh-grade English the year before.

Richie thought about that as he swung around the sharp curve on Riviera Drive and headed away from the water. He liked Veronique, he conceded to himself. She was one of the few people who had treated him kindly. She never talked down to him. Never, that is, until they had that misunderstanding at the movies a few weeks ago. There was something a little screwed up about Veronique, he mused. She didn't know her place somehow. But he liked being with her, and he liked her family. No, he didn't want to get Veronique, he wanted to get that asshole who was her date at the prom. He wanted to show Veronique that he would fight for her. Deep down, Richie did not want Veronique to leave him, like his brother Carlo had left him in the accident on the train track.

He drove to the park in his neighborhood. Several of his buddies were hanging around there. They walked over to the driver's side of the car.

A broad Long Island accent came over the line. "Hey, Richie. We went by the shop. Your uncle said you got the rest of the week off."

Richie, his own accent getting thicker around his buddies, said, "Yeah. I got a idiot who needs to get a education. You guys can help. Get the other guys, and be at Johnny's house in half an hour. I want to drive by Veronique's house again and see if she's home." With that, he spun his car around and headed back to Riviera Drive.

When Richie drove by the Adriatico's house again, Bob was sitting in the driveway. "Holy shit," Richie said aloud to himself as he saw the maroon Lincoln in the driveway with its owner sitting in it, "This is my lucky day."

He made the sharp turn casually. As soon as he was out of sight of the house, he sped to the gas station at the corner, and used the pay phone to call John Mosca's house where his friends were meeting. It rang two very long times.

Finally, Johnny answered. "Yeah. Hello."

"Johnny. It's me, Richie. Get over to the Adriaticos with the guys. Our bird's in the driveway right now."

"This must be your lucky day, Richie. They're all here. We'll be right over."

"I'll be waiting in the parking lot of the bar on St. Johnland Road."

❦ ❦ ❦

Bob Voldaris was sitting behind the wheel of his shiny, factory-new maroon Lincoln Town Car. The soft sounds of the waves rustling the cattails on the other side of the street combined with the startled calls of sea birds. Every once in a while, the gentle sea breeze would change direction, and he would smell the sand from the road side or get an occasional whiff of a lawn being mowed. The heat and the quiet made him drowsy, and he loosened his tie and reclined in his car, dozing, waiting for Veronique to come home.

When Richie pulled up to the Adriaticos' driveway, blocking it with his Mustang, Bob was dreaming about large bumble bees buzzing around and flying in and out of a snow-covered mound. A grey Volkswagen van, a chartreuse Jeep, and a zebra-striped Dodge Dart, each carrying five boys, pulled up behind Richie's vehicle. Bob was startled awake, realizing that the buzzing of the bees in his dream was actually the sound of the cars' engines behind his car on the street. In his rearview mirror, he could see fifteen teenage boys with baseball bats piling out of three mangy-looking cars, while another boy bounded from a Mustang that blocked his car in the driveway.

"Hey you, kid. Move that car. You're blocking me."

"You ain't going anywhere, moron," the boy said, advancing upon him menacingly.

Instinctively, Bob power-locked his doors. "Look, I don't live here. I'm just waiting for someone."

"Yeah, I know that. You're the one I want."

"I don't know you."

"I know you don't. But I know you. You stole my prom date, and now you're gonna pay."

"Your prom date? I didn't know she had a date. I had a party to go to—"

"Shut up, and get out of the car."

Bob rolled up his windows as Richie slammed a bat onto the roof of the car. As the other boys started smashing the car with their bats, Bob was starting his car and leaning on the horn to attract attention. Jonathan and Wendell, wrapped in towels, came around the side of the house to see what was going on.

Marc looked out the window as Veronique and Luca pulled up in Luca's car, followed by Alec and five of his brothers who were coming over for a swim.

Veronique jumped out of the car before Luca had fully stopped it. Her anger impelled her into the middle of the ruckus.

"Richie, what the hell do you think you're doing?" A bat smashed the passenger's side view mirror.

Her cousins piled out of their car and moved toward the boys with the bats. Wendell, seeing a group of white boys with bats, froze in fear. He cowered behind Jonathan. "I didn't do anything," he muttered.

Jonathan tried to guide the youngster back around the side of the house, but he was locked in place, terrified, and at the same time mesmerized by what was happening.

Meanwhile Veronique, angry and undaunted by the boys or the bats, came up behind Richie. "Get lost, you asshole," she yelled at Richie over the blaring horn. A tail light shattered as Johnny's bat gleefully found its mark. Somehow Veronique managed to grab the bat from Richie as he was taking aim for another swing. He turned to look at her in surprise as she came around to stand between him and Bob's car, brandishing his bat.

"Tell your goons to stop." She kicked the door of the car. "Stop that horn, you moron," she yelled over her shoulder. Immediately the sound ceased, although the banging did not.

"Stop them now," she commanded, still yelling and not letting go of the bat.

Sirens on St. Johnland Road were coming closer. The kids stopped even before Richie gave them the order, and they ran for their cars. Tires screeching, Richie's friends made their getaway. Bob opened his window. "Move your car, you idiot, before I make sure you're held responsible for the damage on my car."

"You're sure in a hurry," Richie drawled slowly. The closer the sirens got, the more nervous Bob was.

"You'll pay for this," Bob shrieked, frantic.

"Move your car, Richie," Veronique commanded. "You're still on probation. You don't want to lose your driver's license."

Richie had not thought about this. Hurriedly, he retreated into his vehicle, and sped off in the opposite direction from where the sirens were approaching.

Without a word to Veronique, Bob sped out of the driveway and followed Richie, leaving Veronique and Luca choking in engine fumes and burning rubber. The sirens suddenly ceased, and moments later, two blue squad cars came around the curve of Riviera Drive. Two officers, a tall blonde male and an equally tall and blonde female, who were dressed exactly the same right down to their mirrored-lens aviator-framed sunglasses, got out of the first car. Veronique fleetingly thought that they looked like identical twins as the female officer approached her and Luca.

"We got two calls of trouble here. A couple of your neighbors called, and said some kids were banging on a car with baseball bats."

Veronique was still enraged at both Richie and Bob. "Yes, officer. Apparently a guy was loitering in this driveway, and when I got home from work just now with my cousins, we drove up and saw a group of kids smashing his car with bats. They all went screeching toward the country club when they heard the sirens."

"Were any of these people known to you?" the officer asked, while her partner went to speak to the officers in the second car who took off in the direction that Veronique had indicated. He bent down to pick up the bat that Veronique had dropped as he returned to his partner's side.

Veronique paused. Jonathan, with the help of the two youngest cousins, had induced Wendell to return to the swimming pool. All the other cousins except Luca also went to the back of the house. She looked at Luca who shrugged. Her anger impelled her to speak.

"Yes. I know the guy in the Lincoln who was loitering around here. He's Bob Voldaris."

The officers looked at each other.

"Of Voldaris Lincoln Mercury?" the male officer asked.

"Yeah. I used to work there."

"Who was in the other cars?"

"Well, the ringleader was Richie Dell'Alma. He must'a come with a bunch of his friends."

"Do you think they planned to meet here?" The female officer continued the questioning.

"I have no idea. I've been at work all day."

"What do you think they were doing here?"

"Like I said, I used to work for Bob, but I got a better job last week, so I don't work there any more. Richie was gonna be my prom date until he started misbehaving, so I went to the prom with Bob." The officers exchanged a glance as Veronique continued. "Maybe Bob wanted to talk to me, and because I didn't return his calls he was just waiting here to talk to me. Richie must've drove by and gotten mad or something, and got his friends to come over with their bats. That's one of the reasons I didn't want to go to the prom with him."

"With Richie?" the male officer asked. He had tucked the bat under his arm and was taking notes on a small pad.

"Right."

A call crackled in over the squad car's radio. The female officer went to the car and responded. Her partner was asking a series of routine questions, so Veronique and Luca were not able to hear what was being said over the radio. When the officer came back, she announced that the other squad car had spotted Bob's car entering a service station on Jericho Turnpike. "He won't press charges, wouldn't say what happened and didn't know who vandalized his car."

"He was clean," she said to her partner, adding, "All they could do is give him an equipment violation."

"Do you want to press charges?" she asked Veronique.

"For what, trespassing or something? It's probably not worth it." Veronique shrugged. Then she added, "Maybe some of my esteemed neighbors will want to press charges."

"Well, I don't see them here, so I'll assume that if they do, they'll call us," the female officer said to her. She took a card out of her pocket and handed it to Veronique. "Here's my card in case you need to get in touch with me for any reason." Her partner took out a card and offered it to Veronique as well.

"Thanks for coming by." Veronique said, as they got into their car.

As the squad car went around the corner, Veronique went to the house and dropped her purse inside the front door.

"I wonder why Bob was so nervous," Luca mused. "I'll bet that he did have something in the car, but he got rid of it before he got to Jericho."

"If he did, it's probably in somebody's front bushes." Veronique said. By unspoken agreement, the two of them walked down the street in the direction that the squad car had taken, the same direction that Bob and Richie and his friends had driven earlier.

Two blocks away, the squad car was stopped behind a chartreuse Jeep. Johnny was arguing vehemently with the two officers. Most likely, his friends had abandoned the car when they heard the cops coming. "I don't know what's in it. I just saw it by the side of the road. Look. It's not even open."

"What were you doing in this neighborhood?" The male officer was asking him.

"I was just out for a drive. I saw this pink package laying near the side of the road. I stopped to see what it was. I don't know what's in it. I swear."

The female officer saw Luca and Veronique walking toward them.

"Miss Adriatico, was this one of the young men who was in your driveway earlier?"

"It was," Luca answered for Veronique, not giving her a chance to take the heat for accusing Johnny of anything. Veronique realized what Luca was doing, and she did not appreciate it.

"Yes, my cousin's right," she said, rolling her eyes in Luca's direction. "This guy was one of the ones in my driveway."

"Bitch," Johnny cursed her.

The male officer opened the pink paper bag and gave a low whistle. "Smells like pot, looks like pot." He stood and faced Johnny, grabbing one hand and swiftly putting a handcuff on it. He pulled the other hand behind Johnny's back and clipped it inside a steel ring, while informing a loudly protesting Johnny of his rights.

"You just screwed yourself, Johnny," Veronique said to him. "I guess I don't need to press any charges, Officer. It looks like you've got enough without me."

The officer did not argue with her. He merely said, "We'll be in touch with you."

Veronique and Luca continued walking down the street. Beautifully manicured sod lawns sat next to patchy, seeded ones. "If Bob dumped any drugs, Johnny found them," Luca told Veronique. She nodded.

The shadows lengthened as they walked together down the road. The summer solstice was approaching, and the days were getting longer. The sun would not set for another three hours, and the heat of the day exuded from the unprotected blacktop driveways, which had been baking in the sun. Ancient oak trees on either side of the road formed a deep green arc, which protected the black tar-paved street from the sun. A light blue sedan approached. "Hey, it's Father Joe. Mom must be home, or at least on her way." Veronique said.

"Yeah, where your mother is, can that priest be far behind? Or vice versa. As a matter of fact, looks like she's getting a ride home with him," Luca observed. Sure enough, Irene was in the passenger's seat.

"We should get them to pick up any mysterious packages we find," the cousins laughed together.

"My mom and a priest being picked up for possession of pot. That would be interesting," Veronique mused as they waved and the car slowed.

"Let's go back," Luca urged. "I don't want to get caught finding anything." Veronique nodded.

"The two of them sure spend a lot of time together," Veronique said absently, still looking around for suspicious packages as they took the long way back to the house.

"So do we," Luca reminded her.

She looked at him sideways. "That's different."

"Is it?"

"You're my cousin. They're just, like, friends or something. We're relations."

"If you say so."

# CHAPTER 11

❈

The summer passed quickly. Wendell needed two weeks to get over the image of the boys with the bats around the Lincoln. But being around Jonathan and his cousins, the memory eventually receded into the background. By the time he was ready to go home, he was a changed child—outgoing and laughing a lot. Jonathan and his cousins were sad to see Wendell leave.

Unfortunately for Veronique, the incident did not fade from memory so quickly. The day after the incident, phone calls started coming in at strange times of the night. Usually no one would be on the other end. A few times, Veronique could hear strange noises, sometimes like breathing, sometimes not, on the other end of the line.

Then one night in early September, the phone rang at 3:45 a.m. Groggily, Irene answered. Loud music was playing in the background, but no one spoke, and the person did not hang up. Suddenly, Irene was awake and angry. "Listen whoever you are, Bob or Richie or whoever, I do not appreciate being woken up like this, so stop right now." She hung up the phone. This happened two more times in succession. The second time, Irene hung up, not even bothering to listen or say anything. The third time, she picked up the phone, hung it up, and then picked it up again, intending to leave it off the hook, but she could still hear the music. The caller was still on the line. This time, she could hear a high-pitched giggling as the connection was severed.

Pino was awake now. Irene told him what was going on, and he was livid. He called someone he knew at the local precinct who said that he would do what he could.

"There's very little we can do about it tonight, but I'll tell the right people in the morning. In the meantime, Mr. Adriatico, the next time you or your wife gets a call like this, just say, 'Officer, this is the call I was telling you about,' and hang up. Okay?"

"Yes. Thank you, Harrison."

Pino reported what Harrison had told him to Irene, and then added, "I think we need to talk to Veronique right now."

Irene was arranging herself in the bed. "Pino, it's four in the morning. Now is not the time."

"Well, she needs to know that it is not acceptable to us to have people she has had, uh, dealings with, calling like this."

"Pino, it was probably a disgruntled beau who has been rejected. If he had been an acceptable young man, she wouldn't have rejected him. Since he was unacceptable, she did reject him, and he is proving that she was right to do so. What was she supposed to do?"

"She could show a bit more discernment, for one thing. She's a bright girl, but she's reckless, and she has made some horrible choices in this regard."

Irene put her head on her pillow and turned away from him. "At least she's interested in boys," she said, turning out the lights.

As this was one of the few things on which Pino and Irene agreed unreservedly, he tacitly agreed not to speak to Veronique at that instant, waiting instead until the morning.

❦   ❦   ❦

"Veronique, we had several more of those telephone calls." Pino started when his daughter walked into the kitchen the next day. "I called the police, and they instructed us to say 'Officer, this is the call I was telling you about,' and then hang up."

"Okay," Veronique said, putting a piece of Wonder bread in the toaster.

"Veronique, I want to talk to you about being a bit more discerning when you give out this number to people." Pino started but Veronique did not let him continue.

"Since nobody says anything on the other end of the line, why do you automatically assume that it's someone I've given the number to? There are four other people in this house giving out that number, including you. You're the boss of your own company. Don't you think it might be a disgruntled employee? Or what about Jonathan? He's a school teacher. Maybe one of the kids got his number. And then there's Marc. Who knows who he hangs out with? It might even have been someone Wendell gave the number to. Did you ever think about that? Probably not. So just don't go acting like I'm the only one who comes in contact with people who would do that." With that, she turned heel and started to leave the kitchen.

"Come right back in here, young lady," Pino ordered. "Do not leave until the conversation is finished." Veronique paused on the threshold, hand on her hip, but she did not turn around. "Come back in here and sit down." Veronique did an about-face to look at him, but did not move toward the table.

"Veronique, you have to admit that your choices in boyfriends the last two times weren't the greatest," Irene started.

"Let me handle this," Pino ordered. Irene shrugged and turned to the coffee pot. Pino continued, "When your brothers were growing up, we did not have things like this happening."

"Well, my point is that maybe NOW they're doing something to attract people like this," Veronique said through clenched teeth.

"Given their record—doing well in school, working hard after school—it's highly doubtful," Pino said decisively.

"Just because I don't have a straight-A average doesn't mean I'm stupid. I already skipped a grade, and now I have other priorities than being a geek like Marc or a teacher like Jon. And what about you? If you get along with people so well, tell me when was the last time either of you talked to Delfina? And she's your own daughter. Why wouldn't you think it's someone who works for you? I do, and I can't wait for your cop friends to prove me right that it wasn't somebody I gave the number to," Veronique told him. "Look, I gotta go. I'm late for school."

"What about your toast?" her mother asked her.

"I just lost my appetite." She left, letting the screen door slam behind her.

"Why do you accuse her like that?" Irene asked Pino. "If you keep attacking her, she'll never talk to you."

"Somebody needs to be strict with her. We both know it won't be you."

"You're not strict. You're unreasonable. She has a point, too. Maybe it isn't one of her friends."

Pino snorted his disagreement, and they both lapsed into silence, having had this type of argument about Veronique before and knowing that neither would change the other's mind.

❦ ❦ ❦

Veronique slammed her orange locker shut and clicked the combination lock into place. Her best friend Dawn walked up to her followed by Luca and Renee. Veronique had tentatively renewed a friendship with Renee, although the two were in different grades, and Renee was never allowed to stay after school or socialize with anyone. Veronique had never again broached the subject of what she had seen, and Renee seemed to forget that Veronique had ever brought it up.

"What's wrong with you?" Dawn asked, responding to the slam of the locker.

"My damn parents. That's what. Really, my father. I'm really beginning to hate him. Someone's calling the house at three in the morning, and he's blaming me. It could be anyone, but it's me who gets the flack."

"Yeah. My parents have been jerks lately too," Luca told them. "My mother's turning into some kind of Jesus freak. Like she's not happy just going to church on Sundays anymore. She's doing these weekend retreats and going to these weird prayer orgies or something where the priest pushes people over when he's praying on them—really creepy shit."

"Well, as long as she's not dragging you there, you're okay." Dawn said to him.

"Well, my little brothers have to go, and that's not good. After they come back from one of those things, the twins and I have to debrief them—or detox them really." He paused a moment as Renee laughed oddly.

"I was at one of those things once," Renee told them, by way of explanation. "It really was weird." She got self-conscious suddenly. "I'll see you guys later." She left abruptly.

Luca and the others were accustomed to Renee's sudden comings and goings. Luca resumed his train of thought. "As much as we miss her, it's probably better that Delfina's out west rather than around my mom right now."

"Well, your mom had just better watch herself too." Veronique, still angry about her parents, was even more enraged at the thought of anyone attacking Delfina. "I wish I could just graduate and get the hell out of here."

"My brother's taking the GED in December," Dawn mused, half to herself. "After he got kicked out of school and started working, he never went back and never graduated. But he's nineteen. He'll be twenty by the time he takes the test."

Veronique's mind started working on the beginning of an idea as the three walked outside the three-story, brick building. As they walked down the hill toward the parking lot, a dark green Lincoln Town Car drove slowly around the circle at the front of the building. The car seemed to slow down deliberately as it neared Veronique, but its windows were darkened so much that the driver of the car could not be seen. Veronique, who was closest to the car, had her head turned away listening to Dawn talking. Luca saw the car slow down, and decided to say nothing. Instead, he suggested that they walk down the hill to a different parking lot.

They climbed over a low dividing rail. The Lincoln made another pass around the circle, but it was unable to follow them there.

"Goddamn bastard," Luca swore softly under his breath.

"What?" Veronique, roused from her private musings, wanted to know.

Nothing," he answered, trying to be nonchalant.

Dawn looked up, dubious. Veronique was angry, her burgeoning plan momentarily forgotten. "You never swear unless it's something. So what gives?" She stopped and faced him directly. "Don't lie to me."

Luca told them about the Lincoln which was pulling away after ascertaining that the only way anyone could follow them at that point was on foot.

Veronique was livid. "So why didn't you tell me?" She said, looking back at the retreating car.

"Why? So that you could do something st- rash?" Luca defended himself.

"You were going to say stupid?" Veronique accused him. "No. I would have just walked up to the car and seen who it was." As she looked up the hill, the car slowly cruised by again. Veronique threw her backpack into Dawn's arms, and ran up the hill toward it.

Luca tried to stop her, but she was too far ahead of him.

"Goddamsonofabitch," he cursed, trying to catch up with her. They both vaulted over the traffic divider at the same time. Luca grabbed her arm, but she shook it off and continued charging at the car. As she got close enough to pound on the driver's window, the car sped off toward the exit. Luca and Veronique followed it, running. But by the time they reached the speed bump by the entrance to the school, the Lincoln was at the bottom of the hill, careening around the turn onto Plymouth Boulevard and quickly disappearing out of sight.

Veronique bent over, hands on her knees, to catch her breath.

"How can you be so—so—" Luca faltered for a word other than stupid.

"So what?" Veronique challenged him, still panting.

"So, I don't know, like you don't care what happens to you," Luca was still trying to find the word he was looking for.

"I do care," said Veronique, "but I don't let that paralyze me. If some asshole is tailing me, I want to know who it is. I don't intend to just be some meek idiot who gets frozen every time someone else acts like a jerk."

"But what if they want to hurt you?"

"Now it's 'they'? Luca, let's face it. It's a Lincoln. It's probably Bob, right?" Her cousin nodded, but Veronique continued without waiting for his response. "Bob doesn't have the balls to do anything. Plus he's stoned most of the time. He's just trying to scare me. Looks like he did a job on you."

Luca was angered by the accusation, but did not say anything as Dawn walked up to them carrying both Veronique's and Luca's backpacks.

"Thanks, Dawn," he said, taking his bag. He looked at Veronique darkly, and then stalked away without another word.

"What's wrong with him?" Dawn asked, mystified. The two started walking back toward the school.

"He's being overprotective, and he's shocked that I don't appreciate it," Veronique said through clenched teeth, watching him stalk away. "He can be such a pain."

Dawn laughed. "Sometimes you two seem like an old married couple."

Veronique looked at her oddly. "We've been together most of our lives. We're, like, one month apart in age, and I can't imagine life without him, except when he tries to fight my battles for me."

"See what I mean? Just like an old married couple."

"Don't you have anyone in your family that you're close to?"

"Not that close. I guess you're lucky in a way. But doesn't it ever get weird, like, he's so cute, don't you ever want to make out with him?"

"I know you do," Veronique laughed at her. "I never really thought about it. Not really," she responded to her friend as she rolled her eyes heavenward. "When you're with someone your whole life, especially before you know about being turned on, I mean, it's weird to start thinking about them that way, especially if they're your relations."

"You mean your family?"

"Yeah, family, loved ones, all your relations."

"That's a weird word. The way you use it, anyway. It seems different," Dawn mused.

"Delfina took me to this Native American ceremony for my birthday once. I learned it there. An old man there asked me who is my father—I'm beginning to hope it's not the one I got. I hate him. Speaking of Del, I haven't talked to her in over a week. She didn't call me back. She usually does."

"Call her again," Dawn urged as the bell rang. "Shit, I'm late. Call me later."

Veronique was late too, but she decided to skip class and go to the guidance office. When Veronique walked in, Miss Stanton, her guidance counselor, was standing at the counter that separated the waiting room from the secretarial desks.

"Hi, Veronique," Miss Stanton said brightly. Juliet Stanton was a petite brunette with sparkling, hazel eyes and an energetic personality. Veronique guessed that she was probably as old as Delfina, but with more effervescence and less intensity.

"Hi, Miss Stanton. Can I talk to you a minute?"

"Come on into my office," her guidance counselor said, leading the way.

Once inside the small office with its glass-paneled front wall, Miss Stanton closed the door. "Veronique, you're supposed to be in class. You know that. You're just lucky that my seventh period appointment went home sick today."

"Yeah, I'm lucky. Look, I need to talk to you. Okay?"

Miss Stanton sat down behind her desk in a position of listening.

"I'm gonna be sixteen in a week, and I was thinking about getting my GED instead of wasting another whole year here." Miss Stanton opened her mouth to protest, but wisely shut it, letting Veronique continue. "I hate most of my classes. Everything's boring, because I've heard most of it before. No one's as exciting a teacher as Jonathan. Also, in the Academy, we got such a smattering of everything and enough free time to really explore the things we liked. This is almost a nightmare, but I don't want to go to another high school either. I want to go out west to where my sister Delfina is, go to college out there, and do it now."

Miss Stanton waited a moment, letting the silence in the room punctuate Veronique's declaration. She could see that Veronique was surprised to hear herself speak her plan aloud. Then she cleared her throat.

"Um, for how long have you been thinking about this plan?"

"For quite a while," Veronique told a white lie. "It just makes sense. As much as I like being in school with my friends and, of course, with my cousins, I miss my sister, and I think I'm ready for college."

"Have you talked to your parents about this?"

"Not yet. I needed to get the information from you first. You know, when I can take the test, how to study for it, all that stuff. How much it will cost?"

"I'll need an okay from your parents before you take the test, especially if you're under age. You'll also need a document from an employer or a college saying they want a GED to accept you. Since you'll only be 16, I'll have to pull a lot of strings. So, Veronique, I want you to think this through."

"Okay. I have been, and I will keep on thinking about it. You're right about my parents, but before I talk to them, I need to see whether I really want to take the test or not. If I decide not to, I'd prefer not to hear about it for the rest of my life from my father. And I would hate to get all the grief from my mother about her baby leaving her." Veronique made a face. "She's really cool in some ways, but she can really go on and on about that. I figure, why put her through that if I don't really want to do it."

Miss Stanton agreed. "Okay, Veronique." She reached into her desk drawer and pulled out a newsprint booklet. "Here's the information. I can get some study guides for you, but before I do, I want you to come back here in the next few days with applications for colleges you're thinking of attending."

"In the next few days?"

"Well, however long it takes to get the applications is as long as it'll take you to get the books to study for the test."

"Will you write me a pass for class?" In order to have an excused absence or lateness, students needed a pass from the adult providing the excuse, in this case the guidance counselor.

"Which class?"

"Gym." Veronique grimaced.

Miss Stanton paused a moment, and then looked at the clock outside her office through the glass wall. "You only have twenty minutes more. This is your last class of the day, right?"

Veronique nodded.

"You're working this afternoon?"

"No. I work Tuesday, Thursday and some Saturday mornings. If I work Friday too, that's too many hours."

"Well, stay here for a while, and look through the college catalogues and some of the other college material I have in the next office. You may be able to get that list together and make some calls in the next hour."

Veronique agreed readily. She got up to go into the next room. "Miss Stanton, do you think I could call my sister? It'd be a collect call."

Again the guidance counselor paused, but then agreed. "I'll do the dialing. Okay?"

"Okay. Del says make it person to person."

Miss Stanton nodded. A few minutes later, she closed the door to the office as Veronique listened to the phone ringing.

"Rectory," said the voice on the other end of the line.

"Person to person for Delfina Adriatico," the operator said.

"I'm sorry. Ms. Adriatico has moved to another number: 212-555-2418."

"Wait," Veronique said, scrambling for something to write with. She found a pen, but no paper.

"Two-one-two, five-five-five, two-four-one-eight," the voice from the rectory repeated. Veronique wrote the number on her hand.

"Okay," said the operator.

"Thanks," Veronique's mind was spinning as she hung up the telephone. She dialed the new number, not bothering to ask Miss Stanton for permission.

After six rings, a deep female voice answered. "Yeah. This is Rowan."

"H-Hello." Veronique did not know why she was hesitating.

"This is Rowan. Who's this?"

"I-Veronique. This is Veronique. Can I talk to Delfina?"

"Veronique, eh? Listen, Veronique, Delfina and I are living together. I don't want any girlfriends from her past calling here. We're together now."

Veronique blanked. What seemed like an interminable pause followed.

"Okay?" Rowan said. "I guess you got the message. 'Bye."

"No. Wait!" Veronique almost yelled into the phone, coming to her senses. "I'm her sister. I—I need to talk to her."

"Her sister, eh? We're all sisters. Don't use code with me."

"No. I'm really her sister. My name's Veronique Adriatico. Delfina's my real sister."

Now there was a pause at the other end of the line. Then, "How old are you?"

"Fifteen. I'll be sixteen in a couple'a weeks."

"I thought her sister had a boy's name."

"Ronnie."

"Yeah, that's right."

"Ronnie's short for Veronique. Only my really close family calls me Ronnie now."

"Okay, Ron- er, Veronique. Look, forget what I said at the start of this conversation. Okay? I was just kidding. Delfina's out right now. She'll be back soon. You want to call her in about an hour?"

"I'm calling from school, and I'm not sure I'll be home in an hour. Where's two-one-two? Is it closer than Arizona?"

"Shit. She didn't tell you?"

"Tell me what?"

The voice at the other end of the phone hesitated again. "Veronique, you and your sister should be talking. I don't want to be telling you her news, so you call her back later, tonight, whenever you can. I'll tell her you called. You can call late too, up to midnight or one. I'm at work then."

After Veronique put down the receiver, she started leafing through the GED booklet, her mind racing. She was absently looking at test site locations when she saw the 212 area code. New York, New York. She put the booklet down. Was Delfina in New York? There was a reason she didn't tell anyone. Maybe she didn't want their parents to know.

Miss Stanton looked in to see how she was doing.

"My sister suggested that I look at colleges in New York. She said that might be better."

"She was right, actually. As a New York resident, you can go to New York State or even City colleges at a fairly decent tuition rate."

"Tuition?" Veronique said the word aloud after Miss Stanton left. She had not even thought about how she was going to pay for her little endeavor. Over the years, Pino had made asking for money extremely difficult. Maybe it would be different with education, Veronique mused. Still, if her father was not happy about her leaving high school early, he was probably not going to support her going to college away from home. Veronique made a list of schools in New York City. The two schools on the top of her list were FIT—the Fashion Institute of Technology—and the Pratt Institute.

Miss Stanton came back half an hour later.

"Miss Stanton, can I have them send the catalogues to you here instead of to me at home? I don't want my parents—"

"Veronique, I don't think it's ever a good idea to keep secrets from your parents," Miss Stanton started. Then, seeing Veronique's downcast face, she added, "On the other hand, I could always use the updated catalogues for any other students who might be interested in attending the colleges you're looking at."

Veronique brightened at that. The bell rang, indicating that the seventh class was over and in five minutes the last class of the day was going to start.

"I can go home now," Veronique announced.

"While you're here, since you're not working today, why don't you call for those catalogues? I'll give you the address for the school."

Half an hour later, after Veronique had called for ten catalogues, she was ready to leave. Miss Stanton came into the office carrying her jacket. "I'm leaving. If you want to get your things, I'll drop you off at home."

"I live in Kings Park."

Miss Stanton shrugged. "Whatever you want to do. I live in Rocky Neck, so it's not out of my way."

"Okay. I'll get my stuff."

Fifteen minutes later they were in Juliet Stanton's red Sunbird. As she drove, Miss Stanton asked Veronique some questions about her sister, and after talking about Delfina for a while, Veronique brightened up considerably. When they turned onto Riviera Drive, Bob's maroon Lincoln, sporting new body work and new lights, was parked in front of the house, not in the driveway. Instantly, Veronique's mood darkened again. "Shit. Oh, excuse me, Miss Stanton. There's that jerkoff, Bob."

Miss Stanton stopped the Sunbird behind the Lincoln. "Do you want me to talk to him?"

"No thanks. I can handle this. Thanks for the ride. I'm gonna get rid of this jerk once and for all."

"I'll wait here for a couple of moments, just for my own peace of mind."

"Suit yourself. Bye."

Veronique stalked around the back of the Lincoln, and banged on the driver's window. Bob had dozed off, and he jumped at the sound of the banging.

"Roll down your window, Asshole."

The window opened.

"What in the hell are you doing here? Didn't you get the message last time? I don't want to have anything to do with you. You're lucky I didn't press charges, but I will. Now just get lost." She kicked the side of the car.

"Hey, you watch that paint job. I wanted to apologize. And I wanted to go out with you on Saturday night."

"What, are you stupid or just retarded? I DO NOT WANT TO GO OUT WITH YOU. Not ever. I don't ever want to see you again. I hate your stupid friends, your stupid drugs, and your boring parties. Why would I ever want to go out with you again? To watch you fall asleep with a bunch of old people in Yonkers? No way. Beat it. Go out with Laura. I don't ever want you to call or come around here again. Now get lost before I call those two cops that came here last time you parked by my house."

"Veronique—"

"I mean it. Get lost." With that she stamped toward the house, let herself in and slammed the door behind her. Juliet Stanton watched the scene, and smiled to herself as she backed away from the Lincoln, pulled around it, and drove past it down the street.

❧ ❧ ❧

Inside the house, Veronique dropped her books on the counter. The telephone had started ringing as soon as she slammed the door.

"Hello."

No one was on the other end.

"Damn you." She hung up.

As she started walking toward the refrigerator, the telephone rang again. "Hello?"

In response, she heard a sick, high-pitched laugh on the other end of the line. "Operator, this is the moron caller that I was telling you about." She hung up.

"I guess that rules out Bob," she said aloud, watching the maroon Lincoln make a U-turn and drive slowly in the opposite direction that Miss Stanton had taken. Ten minutes later the phone rang again.

"Listen, if you call again—"

"Veronique. It's me. Delfina."

"Del. Where are you?"

"On the other end of the line." Her sister could not resist the wisecrack.

"Yeah, it's really you. No, seriously, I called this afternoon, and they said you had a new number. Where are you?"

"I'll tell you, but you have to swear not to tell Mom and Father. Okay? I don't want to deal with them right now. If you don't think you can keep it from Mom, just let me know. I can tell you other things without giving you that information."

"Why? Do you think I can't keep a secret? I never told about the Chamber, did I? Where are you?"

"New York City. My friend Rowan and I are moving into an apartment in Brooklyn next week.

"That's great. Del, remember when you said that I could come live with you after I graduate? Is that still true?"

"Of course it is. You're in, what, ninth grade?"

"Eleventh. I turn sixteen in a month, and I'm taking my GED so I can go straight to college. I want to get out of here. Mom's always gone somewhere or another with Father Joe, and Father's a jerk. Someone's been calling here at weird hours, and they're blaming it on me. Oh, and, shit, there it is again." Veronique looked out the window to see the green Lincoln drive slowly past her house.

"There what is?" Delfina's concerned voice came over the receiver.

"Listen, Del, call me back in five minutes. Promise?"

"Only if you swear that you'll tell me what's going on when I call back."

"I swear," Veronique promised and then hung up.

Quickly, she pulled out the police officer's cards that she kept in her backpack. She dialed the number and watched as the green Lincoln cruised by again, this time in the opposite direction.

Her call was answered on the second ring. A male voice said, "Torre here."

"This is Veronique Adriatico. You came to my house about a week ago because some guys were banging on a car."

"Oh, yes, Miss Adriatico. What can I do for you?"

"There's a green Lincoln that's been following me around all day. It was in the high school parking lot at lunch today. Now it's driving back and forth in front of my house. The windows are too dark to see who's driving. It doesn't have a front license plate, and the back one's bent, so you can't read it."

"Any idea who it might be?"

"No. I know it's not Bob Voldaris, the guy whose car got wrecked last week, because he was just here in a different Lincoln, and there's no way he could have switched cars that fast. This car just keeps driving by—there it goes again—and I'm getting creeped out."

"I'll send someone over right away." The line went dead.

Veronique hung up slowly. Five minutes passed, but it felt like two hours to Veronique.

The telephone rang again. "That's probably Delfina," Veronique thought.

"Hello?"

Over the line came a strange computer-like noise and then the high-pitched laughter. Veronique hung up and then took the telephone off the hook. She did not keep it off, wanting Delfina to call back.

The next time the telephone rang, it was her sister.

"Okay, Ronnie. Tell me what's going on."

Veronique told her the whole story, ending with, "And now these weird phone calls started coming in, and Bob, the moron drug dealer, is not making them. That green car keeps cruising past the house. I called the cops. Of course, they haven't done anything. Oh, finally. They just showed up now—twenty minutes later. Of course, the green Lincoln is gone. But Del, the reason I called today is that I want to get out of that high school, out of this house, and especially away from Father. Even Luca is acting like a possessive jerk."

"I thought you loved Luca."

"I do, but he can treat me like he wants to own me, just like the rest of them."

Delfina heard a burgeoning spark of feminism in her sister's umbrage. "Okay. You pass the GED and get into a college around here, and you can come and live with us. Remember. Not a word of this to Mom and Father."

"The same goes for the GED. Thanks Del. I gotta go now. The cops who have been sitting in the car for the last few minutes—It's a police car, do you think they could have been more obvious?—are coming to the front door."

"Are their red lights flashing?"

"No."

Delfina's laugh came across the phone line. "Then they could be more obvious. I'll call you in a couple of days. Maybe Jon and I will take you out for your birthday."

"Jon knows where you are?"

"I'm going to call him tonight. Then we'll make some plans."

❦   ❦   ❦

"You passed."

"What?" Veronique had been sitting in the waiting room while Miss Stanton corrected her practice GED test. She jumped from her seat. "Really?"

"It's not the most spectacular showing I've ever seen, but you passed by a comfortable margin. With a bit of work, you would have aced it. Congratulations. I thought you should wait and study, but you did well enough."

"My birthday was last weekend, but Jon and my sister are taking me out tonight. As a matter of fact, I've got to meet my brother at five."

"Well, have a great time. Have you said anything about the GED to your brother or sister?"

"Not yet. I was waiting to see them both together. I'll tell them tonight, because God only knows when I'll get another opportunity to see them in the same place at the same time again.

"Where are they taking you?"

"I think the Bonwit Inn in Commack. I've always wanted to go there."

"Set up an appointment with me next week. And call me if you need some help talking to your parents."

"Thanks." Veronique left quickly, elated that she had passed and wondering to herself if it mattered how well she did as long as she just passed. She did not want to get into a discussion about that with Miss Stanton at that moment. Excited to see Delfina, she hurried to the junior high parking lot, hoping that Jon might come out a few minutes early.

❦   ❦   ❦

"...so I'm going to study for a couple of weeks, and then take the GED in November. That way I can fill out all the college applications and maybe work until September, save up some money, and then start college."

In the subdued atmosphere of the Bonwit Inn restaurant, Jonathan and Delfina had exchanged glances several times during Veronique's declaration. Their unspoken conversation was a subtext to Veronique's words. Delfina's raised eyebrows to Jonathan said, "Reckless?" His furrowed brow answered, "Probably."

Jonathan had known for some time that his younger sister was bored in school, but he had never thought that graduating early was an option. Still, he could think of no really good reason for Veronique not to go through with her plan. Delfina, whose absence had made her unaware of the extent of Veronique's unhappiness at school and home, was a bit more surprised.

"Aren't you involved in any clubs or afterschool activities?"

"No. I have early release, and I work two days a week after school plus Saturday."

"Oh, well. If there's really nothing keeping you, far be it from me to object." Delfina said.

"If you do object, then I guess I can't move in with you."

"Oh yes. We haven't talked about that part of your plan, have we?"

"You said when I graduated I could come and live with you."

Jonathan shrugged and nodded, agreeing with Veronique. Delfina laughed. "You always were tenacious," she said to Veronique. "And you," she continued to Jonathan, "could always be counted on to stick up for her. Well, I'm living with someone right now, so it'll have to be okay with her too. If you're helping out with the rent and paying your own bills, it shouldn't be a problem. Before we even talk about that, you've got to get accepted to a college."

Their conversation was interrupted by a loud voice behind Veronique. "Oh, there you are. What a nice coincidence, running into you like this." The slurred speech was Bob's. He walked haltingly toward their table. "You little slut. I give you a job, treat you real nice, and then you throw it all in my face."

Veronique was up before Jonathan or Delfina could stop her. With one hand on her hip and a long, red-painted nail on the other hand one inch from his nose, she confronted him. "Bob, you idiot. The reason I refused to go out with you any more is because of how you act, like you're acting now. Like a jerk. I'm sorry. I refuse to go out with jerks. *You* and your little drug-dealing goons"—she grimaced in the direction of the two large men standing behind him—"may not understand that, but that's the way it is."

Bob was so angry that his neck turned purple. "Stop screaming like a kid," he sputtered.

"I am not screaming," Veronique informed him haughtily. "However, I will not tolerate being called names by some guy who just walks up to a table where I am having a private dinner."

The maitre d' had heard the commotion, started coming toward Veronique's table. But when he saw that Bob, a regular customer, was arguing with one of Pino Adriatico's children, he hesitated. Veronique saw him.

"Mr. Antonelli, this guy doesn't seem to know where the exit is. He was sitting way over there, on the other side of the restaurant, right next to it. Now all of a sudden he's over here."

"Don't make a scene, you little bimbo," one of Bob's companions growled at her.

"Don't tell me what to do, especially when your boss is the one causing the scene."

The man standing behind Bob glowered at her.

Veronique, angry, but not intimidated in the least, taunted him, "What are you going to do, rough me up in the parking lot?"

Mr. Antonelli came over cautiously, looking very upset. "Is there a problem here?"

Veronique waited as Bob got angrier and more flustered. Both Jonathan and Delfina had gotten up from their seats by this time.

Delfina felt sorry for the maitre d', and spoke up quickly. "Uh, look, Bob. That's your name, right? I don't know what business you think you have with Veronique. I can tell you that she's a minor, and whatever it is will have to wait a few years until she turns eighteen. So, as she pointed out to you, the exit is back the way you came. You'd better use it now."

"Or else what?"

"Since she's under age, and she worked in your office, *and* you seem to think you have a more personal relationship with her, I'll leave the 'or else' up to your imagination, and your lawyer's."

Delfina, taller than Bob in her stocking feet, towered over him in her cowboy boots. She stared down at him. Bob looked over at Jonathan, who flanked Veronique's other side and was also staring at him impassively.

Muttering to himself, Bob turned around and walked out of the restaurant followed by his associates. Mr. Antonelli breathed a sigh of relief as the three men crossed the threshold. He returned to his station. The low murmur of patrons' conversation, which had ceased during the exchange, resumed, and the three Adriatico siblings sat down.

"That, I take it, was Bob," Delfina said, replacing her napkin in her lap.

"You take it correctly," Jonathan told her.

"You're sure he's not the one making the phone calls?"

"Positive," Veronique answered her. "There's no way he could have called the last time. He was in the car outside the house when the phone rang.

"They have car phones now."

"I know, but with these calls, there's usually music in the background. And besides, when you get a call from a car phone, it's like they're talking in a tin can, and there's a lot of static. I don't want to talk about that now. Aren't we going to the movies?"

❦   ❦   ❦

Three hours later, as they were walking out of the Commack Multiplex Cinema, they encountered their aunt Ellie who was escorting her two youngest children from another theater within the complex. The two groups saw each other, and before Delfina could even think about avoiding being seen, her two youngest cousins broke away from their mother and ran toward her.

"Delfina, you're back," Gordon yelled, body slamming her and hugging her legs.

Cameron, the youngest cousin, was three steps behind his brother. Delfina crouched down to give them both a kiss and a hug. Ellie, who had gained a significant amount of weight in the past two years, lumbered up behind them.

"Hi, Aunt Ellie," Jonathan said, coming forward to give his aunt a hug. She submitted her cheek for a kiss and then looked at Delfina.

"Well, you've finally returned," Ellie said slowly.

"I'm just visiting, Aunt Ellie," Delfina said, getting up and taking a step toward her to give her a hug.

Her aunt put up a hand, stopping her. "Let me get a look at you. I've heard rumors you've gone down a sinful path, the path of homosexuality."

The attack was so sudden and unexpected that Delfina froze in her tracks. Jonathan gasped as though someone had hit him in the stomach as Veronique rolled her eyes. Then Delfina laughed. "Aunt Ellie, that sounds like a line from a bad movie. Since when did you start preaching about sinful paths?"

"I have seen the light, and I know who you are," Ellie responded haughtily. "Belittle my words if you will. You and your kind may see fit to ridicule me, but read Leviticus. You'll see you're on a path that's headed straight to hell. Forsake your sinful ways now. Repent and be saved."

"You've GOT to be kidding," was all Delfina could say in response. Her cousins sadly shook their heads as if to say, we wish she were, but she's not.

"Look Ellie," Delfina dropped the familial prefix, seeing the response of her cousins, "I am definitely a lesbian—"

Her aunt interrupted her with a gasp, and pulled her sons toward her. They shook her off and stepped closer to their cousin again. "I will not have you speaking like that in front of the children," Ellie told her.

"You brought it up. If I were to hide who I am, it would be like I'm admitting something's wrong with who I am, and there isn't.

"Read your Bible, child. You'll see the path you have chosen is the path of the devil."

"The path of the devil, to use your words, is to lie about who I am.

"This will bring shame to your whole family."

"I doubt it. If you feel shame, that's your problem, Ellie. God help any of your kids if they turn out to be gay."

"You go out West cavorting and living a bohemian artist's life. I am home for my children. I make sure they stay on the right path," her aunt snorted.

"God help them." Delfina repeated.

"Go right ahead and have a laugh at my expense. You'll see in the end. Not only will you cause your parents pain, but you'll feel the wrath of God on judgment day. The Bible says in—"

"Let's go," Delfina said, turning away and not waiting to hear any more. Over her shoulder, she said to Ellie, "Out of respect for my father, I won't tell you what I'm really thinking right now."

"Your parents won't be as forgiving as you think," Ellie yelled, following the three as they retreated to Jonathan's car.

"What is wrong with her?" Delfina was saying, as they walked to the car.

As she unlocked the car door, Veronique interrupted her. "Oh shit."

Bob's maroon Lincoln was parked next to Jonathan's car. Bob was standing outside the driver's door, waiting.

"What do you want, you idiot? Didn't I tell you to get lost at the restaurant?"

Bob, alone now, had a very different attitude. "I need to talk to you, Baby," he wheedled. "I miss you. My life's a shambles. I just want to talk to you privately for a few minutes. I don't have anywhere else to turn."

"Go talk to a shrink or to Laura or someone. I don't want to have anything to do with you, so get lost."

"We meant so much to each other…"

"You've got me mixed up with someone else. I went out with you once. That's all. Now move your car and beat it."

"I've been suicidal."

"Do us all a favor and get it over with."

"I have."

"Bullshit asshole. Get lost." Veronique moved past him to get into Jonathan's car, but Bob blocked her.

Ellie, with her two sons in tow, came huffing toward the car just in time to witness the whole exchange. She took a step toward Bob. "Leave your adulterous ways. That's why you're suicidal. Poor man. Repent, and God will provide eternal bliss for you."

Bob looked at Ellie askance. "When I need your advice, I'll ask for it."

"No, listen to her, Bob," Veronique said, slamming the car door and opening the window slightly. "You wanted someone to talk to. Now you've got someone. It's perfect. I'm telling you to go to hell, and she knows all the ways to get there." Veronique closed her window. Jonathan slowly backed out of the space while Ellie accosted Bob, and Gordon and Cameron stood next to their mother miserably.

Ellie was still talking and following Bob as he almost ran to the door of his Lincoln.

"I can't believe she's related to us," Delfina said, shaking her head.

"Technically, she's not," Jonathan told her. "Uncle Otto and Father are brothers. She's not a blood relative."

"That makes me feel better."

"Still, we're all relations," Veronique, in the back seat, said under her breath.

# CHAPTER 12

The letter arrived on Saturday, a week after Veronique, Jonathan and Delfina celebrated Veronique's sixteenth birthday. The sun was shining on the brilliant fall foliage when Veronique went out to get the mail, barefoot in shorts.

She leafed through the bills and catalogues as she walked back to the house. A handwritten envelope addressed to her caught her attention. It did not have a return address.

She opened it. It was a one-page letter. She recognized her aunt Ellie's name scrawled at the bottom of the powder blue paper.

*October 20, 1990*

*Dear Veronique,*

*I know about your boyfriends who do drugs and smoke. I've seen the man you're dating who's old enough to be your father. I wanted to write you a letter to let you know, as your aunt, how concerned I am about you. I know that being around people who smoke and do drugs will only lead you down the same road. After the drugs comes drinking and then fornication, and your whole life will be ruined. I know you would never want your parents to know about the things you do. I won't tell them. That's why I'm writing to you rather than calling or visiting. This will be our little secret, our private understanding. I wanted to let you know that I know, and I want to help you. I don't want to see you get into trouble. I also want you to know that I'm here for you. It's not too late to find the right way.*

*God bless you. Love,*

*Aunt Ellie*

"I don't believe it," Veronique exclaimed as she walked into the kitchen.
"What is it?" Irene asked.
"Aunt Ellie. She thinks she's the dating police or something. Look at this letter."
Irene read the letter in silence and then handed it back to Veronique.
"Well, she was wrong about one thing."
"Only one? I think she's wrong about everything."
Even though Irene was irate, she smiled at her daughter's indignant face. "I was thinking about her saying you wouldn't tell your parents."
"She's a jerk, that's all. What am I going to do, keep a secret with her from you? I don't think so."
"When your father gets home, I think we should sit down and discuss this."
"He'll say it's all my fault. He always does that. He's not going to care what Aunt Ellie The Elephant does. He's going to say she's right, and I'm going out and smoking and doing drugs and everything."
"Are you?"
Veronique rolled her eyes. "Yeah, sure. That's why I'm showing you the letter, right?" She held her breath, waiting for her mother's response.
Irene nodded, not noticing that her question had not been answered. "That's true," she responded to Veronique's question as her daughter let out a sigh of relief at not having to lie. "I'll make sure your father stays on point about this letter," Irene continued. "After all, Ellie's insulted him and me with this insinuation that she sees something that we don't, not to mention the fact that she thinks she can communicate with you better than we can."
Veronique was out doing grocery shopping for her mother when Pino came home. Irene showed him the letter his sister-in-law had written.
Pino sat in silence at the kitchen table, having read the letter twice. Irene could tell that he was furious. He was also caught between family loyalties. He and his wife were, in effect, being treated as though they were unfit, or at least unconscious, parents. The accuser was his brother's wife. His daughter was being accused, but some of the things his sister-in-law wrote did not seem to

be too far off the mark for Pino. After all, those calls were still coming in. They might well be the work of some deranged drug user. Pino voiced this last thought to Irene as Veronique came through the front door carrying the groceries.

"Pino, that's ridiculous. If she were involved with people of that sort, she'd be acting differently. Besides, she never would have let me see this letter."

"I don't know about that. She seems intent on causing disharmony."

"Let me remind you that it's your sister-in-law who's causing the disharmony. I know my kids. If Ronnie were using drugs, I'd be able to tell. She's bored in school, and socializing is more important to her than good grades. For all that, she's not doing badly with a B average. Don't forget she skipped a grade. Just because she's not a straight-A student like Delfina doesn't mean she's using drugs. She has other priorities, like boys, which is a good thing, I think. Anyway, that's not the point. The point is that Ellie thinks we're not responsible parents. Basically, she's asked Veronique to go behind our backs by saying she's willing to collude in keeping a secret from us."

Veronique held the screen door and let it close quietly, listening.

"Veronique showed this to you?" Pino asked, speaking slowly as he was thinking.

"Yes, which is another reason I don't believe a word of it."

"Is she going out with someone my age?"

"No. That's an exaggeration. Bob, the car dealer, is too old for her, but I think she went to the prom with him because of the way Richie treated her just a few days earlier. She didn't want to go to the prom with Richie, and she didn't want to miss it either. So she went with Bob, who apparently asked her out that day. She only went out with him that one time. Even though he's been insistent about calling her ever since, she hasn't shown any more interest in him. And, by the way, how uninvolved could I be in my kid's life if I know all this? The point is, we've been insulted by Ellie. What are we going to do about it?"

"You seem to have an idea about what you want to do."

"Yes, I want to tell Ellie that I do not appreciate anything she did or was trying to do in this letter."

"What would you do? Walk up to her, letter in hand, and say…what would you say?"

"I would say that as a mother she should know how invasive a letter like this can be and how irresponsible it is to go behind parents' backs this way. I would ask her how she would feel if I wrote a letter like this to one of her kids."

Pino listened to her and paused, thinking, before he answered. "And she would say that none of her children dates or does drugs like Veronique," he predicted, playing out the scene in his mind.

"You talk like you believe her. I know Ronnie. She may not have the best taste in men, but she doesn't smoke or do drugs."

"You're so sure?" Pino sneered. "Well, you'll have to find a way to do it that does not involve insulting my brother."

"Insulting your brother? What about my being insulted by your brother's wife? Or doesn't that count for anything?"

At this point, Veronique stormed into the kitchen. She had heard enough. "No, Mom." She was talking loudly and quickly so that she would not be interrupted. "Apparently me or you being insulted doesn't matter at all to him. All that matters is appearances to the outside world. He thinks I'm a smoking, drug using slut, and he's not going to do anything to stop anyone else from thinking that way. As for you, you're just his wife. You get to see all the dirty laundry, but as long as it stays behind our closed doors, all is right with the world. He doesn't want to make waves. He's never going to defend you, much less me."

Pino stood up and slammed his hand down on the table, making his wife and daughter jump. "I will not be spoken to in that way," he said through clenched teeth.

"You're not going to do anything different from what I said either," Veronique challenged him.

Pino raised his hand, looking as though he was going to hit her. She did not shrink away from him, and he stopped. "None of the other kids brought us trouble like you do," he told her, quietly, gravely. "None of the other kids had problems like people making prank calls at all hours of the night, police coming to the house because of kids with bats doing vandalism in our driveway, and not doing the best they could in school. Maybe Ellie has a point. Maybe she's fanning smoke, but where there's smoke, there's usually fire. I don't know what to do with you anymore." With that, he walked out of the house.

"Yeah. Blame it all on me. That way you don't have to stick up for Mom with your brother's wife," Veronique attacked his retreating back.

She turned to her mother who had stood quietly during the exchange. "You said that this wasn't going to happen. Right. He's already written me off. Sometimes I wonder if he's really my father," Veronique yelled at her.

Irene breathed in sharply.

Unheeding, Veronique continued. "There are times when I wonder if I was switched at the hospital."

"You weren't switched at the hospital," her mother told her. "Your father is angry, and he has a funny way of showing it, that's all. Don't worry, Honey. We'll take care of this."

Veronique shook her head, not believing her mother. "I'm going out. I won't be back for dinner."

"I thought you wanted me to make ravioli, which is why you went shopping," her mother reminded her.

"I'm not hungry. Make it for your husband if he decides to come home."

Dejected, Irene watched her leave, and then picked up the phone. "Ellie? Irene. You and I need to have a talk."

"Irene. Is something wrong?"

"I'd prefer not to talk over the phone. Do you want to come over here?"

"I'm in the middle of preparing dinner. I still have kids at home, and you know—"

"—Then why don't I come over to your house later, say around seven?" Irene cut her off.

"Make it nine. I need to do homework with the boys."

"Nine it is," Irene said through clenched teeth.

❦ ❦ ❦

What upset Veronique the most was her mother's backing down in front of, and subsequent defense of, her father. When she left her house, without thinking she got into her car, turned up the volume on her radio, and drove toward Luca's house. Her habit was to discuss everything with Luca.

As she was about to round the corner onto his street, she realized she could not go there. Her aunt, Luca's mother, was the source of her current angst. Veronique would not be able to avoid Ellie if she went to Luca's house.

She drove to the beach instead. Parking in the farthest lot at Sunken Meadow, she grabbed a large towel from the back seat of her car, and walked down to the water. The Indian summer air was still warm, and the low tide was beginning to turn as she headed east along the shoreline to the remains of the driftwood oak tree. When she got there, she saw that a small fire had been lit to one side of the tree, away from the beach house and the parking lot. A large green towel had been abandoned near the fire. Veronique could hear the rustling of someone walking through the tall grasses that led to the beach.

The red-orange sun was touching the water to the left of her. She could not see anyone in the grasses to the right. By the familiar deep green color of the towel, she surmised one of her cousins was nearby. Instead of announcing her presence, she wrapped her own white and yellow striped beach towel around her shoulders and sat back against the tree to watch the indigo water consume the fiery orb.

"Hey, Ronnie," Luca recognized her as he stepped from the grass behind her.

"Hi Luc," Veronique did not turn away from the sunset. "Shhh, wait 'till it's over."

Luca understood the solemnity of his cousin's sunset ritual. He sat down quietly beside her. Shoulder to shoulder, they watched the quick descent of bright red day into subdued amber twilight with a deep blue cover. When the final hint of amber turned deep red and then disappeared into the smooth blackness of the nighttime Long Island Sound, Veronique sighed.

"Were you holding your breath that whole time?" Luca asked, teasing her gently.

"It's weird," she confessed, still speaking in a subdued tone. "It's so beautiful, I'm afraid that if I breathe I'll disturb it, or miss something. I feel like I don't want to miss a single second."

Luca smiled in agreement. "It's like if you breathe, the quiet might be spoiled, or the smoothness of the low tide might be disturbed." He also spoke quietly, not wanting to intrude on the feeling. They sat quietly until the last deep red glow was consumed by the dark horizon. Then Luca got up to put more logs into the fire.

"No dates tonight?" He spoke casually.

"Do I look like some kind of dating machine? No. But I'd like to kill your mother and my father." He sprawled down beside her, head in her lap, as they had done for years, and she launched into the story about the letter and what had transpired in her kitchen that evening. She ended with, "Sometimes I wonder if such a big jerk could really be my father."

Luca laughed at that. Then, after a silence, he said, "Times like this, I wish he wasn't."

Veronique was stroking his side burns as he said this, and her hand paused momentarily, letting his words sink in. Then she resumed. "It would make things a lot different," she mused, half to herself, still thinking what life would be like without Pino as a father. "But then we wouldn't be relations."

"You've always been so into that relations thing. Just because we weren't cousins doesn't mean we couldn't be relations in another way."

She looked down at him. "Remember how we used to go to the Chamber, sit like this and talk for hours?"

"Yeah. I miss talking to you like that."

"Well, sometimes you can be really bossy, like you don't think I can take care of myself."

"I know. I can't help it. I don't want anything to happen to you."

"I'm not a helpless female. The sooner you get that through your thick head, the better." She changed the subject, not wanting to start a fight. "Remember how we used to play 'make weird upside down faces' when you were lying like that?"

"Yeah."

"Remember 'touch tongues'? It was like licking an eel or something."

"We'd pull away really fast and wipe our tongues on our sleeves," Luca laughed, remembering. "I think that ruined me for life. That girl I went to the prom with, I forget her name now, she said I was a lousy kisser."

"I can't believe that. Maybe it was her. It takes two, you know."

"I don't know. She seemed pretty definite."

"Richie was a really rotten kisser. I never thought it was me." Veronique stopped to contemplate the possibility for a moment. Then she shook her head. "No. It was him. He was an asshole all the way around. But with you, it's gotta be different. Here, show me how you kiss."

"Kiss you? But you're my cousin. That would be sick." Luca was shocked.

"You know we like each other best. If we can't practice kissing with each other, who can we do it with?"

"I don't know. It sounds like we'd be breaking at least two of the ten commandments."

"Where does it say 'Thou shalt not kiss your cousin'?" Caution was not an issue for Veronique.

"What about the one about adultery?" Luca was beginning to be tempted.

"It's just a kiss. And, plus, it's not a real one either. It's an example. Like an experiment for the real thing."

"Okay." He moved to sit up.

"No, stay like that first. I'll show you how I kissed Richie. Then you can show me how you kissed what's-her-name." She put one hand on top of his head and the other one under his chin.

"This feels like you're doing CPR," he started.

"Shhh—be serious," she ordered, slapping the top of his head lightly.

He settled back, resting his hands on his stomach. She leaned over and kissed his mouth, which he held firmly closed.

She raised her head slightly. "Did you keep your mouth closed like this with her?"

"I don't know. Probably," he mumbled from somewhere under the veil of her hair.

"No wonder she said you were lousy. Relax, and let your jaw hang open a little." She moved her hand from under his chin to beneath his neck, lifting it slightly. Her tongue separated his lips and found its way between his teeth. When she found his tongue, he started to sit up, but she pushed him back down lightly. "This is not touch tongues," she reminded him with a schoolteacher-like manner. He settled back and tried again. This time his tongue met hers, and a few seconds later, as she started to raise her head, he put his hand lightly on her neck, keeping it there a moment longer.

"That was better," she said a minute later. "Let's change places and try it again."

Luca complied willingly. She lay down, and he bent forward quickly to kiss her, but not quickly enough to hide the bulge that sprang up between his thighs. He kissed her hungrily, and out of the corner of her eye she looked down the front of his open shirt, watching the bulge grow. Still kissing her, he rested one hand on her stomach. Watching his crotch with a sense of exhilarated abandon, she unclipped her bra and moved his hand up to her breast. The bulge was now stretching the seams of his khaki shorts.

When he finally came up for air, she said, pointedly, "What's-her-name didn't stick around long enough for the real treat."

Embarrassed, he started to pull away from her.

"No, don't. It's awesome."

"You, you think so?" He said it shyly, unsure of what to do next.

"Lie back down. Let's see how big it is. Go ahead, you big baby," she said as he hesitated. Then he complied. "Looks like a tent," she mused. "From here, your fly looks like the opening, but it seems more like a teepee than a regular camping tent."

He laughed at that.

"Once, I saw a woman take some guy's dick in her mouth. That was pretty gross."

"Where did you see that?" he asked, curious.

"It's a long story."

They kissed again, more deeply than before. She was enjoying the sensation of his tongue on the roof of her mouth, not noticing how uneven his breathing had become.

"Oh, Jeeeesus," Luca groaned suddenly, pulling away from her roughly and rolling to lie almost face down in the sand, his back to her. In the dying firelight, she watched his body shudder for a few moments. Then he stopped, still breathing heavily. He punched the sand as the fire went out.

"This is wrong." He sprang up, keeping his back to her, grabbing his towel and wrapping it around his waist. Without waiting for her to answer, he fled down the beach toward his car.

Her eyes adjusted quickly to the darkness, and she watched him go, the silhouette of his head bobbing up and down against the reflection of the lights of Connecticut on the horizon. She felt a mixture of relief and regret as she listened to his car start in the parking lot, crunch of wheels on gravel and then a looming, hollow silence after he was gone. Instinctively she knew that this shared episode in their lives would not bring them closer together. She sat for a long time in the humid sea-salt night, knowing that she had just lost her best friend.

After what seemed like a lifetime had passed, with the quarter-moon high in the inky sky, she felt cold enough to head reluctantly toward home.

"I've got to get out of here," she said aloud to herself as she headed back to the parking lot, following Luca's footsteps in the sand.

## CHAPTER 13

❁

"He *is* old enough to be your father." Irene met Veronique at the door as she came home from school.

Instantly, Veronique was on her guard. "Who? Father Joe?" she responded, picking the first name that came to her head.

Having been awakened three times the previous night by the ongoing anonymous phone calls, Irene was already working on a short fuse. She reacted to her daughter's remark as though she had been slapped. "Do not use that tone of voice with me," she warned Veronique menacingly. "I am talking about that, that, whatever he is, Bob. The one you went to the prom with. He was here an hour ago, looking for you."

"Did you tell him he could go straight to hell?"

"I told him to leave or I'd call the police. I also threatened him with statutory rape."

Veronique rolled her eyes. "*Mom*. I didn't have sex with him. That's probably why he keeps calling."

Irene looked at her daughter impassively. "Have you had sex with anyone?"

"NO," Veronique yelled, thinking guiltily of her close call with Luca. Her cousin had been avoiding her since the night on the beach. "Honestly, what is wrong with you, Mom?"

Irene walked into her studio. Veronique followed, knowing that her mother found it easier to talk lucidly when she was pounding clay. Sure enough, Irene took some clay, threw it on the work table, and started pounding it as she began to speak. "I finally spoke to Ellie. She's been putting me off for three weeks. I confronted her about the letter, told her how un-Christian it was to meddle. Do you know what she told me?"

Veronique shook her head, not knowing what to expect.

"She told me that she had met you and Bob with Jonathan and Delfina, of all people, outside the Multiplex. I thought you said you weren't seeing Bob. But worse than that—" she held up her hand as Veronique started to interrupt "—worse than your being with Bob, the fact that you saw Delfina and didn't tell me that she was here. She asked me if I had ever met Bob. I had to say no, so I could not really refute what she was saying. Then she asked me why I hadn't mentioned that Delfina was back. Again, I couldn't say anything. That really hurts, Veronique. Since when do you keep these things from me?"

Veronique felt herself getting angry. "Like you'd really care if you ever saw Delfina again," she yelled, remembering the awkward Christmas dinner two years earlier, when Delfina showed up with her girlfriend Lee from Arizona. "You practically disowned Del as soon as you and Father found out that she's a lesbian—"

"—Do NOT talk about your sister that way," Irene recoiled, shocked.

"Mom. She is. There's nothing wrong with it. What's wrong is how you and Father treated her and her girlfriend, practically throwing them out of the house. Now THAT's un-Christian. Almost worse than Ellie." Veronique echoed the reasoning of her brother, Jonathan. Jon had long maintained that their aunt's radical Christianity was antithetical to the whole idea of the religion. "Hitler or Holy Roller, there's no difference," Jon had said. "Both want everyone to be exactly alike, according to their version of what's right."

"I don't appreciate your Aunt Ellie telling me about the whereabouts and activities of my own children," Irene said, testily, also remembering Jon's argument.

"Well, maybe if you paid more attention, you could get the story straight. Pay attention. Number one, I was not having dinner with Bob. Jon and Del took me out to the Bonwit for my birthday. Bob was there. He followed us to the movies with his goons. Ellie was at the movies with her little kids. We all met by accident in the parking lot. She was preaching to Bob when we left. NO, now it's my turn to talk," Veronique added forcefully as Irene began to interrupt. "Number two, Delfina is a lesbian." Irene winced, but Veronique continued relentlessly. "She is fine with it. What she's not fine with is how you're treating her. Get over your stupid hang-ups and apologize to her, unless you're as much of a Holy Roller, and as un-Christian, as Ellie."

Pino had walked into the studio to hear the last of what Veronique said. She walked past him, out of the studio, slamming the door, without acknowledging his presence and without waiting for Irene's response.

Veronique was in the hall, on her way out the door, when she saw an envelope bearing her name on the entrance table. It was her GED results.

Veronique opened the envelope as Pino came into the hallway saying, "It's *Aunt* Ellie to you." He stopped her. "Listen to me, young lady. I've been putting up with a lot—these phone calls, unsavory men coming to the front door, your aunt trying to keep you out of trouble in her own convoluted way. And why? Because you get into trouble. As long as you live in my house you will speak with respect to your mother and to me. You will speak with respect about your aunt. And you will shape up. Do you understand me?" Veronique looked from her test results to her father's angry face.

"Oh, yeah. I understand you perfectly." She turned and left the house without another word.

🍁   🍁   🍁

Twenty-four hours later, Veronique stepped off the Long Island Railroad train from Huntington to Pennsylvania Station. It was the first week of November, and the weather had suddenly turned cold. She was wearing high-heeled, black boots and a long, leather coat with a fur-trimmed hood. She was dragging two heavy suitcases. When she got to the middle of the platform, she looked around uncertainly.

"Can I help you, Miss?" a young conductor asked, coming up behind her.

"I'm supposed to meet my sister by the ticket windows, but I'm not sure how to get there."

"I'm going that way. Let me take your bags." Veronique relinquished them to him gratefully. "My name's Kevin. What's yours?"

"Veronique."

"That's a pretty name. Are you staying in town?"

"Um, no." They were climbing up the stairs to the main floor now.

"Oh, I see. Getting ready to fly somewhere with these two heavy bags?"

Veronique smiled. "I'm meeting my sister. Then we're going to decide what happens next."

When Veronique left her parents' home the day before, she drove straight to Dawn's house. She told Dawn what had happened with her mother and father, ending with, "He said as long as I live in his house, I'd better do as he says. So I decided to get out."

"What about school?" Dawn had wanted to know.

"I passed the GED. With a little help from Miss Stanton, I'm out of school."

"Oh. Congratulations." Dawn had looked crestfallen, but she had accompanied Veronique to the bank while she got some money from her savings account. Then the two of them had driven back to the Adriaticos' house, and Veronique had packed. Irene had gone out, and Pino was working in his home office with the door closed. So the house was, in effect, empty.

When they finished packing, they returned to Dawn's house where Veronique had called Delfina. Her sister's words from long ago had been ringing in her head: "If you ever need anything, call me." Veronique knew she meant it. She told Delfina the whole story, and asked if she could stay with her for a while.

"Come on. We'll talk about it when you get here. You may not like it once you're here," had been Delfina's answer. So the next day Dawn had driven Veronique to the station, having agreed to sell her car for her and send her the proceeds.

Delfina was waiting for her as she came out of the stairway following Kevin, the conductor who was carrying her bags. While the two sisters embraced, the young man put down her bags, pulled out a small pad, and started writing furiously. When Veronique turned around to thank him, he put a piece of paper in her hand.

"Don't tip me or whatever. Just call me, and maybe we can go for a drink sometime. Okay?" he said quickly, red-faced. Without waiting for an answer, he turned and almost ran in the opposite direction.

"Well, you seem to have made a good impression in your first ten minutes in New York," Delfina observed wryly.

"He offered to carry my bags. I wasn't going to say no," Veronique replied, feeling defensive.

Her sister laughed. "Don't worry about it. Listen, Ronnie, I have to be at work in about an hour, so I can't go back to Brooklyn with you. I'm going to put you in a cab. Here's thirty dollars. It shouldn't cost more than twenty, even though rush hour's about to start. Rowan knows you're coming. She'll let you in, and tomorrow I'll get you a set of keys." They took the escalator up to the street level where Delfina hailed a cab. Veronique got in while Delfina put her bags on the seat through the opposite door.

"She's going to Brooklyn. Park Slope." Delfina gave the driver an address, and he nodded. "Which way are you going to go?"

"I'll take Thirty-fourth Street to the FDR. Then we'll go over one of the bridges, whichever looks best." He smiled, and his dark skin shone against his perfectly straight, white teeth.

Delfina nodded, satisfied. "See you later, Ronnie. Call me at work when you get to the apartment."

After being bumped, jostled and thrown around the back of the cab for forty-five minutes, Veronique found herself at the apartment house where Delfina lived on Eighth Avenue in Park Slope. The red-stone building looked like it was at least a century old. She rang the ancient intercom buzzer with Delfina's and Rowan's names beside it, and identified herself to the static. An answering buzzer unlocked the huge wooden front door. She found herself in an immense parlor, complete with fireplace, dark wood paneling and wide carpeted staircase. She entered the double doors as a muscular dark-haired woman who seemed to exude energy was jogging down the stairs. She stopped when she was two steps from the bottom, and pushed her short hair out of her eyes.

"You're Ronnie," she said, blinking as though she could not believe her eyes.

"Yes," Veronique said shyly, looking down.

"Wow. Del told me she had a sister. She didn't say how good looking she is."

Veronique shuffled, embarrassed, feeling like she was eleven years old.

"Um, sorry. Didn't mean to put you off or anything. I'm Rowan, your sister's...friend. We talked on the phone."

"Yeah. Hi." Veronique was suddenly feeling very self-conscious.

"Well, come on up." Rowan said, picking up her two suitcases as though they were empty. She led the way up two flights of stairs to a wooden door that was a smaller version of the front door. She opened the door and let Veronique go in first. The large, sunny living room she stepped into was warm and inviting. A large couch faced a fire place, and two overstuffed chairs stood on either side of the couch. A low teak table, accessible to all the chairs, was in the center. To the left was a kitchen in which three women were sitting, reading.

"Sue, Drake, Chase, this is Del's little sister Ronnie."

The three women looked up and acknowledged her.

"Some little sister," Sue observed, taking a slow drag on a joint and looking Veronique up and down appraisingly before returning to her book.

"Just what I was saying to her downstairs," Rowan agreed. "Come on, Ronnie. Let me show you where to put your things. We cleaned out the spare room and made it into a bedroom for you. It's over here." She was leading the way past the kitchen to a small, sun-lit room with a futon and chest of drawers in it. "Our bedroom is on the other side of the living room, so we can all have our privacy, if you know what I mean." She winked as she set Veronique's bags in the center of the room. "The bathroom's next to the kitchen. If you choose the wrong door, you'll end up in the closet. That's a place none of us want to be." She laughed at her own joke.

Veronique smiled.

"Okay," Rowan continued, not missing a beat. "I'll leave you to unpack. I work the midnight shift. Del usually gets in by one. Make yourself at home. If you're hungry, and there's nothing in the fridge, Seventh Avenue has some great restaurants including my favorite, the diner at Second Street. It's called the Grecian Corner. Just take a right when you get to Seventh Avenue and keep walking." Veronique nodded, not taking in what she was saying.

"I'll probably have to ask you again later," she said. "I'm suddenly feeling really tired."

"Of course. You've had a rough day. Make yourself at home. Like I said, Del will be home around one." With that, Rowan left the room.

❦   ❦   ❦

For the next month, Veronique acclimated herself to life in Brooklyn. Delfina and Rowan had agreed that she could live there for a month without having to pay rent until she decided whether she wanted to go back to her parents, to school or to work.

The building that Delfina and Rowan lived in seemed to be more like a sorority house than an apartment house. The ten units in the building each housed women, some single, most living in pairs. Many were involved in Twelve-Step activities, and most attended at least one meeting of some kind each week. One of the women who was single and living in the building was Delfina's old girlfriend from Arizona, Lee.

Veronique met Lee on the stairs one day as they were both going out.

"Hi, Ronnie. I heard you were here. I haven't gotten a chance to stop by and say hello," Lee said, smiling at her.

"Hi, Lee. I would have come by to say hello if I'd known it was you they were talking about," Veronique said to her.

"I'm going to the Prospect for a late breakfast. Want to join me? We can get caught up on things," Lee invited, turning on her dazzling Southwest smile.

Over breakfast at the diner, Lee and Veronique talked about many things. Veronique was surprised at how relaxed she felt with Lee, although she had only met her once before. Lee's hazel eyes sparkled when she talked. She did not seem to be as uptight as many of the other women in the building, most of whom, Veronique felt, were sizing her up to see if she was really a lesbian or not.

When she had mentioned this to Delfina, her sister had laughed. "You're right, they are. Boy's name like Ronnie, makeup like a straight woman or a femme. My advice is, keep them guessing. It can't hurt."

Veronique had taken her sister's advice. Now, sitting at breakfast with Lee, she was reminded of that advice again when Lee's conversation took a subtly flirtatious turn. "Listen Ronnie, I'm having an extremely good time, but I have to run a meeting over at the AA center in a little while. You want to come and sit in? Maybe we can go out for drinks or something afterwards and continue the conversation, unless you're doing something else this afternoon?"

"I'm not. What meeting is it?"

"It's not a Twelve-Step meeting, but it's run in conjunction with them. It's an incest survivor's meeting. It's an introductory meeting, one where newcomers and old-timers are together. It's kind of like advertising for the groups that I'll be starting in a couple of weeks. Those meetings are closed, but this one's open. If you want to come, you're welcome."

"Okay," Veronique said, reaching into her purse to pay her tab.

"I'll get it," Lee offered and would not hear any protests from Veronique.

They walked down Seventh Avenue together, Lee touching Veronique's arm from time to time as she was pointing out places of interest that they passed. They turned down a side street, and soon they were entering the basement of a neighborhood church. "What will happen is that I'll start with an introduction, then everyone goes around and tells their name. A few people who have been to my meetings before have agreed to tell part of their story so that newcomers can get an idea of how the meetings go. You don't have to say anything but your name. Is that okay?"

Veronique nodded.

"Great. Make yourself comfortable. There's coffee over there. I've got to check on a few things." Lee started to walk away, but then she turned, her eyes twinkling, "Don't disappear on me, okay?"

Veronique smiled. "I'm staying right here," she assured her new friend. She got a cup of coffee and tried to choose the least obtrusive seat in the circle. There was no sitting in the back of the room at these types of meetings.

For two hours, Veronique watched Lee "in action." Lee was even more energetic than Rowan, if that were possible. But Lee's energy was more focused, and, somehow more kind. Her vitality and charisma set people at ease. Veronique could not take her eyes off her. The meeting opened with a moment of silence. Next, Lee read a short prayer from a book she had brought with her. Then, as she had said, everyone sitting in the circle took a turn at announcing their names. Some added the phrase "and I'm an incest survivor" after announcing their name. Most did not. Then one of the women got up and began to tell the story of how her parents were part of a satanic cult, and of the ritual abuse she had suffered as a small child.

Veronique was horrified, but her reaction was quiet, compared to others in the room. One man wept openly. A woman sitting across the room was continuously blowing her nose. After the story was over, Lee offered some advice for the people who were obviously being affected by what they were hearing.

"Some of you may be hearing parts of your own stories in the one we just heard. If you need to talk with someone right now, we have set up a safe room in the office next to this room. Anyone can go talk to the counselors there." Two people got up and moved toward the office she had indicated.

Another woman told of being abused by her twenty-year-old cousin when she was six. The third speaker was a young man in his late twenties named Kevin. He looked familiar to Veronique. Kevin told his story. He had been raped by a priest when he was twelve. As he spoke, she recognized him as the conductor who had helped her with her bags in Penn Station a month earlier. She had not noticed him before the meeting started. Kevin looked around the room as he spoke, but his eyes did not seem to be focused on anything or anyone. Veronique made a mental note to say hello to him after the meeting.

In between their talks, Lee offered advice to the newcomers in the circle, inviting them to sign up for one of the groups she was offering. She was so skillful in her presentation that Veronique considered signing up for a group, even though she did not feel that any of the stories she had heard reminded her of any part of her life, except for when she had seen Renee and her father while hiding in the guest room closet.

When the meeting was over, she went over and said hello to Kevin.

"Hi," he said quietly but enthusiastically. "I saw you come in with Lee. I didn't know if you'd remember me or anything. Are you just passing through, or are you here to stay?"

"I'm trying to decide," Veronique answered, truthfully. "I really like it here."

"Good. Listen. If you decide to stay, maybe we can get together for coffee or something?"

Something made Veronique hesitate. She was not sure what. Then, as Lee started walking toward them, she remembered her sister's advice and weighed the politics of her answer.

"Oh, I guess you're with Lee," Kevin, sensitive to her hesitation, turned as Lee walked up behind him.

"Right now, everything is sort of up in the air for me. I'm trying to decide where to live, and whether to go to school or work. There are so many things I need to think about."

Lee smiled, overhearing the last part of her remark, and said, "Life's tough when you're young, smart *and* good-looking. You have so many options."

Later, over dinner, Lee said to Veronique, "Kevin seemed interested in you."

"It was funny, actually," Veronique told her, ignoring her unspoken question. "I met him when I first got off the train at Penn Station. He was the conductor. He carried my bags from the train to the ticket booth where I met Del."

"You rarely get that kind of service on the LIRR."

"Del said the same thing. He said, instead of giving him a tip, we should go for coffee sometime."

"He doesn't often do that. He must have really liked you," Lee observed. "Do you like him?"

Sensing a trap, Veronique changed the subject. "This afternoon, all the stories were terrible. It was like soap operas. The worst was Kevin's story, with the priest. I couldn't believe that people would do stuff like I heard those people talk about with kids. However else my family was screwed up, it wasn't bad in that way. But when he was talking, I got to thinking about this one priest who was at our church for a while, Father Rex." Lee looked interested. "He was interested in boys, so he never really paid attention to me. My brothers always kept an eye on him though, especially since we had nine boy cousins."

"Nine? From one family?" Lee was surprised.

"Yeah. My family's Catholic—don't believe in birth control or anything," Veronique explained. "You know that stuff you said about incest? What if it's, like, a brother and sister who are, like, the same age or really close, like twins or something?" Veronique, still processing all the information she had gotten that afternoon, was thinking about Luca. "If they're the same age, who's the, um, perp?" She used vocabulary she had heard from Lee.

Lee smiled. "Usually, when kids are playing and experimenting with each other, it's different. It's not a power thing. It's just kids' curiosity. That doesn't cause the same kind of life-long damage that an older cousin or a priest or some other significant adult causes when sexually exploiting a child who's not in a position to say no. Why, Ronnie? Did you and your cousins ever play doctor?"

Now it was Veronique's turn to smile. "Not really. There were so many boys, and I was really the only girl. Delfina, Jon and Marc were really a lot older than my cousins and me. The boys used to have contests to see how far they could pee. I'd watch until I got bored, which wouldn't take too long."

They had paid for their dinner, and were leaving the restaurant as they continued their conversation.

"I know what you mean. My brothers used to do that too." Lee changed the subject swiftly. "So, Ronnie, which side of the fence do you really fall on?"

Veronique was confused for a moment. It must have shown in her face, because Lee laughed, a warm, friendly laugh and said, "Maybe I should rephrase the question." She paused a moment and said, "To put it bluntly, what I'm trying to ask is, are you gay?"

Veronique felt her mouth forming a small "o" as her mind raced between her knee jerk reaction, which was, no, of course not, and her sister's advice to keep a low profile. "Mmmm. I don't know," she started, about to say something about being on the rebound and not wanting to be involved with anyone for a while, but Lee interrupted her.

"Well, Ronnie, I guess that's what makes you so alluring to everyone in the house."

"*Every*one in the house?" Veronique repeated, disbelievingly.

"Okay. Not your sister. But practically everyone else."

"Gee. Great. Thanks for telling me."

"It's no big deal, really. It's not like people are hiding in the shadows to jump your bones or anything. They just think you're hot. A lot of them would like to give you your first experience."

Veronique felt herself go red. "Like they think I haven't already had my first experience," she blustered, feeling half angry, half exposed.

"Hang on there, Sweetie," Lee soothed. "Nobody means any harm. You're just an enigma, and therefore a topic of conversation and, of course, gossip." They were walking up the stairs to the apartment then.

"I'm glad that Del and Rowan are together. At least I don't have to worry about turning either of them on when I'm in the shower or something."

"Well, I know that's true of your sister, of course. But keep your eyes on that Rowan," Lee warned, stopping at her door. "Look, I'd invite you in, but my place is a mess, and I have a really early day tomorrow."

Veronique nodded. "Yeah. I'm supposed to start signing up at temp agencies tomorrow afternoon."

"Oh. I'm done at five-thirty. You want to meet me downtown when you're done?"

"I guess so. I should be done by then. Where do you want to meet?"

"How about Henrietta's in the Village? Six?"

Veronique nodded, and Lee wrote directions to their meeting place on a small pad that was hanging inside her door. Then they said good night. Lee gave her a quick kiss on the cheek as she turned toward the stairs.

When she opened the door to Delfina's apartment, she was surprised to find her sister sitting on the couch in front of the fire place.

"Hi Del. What are you doing home?"

"Hi Ronnie. There was a system shutdown, so I got to leave early. What have you been up to?"

"I spent the afternoon with Lee. I went to a meeting she was running, and then we had dinner."

"That was some late dinner. It's almost eleven. I know those meetings are over by five."

"Yeah. We talked about a lot of stuff. Some of the stories those people tell are terrible. One of the people who spoke was the conductor who brought my bags from the train. Remember him? Anyway, he was raped by a priest. I remembered Father Rex and the boys. I also remembered Renee and her father that time I hid in the closet for your graduation. Del, do you think Renee was—is—an incest survivor?"

Delfina looked at her soberly. "I don't know, Ronnie. What do you think?"

"From what I heard today, it sounds like it. But I don't know what to do about it."

"Why don't you ask Lee? If I know her, and, believe me, I know her, she'll probably be glad to see you again."

"She's taking me to Henrietta's tomorrow."

"She is? Henrietta's is a bar. You're not old enough to drink."

"They didn't proof me tonight."

"Well, you're a big girl, and so is Lee. I'm not playing Mommie, so do what you think is right."

"Del," Veronique wanted to ask a question that had been popping into her head at various points all night. "Do you think Lee would like me even if I wasn't gay?"

Delfina sighed and shrugged. "I couldn't tell you, Ronnie. I really don't know if most of the women here would like any of the others if they weren't gay. For some of them, it's like the first criteria for them giving you a chance.

Sometimes I really get sick of it." She paused for a moment as though thinking about something. Then she turned back to Veronique. "The only thing I can tell you to do is ask Lee yourself."

"It's weird. I think she's flirting with me. But after seeing how she was in that meeting, you know, sort of making eye contact with everyone in the room, I'm not sure if that's just the way she is with everyone."

"Ronnie, I know Lee as well as I know anyone. Hell, I lived with her for three years in Arizona. When you're living with someone who's your lover, you really get to know a lot about that person, male or female. I know that Lee never goes out with someone two nights in a row unless she's interested."

"Wouldn't that be weird though, me going out with your ex-girlfriend?"

"Why?" Delfina countered. "I'm not going out with her. Even if I were, and she was interested in someone else, she's not an object that I can own. I can't control what she does. If you did end up having sex with her, I'd be more interested in why you were doing it. You always seemed interested in boys. By the way, what happened with Luca?"

Veronique looked down at her hands. "Nothing," she said, too quickly. "Why do you ask?"

Her sister gave her a searching look. "Well, you two seemed to be so close. Last time I saw you, all you talked about was what you and Luca had done. Jon even said that the two of you were inseparable. I was just wondering what happened to change that."

"Sometimes he can be a possessive jerk," she told her sister, wishing there was a way to describe what had happened at the beach. "He wasn't happy about my taking the GED and leaving high school early either."

"Maybe you two should try to kiss and make up," Delfina suggested.

"That might be easier said than done," Veronique replied, startled at her sister's choice of words. But knowing better than to ask or react in any way, she changed the subject. "So, you don't care if I go out with Lee?"

Delfina smiled at her. "Go out with anyone you want. Just be careful, and be prepared for the consequences of experimenting with something that other people take as their identity. I don't want to see you getting hurt. It would also be nice if you didn't hurt too many of my friends either, you little heartbreaker. By the way, how did the job thing go yesterday?"

"I went to a couple of agencies, but I don't type fast enough."

"I was afraid of that. Let me show you something on my computer." Delfina had a computer typing program that she had loaded onto her computer. She showed Veronique how to turn it on. "Practice on this for a week, and we'll start having typing races. Use it for a while in the morning, then go and sign up at two agencies. See if you're typing any faster by tomorrow afternoon," Delfina suggested. "I'm going to bed now. If I don't see you in the morning, have fun with Lee." Her voice was teasing as she said the last part. Veronique stuck out her tongue as her sister left the room.

※ ※ ※

The next evening Veronique met Lee at Henrietta's.

Lee was already seated near the center of the long bar when Veronique entered. In the smoky darkness, Veronique could make out many figures huddled together, a few sitting alone. All were women. Lee pulled the stool she had been saving for Veronique closer to hers. A television above the bar was showing sports highlights. Somewhere across the dance floor a jukebox was playing loudly enough to make the bar vibrate.

"What'll you have?" Lee yelled to be heard above the din.

"How about a Long Island Iced Tea, the drink of my homeland?" Veronique yelled back.

Lee laughed. "Your sister always says that." Then she ordered from the petite bartender with the shaved head and at least fifty earrings along the perimeter of her right ear. Lee turned back to Veronique. "Ever been in a gay bar before?"

"Not really. I usually go to dance clubs with my friends," she answered truthfully. The truth was Veronique was under age, and the only places that she and her friends could go were to clubs that had no-alcohol teen nights. The bartender brought her drink, and Veronique held her breath, waiting to be asked for proof of her age. To her immense relief, the bartender left as quickly as she had come, without asking Veronique or Lee anything other than if Lee needed change.

"So. You dance?" Lee looked interested. "The band starts in about an hour. There's a dance floor here. You can't see it right now, but take my word for it. It's there—small, but serviceable."

Just then, a woman walked up to Lee. Apparently, she had been in one of Lee's groups. As Lee turned to talk to her, Veronique looked around at the assortment of women sitting around the bar. She was fascinated.

Then the bartender brought two more drinks, one for her and one for Lee. "From the couple in the corner," she yelled above the din, indicating two women at the far end of the bar who raised their glasses when she looked over. It was Sue and Drake. Veronique waved back. Lee turned back, saw who she was waving to, grabbed her fresh drink, and nudged for Veronique to follow her.

They hung around with Sue and Drake until the band started playing, and then the four of them went out to the dance floor. Veronique was a good dancer and she enjoyed dancing with the three women. When the band slowed down and started playing more romantic songs, Lee grabbed her hand and pulled her close. Another woman cut in. Then Drake cut in. Then Lee was back. This happened for most of the night. Finally, the band announced the last song.

"Last dance. Find your partners, girls. The ones you're going home with. There'll be no cutting in on this one." The band started playing Eric Clapton's *Beautiful Tonight*. Lee had already claimed Veronique for this dance. Standing almost six feet tall to Veronique's five-foot-six, Lee leaned over and started singing the words into Veronique's ear. Veronique felt a shudder of something, a mixture of excitement and fear, and kept dancing.

It was late when the four of them hailed a cab back to Brooklyn. Veronique, having had three Long Island Iced Teas, fell asleep on Lee's shoulder. She barely remembered being led upstairs to Delfina's apartment by Lee, getting a quick goodnight kiss at the door, and stumbling, alone, into her bed.

❦   ❦   ❦

The next week was a blur of activity for Veronique. Delfina's strategy of playing to her sister's reckless competitiveness worked. Veronique woke up each morning and spent three hours at the computer, working on her typing speed. Each afternoon before Delfina left for work, they would have one typing race. By Friday, Veronique's speed was vastly improved.

"Wow. That's really good work," Delfina was impressed. "I'd say you were, uh, up to speed, so to speak. Now, all you have to do is learn a couple of programs, and I'll introduce you to a friend of mine who can get you all the temp work you'll ever want." With that, she left for work.

Veronique was having dinner with Lee that night. She had never been in Lee's apartment, but Lee had said that she was getting a cleaning person to come in, and she was going to cook dinner herself. Veronique thought it would be fun. Despite her uncertainty about Lee's flirtation, Veronique really liked Lee and had a lot of fun with her.

❧   ❧   ❧

At precisely eight that evening, Veronique presented herself at Lee's door carrying a bottle of Long Island White Zinfandel. Her hair was up, and she wore a silk wrap-around dress and slip-on high heels. Lee also seemed to have taken time with her own outfit—pressed black jeans, newly shined black, cowboy boots with silver tips and a crisply starched embroidered cowboy shirt. She stopped and gawked for a moment before moving aside to let Veronique in.

"Wow."

Veronique felt a surge of something. She could not quite identify it, but she felt like she was in control of the situation. Lee momentarily regained her senses, taking the proffered bottle and bringing it into the kitchen.

"Come on in," she called over her shoulder. "Make yourself at home while I finish getting this ready." The smell of pasta and sauce was emanating from the kitchen.

"Smells good. Can I do anything?"

"Just sit there and be beautiful," Lee's voice was teasing. "I'll be out in a minute." After some banging of the pots and pans, Lee called from the kitchen, "The wine will go great with the pasta, it's chilled and everything."

"Yeah. I didn't have too far to travel. I guess it stayed cool."

"Smartass." Lee laughed, emerging from the kitchen with two glasses, which she put on the impeccably set table. She lit two candles and turned on the stereo. Instantly, Billie Holliday was crooning quietly in the background. "Why don't we just start eating?"

Veronique looked at Lee as Lee held a chair for her. Remarkably, Lee seemed very nervous. Veronique sat and watched Lee take the seat across from her. The dinner passed quickly. As it turned out, Lee was both a good cook and an excellent host. She had many interesting stories to tell, and the conversation never lagged.

Finally, after homemade cannoli, Lee suggested Irish coffee in front of the fire. Veronique accepted willingly; she was having a wonderful time.

Sitting together on the couch, sipping their coffees, Lee said, "Tell me about your cousin, Luca. The two of you seemed to have spent a lot of time together. How come you're not in contact now?"

Whether it was the heat of the fire, the wine, the Irish coffee, or the combination of them, with Lee's soft-spoken voice and alluring eyes, Veronique suddenly found herself telling the story of Luca and the beach.

She ended with "We used to talk every day. Now he doesn't even know where I am, and he probably doesn't care." Then she laughed and added, "I don't know what would make my father madder, seeing me with Luca or seeing me here with you." Laughter turned instantly to tears. Veronique had put down her empty mug and was wiping her eyes. Somehow her head found its way to Lee's comforting shoulder. She relaxed as Lee rocked her. Over and over, Lee softly intoned, "It's okay, Baby. Everything will work out."

Lee was stroking her head. Then she brought her index finger around Veronique's jaw and under her chin, bringing Veronique's face up an inch from her own. "I've been wanting to kiss you from the moment you walked in here." Something in the now-familiar hazel eyes sparkled, and Veronique closed her eyes and moved her lips to Lee's without thinking about anything.

Kissing Lee felt natural to Veronique, even though she was nervous at first. She began to relax as Lee did not seem to be in a hurry for anything more. Veronique was vaguely aware that she didn't really know what to do next. Lee seemed content to explore her mouth for the moment and to allow her mouth to be explored by Veronique.

Lee's face was smooth, not stubbly-chinned like Luca's, and Lee's tongue was more alive, more playful and more insistent. Lee also seemed to be more aware of Veronique, while Luca had been more conscious of himself. Within minutes, the comparisons stopped, and Veronique's thoughts of Luca faded. When Lee's hand, which had started on Veronique's cheek, moved to her neck and then to her breast, Veronique again thought fleetingly that she had no idea what to do. But she knew that Lee did.

Lee had nudged her into a lying-down position on the couch, while Lee's own body was sprawled half on top of, half next to, hers. "How old are you, Ronnie?" she asked lazily between caresses.

"Um, eighteen," Veronique mumbled the lie, not wanting the touches to stop.

"I'll be forty in a month," Lee said in a low voice. "I thought you should know before we go any further."

"I don't care," Veronique groaned slightly as her chest arched to Lee's touch. "And I'm too old for you to worry about statutory rape," she added, grinning through clenched teeth in an effort not to groan again.

"Well, now that we have that out of the way, maybe we should graduate to the floor in front of the fire?" Lee invited in a ragged whisper. She rolled off the couch and onto the plush rug that was lying in front of the fireplace. Lying on the rug, leaning up on one elbow, Lee gestured for Veronique to join her there, which she did.

On her back, lying in the crook of Lee's arm, Veronique and Lee continued kissing while Lee's hand went on a scouting mission, loosening the tie of Veronique's dress and letting it fall open. She also opened the buttons on her own shirt, revealing her naked breasts below.

Somehow, with Lee's hand on her stomach, playing with her navel, the sight of Lee's hardening nipples sent an erotic shudder through Veronique's body. She started to kick off her shoes.

"No, leave them on for now," Lee said. It was a request. Veronique complied, cupping one of Lee's breasts in her hand, more out of curiosity than out of lust. The effect that simple act had on Lee was gratifying. Lee kissed her with more passion, breathing heavily, her body undulating slightly.

With one hand, she unclipped Veronique's bra. Then she moved her hungry mouth from Veronique's mouth to her uncovered breasts, giving each one attention. Veronique felt her own breaths deepening.

As Lee was stroking her thighs, her belly, her pubic bone over her panties, Veronique panicked for a moment. Lee, feeling it, whispered, "Just say stop whenever you want me to." Veronique nodded. Lee continued to caress her over her panties while Veronique ventured to let her hands run down Lee's sides. She loosened the older woman's belt, undid her jeans zipper and button, and let her hands move down her smooth back to her buttocks. No underwear, Veronique discovered with surprise and an unexpected rush of lust. She moaned slightly, moving her hips slightly in a circular motion.

She felt Lee slip one finger under her panties. Embarrassed, she realized her excitement had left its mark, but her embarrassment melted into a flood of sensations like the ones she had felt with Luca. They grew more intense with each new contact from Lee. She tried to imitate Lee's actions, but Lee's body was too long.

"Relax, gorgeous," she heard Lee whisper in her ear. "Let's do this one at a time, okay?" Veronique nodded, relieved, as she realized that she wouldn't know what to do. Lee knelt up, jeans slipping off, as she started to massage Veronique's inner thighs with her hands. She started working her way up to the panties again while she teased Veronique's breasts with her lips and tongue.

Finally, hearing the groan Veronique could not suppress, Lee said, "Is it time to take these out of the way?" Veronique nodded, swallowing. She was vaguely aware that Lee had also removed her boots and jeans.

"Ohmygod." Veronique heard her own voice unbidden as she felt Lee's tongue move from her breast to her belly and then down. She felt Lee position her still-high-heeled feet beneath her bare bottom, and then she felt Lee's hand—or was it hands—lifting her bottom to Lee's ever-inquisitive tongue.

"Ohmygod." Lee's tongue and fingers were all over her. Veronique gave up trying to know what was where.

"Ohmygod." She felt Lee enter her, and then start a slow in-and-out rhythm that increased as Veronique's own unconscious tempo increased to a shuddering, uncontrolled crescendo. "Ohmygod. Ohmygod. Ohmygod."

❧ ❧ ❧

The next day, back in Delfina's apartment, Veronique felt both excited and confused. She and Lee had spent the night in front of the fire. With a little coaching, Veronique had succeeded at making love to Lee. She had marveled at Lee's unselfconscious way of showing her what felt good. She marveled at the force and number of Lee's orgasms. Lee had as much charisma as a lover as she did when she was leading a group. Veronique was fascinated.

Now, back in her own room, Veronique needed space to think. Neither Rowan nor Delfina was home; she had the apartment to herself, so she decided to take a hot bath. She washed her hair in the sink as the bath was filling, and then, hair wrapped in a towel, she immersed herself in a bubble bath, and was sitting in the sauna-like bathroom when Rowan walked in.

"Wow," Rowan breathed out the word in a husky voice.

For the second time in two days, Veronique heard the breathy exhalation in response to the sight of her. She liked the sudden surge of power she felt at the energetic woman's reaction. It was different from Lee, but just as powerful with Rowan, who stood immobilized at the door, staring. Veronique laughed.

"What's so funny?" Rowan wanted to know.

"I never thought I'd see you so, I don't know how to describe it, still or something."

Rowan, who had not taken her eyes off Veronique, edged closer to the bubble-filled tub. As if mesmerized, she knelt behind Veronique, and started rubbing her neck and shoulders. Half curious, but feeling herself getting angry because of her loyalty to Delfina, Veronique waited to see what would happen next. She remembered Lee's warning.

Rowan, hands now on Veronique's collarbone, bent forward to kiss her mouth. In that moment, Veronique put her thoughts of her sister aside, kissing

Rowan, comparing her to Lee the night before and to Luca. She shook her head.

"What is it?" Rowan asked, remarkably gently.

"Um, two things. First, in a word: Delfina." Rowan's hands jumped guiltily. "Second, you wouldn't be the first. I've already had sex with Lee. It was great."

"Oh." Rowan's voice was tinged with disappointment. Then, instantly, she seemed to snap out of her zombie-like stupor. "You don't need to tell your sister about this, right? It'll be our little secret, okay?" Her face was clouded with worry, her usually merry eyes seemed hollow. Veronique remembered Delfina's words, "she's not an object to be owned…" She knew it was between Rowan and Delfina.

"You really should talk to her. I sure as hell am not going to say anything."

# CHAPTER 14

"Mom's been bugging me about where you are," Jonathan's voice came over the phone.

"Why would she think you know where I am?" Veronique's voice had a hint of sarcasm. "I'm sure Father doesn't give a damn."

"He's worried, even if he doesn't show it. Father Joe has asked if I know of any way he can get in touch with you. I said no. If I had told him to write to you, to send it to Delfina and ask her to forward it to you, he'd figure out where you are. So I just play it like I do with the rest of them—I don't know anything. Oh, and, uh, Luca wants to see you."

Veronique was silent for a moment. Then she said, "If he can get into the city in a couple of weeks, maybe we can meet somewhere." She missed Luca, even though every time she imagined their first meeting, she knew it would be an awkward one.

"By the way, Richie Dell'Alma stopped by the school to see me the other day."

"Oh yeah? What did that creep want?"

"He's not so bad, Ronnie. He actually came by to apologize for the way he acted this summer. He said he's been thinking about it a lot, and he really likes you. He didn't want to be acting like Bob. That's why he came to apologize. He came to me because I used to tutor him. He hoped I'd give the message to you. Actually, to you and to the whole family. Family's very important to Richie since his brother died."

Veronique ignored the information about Richie. "Oh, by the way, Jon, I went to this meeting where all these people talked about being abused by adults in their lives when they were children. I keep thinking about it. What people do to their kids…" her voice trailed off for a moment before continuing. "At the meeting one guy, a train conductor I met on the way in, told about how he was raped by a priest. I got to thinking about Father Rex and how weird he was. In this meeting some people talked about wanting to commit suicide. When you mentioned Richie just now, I thought about his brother Carlo. Maybe he killed himself because of Father Rex."

"Maybe he did, but there's nothing we can do about it now. I just wanted to let you know that Richie apologized, and I think he was sincere. Bob, on the other hand, is making a royal pain of himself. Mom's just about had it with him. She finally told him to look in the city. She was really mad the day he came to the door last week. She was in the middle of making a pot that fell when the doorbell rang. It was Bob, and she let him have it. Just about the only thing she didn't do was throw clay at him. I think she pushed him out the door—must'a got clay all over his suit." Jon laughed.

Veronique would have thought it was funny, except that Bob now knew she was in the city.

"How does she know Del's here?"

"She doesn't. It's just intuition, I think. I haven't told her anything. She knows Del's not in Arizona anymore. She may have gotten some information from the mission when she called out there. She doesn't know Del's living in Brooklyn, and she can only assume you're with her, which is logical. By the way, what have you been doing?"

"I've been temping, but I think I need a permanent job for a while."

"How do you like working?"

"Temping's fun, because I get to meet a lot of interesting people—artists, writers, idiots."

Jon laughed. "And the work?"

"Pretty boring now that I know what I'm doing. Lee, um, you remember Del's old girlfriend—"

"Yeah. She was pretty cute, as I recall."

"I guess so. Anyway, she's been getting me really good jobs. Good, as in they pay well."

"It's nice that she's taken such a personal interest in you," Jon observed, casually. "From what Del says, you're pretty popular with most of the women in the house."

"I guess so." Feeling partly guilty, partly exuberant, she thought to herself as she had so often in the weeks after she had been with Lee. "I'm a temp lesbian." The truth was, news of the affair with Lee, via Rowan, had done wonders for

Veronique's reputation among the women in the Slope. It felt good, in a way. Veronique felt that she was a guest member in a very exclusive all-female club, and she was enjoying it.

A few days later, Jonathan called again. This time Delfina answered the phone. "Do you mind if Luca and I come in to Brooklyn for a visit?"

"That would be great, Jon. I miss you, and I know Ronnie does too. She must miss Luca as well, although she doesn't talk about him."

"Tomorrow's Saturday. I'll definitely drive in. If Luca can come, I'll bring him too."

Delfina hung up the phone. Almost immediately, it rang again.

"Hello?"

A crackling sound came over the line as though it was a very bad connection, then high-pitched laughter before the line went dead.

"Prank," Delfina said aloud as she hung up.

※ ※ ※

"Luca's sitting in the car. He wanted me to go in first. He thought Ronnie might not want to see him." Jonathan paused. He was sitting in Delfina's kitchen at 9AM, a cup of coffee on the table in front of him. "Actually, he's been drinking a lot lately. I had to haul him out of bed and strong-arm him to come."

"How'd you do that?"

"Told him I'd tell his mother he's been out getting blasted. She'd make him go to church or something. He knew his life would be a living hell. So he's in the car, dark glasses, hangover and all. He's actually pretty miserable." He gave a sad half-laugh. "I thought seeing Ronnie would be good for both of them. I don't know what's with him. Anyway, I thought he'd be excited to see her. When he said he didn't want to, I knew he had a problem."

"They might both have a problem." Delfina told him.

Jonathan looked at her questioningly.

"Lee had a little talk with me, now that she and Ronnie are an item."

"*What?*"

Delfina laughed. "It's not that tragic, is it, having two dyke sisters?"

"That's not what I meant. Ronnie always seemed so, well…so straight."

"I think she is. She's just a wild kid taking a walk on the wild side. She'll be back to your side of the line before too long. Being gay is too hard of a lifestyle to live even when you actually are gay. When you're straight, there's absolutely no reason to pretend you're gay for very long."

"Why on earth is she pretending at all?"

"Lesbians have been pretending to be straight for centuries. There's a big payoff that way, you know—money, social acceptance." Delfina paused. "But to answer your question, I think Ronnie enjoys being 'in,' you know, with the in crowd, the cool ones, wherever she is. She's really popular here. Lee can make anyone feel like they're more precious than gold. But Ronnie's straight, and we know that. Even Ronnie knows it. I think she's trying to figure how to get out of it."

The phone rang. Delfina got up to answer it as Jonathan thought about what she had said.

"Another hang up. We've been getting about three a day for two weeks. Most come late at night. Sometimes there's this sick, high-pitched laughing on the line. It's really annoying. I called the phone company. They said there's not much they can do except change the number, which would be a royal pain for both Rowan and me."

"Strange. Mom was getting those kind of calls for a long time. They stopped about two months ago. They never figured out who it was. Father, of course, blamed it on Ronnie's bad choice of acquaintances and boyfriends. Marc and I always thought it was Bob, not that Marc's around very much these days." Their brother Marc had decided to become a professional artist, much to their father's dismay. Marc had been doing erotic sculptures since he was a teenager. When he started doing homoerotic sculptures, his father had thrown him out of the house.

"Marc called me last week from Albuquerque. He said he's living in a little town in Arizona called Sedona. He's sharing a house with some woman. Says his hair's longer than mine and he's making a living sculpting. Said father would be furious if he saw his latest. He calls it 'Doggie.'" Delfina laughed, but then turned serious. "Do you think Bob found her here?"

Jonathan shrugged. "Could be. Mom got really mad at him last week when he made her lose a pot. She got clay all over his suit pushing him out, but she did say something about maybe Ronnie was in New York City with you."

"It seems crazy that he would be able to find her with just that much information."

"Yeah, but it's a really weird coincidence that the phone calls stop there and start here."

Delfina nodded, thinking.

"Should I go in and wake her, or should I get Luca?"

"There's something you should know about Ronnie and Luca," Delfina said slowly. "Then you can decide. When I was mentioning the other day that I thought it was weird that Ronnie never talks about Luca, Lee told me that Ronnie and Luca had been doing some heavy petting down at Sunken Meadow."

"They were bound to get to it sooner or later." Jonathan was only mildly surprised.

"I guess you're right. Ronnie's been talking about kissing Luca since she was seven." Delfina nodded. "Anyway, it seems, according to Lee, that Luca couldn't handle it or something. I'm not sure how much of the editorial comments we can believe. After all, consider the source, who, at the time of the telling was, I believe, trying to seduce our sister who is a good twenty-five years younger than she is. Ronnie told her she's eighteen. Lee almost died when I told her Ronnie's sixteen."

Jonathan lifted an eyebrow. "What a difference a couple of years makes. What's even more interesting is that your ex, Lee, told you. Now that, I would say, is weird."

Delfina laughed wearily. "There's an old lesbian joke: my lover and I went on vacation with my ex-lover and her girlfriend...For a dinner party, we need a flow chart." She shrugged slightly. "The thing with Luca came up when you called yesterday. Lee was over. I guess she thought it was pertinent."

Jonathan sighed and got up. "Well, I guess the best thing to do is talk to Ronnie. I'll wake her." He went into the room where Veronique was sleeping.

Delfina went out to Jonathan's car where Luca had dozed off. He jumped violently when she got in and shut the door. "Hi Luca," Delfina said, kissing his cheek. "I hear you've been drinking a lot lately."

He slouched down in the passenger's seat, his lanky six-foot-two frame barely fitting in Jonathan's tiny TR7, a sports car with no back seat. He crossed his arms and stared out the window at the car in front of him.

On impulse, Delfina said, "Don't worry about what happened. Ronnie's been talking about kissing you since she was seven." She watched Luca react and knew she had his attention. "She misses you. Why don't you come on in?"

With that, Delfina watched as something in Luca shifted. He was still groggy from his hangover, but his energy had changed. He took off his sunglasses, ran his fingers through his blonde hair, and put the glasses back on again. "Okay. I'll go talk to her."

Without another word, Luca followed Delfina into the apartment. He went directly to Veronique's room as Jonathan was leaving it. Luca sat down on the bed next to her. He was stroking her hair as Jonathan glanced back through the door.

An hour later, Luca, his eyes bloodshot from the night before, emerged with Veronique whose eyes were red from crying.

"Hey, nice to see you," Jonathan said to Veronique softly.

At that moment, the phone rang. Veronique, who was standing next to it, answered.

She cursed and hung up quickly. "Shit. It's those weird hang ups I was getting at home. It's probably Bob. I wish there was a way to teach that asshole a lesson and make him stop calling."

"We need to do something about him," Jonathan agreed. "I told you he keeps coming to the house. I talked to Lou about it," Jonathan said. "He just got home from basic training. He was in a wild mood, and gave me some ideas about what he'd like to do to Bob. One of his ideas seemed harmless enough, but also enough to scare the bejeesus out of Bob. That might be enough to make him get lost." To Luca, he said, "We'll talk about it."

"Don't do anything without me," Veronique warned.

"I won't," Jonathan promised.

"Count me in, too." Delfina reminded him.

The doorbell rang. Jonathan, standing nearest to it, opened the door. It was Kevin, bringing flowers. He stepped into the apartment as the four Adriaticos looked at him.

"How'd you get in without buzzing?" Delfina said, startled at seeing someone who did not live in the house.

"I was at Lee's," the young man said, apologetically, shrinking back towards the door. "I didn't want to intrude. It's just that Lee said Ronnie might be in," he answered Delfina. To Veronique he said, "I just wanted to give you these flowers." Thrusting them at her, he fled toward the door. "Bye." He left without waiting for an answer.

"That was the conductor?" Jonathan said, bemused.

"He's actually a nice guy," Delfina said, feeling bad about the abrupt way she greeted him. "It's just that with the prank phone calls and everything, I don't want the security in this place to be compromised."

"If he really cares, he'll be back," Jonathan said gently. "How about we all go out to eat?"

Veronique suddenly found that she was very hungry. Luca, who had been quiet before Kevin had showed up, was quieter after he had left, and was less enthusiastic about eating. He did not say anything though. The four spent two hours at the crowded New Prospect Diner, first waiting for a table and then sitting in a sunny booth overlooking the street, getting caught up talking about putting a stop to Bob's annoyances. After the meal, Delfina and Veronique walked Luca and Jonathan to the car.

When they returned to the apartment, they were surprised to see Father Joe sitting on the front steps. They were too far away to talk to him as Rowan bounded out of the front door. Seeing a man dressed in black, wearing a Roman collar, sitting on the steps she seemed to screech to a halt. As the Adriatico sisters came closer, they heard Rowan say contemptuously, "What do you want, Priest?"

Joe was opening his mouth to answer when Delfina called, "Hey, Rowan. It's okay, he's with us."

Rowan backed off slightly. "He's coming up to the apartment?"

"It's okay. The maid came yesterday."

"That's not what I'm talking about," Rowan said through clenched teeth. "We'll have to have her come back tomorrow." With a baleful look at Joe, she ran down the steps. To Delfina, she said, "See you later, Babe."

Joe hugged both Veronique and Delfina.

"It's so good to see you both again," he said. "Is my being here a problem?" He asked Delfina. "We could go to a coffee shop or to the park to talk."

"Well, Father Joe, the Catholic Church isn't very popular amongst the lesbian crowd. With all the homophobic preaching, many of the people here see you as a source of the violence that affects us."

Joe was silent for a moment, thinking. "Love the sinner, but not the sin," he started.

"That statement makes so many wrong assumptions and hurtful insinuations that my head is spinning," Delfina said heatedly. "We should discuss it some time, but not on the street and not now, since I'm sure you came looking for Veronique, not me." Veronique stood by silently.

Joe looked at Delfina kindly. "I've been wanting to keep in touch with you, Delfina, but you didn't seem to be inclined. Ronnie's parents are worried about her. She's not eighteen yet, and I thought I'd try to reconcile the family."

"Well, come on in, and you two can talk." Delfina unlocked the front door.

As she led the way up the stairs to her apartment, they met several women, all of whom had the same reaction as Rowan to seeing a man dressed in black with a Roman collar. Most muttered epithets as they passed. If Joe heard them, he gave no indication.

Once inside the apartment, Delfina gave them each a glass of water and then retired to the living room while Joe and Veronique sat at the kitchen table.

"How'd you find me?" Veronique wanted to know.

"I called Luca this morning to help me at the rectory. He said he was going to Brooklyn with Jon. I asked him if he knew where in Brooklyn he was going. He didn't know the address, but he knew he was going to Park Slope. I drove in hoping to find them and meet up with you. I saw Jon's car, so I asked a few people if they knew where you or Delfina lived. The guy in the deli knew you. He gave me the address." Joe paused before starting on the subject that brought him to Brooklyn. "Listen, Ronnie, it's not right that you've left home this way. You're only sixteen. You should still be living with your parents."

"Instead of in this house of ill repute?" Veronique was defiant. "My father doesn't give a damn about me or where I am. When I'm in his house, everything that goes wrong is my fault. Why should I stay there? I've got a good life here. Everyone likes me. I'm making my own money, and I don't have to live with a guy who thinks that I'm a fuckup."

Joe ignored the expletive. "Your parents miss you. I know your father's not the easiest person to get along with, but he tries to do the right thing. You're still a teenager, and you should be under the supervision of your parents, even if it's only for a couple more years. I know you've started to make a life for yourself here, and you have entered into relationships with many new people. They'll still be here in two or three years. In the meantime, instead of working, you could be going to college and getting an education. Your mother misses you, and so does your father, even if he doesn't always show it."

"I often wonder if he's really my father. Life would be so much simpler if he wasn't." For a moment, Joe looked at her, musing. Then he said, "We all have our crosses to bear. Your father loves you, even if he doesn't always show it in the way you'd like. At least think about what I've said."

"I will, but I don't want you telling my parents where I am."

"I can't promise that."

"Fine. Then I'll disappear again." She got up as though she was getting ready to leave at that moment. "This is Delfina's place, not mine. I didn't ask you to come here. If my parents really wanted to find me, they would have. Face it, this is really for the best."

Joe had gotten up too. "I disagree, Ronnie. I tell you what: if you call them and talk to them, I won't tell them where you are right now."

"I'll promise to call them if you promise never to tell them where I am."

"Never is an awfully strong word, Ronnie. What if something happens?"

"Tell Jon. He'll take care of it. If they really care about Delfina, they should find her on their own, not have the information handed to them on a silver platter. So far, they haven't bothered to find out, which tells me they don't really care. But if they know where she is, and still don't give a shit about getting in touch, that would really suck." Veronique's language was regressing as she got angrier. "Don't tell them, Father. Because if you do, and they don't call her right away, I would decide that this is a family I never want to deal with again." She paused for a breath and then threw at him, "I can't imagine that you would want to associate with such un-Christian people either."

Joe could see how she had changed in the months she had spent away from home. "Okay, Ronnie. That's enough. If you call your parents today, I won't tell them where you are or where Delfina lives."

Rowan returned as Veronique was letting Joe hug her goodbye.

"God. Are you two related? You have the same eyes," she noticed. Delfina, reading on the couch, looked up, startled and then went back to her book with a troubled look in her eyes.

Joe and Veronique looked at each other. She shrugged off Rowan's observation. "Lots of people have blue eyes. My father does too, and sometimes I wonder if he's really my father."

Joe, standing at the door, did not respond to Rowan or to Veronique. He left saying, "Goodbye, Delfina. Don't forget our agreement, Veronique."

# CHAPTER 15

"Hey, Marcoooo!" Jonathan got up from his seat at the diner at the intersection of Main Street and the Smithtown Bypass. Jonathan was sitting at the head of a long table, keeping one eye on both busy streets, waiting for Marc's arrival. He was sitting with both of his sisters, seven of his cousins and Richie Dell'Alma.

Veronique looked up and saw a tan, broad-shouldered man with a blonde beard and a long, white-blonde pony tail. She recognized Marc's eyes in that new body, and ran to hug him. He had already greeted Delfina and was making his way toward her. Behind him was an athletic-looking woman with ash blonde hair in a similar pony tail, sporting a similar Arizona tan. After Marc hugged Veronique, he turned to this woman.

"Everybody, this is Sandy, my muse and the love of my life." Jonathan had already greeted her. Delfina was saying hello as Marc continued, "We just got a place in Sedona. I wanted her to meet the family. I thought this would be a great opportunity. She met Mom and Father last night." Collective groans. "Sandy, this is one of the few times you'll ever get to see most of the gang in one place at one time. You already met Jon and Del. This is my *baby* sister Veronique," Marc said teasingly. Veronique came forward, surprisingly shyly, to say hello. "And now let's see if I can remember everyone else," he laughed. "Next to Ronnie, always, is Luca. Over there is Lou, Gavin, Alec, Andy, Richie—Richie, what are you doing here? Like the goatee, Rich. He's not a relative, Honey—Barr and Kyle."

"Hi everyone," Sandy's sultry voice was low and silky. "If you don't all wear name tags, it might take me a while to remember your names. But I'll do my best."

"That's all we can ask," Marc assured her jovially. He ushered her into a chair next to Veronique, and sat down beside her. "We're used to traveling in a pack. Makes it hard to get to know our individual names. But at places like this, they know to save a huge table for us, and we know we'll get tagged with the eighteen percent gratuity."

Sandy laughed. Veronique decided that she liked Sandy. And as she watched Jon and Delfina, she could tell that Jon and even the more reticent Delfina both liked Marc's girlfriend.

"Where are the little guys?" Marc asked Gavin, who was sitting at his right.

"Gordon's not so little anymore, but he and Cameron are still a bit young for the business at hand." Marc nodded, knowing that the gathering was more than merely a family brunch.

After everyone had ordered and the waitress left, Jonathan said, "Okay, listen up." Veronique, listening to her brother, thought about how much being a teacher was ingrained in him. Jonathan continued, "Everyone knows that we're here for a couple of reasons. In addition to getting together for the first time in a very long time, we have a little problem that I've already talked to most of you about. Lou has actually come up with an interesting solution, but it would involve all of us. And it would involve the Chamber. But before I tell you about it, I want you to think about whether we want to tell Richie and, of course, Sandy about the Chamber, which has always been a place just for us cousins."

Jonathan paused for effect, looking around the table to make sure everyone was listening.

"Hey. How ya doin'?" Marc leaned over and addressed a diner who was staring at the large family group from a corner booth. The stranger looked away, finished his coffee and left hurriedly. It was mid-afternoon on a warm April Saturday. They were now the only patrons in the back room of the restaurant.

"I'm going to tell you what the problem is," Jon resumed. "And because part of the solution involves the Chamber, I want you all to think about whether it's okay to let them know where it is, and tell me at some point in the next two days. That way, maybe we can take care of this by next weekend." His relatives nodded their assent.

"Okay. Here's the problem," Jon started. "A certain old guy, whose name I won't broadcast here, took Ronnie to the prom last year." Richie mumbled an expletive in a low voice. Jonathan ignored him. "This guy became a nuisance and a real pain in the derriere. He keeps showing up at the house, asking for Ronnie, sitting in the driveway waiting for her, calling and asking for her. The last time I answered, he said he was suicidal because his wife left him, his franchise is in danger of being taken away from him, and he couldn't get in touch with Veronique."

"Boy, Ronnie. You sure know how to pick 'em," Marc teased her. Veronique responded by kicking him under the table while sticking out her tongue at him. Sandy laughed at their repartee.

"Someone should put this guy out of his misery," Luca said.

"We should put this guy out of our misery," Delfina observed laconically. "Especially if he's the one who actually is making all those phone calls." Several of the people at the table asked what she was talking about. She told them about the midnight phone calls which had recently stopped at her mother's house and started at her apartment. "Someone seems to be following Ronnie around. Bob seems like the likely candidate."

"That's exactly what Luca and I thought," Jonathan agreed. "Lou came up with a nifty little plan to scare the shit out of him, as sort of a warning, kind of like a way to tell him once and for all that Ronnie is not interested in him, and a pack of people are willing to remind him of that fact." Jonathan winked.

"What's the plan?" Luca, fired up all of a sudden, wanted to know. Delfina looked across the table at him, musing. He looked haggard, she thought and his eyes seemed to be perennially bloodshot. She knew from Jonathan that he was drinking more and more, and Delfina wondered if her cousin's encounter with her sister was the source of his angst.

"We have to decide about the Chamber, because this isn't the place to go into detail about it," Jonathan was answering Luca. "So, everyone, let me know as soon as possible whether you think two new people can know the whereabouts of the Chamber. Meanwhile, Ronnie will set up a meeting with this guy for next Saturday. She'll ask him about the hang ups. She'll also make it clear that she's letting him know it's over and that he shouldn't come around or call anymore. We'll be there to reinforce the message."

After the family finished their brunch, they all went to the high school and played baseball until it became too dark to see the ball. By the time they parted, it was clear to Jonathan that everyone was fine with Sandy knowing the whereabouts of the Chamber, but he was the only one who thought Richie trustworthy enough to know.

"Okay," Jonathan said to Lou as he sat with Lou and Delfina later that night in the Chamber. "We'll have to go to Plan B, which is a modified version of Plan A. I told Richie, and he's okay with it—says he doesn't really care about a kids' hideout. All he really wants to do is teach Bob a lesson. So, Plan B." Jonathan looked at the huge garage-like aluminum door that formed one of the walls of their hidden meeting place. "Alec got these doors to open last year. Because they're aluminum, they're fairly light, and he's been able to make them open virtually silently. Each of us has a car. Richie said he'll get cars for Del, Andy and Barr. We can fit eight cars here in two rows. I'll camouflage two other cars on either side of the entrance to the upper parking lot. Bob will like meeting Ronnie in a secluded place," Jonathan smirked.

"We'll have the cars here the night before," Lou interjected, "just in case paranoid Bob gets here early or something. Richie will park his car with a trailer hitch in the lower parking lot as close to the upper lot as he can. He'll park it early and unhitch the trailer, but leave them parked together. Then he'll go into the restaurant and wait until he sees Bob drive to the upper lot. He'll call Ronnie who will be waiting by the phone at the church parking lot. Ronnie will use Mom's car."

Veronique had kept her agreement with Joe and called her mother the day after Joe visited the apartment. Irene was overjoyed to hear from her younger daughter who finally promised to visit as long as her mother understood that she would not move back. Veronique stayed overnight with Jonathan in the guest house, which was now Jonathan's permanent residence. Irene let Veronique use her car to get around.

"It'll take Ronnie three minutes to get to the upper lot from there. Once Bob drives in and starts talking to her, we'll let our cars roll out from here silently, no lights—like we used to do. Richie will come in behind him. Marc and I will move the two cars that are camouflaged by the entrance into place to form a circle. When Ronnie slams the door, we'll all let Bob know that we're not going to let him harass Ronnie anymore."

Delfina liked the idea of surrounding Bob and forcing the issue. "I was talking to Sandy. She works in special effects. We should see what she can rig up to make this easier to coordinate."

Jonathan nodded. "I'll talk to her and Marc."

🍁     🍁     🍁

A week later, at seven-thirty on Saturday night, the Old Dock Restaurant was filled with locals from the town of Kings Park and visitors who docked their small boats and came ashore for dinner. Richie Dell'Alma, small and wiry, was seated at a table facing the window. A small candle was in the middle of the table. Richie, his back to the other diners, watched as Angie placed a steaming plate of pasta and a glass of white wine between him and the candle.

When Richie got excited, he got hungry. This particular evening, he was ravenous.

"Thanks, Angel," Richie said, looking up at her, eyes twinkling.

"No problem, Rich. Call me if you want *any*thing," she said, her vapid blue eyes looking seductively into his brown ones, and holding the glance as she turned away from the table.

"Oh, Anj," Richie called her back.

Her eyes never broke contact. "Yes?"

"I'll take some grated Parmesan."

"With or without Romano," she purred.

"The works."

Richie had an hour and a half to eat. Bob was due to show up around nine-thirty, although, according to Veronique, he was usually late. Richie was taking no chances. He would be ready to leave by nine.

Richie spread the white cheese over his spaghetti and started eating slowly, twirling the long strands of tomato-covered pasta on his fork and savoring every mouthful. Every once in a while he would stop to sip the wine, letting it swirl in the glass and then in his mouth appreciatively before swallowing it. From time to time, Angie would come hovering by, making sure everything was all right.

By five minutes to nine, Richie had partially consumed a cannoli and was sipping a cup of cappuccino. The check was in front of him. He put the exact change under the check and a tip under his empty wine glass. He sipped his cappuccino and waited.

At nine twenty-five, his cannoli almost gone and nothing but foam left of his cappuccino, Richie saw a black Lincoln Continental drive slowly past the restaurant. The large car rolled towards the dock along the parameter of the parking lot. The brake lights went on as it turned to pass the launching platform where boaters with trailers could deposit their vessels in the water. It crawled around the perimeter of the parking lot, past Richie's own car, parked in front of the unattached trailer, and back toward the restaurant. Richie could not see the driver of the Lincoln, but he knew instinctively that this was the car he had been waiting for. His instincts were confirmed when the Lincoln, making its second slow sweep of the parking lot, passed his car again and turned into the narrow opening that led to the upper lot.

"Hey, Angie." Richie beaconed to the waitress who came over as he got up. "Listen Doll," he said in a low voice, "I think there's a drug deal going down in the upper lot. But I'm not sure, so I'm gonna go check. No, shhhh," He covered her lips with one finger while putting a twenty-dollar bill in her palm with his other hand. "I'll be fine. Just do me a favor, okay?" She nodded mutely. "If you see anyone driving out of there like a bat outta hell, call the cops. Promise me?" She nodded again, and he left the dining room.

In the foyer of the restaurant, he called Veronique from a pay phone. After half a ring, she picked up. "Yeah?"

"He's here." Richie was terse. He hung up as she was saying "Okay."

He went outside, lit a cigarette, walked to the launching platform and looked toward the upper parking lot where he could see the parking lights of the Lincoln as it was idling, waiting. He knew he was too far away to be identified by the driver. From the launch, he strolled the long way to his car, an Impala, moving beyond the tree line, out of sight of the Lincoln. He was approaching the Impala from the back, walking past the trailer, when Veronique drove up.

Richie got into his Impala quietly. He had rigged the Impala and all the hidden Adriaticos' cars, so that the dome and dashboard lights, as well as the brake lights were wired in each car to a kill switch disguised as an alarm light. That way, everyone would be able to surround Bob without the automatic lights attracting his attention. The kill switch idea was one that Richie had dreamed up when he first started working at his uncle's garage. He had worked happily on all the Adriaticos' cars all week, spending up to two hours to rig each car. He turned the key in the ignition and let the car idle while he fitted the ear piece of a walkie-talkie around his right ear.

Sandy had been so enraged when she heard Veronique's story about Bob, that she had thrown herself whole-heartedly into the Bob project. Somehow she had managed to get earphones for each of the eleven drivers. She did not want two-way radios in case Bob was listening to his radio and picked them up as interference. Everyone knew what they had to do and did not have to report in, Sandy said. She would ride with Jonathan and coordinate the drivers. They had run through the plan two nights earlier and had gotten through with only a few hitches. The biggest problem had been that the camouflage Jonathan had set up for his and Marc's cars had not come off when the cars rolled forward. It made two of the cars look like moving bushes as they rolled into position. Jonathan had fixed this problem. "You don't need that much cover," Sandy had advised. "It'll be dark, and Veronique will be so engaging that Bob won't be looking at the scenery."

❦ ❦ ❦

Hidden in his car with the engine idling, Jonathan saw Bob's Lincoln roll into the upper parking lot and turn around to face the entrance. Jonathan knew that Marc's car, engine also idling, was directly across from his in the darkness.

"Okay, move the vines," Sandy, sitting next to Jonathan, hissed into her microphone.

Fifty feet behind Bob's parked car, Lou, Gavin, Andy and Delfina rustled a low fence of vines softly forward, revealing a row of four cars. Then they climbed back through open windows into their cars and took their places behind the wheel. Behind the first row of cars, with their front bumpers against the rear of the cars in that row, were four more cars, their engines idling quietly.

Three minutes later, Veronique sped into the upper parking lot, her bright lights on until the moment that she saw Bob's car. Then she flicked her lights to low beam, temporarily blinding Bob, and making sure that her lights did not catch the headlights of the cars waiting behind him. Veronique pulled her car along the passenger side of Bob's car, got out and went to sit inside the Lincoln. The dome light went on in Bob's car. Jonathan and Sandy could see Veronique engaged in a heated conversation with Bob, gesturing at him and shaking her head.

"Okay, quickly, first row, move out," Sandy ordered into her speaker.

The four cars in the front row were pushed out of their hiding place by the cars behind them. They rolled down the incline and quietly fanned out in a large semicircle. Delfina, Luca, Alec and Lou sat in their cars, while in the second row Andy, Barr, Kyle and Gavin waited for Sandy's cue.

"Second row, go."

The next four cars moved into place as Veronique opened the door, yelling at Bob. "I will not tell you again. I will not go out with you, ever. Stop calling my parents. I don't live there anymore. Stop making those prank calls in the middle of the night. In other words, for the last time: leave me alone."

"Marc, Jon, Richie. Now." Sandy's voice came over the earphones, and the last three cars completed the circle.

"I'm not making no calls in the mid—" Bob's voice was stopped by Veronique slamming the door to the Lincoln. The cousins could hear Bob's muffled protests as he got out of his car to plead with Veronique, who was getting into her car.

"Okay, Richie." Sandy's voice came into his ear. Richie was out of his car in a flash. He turned on his headlights, and stood in front of his car while the other drivers waited in their cars for Sandy's cue.

"The lady said leave her alone, man," Richie said loudly.

"What? Who's that?" Bob's slow tongue had not picked up any speed since Veronique had left his dealership. Bob turned to the lights blocking the only exit from the upper parking lot.

"That's all my relations, here to reinforce my message, because you don't seem to get it when I tell you myself," Veronique yelled at him, getting into her car and starting the engine.

"Why, you little, conniving..." Bob's slow words were lost.

"Marc," Sandy cued him.

Next to Richie's car, Marc's headlights went on, and he stepped in front of his car, yelling, "Leave her alone."

Meanwhile Sandy cued Gavin, who did the same thing, as Sandy in turn cued Kyle, then Lou, Alec, Luca, Delfina, Barr, Andy and, finally, Jonathan in her car. As this was going on, Veronique had backed her own car into the space between Alec and Luca's cars.

By the time Barr and Andy had turned on their headlights, Bob had finally realized that he was being surrounded.

"Everyone back into your cars," Sandy cued as Bob jumped into his own car and started the engine while Jonathan turned on his headlights to complete the circle.

"Okay, start moving forward," Sandy called into the speaker as the four drivers, whose cars had not been on, started their engines. But before they were able to tighten the circle, Bob, showing that he was quicker at the wheel than he was at the mouth, managed to thread his car between Jonathan and Richie's cars. He scraped the passenger side of his car against a tree and tore off part of the bumper as he made his escape to the lower lot.

Inside the restaurant, Angie, hearing wheels squealing on the gravel and blacktop, looked up from the table she was serving to see a black Lincoln, its side badly damaged, careening out of the upper lot and speeding past the restaurant. She put the last plate down and went to the telephone behind the bar. She was dialing the police as she looked out the window, searching for Richie's car. She saw it driving past the restaurant moments later as the phone rang in the police station. Sure that Richie was all right, Angie spoke into the receiver with confidence.

"Yes. This is Angie at the Old Dock. I just wanted to let you know that a black car with its side all smashed in drove out of here at about eighty miles an hour. One headlight was out. One of the patrons here said it might be drug business, so I thought I'd call you."

In the upper lot, Sandy was still on the walkie talkie. "No time to celebrate yet," she instructed. "Let's clean up and get out of here. See you at the diner in an hour."

Richie turned his car around and left the parking lot, following Bob's route. Gavin backed his car into the Chamber. Luca cautiously moved his car, lights off, into the lower lot and backed into the spot Richie's car had occupied. Veronique's other cousins moved their cars into the Chamber and piled into Irene's car, with Veronique behind the wheel.

Veronique drove the car out from the upper lot and turned right, away from the restaurant. She drove to the far end of the lower lot where local high school couples parked for their romantic encounters. Marc moved his car into the Chamber also, closed the huge aluminum door, replaced the camouflage wall with Jonathan's help, and the brothers got into Jonathan's car with Sandy. Then Jonathan, lights off, drove his car into the lower lot and parked by the water.

Ten minutes later, when Veronique drove out of the lot, Angie's back was to the window, as she took an order from a new set of diners. After watching Veronique's tail lights disappear, Luca left his car and headed toward the restaurant.

Jonathan, Marc and Sandy got out of their car, walked into the half-filled restaurant and sat down at the bar. Luca joined them. They ordered Guinness on tap and were talking quietly, watching the patrons when two police officers walked in and asked the bartender for Angie.

She met them in the foyer outside the main dining room. "Ma'am, you called the precinct about a possible drug deal and an automobile being operated dangerously?" The taller of the two did all the talking in a quiet voice.

"Yeah, a black Lincoln drove out from the upper lot about twenty minutes ago. The passenger side and light were smashed, and the bumper was hanging off it. He must'a been going eighty." Angie led them away from the diners.

The officers looked at each other as if to say "I doubt it." The officer continued. "What made you think it was a drug deal?"

"Um," Angie's pretty brow furrowed with the effort of remembering. "A guy who comes in here from time to time said he saw something funny going on in the upper lot. He said he was going to take a look, and if any cars came speeding out, you know, looking strange, that I should call the cops. So when that car came out of there, I called you guys."

Jonathan, Marc, Luca and Sandy exchanged glances. Marc's beer mug was half empty, and Jonathan moved his untouched mug in front of his brother, taking the half empty one. Marc toasted his brother with the new beverage as Luca signaled for another.

"Do you know the name of your customer?" the officer was asking Angie.

Angie smiled. "Nah. I never get names. He's cute though." Her brow furrowed again. "I hope he's okay."

"We'll go up and take a look around," the officer told her. "Thanks for your time. We may be calling you again." He wrote down her name and address, and took some other information. Then the officers left the restaurant.

When Sandy finished her beer, Marc downed the rest of his new mug and said, "Let's get out of here." Luca tossed off the rest of his beer and threw a tip on the table as he swivelled off the bar stool. As they walked back to the car, they could see the two police officers flashing lights around the empty upper lot. "Nothing but some leaves and a bunch of tire tracks," Sandy said, satisfied. They drove out of the lower lot to meet the rest of their cohorts at the diner.

"I can't believe Richie told her to call the cops," Luca fumed.

"That was a really stupid thing to do," Marc agreed, "especially since he put kill switches in all the cars."

"Maybe he doesn't know they're illegal," Jonathan pointed out, reasonably.

"Worse, maybe he does," Luca said darkly.

❦    ❦    ❦

Richie had known that the kill switches were illegal, but the consequences of calling the police had not gone as far as the illegal switches in his thought process. Richie knew that Bob dealt in drugs, and Richie was fairly certain that on a Saturday night Bob would have some drugs in his car. When Richie left the Old Dock Restaurant parking lot, he surreptitiously followed Bob's route. At the first intersection, he went straight ahead. By the time he reached St. Joseph's Church, he saw Bob's damaged Lincoln in front of him, stopped at the traffic light. As Richie approached, the light turned green. Bob, followed by Richie, drove toward Main Street.

At the next intersection, Bob signaled to make a left hand turn, which he did as two police cars approached from the right. Much to Richie's satisfaction, the flashing lights of both police cars immediately went on. The two cars followed Bob and pulled him over several yards ahead. Richie drove past as the officers were getting out of their cars, an ashen Bob staring forward through the windshield. Richie decided to pull into the Carvel parking lot across the street, get an ice cream and watch.

The officers in the first car were asking Bob to step out of his vehicle as Richie went in to get his cone. When Richie returned to his car with the franchise's trademark soft vanilla cone, the officers were telling a disheveled Bob to open his trunk. Bob was refusing vociferously.

Richie smiled with satisfaction, noting Bob's wrinkled and stained suit. By this time, all four officers were out of the car. One was holding a flashlight while her partner opened the trunk.

"This is an illegal search," Bob yelled and made a sudden move toward them. Instantly one of the other officers pushed him against the damaged Lincoln while his partner put hand cuffs on the struggling car dealer. Meanwhile, the trunk had been opened. From it, one of the officers pulled a large brown package.

"What have we here?" the officer holding the flashlight asked, knowing the answer.

The first officer opened the package and took from it a smaller plastic bag containing white powder. He gave a low whistle after determining that it was cocaine. "Yep, it's the real stuff."

"Three more of those in here," his partner informed him as she scanned the trunk with her flashlight as one of the officers holding a struggling Bob read him his rights. Two more police cars had arrived by this time.

"Everyone wants to be in on the biggest drug bust in town this year. Either that, or nothing better to do on a Saturday night," Richie said to his half-eaten cone. He stayed until Bob was put forcefully into one of the police cars and taken away. Then Richie went to join the Adriaticos at the diner in Smithtown.

When he got to the diner, Jonathan, Marc and Luca met him at the door.

"Why did you tell Angie to call the cops?"

Richie looked from Jonathan's angry face to Marc's and then at Luca's.

"Look, Ronnie wanted to scare Bob, and I was happy to go along with it. But we all know that idiot Bob doesn't learn lessons for very long, and I figured he would be back. Now I know he won't be back for a very long time." Richie told Jonathan and Marc what he had witnessed. "I knew he'd have drugs of some kind on him. I didn't think he'd be stupid enough to drive around with a kilo of coke, but good riddance. Seeing him taken away in cuffs was for me, not for Veronique. I think he pissed in his pants. It was great." Richie laughed, remembering his rival being forced into the police car. "Let's eat." He turned to the dining area, ending the discussion.

Jonathan and Marc followed him into the back room of the diner where the rest of the cousins and Sandy were already starting a midnight snack. Luca, who was still fuming, came in a few moments later. Over another plate of pasta, Richie quietly but gleefully retold the end of the story with Bob.

A little while later, Luca pulled Veronique aside. "Let's go get my car," he urged her.

Veronique looked at her cousin's haggard face. "Are you all right?"

"Yeah, never better," Luca answered flatly. "I just want to get my car and go home."

"Okay. The coast should be clear now that they've got Bob," Veronique assented. "I'll get my stuff."

Five minutes later, they were leaving the diner parking lot. As they drove through Smithtown and into Kings Park, Luca said, "We haven't talked in a long time. Want to get some beer and go to the beach?"

Veronique, who had just been thinking the same thing, nodded. She turned the car away from the Old Dock, heading toward the Seven-11. Ten minutes later, having purchased a six-pack of Bud using Luca's fake ID, they went to the Old Dock parking lot, got Luca's car and drove both cars to the beach. Once there, they made their way to their old spot at the beach, carrying blankets. They made a small fire and sat shoulder to shoulder, backs against the old oak driftwood which, by now, was partly buried in the sand.

They sat in silence for a long time, drinking beer and listening to the sound of the waves in front of them and the wind in the dwarfed pine trees behind them.

"So what's up?" Veronique finally broke the silence.

Luca shrugged, pouring more beer into his mouth. "What's up with you?"

"Not much, I guess. You know my story. Got my GED, moved in with Del, got a job, got weird phone calls, got a message to Bob, I hope, tonight."

"That's good, real good." Luca was not communicating too much.

"What's up with you?"

Luca shrugged again. Veronique decided to take a chance.

"I thought you wanted to talk. Jon tells me you've been drinking a lot."

"What the hell does he know? Mister School Teacher. He should mind his own damn business."

"So you have been drinking too much." Veronique knew she was pushing Luca's buttons, but she was worried about him. "Ever think of what happened last time we were here?"

"No." Luca opened another bottle of beer.

"Liar," Veronique muttered under her breath. To Luca, she said, "I do. A lot."

"I heard you're a lesbian now." Luca was blunt.

"Where'd you hear that?"

"Delfina's girlfriend told me."

"I'm not exactly a lesbian."

"You're just sleeping with women."

"Tell me you've never experimented with anything."

"I never fucked a guy."

"Ever do anything with anyone?"

"Yeah, sure." Luca finished another beer.

Veronique looked at him quizzically. "You seem so, um, I don't know, unhappy now. What would make you happy?"

"Happy?" Luca gave a hollow laugh. "Ever think what life would be like if you came from a different family? My mother's a religious nut, and my father acts like nothing's happening. My little brothers are walking around like brainwashed zombies, afraid to say anything for fear of a lecture. It's nuts." He was quiet, drinking.

"Yeah," Veronique agreed. She started a thought, but Luca interrupted her.

"You look more like that priest than your father anyway." His voice was high-pitched, and his words were coming fast.

"That's stupid. That priest and my father look alike—blonde and blue eyed."

Luca ignored her. "Just think, if your father and mine weren't brothers…" his voice trailed away.

"If they weren't brothers, what?" Veronique prodded him. "We wouldn't be relations." She watched his internal struggle on his face as he debated whether or not to be honest.

"If they weren't brothers, maybe we'd be a different kind of relations. Or have a different kind of relationship. Maybe you'd be sleeping with me instead of with that woman," Luca blurted out.

"Oh Luc," Veronique started, touching his hand, which was holding a beer. He pulled it away as though he had been touched with something hot. He spilled some beer on the sand.

"Shit." He wiped it off his leg with the corner of the blanket.

"Luca, if we slept together, things would be so different between us."

"Things *are* different between us. After that night, you left. We don't talk like we used to, or hang out. I'm still in school, and you're not. It's like you're a bazillion miles away."

Veronique felt guilty for her long separation from him. She had not thought about it before. She assumed Luca would not want to see her again after running away from her on the beach that night. "I'm not that far away. You know where I am now."

"I do, but it's not that simple. It's like I can't stop thinking about you that way. I think, would it be so wrong? We really love each other. What's the big deal? I went to confession. The priest said it was definitely a sin." He started another beer. "Sometimes I think I really don't care."

Veronique looked at him, his lanky, muscular frame, his tortured eyes, hair being blown by the sea breezes. She was tempted. Luca seemed to feel her thoughts. He turned to her suddenly, his eyes burning into hers. "Right now I think, what do I have to lose?"

"Things would change between us, sin or no sin," Veronique warned.

"I don't care," he said roughly. He put his hand behind her head and pulled her face towards his, kissing her deeply.

Although repulsed by the taste of beer on Luca's breath, Veronique was surprised by her physical reaction, and tempted by his daring. After all, sleeping with Lee was a sin too, according to the priests. But being with Lee did not feel like a sin. The beer was starting to make her mind go in circles. Maybe the priests were wrong. After all, how could a bunch of old celibate guys make up rules about who women had sex with, or who anyone had sex with for that matter.

Veronique decided to ignore her misgivings. She kissed Luca back with abandon. He pulled her closer to him, and as she shifted, she could feel his erection. Her unexpected touch surprised him, and he came all over himself and all over her.

"Jesus fuckin' Christ," he swore aloud, jumping up, grabbing his own towel and wrapping it around himself. "It must be a sin," he mumbled, more to himself than to her.

"Luca, don't worry about it."

He was too ashamed to look at her. He shook his head and stumbled down the beach. She abandoned the towel and ran after him. When she caught up with him, she grabbed his arm.

"Wait. Don't leave."

"Leave me alone."

"Where are you going?"

"Home."

"You've had too much to drink."

"No more than you. Now you think I'm too much of a shithead to be able to drive after a couple of beers? I'm fine. The best thing you can do for me is leave me alone." He pushed her away hard. She fell. More shocked than physically hurt, she sat on the sand and watched him plod through the high grass to his car. Tires squealing, he pulled out of the parking lot and left her alone, still sitting on the beach.

After what seemed to be an interminable time, she went back to the remains of the fire to get her belongings.

❦   ❦   ❦

When Luca left the parking lot, he knew he was driving too fast, but he felt he had to get as far away from his cousin as he could, as fast as possible. He left the beach parking lot and careened toward Saint Johnland Road. He spun around the corner, tires squealing, and took the straightest way possible down the curving road, narrowly missing a stone bridge support on his right and an oncoming Jeep on his left.

He barely saw these, swimming as he was in his misery and shame at the night's events with Veronique.

"Asshole," he said to himself. "Can't fuckin' even control it when you do get it up."

His car flew through the State Hospital grounds. He barely managed the sharp left turn at St. Anthony's, the all-boys Catholic high school, grazing the curb with his back tire as he tried to negotiate it. The car fishtailed. He got it back on track. Then he tried to make the quick right turn, losing his side mirror and badly scraping the passenger side against a giant oak tree.

"Moron, can't even drive," he berated himself. "Can't fuckin' do anything right. Fuck her. Fuck her. Why did she have to go and touch me? She made me do it, maybe on purpose." He was angry as he drove down Landing Avenue, past the old cemetery, over the speed bumps and around the heavily wooded, curving road. He saw the yellow arrows pointing to the right as he swung around the first curve, and the road started a steep downgrade.

The car was picking up speed as he straightened the wheels, belatedly seeing the yellow arrows pointing to the left. He tried to compensate with the steering wheel, but the last beer was beginning to take effect. His foot hit the gas, intending to slam on the brakes. He saw the sign warning of the narrow bridge too late. The sign should have been to his right. It was on his left. This time he could not compensate as his car picked up more speed. He hit the right bridge abutment with the left side of his car.

He felt a second of exhilaration as his car went sailing over the steel guard rail, landing upside down in the reeds of the Nissequogue River.

※　　　※　　　※

Back by the old oak driftwood, Veronique was staring at the remaining red logs of the fire. In the changing light, she thought she got the image of an old man. He reminded her of the man at the Native American ceremony so many years before. As the last embers went out, the image disappeared. Veronique shuddered. She picked up her towel and the six empty beer bottles, and slowly headed back to her car.

# CHAPTER 16

❦

The phone was ringing. Veronique's answering machine began to pick up, but the caller hung up and redialed. After the third time, Veronique was roused. She rolled to the other side of her bed, feeling for the phone and scattering her cats Angel and Isis who hissed at her grouchily. Picking up the phone she mumbled into the receiver, "Yeah?"

"Ronnie, it's Father Joe. Did I wake you?"

"Well…"

"I'm sorry. I should have realized that it may still be early for a Saturday."

"It's okay. It's almost noon. I just worked late last night."

"Sorry. I forget the hours you keep. I thought we might get together this week. I'll call back around three." He hung up.

She groaned and tried to hang up the phone. She missed the cradle, and the receiver dropped to the floor. She did not care. As she tried to go back to sleep, her mind went back to Luca as it had so often since that night on the beach three years earlier.

Veronique did not recall anything about Luca's funeral other than Delfina staying at her side through the whole ordeal.

Joe said the funeral mass. All of Luca's brothers were the pall bearers. Luca was very popular in school, and many of his classmates and teachers attended the service. In the pew behind Veronique, Dawn wept openly. Next to her, Renee kept whispering, "It should have been me," as tears streamed silently down her cheeks. Ellie was overcome and had to be lead from the church by Otto and Pino. Jonathan eulogized Luca as did two of his high school friends.

After the proceedings were over, Veronique returned to her old bedroom in her parents' house. She stayed there for a month. Some days she was so sad she could not get out of bed. Other days, she was enraged.

One day, Delfina came to bring her back to Brooklyn.

"I'm so mad at him, I want to kill him," Veronique had ranted to her sister. "But then I remember..." the rest of the thought was choked in a sob.

"Ronnie, Honey. You can't stay here like this. Come back home to Brooklyn." Delfina had spoken softly, her heart aching for her sister's pain.

"Del, I don't feel like I belong anywhere. I can't stay here without Luca, and I can't face going back to the Slope. I'm not really a lesbian. Luca was always the one who turned me on. When I was with Lee, I'd find myself thinking about him. But it was so...I don't know, cool or something, being with all those women, being treated like an adult, like they really cared about me, cared about what I thought. It was like if I was one of them, I was in some really great club. But if I wasn't a lesbian, I was out." Veronique had stopped. Then, looking into her sister's eyes, she continued. "And Lee was so sweet. She made me feel really good when I was with her and all, but Luca kept creeping back into my head."

Delfina nodded with understanding.

"And, plus," Veronique fell back into her regional idioms, "Lee wasn't the only one who seemed to want me." She told her sister what had happened with Rowan. Delfina ingested the information quietly as Veronique finished. "It only happened that one time, just that one kiss. I told her about Lee, and she backed off."

"I wondered how Rowan found out so fast," Delfina mused, her eyes smouldering.

"Are you mad at me?"

"No, Ronnie, I'm not mad at you. I'm disappointed in Rowan for not being forthcoming with me and for telling you to keep something like that a secret. But she's not an object that I can own. She's free to do whatever she wants. Even hit on my little sister." Delfina paused before changing the subject. "Oddly, I can understand why you can't go back to Brooklyn. It would be like asking me to live my life married to some guy. I don't want that for you. I know that some of those women can be tough. I'm not as social as you, so I don't stay around to listen to their bullshit." She gazed fondly at her sister. "God knows I can't say you didn't give it the old college try." Looking pale as she talked in the lengthening shadows, she said, "If you still want to live in the city, I know a place for rent on the Upper East Side. Let's go talk about it over dinner."

Veronique roused herself. "Let me get myself together. Is it okay if I use your brush?"

Her sister smiled gently. "What happened to the one I gave you?"

❦    ❦    ❦

True to her word, Delfina had helped Veronique to find a studio on the Upper East Side. Veronique went through her days mechanically, not interacting with people, and trying to avoid people she knew from her "old" life in the Slope as Lee's girlfriend. Veronique was working at temporary computer jobs around the city. She kept running into people she knew, even on the third shift. She hated working third shift. Too tiring. The first shift was too straight-laced. The second shift, the one Veronique preferred, was when most of Lee's friends worked.

One night, as she struggled out of her high heels after another double shift at yet another law firm, Veronique looked at herself in the full length mirror behind the door. "I need a change," she announced to Angel and Isis.

She had no idea what that would be though, and so she continued moving around, working temporarily at one firm or another.

❦    ❦    ❦

Later that Saturday, the phone rang again. This time Veronique was sitting in front of the television, sipping a cup of coffee.

"Ronnie, it's Father Joe again. Sorry I called too early before. I'll be in town Monday afternoon, and I was wondering if I could take you to dinner after I finish teaching. Joe had taken much of what Veronique had said to heart when he had visited Delfina's apartment. He tried to have lunch with Veronique at least once a month.

"Okay. I'm not working Monday. I'll wait for you in your office at five." Veronique was accustomed to Joe's schedule, although she knew that he had never adjusted to the idea that she usually started working late in the afternoon. Joe was always very pleasant and unimposing when he met her in the city, and Veronique was usually happy to see him.

❦    ❦    ❦

The next day, Veronique walked into Father Joe's office at Manhattan College to find a young man there, his back to the door, studying one of Irene's fog vases. Although she stepped into the doorway silently, the young man jumped and turned around. He had a goatee, but as Veronique recognized him, she felt an unexpected rush of enthusiasm.

"Kevin, the LIRR conductor, right?"

"Uh, yeah," he started, suspiciously. Then he recognized her. "You're the girl from the meeting in the Slope, Lee's girl."

"Well, not really," Veronique began cautiously. "I hung out with Lee and my sister's other friends for a while, but I'm on my own now, on the Upper East Side."

Just then, Joe walked in. He put his briefcase on the desk. "Veronique," he kissed her cheek. "Kevin. I guess you two have introduced yourselves."

They both nodded. "Kevin, Veronique and her family have been dear friends of mine for a very long time. Veronique, Kevin is my newest assistant from the seminary."

"You're a priest?" Veronique could not stop the question.

"I took a year's leave of absence to see if I wanted to do anything else." Seeing Joe's confused look, Kevin explained. "Joe, this is actually the third time Veronique and I have met. The first time was when I was working as a conductor on the Long Island Rail Road. The second was in Park Slope." He gave a sidelong glance to Veronique who noticed that his shoulders seemed extremely tense. She also noticed that he did not elaborate that his reason for being in Park Slope was a survivors' meeting. Veronique, knowing the meetings' rules about anonymity, also said nothing.

Joe did not seem to notice Kevin's evasiveness as he reached into his briefcase and started pulling blue test booklets from it. "Well, that's an interesting coincidence," he noted before changing the subject. "Kevin, Veronique and I are going to dinner. Why don't you get started on these, and when I get back in about an hour, I'll take over."

Kevin started gathering the books. "No, stay here," Joe told him. "You can work at my desk. Less distractions for you, and I'll know where to find you when I get back." Kevin nodded, his head down, starting to put the bluebooks into neat piles. He sat down at the desk as Veronique and Joe walked out of the office.

They returned to Joe's office an hour and a half later. Joe had a book that he wanted to lend to Veronique. A Bob Dylan tape was playing in the small tape deck behind Joe's desk. From the stack of booklets, they could see that Kevin had made progress grading the exams, although he was not there. Veronique felt a slight pang of disappointment. It was the first stirring of any real feeling she'd had since Luca's accident. Surprised, she said goodbye to Joe, took his book and left the office. As she rounded the far corner, she almost ran straight into Kevin who was equally surprised to see her.

"I'm so glad I didn't miss you," he said. He appeared to be much less nervous than he had been when she was with Joe. Before she could respond, he added, "Do you want to have that cup of coffee or something with me some time?" She nodded without saying anything.

"Great." He reached into the pocket of his shirt and handed her a business card. "Here's my number. Call me." With that, he turned around the corner and was gone.

*❦    ❦    ❦*

When Veronique came in from the gym the next day, she had two calls waiting for her. The first was from Kevin, with Bob Dylan music blasting in the background, saying he'd gotten her number from Joe, asking her if she wanted to go to dinner that Friday night, and telling her he would call back at seven. The other was from Delphina.

"Ronnie, it's Del. Are you there? Pick up if you're there." Her sister's voice was shaking. "I guess not. Um…Listen, Lee's been in an…accident. No. Not an accident. She and her girlfriend were beaten up really badly last night. The police are calling it a bias crime. I'm going to the hospital now. It was four guys. Goddam cops said…Never mind. I wanted you to know. I'll call you later." Click.

Forlorn, Veronique sat at the edge of her bed. She picked up the phone to call Jonathan, and stopped. He was out of town. Then she thought of calling Marc. No, she would not be able to reach him either. She thought of Luca, and her eyes filled with tears. Two hours later, she was roused from her reverie by the telephone.

"It's Kevin. I know I said I'd call back at seven, but if you're not doing anything, maybe we could meet for drinks and dinner, say four?"

"I could never get ready by four. How about five?"

"Same place?"

"Same place. See you then." Veronique hung up slowly. She felt raw inside and outside. But at five o'clock she was sitting at the bar waiting for Kevin. She was watching two young men sitting across from her at the bar. They were obviously in love with each other, holding hands and kissing between sips of beer. She was musing about them when Kevin found her.

As he said hello, he followed her gaze, and seeing the two men, he snorted, but did not say anything.

Veronique decided to ignore his reaction, but instinctively she stopped herself from telling him what happened to Lee. She got off the bar stool and led him to the back, to the dining room. After they ordered, Veronique said, "So, Kevin, first time we met, you were working for the LIRR, next time I met you was in the Slope, and the third time was in Father Joe's office being told you're a priest. What's your story?"

Kevin lowered his head shyly as he took a sip of his beer. "I'm not a priest yet. And I appreciate you not saying why I was in the Slope to Joe."

"They're *anonymous* meetings. I'm not one to break that kind of rule."

Kevin looked across the table at her and nodded.

"So what is your story, Kevin McFee?"

"You really want to know?"

She nodded.

"Well, I've been alone most of my life. I was born in Canada. My mother—she was very sick for a long time, so I was left to my own devices a lot. I ran with a group of boys, a gang, I guess. They taught me how to fight. Mom's boyfriend, Jake—I guess he was my father, she never told me. When he was around, he didn't really know what to do with me. He was kind of rough, liked to hit me when he'd been drinking. But when he was sober, he liked to play the harmonica. We'd listen to Bob Dylan records, and he'd play along with his harmonica. I still listen to Dylan a lot, although I never got into playing the harmonica…My mother died when I was ten. I was left with the Jesuits, because Jake couldn't take care of me. So I grew up going to Jesuit schools, until I got put into St. Johns for stealing a car."

Veronique remembered his story about being raped by a priest. She hesitated, but could not stop herself from asking about it. "The story you told at the meeting, about that priest—How old were you?"

Kevin took a deep drink of his beer before answering.

"I was about eleven the first time. I had been there a couple of weeks. There were a few of them. The first one was Father Rex, then Father John, and after him Father Peter. At first, Rex would take me out, let me ride his Harley, treat me special. With him, it was okay, I guess. But he left, and the others were awful. They'd call us into their office for anything, whether we did it or not, and they'd 'punish' us. We never knew which of us it was going to be, or when. I was always afraid, but I kept thinking Jake was going to come back and get me. He never did."

Veronique nodded. "We had a Father Rex too." After a moment, she asked, "With all that shit happening to you with those priests, why would you ever want to become one?"

"A couple of reasons. First, there are really good priests, you know, like Joe. Second, I thought if I were a priest, I could maybe protect the kids who are in the position that I was in back then, and also maybe get the credibility to have justice done within the Church."

"That's pretty optimistic."

As soon as she said it, she realized how jaded her words sounded. She changed the subject quickly. "Come to think of it, the Father Rex at our church really liked giving the boys rides on his motorcycle."

Kevin sneered at his beer. "It sounds like the same guy. He was either on the altar wearing a Roman collar or on a motor cycle wearing a leather jacket. He wasn't a Jesuit—I don't think any of the priests at St. Johns were—How many priests named Rex could there be? I mean, it's not a common name like John or Paul." Kevin stared into his beer for a while. Then he said, "I love the Church, but you're right. I am conflicted about it. That's why I took a year's leave from the seminary to sort things out in my head. That's when you met me. Last year I was on leave working as a conductor. Right now, I'm back at the seminary, but I'm still trying to decide whether I want to be a priest."

"Well, what are the pros and cons?" Veronique was good at making lists.

"Pros are being able to study and teach. As a Jesuit, I'd also get to travel a lot. Cons are you never really get to have a family of your own. Pros are being able to combine your beliefs with your work. Lots of people don't get to do that. Many people have to separate their religion from their work."

He was silent for a minute. Then he continued, "Cons are sometimes the system works against people. But pros are that sometimes you can get people to see the error of their ways." He paused and looked at her. "Veronique, I know that you and the other women in the Slope embrace your lifestyle as good and true; but believe me, it's a living sin. I could read to you from Leviticus, from the decrees of the modern Church. It goes against all that's natural and good according to God."

"You've got to be kidding." Veronique was smoldering. Those were the first words that went from her brain to her mouth in any recognizable sequence. "You didn't invite me out tonight to preach to me against homosexuality, did you, Kevin?"

"No, of course not, Veronique. But since we're on the subject—"

"Good, because it's that type of crap that your church preaches that goes totally against that God of Love of yours. And I say yours, because it certainly isn't mine. It goes against the idea of following your conscience, not to mention your heart, to know what's right. That type of bullshit you're spouting is what gets people beat up by idiots who are hatefully crusading in the name of your God of Love. It's what got Lee almost killed last night. That's right. She was beat up really badly by people who think they have a license to kill, granted by your kind of preaching. You know, you're as responsible for her injuries as the people who did it, because people like you who preach hate from places of authority like the pulpit give bigots fuel for their prejudices."

"That's not true!" Kevin, shocked at the news, started to defend himself as Veronique took a breath, but she was not finished. She was not about to tell him that she was not a lesbian at this point.

"You know, homosexuality isn't what happened to you with those priests. Adults who have sex with kids are just on a power trip. You know that from Lee's groups. Those priests don't think they're gay. Ask them," she goaded him. "And, since you obviously don't have a clue, gay love is just like straight love, except that it's not acceptable by some bigoted institutions with a lot of money, like your church. But there's so much child abuse going on in that church of yours, it's no wonder that priests are against homosexuality. It's because of their guilt and ignorance—the guilt of what they allow in their institution, and the ignorance not to recognize it for what it really is." Veronique was so angry that she was spitting her words, which were so forceful that they had pushed Kevin back in his seat.

He got up, and his chair fell backwards. "That is not true," he yelled, shaking a finger in her face. "You're totally screwed up about that." He grabbed his coat. "You're wrong. You'll see," he said, over his shoulder as he left.

A few patrons in the dining area looked up curiously, but went back to eating as he left. The waiter appeared moments later with their food. "Everything all right here?"

"It is now that the idiot has left. I tell you what. There's a couple of guys at the bar, you know, the ones who are really in love?" The waiter nodded and smiled slightly. "See if they want this dinner along with a bottle of wine. This should cover it." The waiter tried not to act surprised as Veronique gave him a one-hundred dollar bill. Then she left the restaurant by the side door.

❧   ❧   ❧

The next afternoon, Veronique was in Kings Park visiting her parents and having dinner with Jonathan. She was on her way to the rectory to return Joe's book. As she came around the row of hedges, she almost ran headlong into Kevin.

"What are you doing here?" he stammered.

"This is my parish. I've gone here my whole life. You out here preaching more hate?"

They could both see Joe coming out of the rectory. As he drew closer, they stopped talking.

"Ronnie, Kevin, good to see you both," Joe said happily.

"Hi, Father Joe," Veronique said, trying to be casual. "I was just stopping by to return your book. Thanks. It was good. Jon's waiting for me, so I gotta go."

"Okay Ronnie. Say hi to your parents for me."

Joe turned to speak to Kevin, and Veronique glared at Kevin behind Joe's back before leaving.

Veronique had barely gotten into Jon's car when he said, "So are you really dating a priest?"

"God, that came out of nowhere. You can say it in the past tense. I dat*ed* him one time, yesterday. He's not really a priest. He's in the seminary, becoming a priest. He invited me out to preach to me about the error of my ways. You know, being a lesbian and all. I told him he was full of homophobic shit, basically, and he left. I paid for the uneaten dinner. Gave it to a couple at the bar. I just ran into him coming out of the rectory before I met you."

"I bet you were upset."

"He's an asshole. End of discussion." Jonathan laughed as Veronique continued. "He thinks I'm a lesbian, because he met me in the Slope. But that's a story for another time."

Jonathan nodded. "Marc's back in town for something, I don't know what. I was hoping to find out tonight, but I guess we'll have to wait. I wanted to surprise you, but he's not coming to dinner with us after all. He called to cancel as I was leaving."

"Damn. And why did he call you and not me?" Not waiting for an answer, she said, "Well, where will we eat?"

# CHAPTER 17

❀

Veronique stepped into the main lobby of the Huntington Towne House. Her father's office Christmas party had been held there for as long as she could remember. She had not attended any of the company functions for many years. Her brother, Marc, in a hurried telephone conversation, had asked her to attend this end-of-the-year holiday event, and she'd promised she would.

"Father asked me not to say anything, but please come so that we can talk after."

Since Marc rarely requested anything, Veronique did her best to comply. She took the circular staircase under the chandelier to the second floor where an attendant dressed in red and gold met her and directed her to the correct room.

"Adriatico's company Christmas party? Through those doors; then turn right."

Subtle Christmas music was playing as a well-dressed group sipped cocktails and ate hors d'oeuvres.

"Ronnie," Jonathan called to her from a corner near the door.

"Hi, Jon." She kissed him and nodded to the woman at his side.

After introductions were made, Jonathan's date moved toward the bar, and Jonathan grabbed Veronique's arm. "So, is Marc being as mysterious with you as he has been with the rest of us?"

"Yeah. He's not saying a thing. He said he wanted to talk after though."

"He said that to me too. And Del made me swear to call her the minute we knew what was up."

Their sister was never at company functions, and not even the lure of a mystery could convince her to attend this one.

Rocco Laurio sauntered over, his son Fortuno behind him. Now in his early twenties, Fortuno had all the greasy arrogance and the same cold eyes of his father. But Fortuno seemed to be more dangerous, because he was obviously smart.

"Hello, Rocco. Fortuno." Jon greeted them. Veronique nodded.

"Nice party. Same as always," Rocco's slurred, Brooklyn accent had not changed over the years. "I hear your father's about to make a big announcement about some promotions at the company," Rocco started importantly, seeming to imply that the announcement was going to be about him. "But we can't talk about that. How's your mother," he asked them.

As pleasantries were being exchanged between Jon and the Laurios, Veronique suddenly addressed Fortuno, "How's Renee?"

The young man, who had been surveying the room as his father was speaking, jumped, realizing that Veronique was addressing him.

He sighed in a false show of something between sadness and piety. "Oh, we don't talk about Renee anymore." Seeing Veronique's confused look, he said, "I guess you didn't know. About a month after your cousin's funeral, we had to check Renee into a rehab clinic. She was drinking, just like Mother used to. We found her passed out by the pool one night, and Dad really freaked. He said he didn't want to come home one night and find his daughter like he found Mother." Fortuno paused for a moment, his head bowed.

Veronique could not tell whether this was part of his act, or whether he was really feeling something.

"We sent Renee to the best clinic we could find in the state. She stayed there about a week. Then she left. We were never able to find her, and no one has heard from her since."

"She just disappeared?" Veronique was incredulous.

Rocco, who had been following the conversation, added in the same morose tone as his son, "I wake up every morning hoping to hear from my sweet girl, but it's been more than two years, and I'm beginning to lose hope."

Jonathan started to say something consoling, but something inside Veronique shook with rage, and she interrupted harshly, "Your sweet girl? Don't you mean your 'special' girl? I recall hearing you call her that once when I was hiding in a closet when you came to our house for a pool party. You made her change her clothes in the room where Mom hid Del's graduation presents. But that's not all you made her do."

Rocco Laurio's eyes slanted as Fortuno reacted. "What the hell are you insinuating?" The younger Laurio started to move closer to her threateningly.

Rocco Laurio put an arm on his shoulder, pulling him back. "Don't bother with her," he advised his son. "When her sister graduated from college, she couldn't've been more than seven. Kids don't know anything. And this one, she always thought she was so smart, better than us. From the time she was real little, wearing those short skirts at her father's office, she was always trying to cause trouble." To Veronique, he added, looking critically at her dress, "Haven't changed one bit, I see. Still trying to cause trouble. Of course, Renee's not here, so it's just the memory of one seven-year-old brat talking. F'get about it, Fortuno. We can find better company at this party." He turned his back on Veronique and Jonathan, signaling Fortuno to follow.

"Jeez, Ronnie. Nothing like causing a scene."

"That wasn't really a scene."

Jonathan rolled his eyes at her as seating for dinner was announced.

Jon and his date were seated with Veronique, four of their cousins and their dates. Ellie and Otto were seated at another table with the rest of their clan. Irene and Pino were seated on the dais with Marc, Joe, and some company board members. Rocco and Fortuno sat at the next table with members of the press and the company's public relations department.

Before the serving started, Joe stepped to the podium next to the dais to offer an invocation. After champagne was poured, Pino Adriatico stepped to the microphone.

"As some of you may know, the announcement of some changes in personnel have been planned to coincide with this holiday party. This has been a very good year for the company, but we will also be losing one of the key men who has been with me from the beginning. Howard Rotundo, my executive vice president and close associate, will be retiring, effective December 31. Howard has done a fine job for the last twenty-five years, and the company would not be where it is today had he not been a part of it. A toast to Howard: may his life in retirement be long and happy." Pino lifted his champagne glass to his colleague. Everyone in the room did the same. This was followed by a round of warm and enthusiastic applause led by Pino, directed to his vice president. Howard waived his acknowledgement from his seat on the dais. Then Pino continued. "In Howard's place, my Vice President in charge of public relations, Victor Napoli, will become Executive Vice President." Another round of applause, this time more polite and subdued. This promotion had, apparently, been expected.

Again, Pino continued. "The third and last announcement that I will be making this evening—I know we're all getting hungry—is for the person who will take Victor's place as Vice President of Public relations. Many people have spoken to me about new ideas for directions that the company could take in public relations. The best ones have come from the person who will be my new PR Veep. This young man has shown creativity and originality that has impressed me. Now, while some may think I am biased, my own family can tell you that, if anything, I have higher standards for those I am closest to."

As her father was talking, Veronique was wondering what her father was talking about. She looked over at Jon, who looked back with more understanding.

"...so, without further ado, I present to you Adriatico's new Vice President of Public Relations, Marc Adriatico."

She heard a funny croaking noise from Rocco Laurio's table. Rocco looked as though he had choked on his martini olive. As for Veronique, she was truly surprised by the announcement. "I never knew he wanted that," she murmured to Jonathan.

Her brother looked at her and said, "Neither did I, but I guess we'll get the whole story later." He stood and raised his glass to his brother while his cousins and Veronique applauded. Others joined in, although clearly the room had a mixed response to the announcement. Marc smiled shyly from the dais.

"That's all I've got to announce this evening. Thank you all for your work this year. And now, let's enjoy the meal." Pino returned to his seat next to Irene as the music resumed.

Five minutes later, as Veronique was en route to the ladies' room, she saw Rocco Laurio at the coat check with Fortuno. They did not see her, but she could hear Rocco fuming.

"First, that little bitch and her insinuations, and now this. Goddamn nepotism, I tell you. I should'a had that job. I've been with the company since it started. I tell you, there's gonna be hell to pay. No way is that kid prepared for the job. Let's go."

Rocco Laurio stormed out with Fortuno five paces behind.

꧁ ꧁ ꧁

Later Veronique and her brothers were sitting at Jonathan's kitchen table in the guest house. She told them what she had seen and heard Rocco say.

Marc nodded. "Yeah, well, he's not the only one who feels that way. Luckily, I've got the Master's degree to back me up. Otherwise, it would be an even clearer case of nepotism."

"I never knew you wanted to work at the company," Jonathan said wonderingly.

"I never did. Then one day, last time I was here, I stopped in to say hi to Father at the office. He started talking about the company logo and its image. Well, one thing led to another. I gave him some ideas, and he wanted to see more. I sent him a computer slide presentation, and the rest, as they say, is history."

"But I thought you loved Arizona." Veronique was as incredulous as Jonathan.

"I did. Then Sandy broke up with me." He paused. "Arizona didn't look so good after that." He got lost in a reverie for a few moments. Veronique looked at Jonathan who raised an eyebrow. Then Marc continued in a brisk tone, "So this is the next step. Got out of that part of the country. It's really good to be back here. I never really fit in out there. Couldn't get used to not having winter. So now it's almost like I've got a whole new identity, new job, and I don't have to be anywhere near anything that reminds me of Sandy."

"Marc, I'm sorry." Veronique put a hand on his arm.

Marc nodded, tears in his eyes.

The three sat in silence for a while. Then Marc suggested a game of Scrabble. His siblings agreed heartily. Veronique got three bottles of Heineken from the refrigerator. As Jonathan went to get the game, there was a knock at the door.

"Who the hell's coming over at eleven-thirty at night?" Jonathan wondered aloud, putting the Scrabble game on the table and going to the door. "It's not Mom. She never knocks. And Father never comes over," he added, laughing as he opened the door.

"I'm looking for Veronique," Marc and Veronique heard from the kitchen.

"Shit. It's Kevin," Veronique said angrily, recognizing his voice. "I wonder what the hell he wants."

"Ronnie," Jonathan called, "Someone's here to see you."

Veronique stamped her way to the door.

"What do you want, at eleven-thirty at night?"

Kevin looked from Veronique's angry face to Jonathan's implacable one. Then Marc appeared behind his sister, also waiting for an answer.

"I'm sorry to come over so late. Joe just got back to the rectory. He said that you had been at your father's Christmas party. He said you were staying here, so I thought I'd come over and apologize. I shouldn't have stormed out of the restaurant, and I'm sorry to have judged you like that." He paused, looking uncertainly from one Adriatico face to the next. "I was hoping you'd let me take you to lunch and make it up to you, tomorrow maybe?"

"Why should I ever want to break bread with you again?" Veronique spat disgustedly.

"There's absolutely no reason that I can think of," Kevin admitted "except out of the goodness of your heart. I'd like to show you that I'm really sincere in my apology. You're right. I do preach about something that I know nothing about. I'm sorry about that. I'd like to know your side."

Something about his sincerity had Veronique accepting his invitation for lunch.

"I'll be in Manhattan at noon. I have to be at work by five. So, okay, lunch it is. Where?"

"How about we meet at the Plaza Hotel at one? We can either eat there or go somewhere else."

"Okay, but this time you're buying," Veronique told him.

"Happily," he agreed, and then he nodded to all of them. "Well, sorry to disturb you all. Goodnight."

"Who was *that*?" Marc wanted to know.

"Another one-date wonder? Jonathan teased.

"Oh, *gawd*." Veronique started, and she told them all about Kevin over the game of Scrabble.

❦ ❦ ❦

Veronique sat in the lobby of the Plaza Hotel watching the people enter and leave the restaurant, waiting for Kevin. She was a few minutes early, so she sat down by the entrance. Kevin came in soon after and sat down beside her.

"Listen, Veronique. We really got off to a bad start. I wanted to impress you, and instead I really put my foot in my mouth. Can you forgive me?"

"It depends on what happens next," Veronique told him truthfully. "I'm willing to suspend judgment, but that's all I can really promise."

"Good enough." He sounded satisfied. "Shall we eat?" He looked at her.

She nodded, but then she was aware that something beyond her had caught his attention.

"Isn't that Joe?" Kevin asked her as she turned to look. "It looks like he's with that woman."

Sure enough, Joe was walking out of the restaurant with his arm around Irene. They were laughing and talking, their heads close.

Veronique opened her mouth to say, "That's my mother," but she thought better of it.

"Should we go over and say hello?" Kevin wondered.

"No. Let's just go in and eat."

Neither one of them moved. Irene and Joe moved through the lobby, oblivious that they were being observed. They crossed the plaza arm in arm and then they crossed Fifth Avenue hand in hand. As if in a spell, Veronique kept watching until they disappeared into FAO Schwartz.

"Pretty strange, huh? Joe didn't say he was coming into the city today," Kevin mused.

"You didn't tell him where you were going either, I suppose?"

"No. Come to think of it, I didn't. "I wonder who that woman is. I didn't really get a good look at her. Did you?"

Veronique just shrugged. "They're adults. Forget about it. Let's go eat."

Kevin followed her into the restaurant, looking back once or twice at the store where his mentor had disappeared.

Throughout lunch, Veronique was preoccupied. Kevin kept returning to what they had seen.

"Do you think I should talk to him about it?"

"Has he talked to you?"

"Obviously not. You know, it doesn't look good."

With that Veronique lost her patience.

"You ask me out to lunch to prove that you want to stop preaching about what you know nothing about. Here's a different example. You don't know what he's doing, but it seems like you're assuming he's doing something wrong. Ask him or don't ask him, who cares? It's the same with me. I'm living my life. If I wanted your opinion about it, I'd have asked. Since I didn't, and since Joe didn't, you're just meddling."

Veronique was speaking to herself as much as to Kevin. He sat back and let her words sink in.

"I guess you're right. They just seemed so, well, *intimate*."

Veronique rolled her eyes as he continued on his train of thought, seemingly oblivious to what she had just said. In fact, Irene and Joe had seemed intimate to Veronique too, but she was not in the mood to confide in Kevin. He seemed to pick up on that finally, and he changed the subject. "Look, I'm really here to get to know you better, and all I'm doing is going on about Joe and that woman. Last time we met, I told you all about me. Now it's your turn."

"Well, my father owns a company, and he works all the time. We don't really get along. My two brothers, who you saw last night, and I are very close. My mother's a sculptor and potter. That fog vase you were looking at in Joe's office, she did that." Kevin looked impressed. "My sister was a teacher. Now she's a writer who does word processing to support herself. She lives in Park Slope. She's a lesbian. She's always done the best things with me. She took me to a Native American day once. I'll never forget it. I saw an old guy at the fire ceremony that no one else saw. My sister was always doing cool things, and she always had the coolest stuff. I graduated high school early and went to live with her. I wanted to be cool like her, to get out of my father's house and to find myself. The day I met you on the LIRR was the day I was moving to Del's apartment. Later, I met Lee. She and I had a wonderful relationship."

"Had?"

"We broke up. She was my sister's ex. My cousin Luca was killed in a car crash." She paused a moment, then continued. "He and I were very close. After that, everything fell apart. I guess I felt like I was partly responsible for his death. The night he died, we had been drinking on the beach. He got upset and left. Then he had the accident. That was the last time I saw him." Her eyes welled. Kevin listened sympathetically.

"You must have loved him very much."

"Too much maybe. I don't know." Something clicked for a second in Veronique's mind, but then it vaporized.

Kevin, seeing that the conversation had taken a downturn, changed the subject again. He talked about sports, movies, places he had been and musicians, especially his favorite Bob Dylan.

"You like Dylan? That's right. I remember you said that last time. Isn't that sort of retro or something?" Veronique wanted to know.

"No, he's always coming up with new stuff. As a kid, I'd concentrate on the harmonica, but now I listen to the words, which are pretty good."

"Yeah, I guess, if you can understand him."

They managed to keep the conversation going through lunch. When they finished eating, Kevin suggested skating at the Wollman Rink. Veronique agreed, and for an hour and a half they had a lot of fun. When four-thirty came around, Veronique was genuinely sorry to have to go.

"Listen, I've had a great time. Thanks. You're not so bad, really."

"Yeah. When I can shut up and listen, I guess I'm okay. Does that mean you'd do this again sometime?"

"What, go out with you?"

"Yeah, to the movies or something."

"Okay."

"Saturday?"

"No. Actually, I'm working Saturday. How about next Monday?"

Kevin agreed happily, kissing her chastely on the cheek before she got into a taxi on Fifth Avenue.

In the cab on the way to work, Veronique thought again about Joe and her mother. Then the voice of the old man at the fire ceremony rang in her ear: "Who's your father? Who are all your relations?" If Joe was her father...

"Nah," she said aloud, shaking her head as the cab pulled up at her office.

# CHAPTER 18

Beep. The answering machine clicked as Veronique checked her messages. She had just gotten in from working a double shift.

"Veronique, it's Kevin. I'm sorry to call you so soon, but I was wondering if you wanted to have breakfast tomorrow morning? I know you work 'til the wee hours, but leave me a message if you want to, any time. It doesn't matter how late. I'll turn off the volume so you won't wake me. I'll be in the city tomorrow, so I can meet you any time before one."

Veronique smiled. She picked up the phone, looked up his number on the pad next to it and dialed.

"Okay, Kevin. I'll see you at eleven-thirty. I'll be at the Starbucks at my corner. We can figure out where to go from there." She laughed. "I'll wait for fifteen minutes. After that, you're outta luck."

Exhausted, Veronique fell into bed, barely managing to take a shower. She slept fitfully, dreaming of Luca and Kevin who kept bringing her to her mother who was holding hands with Joe, who kept turning into the old man by the fire.

The next morning at eleven-thirty, Veronique stepped into the popular coffee bar at her corner. Kevin was already there, waiting at a table by the window. Two steaming cappuccinos sat on the table in front of him.

"Hi there." Veronique was in a friendly mood. She nodded at the two cups on the table. "You with someone?"

Kevin laughed delightedly. "Nope. Just waiting for an angel. I am going to be a priest, you know."

The way he was acting in that moment, Veronique had her doubts, but she was not going to voice them right then. "So, I'm here," she told him angelically. You can either let that coffee get cold waiting for a winged one, or you can let me have it."

He moved over to make room for her. "Okay, I'll settle for you."

"Just couldn't wait until Monday?"

"No. I really couldn't. I had such a great time yesterday. I felt like we really connected. I haven't been able to talk to someone like that, not even Joe, since I don't remember when. Maybe not ever. And I really need to talk to someone. I hope you don't mind."

Veronique shrugged and sipped her cappuccino. "Not so far. If I get pissed off, I'll let you know."

Kevin laughed aloud. "I know you will. It's a little frightening. But what I really need is honesty, so I'll take my chances, because I might piss you off." He took a long sip of coffee before starting. "Whenever I need to think, I go down to Sunken Meadow and walk east. When I get an idea about what to do, I turn around and walk back thinking about my plan. Yesterday, I walked until it got too dark to see, and didn't figure anything out. In the dark, I kept walking into the water, so I turned around and stumbled back. The thing is, I keep wanting to talk to Joe, but then I chicken out. That's why I'm here talking to you. It's like you're the only other person I can turn to. Since I'm not backing down here, I guess talking to you is the right thing to do."

"Okay, I'm not pissed off. Yet. Maybe we didn't see anything. Maybe they were just friends, you know, close, like brother and sister."

"You and your brother ever cross the street arm in arm?"

"Sometimes."

"Hand in hand?"

"I used to, a lot."

"This year?"

"Um, well, no. Probably not for the last ten or twelve years," she admitted slowly.

Kevin sat back and nodded, satisfied. "So I need to ask him about it, but what do I say?"

"How about, 'Uh, Joe, I saw you in the city walking real close to one of your parishioners. What gives?'"

"How do you know she was a parishioner?"

Veronique started, guiltily. "I recognized her, I think. I didn't get a close look, so I don't want to say anything else. It's all insinuation." She changed the subject. "When you start going to Joe, what stops you?"

"I'm not sure. I think I feel stupid, or meddling or something."

"Well, as I told you yesterday, I think you are meddling. On the other hand, if it were my brother, I'd be able to ask him. What's your problem?"

"He's not my brother."

"He may as well be. You two are pretty close."

"Not that close. Besides, if he is, er, doing something...improper—"

"There you go, insinuating that he's doing something wrong with no proof." Now Veronique was getting angry. "If you're assuming he's guilty without even asking him, you're no better than he would be—IF, and it's only an if—*if* he's doing something wrong."

Kevin was sitting back in his chair again, the way he did whenever Veronique started an angry tirade. "Okay. Now you're mad."

"Yeah. I always get mad if someone is presumed guilty and has to prove his innocence. Some friend you are. Just shut up about it, and ask him already. If you don't, it just shows that you've declared him guilty without a trial. Maybe that's the way they do it in the Church, but it isn't the American way, in theory at least."

"Okay, okay. Uncle. I give up. I'm just saying I don't know how to start."

"Right. And what I'm saying is you not knowing where to start shows that you believe he's guilty of something. You have no problems asking him about his lesson plan for the next class, do you?"

Kevin shook his head. "Veronique, you don't understand. This is very different from a lesson plan. I mean, if he's...*with* that woman—"

Veronique rolled her eyes.

"—he's broken his vows."

"He was obviously *with* her." She mimicked his phrasing. "They were together. Since when did you appoint yourself his confessor?" She did not wait for an answer. "Since you decided he had something to confess, right? That's how they do it in that church of yours. Every little transgression, ten Hail Marys. You're giving him ten Hail Marys without him even going to confession. Maybe it's because his imagined sin is one you want to commit. But don't worry, you can do it. When you do, all you have to do is confess it, Mama Church will not only absolve you, she'll take you back into her fold as if nothing ever happened. That's the problem with you baby priests. You've never had to take responsibility for yourselves." She got up. "You know something,

Kevin? I'm not the one you should be talking to about this. Go talk to those boys at the synagogue."

"Seminary." Kevin managed to blurt out.

She ignored him. "What do you know about anything like that anyway? You've spent your whole life being taken care of by the Church."

Kevin looked like he was about to throw up. For a minute, Veronique felt sorry for him. For about a second, really. He looked like he had shrunk from a full-grown man to a ten-year-old with a goatee. Then he got up without saying a word and left the café.

Veronique sat down and finished the cappuccino. She left ten minutes later. As she rounded the corner near her building, Kevin stepped from the side of the building and grabbed her arm.

She shook him off. "Listen, Buddy. Nobody walks out on me and then tries to grab me."

He let her go instantly. "The things you were saying about the Church, you were way out of line. Maybe I'm jumping to conclusions about Joe, but you're wrong about what you said. Just because I may be judging Joe doesn't mean the Church is the way you said.

"Oh, bullshit. You got mad about me saying that you priests never take responsibility for yourselves. Oh, yeah," she added, bringing her face close enough to his that he could feel her breath on his lips. "And you got mad when I said you wanted to commit the sin of adultery, cheating on the church."

He closed his eyes, but did not pull away from her. She got closer and whispered, "I'm right, aren't I?"

He let out a deep breath, still not moving away. "I—" He put his hands on her waist, he seemed to be trying to decide whether to pull her close or push her away.

"Come on, Kevin," Veronique breathed in her most seductive voice. "I know you really like me, don't you?" She felt one of his hands stray tentatively higher. Feeling seductive and sadistic, she let the index finger of her right hand play around his ear while she hooked the index finger of her left into his belt and pulled him closer to her. "I know what you've been missing. Want me to show you?"

"NO." He pushed her away, pulled his coat around him and ran down the street.

Veronique stood and watched him look back as he turned the corner. Then she walked slowly into the foyer of her building, both amused and chagrined. For all his judgmental attitudes, there was something attractive about Kevin.

"And it's not just that he's a virgin," she said aloud as she closed the door to her apartment behind her.

🍁    🍁    🍁

The next morning at ten, Veronique's phone was ringing. Usually she did not answer so early, but she had not slept well and was awake.

It was Kevin. He sounded hung over. With none of his usual formalities, he started, "You know I'm going to be a priest. Why do you keep seducing me?"

"Why should I even talk to you? You were so rude, walking out on me. Twice. And now you're accusing me? Let me remind you that you were the one whose hands kept moving up my shirt. But that just proves my point about you priests never taking responsibility for your actions. Just go talk to your jerkoff boyfriends in that synagogue that you live in."

"Seminary."

"Whatever." She slammed down the phone.

It started ringing again almost immediately. "Don't hang up. I need to talk to you." His voice was contrite.

"Why?"

"I need to talk to you about what happened. I didn't mean for it to. I just really needed to talk to you about Joe. And I wanted to see you again. But I didn't think..." His voice trailed off.

"So you didn't plan to be turned on by me, and now you want to talk to me about it?" The truth was, Veronique had been turned on too. She hadn't felt like that since she had been with Luca.

"S-something like that. But where can we meet?"

"You mean, where can we meet that nothing will happen?"

There was a long pause at the other end of the line. "I guess."

She was feeling mean and reckless. "You'll be safe if we meet in the Church."

He did not hear her inflection. "That'll be okay, I guess. Yeah. That'll be good. St. Joseph's Church, tomorrow?"

"We shouldn't do it when there's a mass going on or anything," she led him in the thought process.

"You're right. Well, there's the eight o'clock mass. Then the women come for about half an hour and clean up the altar. After that, it's closed until confessions at four."

"Perfect. See you at ten-thirty."

# CHAPTER 19

❀

During the week, the side door to the Church was the only one left open. Veronique had rented a car to drive out to Long Island to meet Kevin that morning. She entered by the heavy wooden door, and locked it behind her.

The heavy smell of wood, incense and votive candles greeted her. She went from the vestibule to the main hall of the Church. The empty wooden pews stood in two silent soldier-like rows. Other than getting a new roof and air conditioning, the Church had not changed much since she was a child. She did not see Kevin at the altar or among the pews, so she went back to the inner vestibule where the priests dressed for mass.

Yellow light from a small stained glass window streamed on a closet of white vestments. Not seeing Kevin there, she walked across the Church in front of the altar to a small room on the other side.

"Veronique," Kevin's voice came from behind her. He was dressed in black, except for the white Roman collar at his neck.

"Hi." She turned half way to greet him, and then continued across in front of the altar to the little room on the other side. Let's talk in here where we won't be disturbed." Ignoring his half-hearted protests, she walked into the room. He followed her. The room was small but comfortable. Two leather upholstered chairs faced each other along the far wall. A long bench had been placed between them under a stained glass window.

Veronique sat on the bench and motioned Kevin to sit next to her. He hesitated, but then came to stand before her.

Veronique felt a rush. "So," she started, "you want to talk?"

"I need to talk, and right now I feel like you're the only one I can talk to. I know we haven't spent that much time together, but still, I feel that way. When

I went home yesterday, I thought of everyone at the seminary, and I couldn't go to any of them. I kept coming back to you in my mind."

"I guess it would be kind of hard to explain, unless you'd been there."

"Yes, it would."

"But you know, Kevin," she started in an authoritative voice, patting the bench next to her, "If you can't talk about it, it will always have some power over you."

He nodded, sitting down beside her tentatively.

"Okay. I was there. You were there. We lived through the actual event. Now, use words to just explain to me your version of what happened."

He nodded.

"I was so mad about what you were saying about the Church that all I could think to do was walk out. But then, right away, I wanted to finish our conversation, you know, about Joe and everything."

Veronique raised an eyebrow in surprise. She had been talking about seeing Joe and her mother. She decided to follow his train of thought. "Is that all?"

"Not really. I wanted you to see that something was happening, and I wanted your help to stop it." Now, she was totally lost. Her confusion showed on her face. "No, not about Joe," he answered her unspoken question. "About me. You see, I'm going to be a priest, I've taken vows, and I'm going to take more vows. So feeling like I do, like I'm starting to, about you…is…a problem."

"You really shouldn't dive into one thing until you've explored all your options."

"That's not true. I know that I want to be a priest. It's all I can remember ever wanting. For me, there are no other options."

It was then that a part of her she did not know existed took over her actions. She took his hand in hers, fully cognizant of the effect, but also liking the feeling of him. "It must be hard, difficult, I mean, to be so set on one course."

He turned toward her earnestly. "No, it's not at all. It's wonderful. I have a plan. It's all set."

She moved closer to him, putting his hand on her knee in the process. She kept her hand on his. "So what's the problem?"

"You're the problem," he started, trying to pull his hand away.

She moved it a few inches up her inner thigh.

"You mean how you feel about me is the problem, don't you?"

"You're going to say I'm not taking responsibility again." He stopped struggling, his hand still on her leg.

"Are you?" She was surprised at how aware of his hand she was.

"I'm here talking to you. You seem to know exactly how I'm feeling, and I have no idea how you feel."

"I have no idea if I can trust you with how I feel," Veronique parried, "You could just slam me with it. You know, use it against me."

"Like you haven't done that with me, even though I haven't exactly told you how I'm feeling."

"Do you want to?"

Reluctantly, he pulled his hand away. "I'm not sure what I'm feeling."

"Well, your ambivalence shows me that you're not a one-sided person."

He turned and looked her straight in the eye. "You really mean that?"

Abandoning any thought of consequences, she pulled him to her and kissed him deeply. His frozen shock melted slowly into a willingly returned kiss. He seemed to lose himself in it.

When he started to hesitate, she led his hand up under her shirt, opening her bra so that his palm grazed her nipple, which hardened at his touch. Involuntarily, she moaned softly. She had not realized how much she was feeling.

"N-not here," he started to protest, but his words were muffled by her kisses. She pulled up his shirt, and her manicured fingers found his nipple. It had the desired effect. He kissed her more demandingly, and she could feel his hardness as she put her leg in his crotch and urged him to lie down on the bench.

When she began to loosen his belt, he started to protest. Kissing him, she brought one of his hands up to her panties. With her other hand, she undid his pants, feeling herself getting aroused by his fingers and the sight of his erection. With her lips never leaving his mouth, she hiked up her skirt and removed her own under garment. Then she straddled him. He strained upward to meet her, and she hesitated, one finger on his lips.

"Slowly, now," she coached him. "Control yourself." He moaned, but with a concentrated effort he complied. She sat back on her heels, knees on either side of his thighs, letting him look at her as she massaged him.

He seemed to become a different person, wild and on fire. Finally he begged her through clenched teeth, "Pleeeease, now."

Straddling him, she slowly let herself down on him, moving up slightly and then down again, taking him in. They started rocking together on the old wooden bench, and he came quickly, forcefully, and she helped herself to come right after him. He held her tightly to him and managed to turn her over. Still straddling him, she was delightedly surprised to find that he had remained inside of her. He started moving again, this time more purposefully. He came again, stroking her hair and whispering her name in her ear.

She did not come a second time, but enjoyed the feeling of him inside her, fully at first and then slowly waning, retreating. He lay on top of her for a few moments, spent. Then, he looked up and saw the crucified Jesus behind the altar, head turned, looking straight down at him. Suddenly he seemed to remember where they were.

"Oh...My...God. Ohmygod. What did we just do? Quick. Help me clean up. We can't do this here."

"We just did," Veronique pointed out, calmly, watching him try to put himself back together and clean up the evidence of their activity in the tiny room at the same time.

"What if someone comes in and finds us?"

"It'll save you from going to confession."

"This is not funny."

"It was good for me too," she said, laconically, straightening her clothes.

"I can't believe this. I can't believe this."

"I guess it was good for you." She paused. Then, unable to resist, she asked, "You do this often?"

He was still running around, not paying any attention to her, trying to put the room back the way they had found it. "What if the altar ladies come back?"

"I locked the door."

"You what?"

"Locked the door."

"Why would you do something like that?"

"You have nothing else to say to me?"

"About what?"

Veronique lost her patience. "About what just happened here, you idiot. Something real and I thought, very special just happened. Don't you have anything to say to me about it?"

"I can't believe you locked the door."

Veronique stood at the threshold of the room, getting ready to leave. He did not notice. She turned back to look at him.

"Well, you wanted to talk about a lot of personal things. I didn't think you wanted anyone to overhear." She started to leave, turning back only to fling one parting thought in his direction. "Besides, I thought you wouldn't want us to be disturbed while we were talking about Joe's infidelities."

# CHAPTER 20

"...meanwhile, two more young men have come forward to accuse Roman Catholic priests of physically and sexually abusing them while they were in Church-run diocesan schools. The Church has no comment. The time is now eleven-fifteen. In sports..." Veronique's alarm clock radio went off, but she was already up, sipping coffee at the pass-through to her kitchen. She turned it off. Kevin had been involved in the initial wave of accusations, but he had been quieted by intense pressure and questioning.

She did not want to think about Kevin. She put on a Madonna CD and tried, as she had been doing all week, to think about something other than Kevin.

When she left the Church that day, she got back in the rented car and drove straight back to the City. She threw herself into her work that night to take her mind off what had transpired in the Church and how badly Kevin had made her feel in the aftermath. When her agency called and asked her if she wanted to work an extra shift for the next few nights, she quickly agreed. The only reason she kept her answering machine on was because she needed it for work.

While she was in the shower, the phone rang. She shrugged, not willing to make the effort to answer it. A hang up. A few minutes later, while she was drying her hair, the phone rang again. This time the caller left a message.

"Veronique," Kevin's slurred voice boomed over the machine. "I know you're there. Pick up the phone." Pause. "Pick up the phone." Pause again. "Fine. Just listen then. You've made me make a huge mistake. I don't know what kind of a game you think you were playing in the Church, but I've confessed. I am set to take whatever punishment might be decided for me. I'll know by tomorrow." His voice paused. She heard the sound of him drinking something. Then he continued, more softly and more slurred, "I thought you were my friend, Veronique. I can't believe you seduced me like that, in my own church. I feel so ashamed about it. I can barely look anyone here in the eye." His voice trembled. She thought he sounded like he was crying. "I hear them laughing and whispering behind my back. How could you have done this to me? How could you?" His voice broke, and he slammed the phone around a few times. It sounded like he was having a hard time hanging up on his end.

"Great, now he's drinking," Veronique said to her cats as she finished listening to the message. "Another one." She walked into her bedroom still talking to herself. "Blaming me for seducing him, with no consent on his part, of course, and then drinking to forget it. Just great."

Her eyes fell on a picture of her siblings and cousins at a cousins meeting. It had been a couple of years before Luca had died. She picked it up. She and Luca were in the middle. She sitting on his lap, his arms around her waist. He was smiling, looking at her as she looked at the camera. She looked at her two brothers—Marc as fair and blonde as their father, with the same ocean blue eyes; Jonathan, curly haired and dark like their mother, with hazel eyes. Delfina, in the middle, behind Luca, had the same straight dark hair as Veronique and her mother, but Delfina was the only one of the siblings with their mother's almost-black eyes. Veronique noticed that all her siblings had their father's strong nose, chin and cheekbones. She looked at her own features. Her chin was much more rounded than her siblings'. All her other facial features were clearly her mother's. Veronique's eyes were a different shade of blue than Pino or Marc. And unlike anyone else in her family, when she smiled, she had dimples high up on her cheeks, under the corners of her eyes.

She thought of seeing her mother and Joe hand in hand. She smiled wryly. The incident in the Church had certainly made Kevin forget about Joe's hand-holding. Then she sobered as her attention returned to the picture. If Joe were her father...Her mind flashed to Luca, Luca's preoccupation with kissing her being a sin...

She shook her head, unable to complete the thought, and erased the answering machine message from Kevin without listening to it again.

That night when she came home, Kevin was waiting outside her building for her. He was unshaven and drunk.

"Veronique, I think we need to speak—Ha, that rhymes." He was weaving as he tried to stand in front of her.

"Listen, Kevin. I'll only say this once. If you want to speak with me, you'd better be sober. Don't ever come around here drunk again." He belched loudly.

"Ugh, that's disgusting. Get out of here. When you're sober, I'll talk to you." She shoved him aside and tried to proceed to the door.

He stopped her. "Not good enough to talk to now, am I? What is it? Once you've made the conquest, I'm out like the trash?"

"No, you asshole. Get sober and we'll talk. Now, if you don't leave, I'm calling the cops."

"Just wanted to fuck me in church, did you? Wanted to spoil me. Why? To teach me a lesson or something? Well, I tell you, I've already been spoiled, raped by those priests. There's no part of me left for you." Something in his tone made Veronique stop.

"Come on, let's get you a cup of coffee." She turned him around and led him to an all-night diner a block away. As they were sitting there, he started coming to himself a bit more.

"Things have been rough with those priests being accused?" she asked sympathetically.

He nodded, his elbow on the table and his forehead being supported by his palm. "I never meant for it to get into the papers and stuff. I just wanted the Church to see what was going on. In the papers, it's like they've all been found guilty already. I didn't want that. I just wanted the Church to make it right for other kids in the future."

"You were trying to do the right thing," Veronique reinforced him.

"I really was. And with everything that's happening now, I'm not sure I can become a priest. There's too much wrong."

"But Kevin, you told me that being a priest is all you ever wanted."

"As in, what else could I do with my life?"

"Of course not. You know that's not what I was saying at all. Don't start that bull, or I'll get up and walk out of here," she warned. She was tired and in no mood to have to defend herself.

"All right. Sorry. I sometimes feel that way. I've never thought of being anything other than a priest. But I guess I could always continue with my education and teach."

"That's more like it," Veronique said, approvingly. She yawned. "Listen, Kevin. It's been a really long day for me. I can put you in a cab and send you to Penn Station, or you could sleep on my couch. Your choice."

Kevin had nodded off at the table. That made the decision for Veronique. She paid the bill and prodded him awake. Then she led him back to her apartment and let him collapse on her couch. Then she took a shower and went to bed.

When she awoke in the morning, Kevin was emerging from the bathroom, a towel wrapped around his waist. At the sight of her, he stopped and retreated, unable to hide his immediate physical response to seeing her in a long t-shirt and short shorts. She decided to ignore him and turned to the kitchen.

"Coffee?"

"Um, yes," his muffled voice came from behind the bathroom door.

She brought two cups of steaming coffee into the living room and turned on the television to watch the morning news. A few minutes later, he came out of the bathroom fully dressed and sat down next to her.

Somewhere between the rush hour traffic report and a Jeep commercial, they found themselves in each others' arms once again. Surprised, but enjoying herself, Veronique decided to follow his cues and see what would happen. Kevin, a very good kisser, showed that he had not used all of his best moves in the Church. His hand started exploring under her shirt, seemingly of its own accord. Then, he moved down to her shorts. Getting aroused, Veronique finally decided to unzip his pants. He did not seem to notice until she started massaging him. Then, suddenly, he pulled away from her and started yelling.

"There you go again, trying to seduce me a second time. What is it with you?"

"You have got to be kidding. Here you are with your tongue in my mouth and your hand in my pants, and you're saying I'm seducing you? What is your problem?"

"Veronique, kissing is one thing. That's okay. Harmless petting is also okay. But when you go for the real private parts, that crosses a line that moves into sin."

"Oh, so you can start by sucking on my boobs and then put your hand in my pants, and that's okay. But I cross some invisible line when I touch your—"

"Oh my God. It's Rex." Kevin was staring, transfixed, at the television. The morning news was covering the priest sex abuse story. Sure enough, behind the priest who was making a statement for the Church, stood Father Rex. Kevin sat down hard on the sofa. Rex looked older, but there was no mistaking him. Veronique turned up the volume.

"...a spokesman for the diocese has pointed out that the last three accusations have come from young men who are of questionable repute. Two of the three are drug users, and the most recent accusations have come from a man who has himself admitted to sexually abusing boys in his care while in the school."

"These allegations are unfortunate," the other priest said to the camera. "All these young men are obviously in need of help, and we pray for them. However, we are not willing to comply when an admitted sex criminal tries to blame us for his deviant behavior. Thank you. That's all."

Father Rex escorted the spokesman away from the camera, turning back to say, "No more questions." The camera switched back to the news anchor who continued her commentary. Veronique stopped listening at that point, but Kevin did not. As she started to say something to him, he waived her away.

"No. Wait. Keep listening."

She sat down next to him.

"...others who have made accusations. One, Kevin McFee, will be ordained a Catholic priest within the next year. With all these troubling reports, the question arises as to why anyone would want to stay within, and even become a part of, a system that they say abused him. We were not able to reach Mr. McFee for a comment. We will keep you up to date on this and other stories as they develop. We will return with sports in just..."

As they broke to a commercial, Kevin sat back, still staring at the television. Veronique pressed the mute button on the remote.

The apartment was very still for a very long time. Veronique sat down on an overstuffed arm chair and waited. Finally, Kevin began to talk.

"When I realized how much damage had been done to me by the priests at my old school—all the torture, the rapes...All those punishments. Living in constant fear that any wrong move, or no move at all, could get you punished..." He seemed to get lost in another time for a while. Then, with a start, he brought himself back to the present. "I went to Joe, and I told him what had happened. Of course, he was shocked. He even cried. He said he never wanted anything like that to happen to me, or to any boy. He was very supportive. But I never told him which priests, and he never asked. Later, when one of the other boys accused Rex by name, Joe went ballistic. He swore up and down that the kid was wrong, that Rex could never have done anything like that. Then I found out by making a few phone calls that Rex was Joe's mentor when Joe was in the seminary. They had some kind of falling out about a year after Joe was ordained. I was never able to find out exactly what that was about, and Joe never would say. Anyway, I'd only seen them together once or twice, and Joe always acted like he didn't know Rex. Rex is the same with everybody." Here Kevin laughed hollowly. "He's really only interested in you if you're under the age of twenty."

Veronique, not knowing what to say, said nothing.

"So now, I'm stuck with the dilemma: To accuse or not to accuse Rex by name. I really wanted Joe on my side. I'm afraid that if I accuse Rex, he won't want to hear it."

"Kevin, what do you think Rex did that caused the falling out between him and Joe? What would cause a falling out between you and Joe, your mentor?"

"Well, for one thing, if I found out he was raping young boys. But Joe isn't in contact with kids. We teach in a college."

"What I'm getting at is maybe Joe really knows the truth about Rex and is protecting him for some other reason."

"Like what?"

"I don't know. But it was weird, Joe being a priest at our parish and teaching all those college courses in the city. Usually parish priests at St. Joseph's don't teach in the City, they work in the community. Joe was an exception, and he was always vague about his past. Maybe Rex knows something about Joe that Joe doesn't want anyone else to know."

Kevin shrugged. "Maybe, but I can't very well ask Joe that, can I?"

Veronique shook her head.

Kevin continued. "It was a very long time ago, thirty years. Joe's been a priest as long as I've been alive. Actually a little longer, about a year."

"So he was in the seminary with Rex as his mentor. Then he takes his final vows. About a year later, around the time that you were born, Rex and Joe have a falling out. Then Joe is sent out west where he stays for a couple of years. Then Rex is sent out west, and Joe is sent to St. Joseph's. Apropos of nothing, a year later I'm born. Do you want me to ask him about Rex?"

For a moment Kevin looked tempted. Then he shook his head.

"No, that wouldn't work. I have to do it. Maybe I should go now while I'm sober and I have my adrenaline pumping. Joe starts his office hours in a little while."

"You're not going to talk to him before his class?"

"It's mid-terms. He's not teaching. I'm giving the exam."

❦   ❦   ❦

Veronique stumbled into her apartment after working a twenty-hour shift. There was one message on her machine.

"Veronique, it's Kevin. Joe fired me today. I'm hoping it'll be okay if I come over. I'll just wait for you in front of your building. I hope it's okay."

"Shit." Veronique undressed and showered quickly. The buzzer to her apartment sounded. Five minutes later, Kevin was in her apartment.

"Hi. I got your message," she said to him gently. "I hope you weren't waiting long."

He just shrugged. "I didn't know where else to go." His voice was flat.

"Come on upstairs."

He sat, catatonic, on one of the kitchen stools while she put out two steaming mugs of hot chocolate.

"So, you told Joe about Rex, and he fired you?"

"Yeah."

"Did he give any kind of an explanation?"

"Nothing. It was spooky. He just said, 'That's impossible. Now get out.' I was in shock. As I was leaving, he said, 'I won't be needing a TA for the rest of the semester. Don't come back.' I don't believe it."

"I don't believe it either. That's so unlike Joe."

Kevin nodded miserably and finished his hot chocolate. "Look, I can't talk about it any more. Could you just hold me tonight? I mean, I know it's a lot to ask after everything, but…"

"Come on. Get ready for bed, and we'll see."

Ten minutes later, Kevin was asleep in her queen-size bed, his head in her lap as she stroked his hair.

# CHAPTER 21

❀

The next morning, Veronique awoke alone. A square yellow stickup note had been attached to her clock radio.

> *Veronique, thanks for the hospitality and the comfort. I need to think about some things. I'll call you later.*

Two hours later, she was driving down the exit ramp to the Sunken Meadow Parkway. She was debating whether or not to stop and see Joe. She drove past the Church, and then turned around. She parked in front, and went into the rectory. The secretary smiled, recognizing her.

"Veronique. How nice to see you. It's been a very long time."

"Yes, it has, Maddie. Is Father Joe around?"

"I believe he is. Just a sec."

A few minutes later, Joe emerged from the mysterious back area of the rectory.

"Veronique, to what do I owe this unexpected surprise?" he asked, smiling and kissing her.

"Can we just go outside for a minute? I have to ask you something, but it won't take too long."

"Sure." He opened the door for her, and the two stepped out into the bright Long Island sunshine.

Veronique was direct. "Kevin told me that you fired him. Come on, Father Joe. That's something that my father would do, not you. What gives?"

Joe's smile had vanished.

"I didn't expect Kevin to go running to you about it."

"I told Kevin that whatever his problems were, no matter how bad they seemed, that you'd be reasonable, and that he didn't have to be afraid to talk to you openly. I guess I was wrong."

Joe opened his mouth to answer, but all he could do was sigh. Then he looked at her and said, "Ronnie, there are some things that I just can't explain. We need to leave it at that."

Veronique ignored him. "As far as I can tell," she pursued, "Rex was your mentor, you and he had a falling out, about a year before Kevin was born, as a matter of fact, and then Rex goes out west. When Rex comes back, you go out west. I know, to a different place. But then you come here, and the rest, as they say, is history. Well, almost. You come out here, but you're different from the other priests here. You teach in the City. And the history starts for me a year later when I'm born, and you become my Godfather." She watched him closely. He was wearing a poker face.

"Are you asking me a question?"

"I'm just trying to figure it out. Like I said, I never dreamed that you'd just fire a guy for talking to you. I feel bad, because I was the one who said to him, 'Don't worry, Father Joe's not unreasonable. Not at all like my father.' And then you go and fire the guy. Of course I'm upset. He's been through a lot. You're the one he always went to. And now you're dumping on him." As she was speaking, Veronique realized that Kevin said that he had confessed about their encounter in the Church. She wondered if he had named names. But then she shrugged it off and waited for a reply from Joe.

"Veronique. There are many sides to this story, and I don't want to go into them with you. Kevin was in the news recently with a revelation that he made about his time in a parochial school when he was growing up. That revelation was about something that happened twenty years ago. Why is he bringing it up now? And why on earth would he ever consider being a priest if it were true?"

Veronique opened her mouth to answer, but Joe held up a silencing hand.

"These questions, on top of his accusation of Father Rex—"

"I remember Rex. He's the one who asked Jon whether he had pubic hair the first time he came to the house."

Joe looked startled. "That's the first I heard of that."

"Yeah. Jon was afraid that if he told any of the other priests, they'd all gang up against him to protect Rex, like what they're doing to Kevin now. Anyway back then, we all decided that what we could do is just make sure that none of our cousins, all boys, was left alone with Rex." She made a face. "He had no interest in girls. Back then, you and Rex acted like you didn't really know each other too well. I don't think anyone would have guessed that he was your mentor."

Joe was silent, so Veronique continued. "I'm out here to ask why on earth you'd just fire Kevin like that? He was a good TA. You told me that yourself, several times. He told me how upset you were when he first said that they raped him in that school. Now you're being really different. Why?"

"Well, Veronique, other things have been brought to my attention," Joe said, his eyes turning on hers seriously. "For one thing, Kevin committed a certain...indiscretion that only recently came to my attention. That, in addition to the allegations he has made, rendered our working situation untenable."

"Oh, come on, Father Joe! Kevin told me that he confessed to his indiscretion, as you call it. Whatever happened to repentance and forgiveness? You know, ten Hail Marys and the slate's wiped clean. Isn't that what they do for all those priests who have admitted to abusing children? Isn't that what happens when anyone goes to confession? After they confess, it's over with? How come not for Kevin? After all, he confessed. It's not like he was caught in the act or anything."

Joe did not answer her. He merely said, "Veronique, there are some things that I simply cannot explain to you. As far as I'm concerned, this conversation is over." He turned and walked back into the rectory.

Enraged, Veronique tried to get into the Church. It was locked.

"I wonder who's in there now," she mused grimly as she turned heel and stalked toward her rented car. Once inside, she gunned the engine and sped toward the Sunken Meadow beach.

When she got there, she parked in the far lot and started walking east. She found Kevin about a mile east of where the boardwalk ended. He was sitting on the sand. He was not drunk, but he looked like a zombie.

She sat down next to him on the sand. He barely acknowledged her presence. He simply stared out over the azure water of the Long Island Sound, rocking forward and back. A light salt breeze played across the water. In front of them, the Connecticut skyline was clearly visible. Farther east, the pristine, white ferry made its way from Port Jefferson to Bridgeport.

She put her hand over his. "You been thinking about things?"

He nodded and said, "I don't know what to do."

"Talk to me."

He shook his head and kept repeating, "I don't know what to do."

Veronique had heard about things like this in the incest survivors meetings she had attended. She let him repeat it for a while. Finally she said, "Why don't you get yourself into therapy?" He looked at her blankly. "Come on, Kevin, we both sat in those survivors' meetings. You know what you need to do. Those assholes didn't kill you with the abuse. They can't kill you now by denying it happened." She grabbed a card from her purse. "Here's Lee's number. No matter what you think of her personally, you know she's the best resource you have to get help. God knows the Church isn't going to do a damn thing for you."

He nodded, seeming to hear her.

She sat next to him for a long time, quietly running her hand back and forth in the sand. Her hand made a deepening furrow in the white sand. Two inches down, the sand became damp and her hand hit something hard. She looked down and saw that what she had uncovered was a piece of the old driftwood that she and her cousins used to sit against when they built their fires on the beach.

She jumped, realizing that the last time she had been to that spot was the night Luca had died. She thought of her cousin, and tears welled up in her eyes. Then she looked at Kevin.

"Come on," she said to him resolutely, standing up and taking his hand. He got up, too. Hand in hand, they walked back to the parking lot. He made a motion to get into his car, but she pulled him to hers. "We'll get your car later. Right now, you've got some phone calls to make." Under her breath, she added, "And I'm not losing you."

# CHAPTER 22

"Hey there, I'm home," Veronique called as she opened the door to her apartment.

A month after they had left the beach together, Kevin had gotten himself into therapy and out of the priesthood. He had asked if he could stay in Veronique's apartment. She hesitated at first. Finally she agreed that he could live with her.

"But if you accuse me of seducing you even once, you're out on your ear."

"Okay, okay. I can't help it if I'm ravenous about sex because I came so close to spending the rest of my life celibate."

"Come here. Let's cross that invisible line into sin."

When Kevin first moved in, Veronique agreed that he could take six months to get himself together, and then they would talk about sharing the rent and other bills.

Kevin was a very good roommate, keeping the place neat and taking out the trash. He brought his computer in and set up an internet connection. He set up his stereo system, and they listened to a lot of Bob Dylan.

When Irene found out that Kevin was living with Veronique, she was unhappy. "Ronnie, you know that goes against our beliefs. You need to be married before you live with a man, or have sex."

"Mom, it's the twentieth century, almost the twenty-first. Get used to it. I'm paying my own bills, living in my own home. As you always told me, when I live in my own place, I make the rules. My rule is that Kevin stays, for now. If you don't like it, you don't have to come visit." Not that she ever had, Veronique noticed to herself.

Irene had sighed heavily and ended the phone call quickly.

In fact, Veronique had tried to keep Kevin and her mother apart. She was not sure how good of a look Kevin had gotten at the woman with Joe. The issue of Joe being seen in the City with a woman had been forgotten in the more pressing fervor of Kevin's break with the priesthood, and Veronique did not want to stir up that old issue if she could help it.

Veronique had informed Jonathan and Mark that she had someone living with her, and so they helped her with "Irene management."

"It's no big deal," Mark said playfully. "It's good, actually. This way we can coordinate holidays easier."

"So," Jonathan had asked jokingly avuncular, "You shacking up with that priest?"

"Ex-priest."

"Thanks to you, right?"

"Not really. He was on his way out. I just, um, facilitated the departure."

Jon gave her a knowing look. "So, how much longer before you're walking down the aisle?"

Veronique looked at him in surprise. "You're crazy."

Veronique returned from her visit with her brothers in a very good mood. "Lay Lady Lay" was playing as she walked in. Kevin was sitting at the computer, surfing the internet. He did not turn around as he started talking to her. "I've just been looking at places for sale on Fire Island. I've been thinking it would be great to have a beach house—you know, a place to get away. It's still the off-season. Come here. Look at these."

"That's great. We should go out there, maybe next month. I'm going to be really busy at work for the next few weeks."

The phone rang.

"Who could be calling at this hour?" she wondered aloud.

She decided to let the answering machine pick up.

"Kevin McFee, leave the priests alone." Click.

Veronique and Kevin looked at each other.

"Great, they've found me."

"I wonder how they did that."

"Joe has your number, doesn't he?"

"Yes, but he wouldn't give it to anyone." Veronique was sure of that.

"Maybe somehow they got it when I put in the second line. I had to use your information as well as mine, since it's your apartment."

As they got ready to go to bed, the phone rang again.

"Kevin McFee. Leave the priests alone." This time the voice was higher pitched.

Click.

"It's two o'clock in the morning!" Kevin exploded.

"Shhh. Let's turn off the phone and the sound on the answering machine. We'll deal with it in the morning."

Kevin agreed reluctantly.

The next morning when they woke up, there were six calls on the answering machine. The messages were all the same. The sound of the voice was the only thing that varied.

Veronique was furious. "We're calling the police right now."

"No. Wait. I think I should call Joe first and see if he gave them the number."

"Like he's going to tell you. No, if anyone should call, it's me." Before he could stop her, Veronique picked up the phone. Instead of calling Joe, she called her mother.

"Hi. It's me." Veronique rarely had any preliminary conversation with her mother. "Listen, Kevin got a bunch of threatening, anonymous calls on my machine today. Would Joe have given anyone in the archdiocese my number?"

"Oh, no, Ronnie. Joe wouldn't do anything to put you in danger, no matter how much he disagrees with what Kevin or you are doing."

"But what?" Veronique was good at reading her mother's silences.

"No buts. I was just thinking…"

"I hope you were just thinking that truly religious people do not go around making threats against other people. I'm getting ready to call the police. I just wanted to know if Joe might have gotten my number and given it to one of these threateners inadvertently."

The stiffness in Irene's voice belied her words as she mumbled something like agreement.

This was another phone conversation in which Irene sighed heavily quite a number of times and ended the call quickly.

All the police did was make a report and tell Veronique what her parents had been told to do with anonymous calls many years before: "Say, 'Operator, this is the call I was telling you about,' and hang up."

"So you're not going to do anything else for us?"

"Ma'am, there's nothing else we can do at this time."

Like hell there isn't, Veronique thought to herself as she hung up the phone.

Kevin was pacing around the apartment. His fear was palpable.

"Listen, Kev. Next time they call, I'll try to keep them on the line. You call the police from the other line."

"It's hooked up to the computer."

"Use my cell phone." She tossed it to him.

Two hours later, the phone rang. Veronique picked it up. "Hello?"

"Kevin McFee, leave—"

"Listen," Veronique put on a thick Long Island accent and yelled over the caller's voice, "You have the wrong number."

"—alone." Click.

"Oh, forget, it. The call's ended." Kevin hissed disgustedly and turned off the cell phone. "They just gave the same message and hung up."

The phone rang again.

"Yeah?" Veronique answered aggressively.

"Trouble in paradise?" Jon's voice came cheerily over the line.

"Oh. Hi, Jon. No. We've just been getting these anonymous calls like every hour on the hour telling Kevin to leave the priests alone. We just got another. Kevin called the police on the cell phone while I tried to keep them on the line. No luck."

"You saved the answering machine tape?"

"Not yet."

"Do it to cover your butt. Let me call Lou. Maybe he'll have some ideas about tracing the call."

Twenty minutes later, he called back. "The next call is due in about half an hour, right? Lou and I are on our way over."

Lou walked into the apartment carrying a large stainless steel suitcase. He nodded when Veronique introduced Kevin to him, and went straight for the phone.

"They call on this one?"

"Yeah," Veronique said. "We called the police from the cell phone, but they got off too fast."

Lou nodded, opening his case. In it was a type of recording device. He went to work, and Kevin paced.

"Coffee, anyone?" Jon made himself at home in Veronique's apartment.

"I think some calming tea would be more in order," Kevin suggested tensely.

"Don't worry. If the calls can be traced, Lou will trace them." Veronique was caught up in the adventure of it. Jon made a pot of coffee.

Lou finished quickly.

"Do we answer the phone or let the answering machine do it?"

"Let it ring four or five times. Then answer it with something that might throw them off. That should buy you some more time." Lou picked up the mug of coffee that Veronique had placed before him.

The four of them sat quietly, drinking the coffee and waiting. Veronique's grandfather clock ticked extraordinarily loudly. Angel and Isis purred from their perch near the window.

The phone rang. Everyone, including the cats, jumped. Veronique sprang for the phone and counted, her mind racing for something to answer with. Two…Three…Four…Five…

"There's no Kevin here."

"This is your sister speaking. Of course he's there. What's the deal?"

"Oh. Hi, Del. We're trying to get these anonymous calls to stop."

"Someone's been harassing you guys?"

"Only since last night. They say 'leave the priest alone' and hang up. Listen, Del, can I call you back later?"

"No problem. Let me know what happens."

Veronique hung up. Almost instantly, the phone began to ring again. Instinctively, she moved to answer it.

"Wait." Lou's voice was authoritative.

Veronique remembered, and waited for the fifth ring.

"THERE'S NO KEVIN HERE."

The caller hesitated.

"Who is this?"

"Leave the priest alone, Kevin McFee." Click.

"Got it." Lou smiled. "I'll give you the number and get you all the information you need when I get back to the office."

"Clever answer," Jonathan congratulated Veronique.

"No charge for family," Lou said as Kevin made a move toward his wallet.

"Thank you very much," Kevin said to him and Jonathan.

"No problem. We want to get those bastards. Anyone who'd do something like that to a kid…" Lou was enraged.

Lou seemed anxious to get back to his office. Jonathan went with him. "I'll call you on your cell for now," he told Veronique. "Meantime, leave that answering machine unplugged. Get anyone who calls you to either send an e-mail or use the cell."

Veronique thought that was an excellent idea.

When they left, Kevin pulled Veronique close to him. "I've been thinking. Maybe for the next week or so you should stay with Jon, and I'll get away for a few days."

"No. I'm not going to let those bastards scare me out of my own house. And what about the cats?"

"Cat sitter. Or maybe Jon can come and stay with you."

She looked at him strangely.

"I don't know who these people are, and I've got the feeling that I'm not making many friends at the police station or anywhere else," Kevin explained. "Besides, if they got this number, who knows what else they can do? I don't think I should be sending e-mails or using the phone to talk to my attorney or anyone else." He paused. "The truth is, I'm spooked."

"If you leave here, where will you go?"

"First thing I need to do is have a talk with my attorney. I'll give him the answering machine tape and any information Lou gets. Then, I figure, I'll just hang with him for a while. We went to high school together. I'm sure he'll let me stay with him for a bit."

"If you're afraid to use the phones, how will I get in touch with you?"

"I'll call you on your cell phone."

"If you're worried about people listening in, that's not the way to communicate."

"My lawyer's name is Van Rogers. Here's his card. You can call him to get in touch with me; and if I need to get in touch with you, he'll make the call."

"Okay, I guess." Veronique was uncertain about this solution.

"It's all I can think of for right now. I need Van's advice. I do wish you'd stay at Jon's."

"Well, I'll consider it. But I don't want to leave my space or my cats."

"I know. But you won't be here too much for the next few weeks, because you'll be working a lot." He paused to kiss her. "This will be over soon."

# CHAPTER 23

❈

Veronique stumbled into the kitchen for a cup of coffee. She had been working double shifts for weeks. She put on one of Kevin's Bob Dylan CDs. Sitting in the living room, petting her cats, she stared at Kevin's dark computer. Kevin had left the apartment exactly four weeks earlier. The anonymous phone calls had stopped six hours after he left. This had chilled and enraged Veronique who asked Jon to get a message to Kevin through the attorney.

For the thousandth time, she wondered where Kevin was. His communications had been sketchy and erratic since he left. He had lived in the apartment only a short time, but their forced separation made her realize how much she had enjoyed having him there. Listening to Dylan's snarling blues, she also realized how much she missed Kevin.

She kept very busy, working every day. Sipping her coffee, she reflected on what she had accomplished in those four long weeks. She thought about the night ahead. She was exhausted, but she needed the security of the extra money.

The phone rang, waking Veronique from her reverie. High-pitched laughter came through a static line. Then silence.

"Who the fuck is this?" Unnerved, Veronique screamed into the phone.

Click. Dial tone.

Terrified into moving on automatic pilot, Veronique slammed the phone down and scrambled to pack some clothes. She got her cat carrier and struggled to put Angel and Isis into it. Miraculously, they cooperated more than usual. Ten minutes later, she was hailing a cab.

"Avis. East Side."

She had no plan other than to take the cats to her mother's.

She got into the rented car a while later and started driving. Zooming east on the expressway at eighty miles an hour, she began to feel calmer. Forty minutes out of New York, she stopped at a gas station on the service road. On her cell phone, she called Irene, but hung up before it started ringing. She called Jonathan instead, and left a message saying she needed to leave her cats with him for a few days.

"I know you're allergic, so they'll stay in the basement. Please, please, please call me on my cell as soon as you get this. Thanks, Jon."

Then, from a pay phone, she called Van Rogers.

"Hello Veronique. Where are you calling from?"

"A pay phone on the Island."

"Good. I'm glad you called. This is a secure line. Kevin asked me to tell you to meet him on Fire Island this weekend."

"Can I meet him there a day early? I've stopped work sooner than I originally planned."

"I think he'd love that. He's staying in a bungalow at Cherry Grove." He gave her the address and directions.

"Damn. Work." She cursed aloud. Then she called her job and tersely told the startled receptionist that she would not be in.

Jonathan called her back on her cell phone.

"Ronnie, are you in trouble?"

"I'm not sure. Kevin's been harassed. I told you that before. But those calls, you know, the weird ones with the high-pitched laughter? They started again. I'm totally frightened, so I left the apartment. I didn't want Angel and Isis to stay in the apartment without me. Would you take them for a few days, please?"

"Yeah. Bring them over."

"Um, could you meet me at the Walt Whitman Mall, near the fountain that doesn't work?"

"I'll be there in half an hour. And Ronnie, you'd better tell me what's going on."

She left the cats in the car when she went to meet him. Brother and sister sat in the mall's health food restaurant while Veronique reiterated the story that Jon already knew: the phone calls that involved Kevin and the fact that they had stopped six hours after he left. And now the new—or was it old?—calls with the high-pitched laughter that seemed to follow her. She ended saying, "I don't know. Something about the laughter sounded dangerous this time.

Maybe it's nerves. Maybe it's those creeps calling Kevin for so long. Whatever. I had to get out of there."

"Do you think it's Bob?"

Veronique paused and then answered slowly. "I did for a long time, mostly because I couldn't think of anyone else that it might be."

They looked at each other, a new idea brewing.

"What about Rocco?" Jonathan read Veronique's thoughts. "He's got the connections. You certainly didn't make a friend out of him with your comment about Renee. But do you think it's gone on since you were a teenager?"

"There was that time in Father's office when Laurio caught me alone in the lunchroom. He said something lewd, and then Father walked in and I asked him about it."

"You were at the Academy then, right?"

Veronique nodded.

"That caused him to get a demotion. I remember Father saying something about it, but not explaining." Jonathan was lost in thought. "So that's what happened…From then, Rocco went on to lose stock options, and then Marc got the promotion that Rocco wanted…But why would he do something as juvenile as phone pranks? And why follow you around for, what is it, almost ten years? And how did he find you?"

"After what's been going on with Kevin, I know Laurio could get my name and address in no time. Maybe I'm a little paranoid, but if he's watching Mom and Dad's house, and I show up…I don't know what, but I'm scared."

Jonathan nodded. "But you can't hide out forever."

They had left the restaurant and were headed for her car.

"Yeah. I know. But right now, I just need to know that my babies are safe with you. That way, I can go out to Fire Island and see Kevin."

"No problem, Ronnie. But call me every few days so I know that you're all right. Okay?"

"I promise I will." She kissed him and handed him the cat carrier. "Oh, would you tell Del I'm okay?" He nodded. "Thanks so much for doing this. I know you're allergic."

"I suppose I'll have to get a litter box? You owe me big time. I'll have to drive with the windows open and hope for the best."

❦   ❦   ❦

Kevin was on the porch waiting for Veronique when she turned the corner to the bungalow.

He rushed to meet her, kissing her, taking her bag and holding her close to him at the same time.

Hours later, after they had made love and talked and made love again, they got sandwiches and walked out to the beach to eat. The wind was too strong to make a fire, so they munched the food, sitting close under a blanket. When Kevin started kissing her again, she stopped him.

"You know, I'm two weeks late?"

"Late for what? You're a day early."

She paused, not knowing whether to be aggravated or amused. "Two weeks late with my period."

She watched the news sink in.

"Ohhhh. You think you're pregnant? Well, don't blame me. I had a vasectomy when I was twenty-one."

"You did? I thought you said that one of the 'cons' of becoming a priest is you don't get to have a family."

"You remember? I did say that. But I was thinking a wife and adopted kids. There are so many children who have been abandoned and need homes. With everything I've experienced and with the population growth as it is, I figured why bring more people into the world. Let's work with what we have."

"Oh."

"Did you want to have kids?"

"I never thought about it. I don't really feel like being pregnant right now."

"Well, you can't be pregnant by me. I hope that relieves your worry."

"Well, maybe it does."

"Maybe? You mean there's someone else?"

"You know I like to keep my options open," she said, playfully. He looked so crestfallen that she recanted immediately. "I'm kidding. You're the only one." He brightened then.

"It's getting cold. Let's go back to the cottage."

"Okay, but we need to pick up some milk and coffee from the deli before we go back."

Hand in hand they walked down the deserted cement pathway to the little row of stores. As they were standing in line, a news radio station was playing behind the counter. Through the static, a name came through that Veronique recognized.

"...Rocco Laurio, the distraught father of Renee, says he has no idea why anyone would do such a grisly thing to his daughter." Rocco's voice was heard, the deep Brooklyn accent mumbling platitudes about his daughter. Back to the news anchor: "Renee had been estranged from her father and brother for several years. Ms. Laurio had experienced a series of emotional breakdowns, starting at the age of fifteen. In fact, Mr. Laurio had reported his daughter missing in 1995 when she disappeared from the private hospital where she was recuperating from yet another emotional breakdown. Last night, his son was having a birthday party at the Kent mansion. There were many guests. Renee could have come in with any group of guests. Police sources say it's likely she hung herself from the front porch of the elite Old Brookville home."

Veronique froze. "Oh God, Renee."

Feeling ill and shaken by the turn of events, Veronique could only think of getting back to the warmth of the bungalow. Together, she and Kevin walked down the long dark path. It was too early in the season for many residents to be there on the beachfront, and most of the houses were dark. Turning the corner, they heard a loud explosion, and the ground trembled. Suddenly a house in the middle of the block caught fire.

Instinctively, Kevin put his arm around Veronique's shoulder.

"Oh my god. It's the bungalow," he said, horrified.

# CHAPTER 24

New York State Trooper Lou Adriatico was angry. He was not getting answers from the Suffolk County police department. He could not figure out why. He and Kevin paced around each other in the newest safe house that Lou had found for Kevin and Veronique. Jonathan, sitting on the couch, listed their dead ends.

"We've got no help from the local police. There's no response from Fr. Joe. Mom can't deal with it. She and Father are going to Florida this weekend. They're spending two weeks in the Keys. In fact, Mom and Father have been spending a lot more time together. They even seem to be getting along. Miracles continue to happen, but we seem to be at a stalemate here. We don't know whether the bungalow was bombed because of Kevin, or because of Ronnie."

"I'm inclined to think it's because of me," Kevin said. "How could they have known that Ronnie would be there?"

"He's probably been on her trail since he figured out what car she rented. Ronnie, you had to give your address and phone number to rent the car, right?"

She nodded.

"With all Laurio's connections out here, he could have tracked her in no time. You said you were on the beach for a few hours, right? They probably rigged it then, more as a warning than anything else."

"The same could be said for the Church people though," Kevin reasoned.

"You two have to go somewhere else for the next two nights." Lou was firm.

"How about the Shinnecock Reservation out East?" Kevin suggested.

"Nobody gets to stay out there," Jonathan vetoed the idea.

"I used to know some people out there. We could visit for the day. Even if we can't stay there, maybe we could go to a bed and breakfast inn near there."

"You can use my car. And use cash wherever you stay," Lou instructed them.

"Why your car?" Veronique thought it might be traceable.

"I can follow it," Lou confirmed her suspicion. "So I'll know where you are. I'll be keeping an eye on you. It's probably best not to use phones too much until we devise a plan."

"Did I hear someone say a plan?" Delfina walked into the room.

"Del!" Veronique jumped up joyfully to hug her sister.

"How did you find us?" Lou was overly cautious.

"Jon told me at breakfast this morning. Someone's got to play with Ronnie's cats. I took the long way here."

Lou nodded.

Delfina continued, "I heard the word plan. You guys got one?"

"Not yet." Jonathan smiled fondly at his big sister. "We were waiting for you."

"How about resurrecting the old Bob trick?"

Kevin looked confused, but the cousins jumped at the suggestion.

"That's a great idea." Lou was enthusiastic. "We should plan it here and then script some phone conversations, since that's probably the best way for them, whoever 'they' are, to pick up the information."

"The trouble with the Bob plan is that in this case we don't know who the 'Bob' is," Delfina pointed out a flaw in her own solution.

"Yeah," Lou said. "But, in a way, it doesn't really matter. I'll get some of my guys on it. We'll see how much coverage we have. In the meantime," he addressed Kevin and Veronique, "you two should take my car and get out of here. It's parked in the garage next to this building. Go to the Reservation. If you can't stay there, go to this bed and breakfast." He handed Veronique a card. "I go there a lot. We'll meet at the Chamber in two days. In the meantime, no phone contact unless there's an emergency. In that case, call me on my cell."

"The guys I knew who were out here left about a year ago," Kevin told Veronique who was looking at some hand-made souvenirs at a stand near the Reservation.

"So we can't stay here," she concluded.

"No. But they're having a fire ceremony tonight. You said Delfina took you to a fire ceremony when you were a kid, so I thought you might want to stay for another."

"You know I do. Maybe we should get set up in Lou's bed and breakfast, and then come back."

Kevin agreed. After they settled in, they ate a light dinner before returning to the Reservation. As they ate, Veronique recounted her memories of the last fire ceremony she had attended. "The thing I remember most," she concluded, "was that old man, looking at me across the fire, saying, 'Who's your father?' It was creepy, but it was cool. Every once in a while he comes back into my mind. I wonder if I'll see him tonight." She paused. "If I do, maybe I'll ask him who my father is."

"You don't think it's the guy you've been calling Dad all these years?"

Veronique made a face. "He always wanted us to call him Father." She changed the subject. "At that first fire ceremony, the guy who led it honored all the plant people, animal people and stone people. He talked about all our relations." She looked lovingly at Kevin. "I guess now that we've had, um, relations, you're part of all my relations." She kissed his palm.

He smiled happily. "Much as I hate to end this, we should go. Don't want to be late."

This ceremony was different from the one Veronique remembered. There were a lot of tourists, and the whole flavor was not what she remembered from her childhood experience. She did not see the old man during this ceremony; but she stood, watching, feeling grateful that she first had the experience of the ceremony when she was so young.

When the ceremony was over, she stood at the edge of the circle, staring at the deep red embers. Kevin stood behind her, looking at the stars. All of a sudden, a slight breeze fanned one of the embers. It flared up, and there he was—the old man she remembered. He was too far away to say anything, but he seemed to look at her, smile and cock his head to one side as if to say, "Figure it out yet?" Then the fire went dark.

"There he is," Veronique nudged Kevin.

"Where?"

She pointed to the empty spot where he had been. They went around to it, but no one was there.

"Maybe it was my imagination," she said, doubtfully, "but it seemed so real."

"If Pino isn't your father, who is?"

"I may not want to know."
"So leave it alone."

※ ※ ※

Two days later, they were sitting in the Chamber with Veronique's cousins and siblings. A quick vote among the Adriaticos admitted Kevin to the childhood hideaway. Even Marc, in his three-piece suit, had managed to get away from the office to attend the meeting.

"Okay, everyone," Lou started quickly. "Listen up. This thing has to happen tonight. I've got some of my buddies unofficially helping me out. One of them will get us some communications and safety equipment. That stuff has to be returned twenty-four hours after we get it." He winked handsomely. "We've got to work fast. Everyone here will have to get their cars up to the Chamber. Meanwhile, Ronnie and Kevin, you'll take a nice long walk through Huntington. Park the car on Main Street. Look for a white Bronco that will start signaling to pull out as you pass the intersection of New York Avenue. Your car will take its place. Once you've parked, get out and go down Main Street to New York Avenue. Stop in the Book Revue. Stay an hour. Go down Main Street, around the next corner to Wall Street, and check out the Mystic Warrior. Stay in there for at least forty-five minutes. Stop at Starbucks and have a leisurely coffee. Then, at four o'clock, leave Starbucks and go to the Dairy Barn. There's a pay phone there. Use it to call your Mom. She knows nothing about this. Tell her your plans for the evening."

"And what are our plans?"

"You're so precocious, Ronnie. I'm getting to it. Tell Aunt Irene that you're in Huntington and that you and Kevin will be having a romantic dinner at the Old Dock. If she wants to join you for dinner, tell her you'll be over to see her tomorrow. Tell her that Kevin has something private that he wants to talk to you about tonight."

"He does?" Kevin interjected.

"I don't know. As far as that goes, you can talk about the Mets for all I care." The others laughed. "The point," Lou continued relentlessly, "is to stay on the phone as long as you can, and give as many details as possible about where you'll be and what you'll be doing. Got it?"

Kevin and Veronique nodded.

"Remember, under no circumstances is your mother to join you tonight."

"Oh great, I'm supposed to tell her everything, and then keep her away?"

"Don't worry, Ronnie," Delfina spoke up, "The Threesome's all going to see 'Rosenkavalier' at the Met tonight. She'll be leaving within the hour after she gets your phone call, if she answers the phone."

"Good point, Del," Lou jumped in. "If your mother's not there, leave the information on her answering machine. Remember, stay on as long as possible, and give as many details as possible. Oh, yeah. Tell her that you'll probably end up looking at the moon from the Point."

"You're kidding. No one talks about the Point with their parents."

"Just do it. Hopefully, the night won't be that long."

He handed them each a heavy black vest. "It's a good thing it's chilly today. Put these on under your clothes. They won't be noticeable with your bulky jackets."

"Are bullet proof vests really necessary?" Jonathan asked nervously.

"Just a safety precaution." Lou was all business. "Unfortunately, I can't put communications on you, because we don't know who else is out there listening. But we'll be watching."

"I think I should do this alone," Kevin began.

"I'd agree, except we don't know whether they want you or Ronnie," Lou told him. "Believe me, I don't want either one of you doing this, but, unfortunately, both of you have to go. My guys will be around you. That's why you have such a specific route."

༺ ༺ ༺

At noon, Veronique and Kevin were in Lou's car, driving down Pulaski Road to Huntington.

"That Chamber is a really cool place," Kevin commented. "You went there a lot as a kid?"

"Jon and Del discovered it around the time I was born. They've been bringing Adriaticos there ever since." She smirked. "Sounds like a travel commercial."

The white Bronco pulled out, and Kevin parallel parked the Buick at its meter on Main Street. Then he and Veronique made their way to the Book Revue where they browsed for an hour. Veronique bought two books on Fire Island. Then they headed to the Mystic Warrior.

Native American flute music was playing as they entered the quiet shop. The soothing sounds and the smell of incense calmed Veronique, who was beginning to get jumpy. They examined each piece of jewelry, artifact and drum on the lower level, and then went upstairs and examined everything for sale there. Veronique purchased two braids of sweetgrass. Kevin got some CDs. After making their purchases, they went to get coffee in Starbucks.

At precisely four, they left the coffee bar and went to the Dairy Barn. They found the pay phone, and Veronique called Irene.

"Helloooooooo," Irene answered cozily.

"Hi, Mom."

"Ronnie. Where are you?"

"Right now I'm in Huntington with Kevin. I've been showing him around, and we've been shopping."

"Father Joe says hi, Ronnie." Irene interrupted.

"No wonder you sound so…up."

"I always sound the same," Irene contradicted her.

"Whatever. Anyway, Kevin and I have been having a great day in town."

"Kevin, Father Joe's nice young TA?"

"That's the one. Tonight we're going to the Old Dock for a romantic dinner. He's been wanting to talk. The Old Dock seems like a perfect place for it." She hesitated. Then, through clenched teeth, she added, "I'll probably even show him the Point, if he's lucky."

"Veronique." Her mother's voice was stern. "I thought that was closed after dark."

"*Mom*. I'm sure you've been up there a time or two."

"If I was, I didn't know it."

"Then how would you know if it was closed after dark?"

Irene paused, not answering, as if listening to something on her end. Joe's voice was muffled in the background.

"Joe wants to know how serious you are about Kevin."

"Why?"

More distraction on Irene's end of the phone. A full two minutes later, in a slightly troubled voice, Irene said to her daughter, "There's something Joe and I need to talk to you about. We're going to the opera as soon as your father gets here. Where are you staying tonight?"

This was a question Veronique had not anticipated.

"Um, the Three Village Inn." It was the first place that came to her mind.

"Oh good, you're staying out here. Maybe Joe and I can meet you for breakfast tomorrow?"

"Yeah, sure. We'll probably want to sleep in, but I'll call you around ten. Maybe we can have lunch at that breakfast place in Setauket."

"Okay, Ronnie, Honey. Your father's home now, so I've got to go."

"Okay, Mom. Have fun. I'll call you in the morning."

Irene hung up without answering.

Veronique heard a second click as she hung up, but she was more interested in what her mother had said.

"Hmmm. That was strange," Veronique mused, frowning as she replaced the receiver. "I wonder what Mom and Joe want to talk to me about." She related to Kevin what her mother had said as arm in arm they crossed the street, heading toward the movie house.

Two hours and fifteen minutes later, having watched *Tomorrow Never Dies*, they emerged from the theater.

"What was that all about?" Kevin wondered aloud.

"Don't you think that there are some people who don't want to get married?" Her voice was teasing.

They were walking slowly back to the Buick.

"Do you?"

"Weren't you one of them for a long time?" she countered mischievously. "For all I know, you're still one of them."

He turned his blue eyes on her. "I was for a while, but about marriage, not about commitment."

Their conversation went back and forth until they got to Lou's car.

"You don't think it's rigged to explode when we turn it on?" Kevin asked apprehensively as he unlocked the passenger door.

"No. One of Lou's buddies has been watching it from the diner."

"How do you know?"

"He told me."

Still, she held her breath as Kevin turned the key in the ignition. The engine turned over without a hitch, and they both breathed a sigh of relief.

"Old Dock, here we come," she said nervously.

❦    ❦    ❦

Preparations at the Chamber had progressed smoothly. Within two hours, the Adriatico cousins, minus Marc who had to be back at work, had all the cars camouflaged at the Chamber, ready to go. Lou periodically got calls from his associates in Huntington who were tracing Veronique and Kevin's progress.

At four-ten, Lou's contact at the Dairy Barn called with a terse message: Mama's message got by Peeping Tom."

"Okay. There's gonna be a party tonight," Lou announced as he clicked off the phone.

Two hours later Lou got another call: "Love birds gone looking for worms."

"Okay. Listen everybody. Ronnie and Kevin just left Huntington. They should be here in the next half hour. My guys will take the front cars. I don't want any of us going out unless it's absolutely necessary."

"What do you mean, we're just supposed to sit here in case?" Gavin was annoyed.

"That's right. I don't know who we're dealing with or how they're going to show up. The more time that goes by, the more I realize how sophisticated they are. We want to get them—Right?—not get ourselves killed. Even if it's only one guy with a magnum, I don't want any of us out there. It's just smart, Gav." His brother was still unhappy about this turn of events. The others also seemed less charged than they had before.

Jonathan, sensing this, told them, "Look. The main thing is to catch the guys and make sure Ronnie and Kevin are no longer at risk. We got our thrills doing this once with someone who was basically harmless. We don't need to do it again with a person, or people, who are dangerous."

"At the same time, stay alert. You never know how things may turn," Lou added.

"I guess we should all just get into our cars anyway," Jonathan said to him.

"Might as well. If I need you to do our old Bob thing, I'll just turn my flashlight on over your windshields. As soon as you see it, everyone start your engines right away, and fan out in the old circle. You know how."

"I guess Marc never got back," Delfina observed as she moved to her car.

"He knew not to come if he was going to be later than six," Lou reported.

"I hope he doesn't do anything stupid," Jonathan muttered to Delfina as he got into his car, which was directly in front of hers.

       ❦       ❦       ❦

Bobby Nell, a classmate of Lou's from the Academy, watched the restaurant from the deck of his Bayliner through infrared binoculars. Kevin and Veronique had been dining for an hour.

"One if by land and two if by sea," he muttered the lines of an old poem to himself over and over again. He and Lou had agreed that Bobby would watch the couple and keep an eye on the parking lot from his boat. If he saw suspicious movements from any of the boats, he'd turn on the double light above him. If the only movement was from the parking lot, he would turn on only the single light in front of him.

He had rigged lights to the top and rear of the boat that he controlled with switches that were next to his chair. He could turn on either the single or the double light without moving more than a finger. The lights cast a narrow beam that were easily observable only from the upper parking lot, not from the water.

As Bobby watched Kevin and Veronique get up to leave, a boat docked near his sounded a high-pitched beep which was followed by a grisly voice saying, "She's moving."

Instinctively, Bobby knew it was about Veronique. Quickly he flicked on both sets of lights. Someone on a boat near his was talking to someone in the parking lot. He looked at the boats anchored in the small bay. All of them were dark. No one on the water was making a move toward the dock. He turned off the double light, hoping that Lou had seen it and guessed his message.

Bobby could see a long limousine roll toward the restaurant from St. Johnland Road. Lou had obviously gotten his signal, because he could hear two cars start almost simultaneously in the parking lot. No headlights had gone on.

Bobby saw two of his colleagues jump off a fishing boat that was on a trailer near the loading dock. They walked quickly toward the restaurant. They were not quick enough. The limousine screeched to the front of the restaurant as Veronique and Kevin, not realizing what was coming, stepped out the front door.

Instantly, two men jumped out, pushed Kevin out of the way and pulled Veronique into the car. Then, with wheels squealing, they took off in a wide circle around the other cars.

The limousine sped out of the parking lot, but its passage was impeded by a blue Jeep Cherokee that was towing a U-Haul trailer in the intersection on St. Johnland Road. The Cherokee was making the left turn onto Old Dock Road. Instead of slowing down, the driver of the limousine gunned the engine and ran the red light, trying to swerve around the Cherokee.

The limousine ran up the nose of the Cherokee, crushing the cabin of the SUV underneath it. Two of Lou's associates had been waiting at the other side of the intersection. They got out of their cars and ran toward the limousine, one of them calling for help on a cell phone.

Kevin was at the door of the limousine by this time. As he opened the door, Veronique, who had apparently been leaning against the door, fell out of the car. He scooped her into his arms, holding her tightly.

Meanwhile, Lou's associates who had been on the trailered boat were struggling with a cursing Fortuno Laurio whose two body guards were lying dazed in the middle of the broken water glasses in the back of the long black vehicle.

As Kevin was holding Veronique close to him, he pulled a small box from his jacket pocket, and took a diamond ring out of it. He slipped the ring on Veronique's left hand and whispered "I love you. Think about it." She smiled at him, suddenly aware that her head had begun to pound.

The Adriaticos who were in the Chamber heard the squawking on Lou's communicator.

"It's over," Lou announced as Delfina and Jonathan jumped out of their cars and headed toward the parking lot, followed on foot by the rest of their clan.

Delfina saw the Cherokee first. "Oh my god. Marc."

Jonathan, who was right behind her, looked in the direction his sister was staring. Both broke into a run simultaneously.

The whine of multiple sirens approached while Lou's comrades pulled the driver out of the limousine. Lou was at the passenger door of the Jeep. He could see his cousin inside, leaning toward him.

"Marc. Hold on. We're gonna get you out of there."

"Marc!" Veronique looked over Kevin's shoulder to see the Cherokee. Her voice rang out above the sound of the sirens. She ran toward her brother's car as Lou succeeded in pulling the passenger door open. Pushing her cousin aside, she reached in and grabbed her brother's hand, squeezing it hard.

His grip was weak, but he held onto her. He was alive and conscious.

"Marc, can you hear me?"

"Yeah." His voice was raspy.

"What were you doing?"

"Did you get them?"

"Yeah. It was Fortuno."

"I know. He was in Father's office today. I overheard him talking to his goons on the phone. They had just finished listening in on your conversation with Mom." Marc's voice was getting lower, and his breathing was more labored.

"You can tell me later, Marc," Veronique assured him.

"No. It's better that I keep talking." He breathed heavily and seemed to lapse out of consciousness for a moment.

"Marc?"

He breathed himself awake. "I heard what they were going to do, pick you up in the limo as you left the restaurant. They had a listening device set up at your table. The waitress..." He faded out again. "...I know Lou was expecting to take him down at the Point. I figured if there was something to slow them down, Lou's guys would be able to pick him up no matter where they started out from." As he spoke, his breath became more and more labored.

Veronique kept talking to him and squeezing his hand, making sure he stayed conscious. She was not sure how much time had passed before the limousine was finally removed and Marc was airlifted to Stony Brook University Hospital. The paramedics would not let her ride with him. In one car, Jonathan, Lou, Kevin and Veronique sped to the hospital. Delfina and Gavin went back to Riviera Drive to wait for Irene, Pino and Joe.

❦     ❦     ❦

Marc was lying in a bed of white sheets and pillows, his head bandaged in white gauze, with many white machines attached to him through plastic tubes. Kevin, Veronique, Jonathan and Lou were gathered around the bed when Irene, Pino and Joe walked in with Delfina. Joe was visibly startled to see Kevin there. Since Kevin had made his allegations of abuse public, Joe's attitude toward him had cooled noticeably.

Kevin was also startled to see Irene and Joe walk in. Veronique knew immediately that Kevin recognized her mother as the woman who was so friendly with Joe at the Plaza. Kevin hid his surprise, lowering his eyes and moving away from the bed so that Marc's parents could come closer.

The room was silent except for Veronique's muffled sobs and the steady beeping of the monitor. Joe raised his hand to make a sign of the cross over the unconscious man, and he said a silent prayer. As he was finishing, a doctor came into the room. He motioned to Pino and Irene that he wanted to speak with them outside the room. Irene turned to leave, silently indicating to Joe that he should join them.

When they came back into the room, both Pino and Irene were crying. Joe was only slightly composed. In a shaky voice, Pino told his children that Marc had suffered a cerebral hemorrhage and that he was being kept alive by the life support systems.

"We've opted to turn them off," Irene quavered as she told her other children. "Markie wouldn't have wanted to be kept alive like this. The doctors said that because of where the hemorrhage was, he will never regain consciousness." The doctor had followed them into the room.

"We'll stay with him," Pino told the doctor, who seemed to be waiting for them to leave.

The doctor appeared to begin to protest, but then he looked at Pino, towering over him and Joe in his black suit with the Roman collar. He nodded.

"Please step into the hall for a moment. There are some papers for you to sign. Then you can come back in."

Joe administered the last rites, and then the Adriaticos began to file out of the room. Delfina and Veronique kissed their brother on the cheek before leaving. Irene, the last one to leave the room, did the same. As she went to the door, she turned back. "I'm going to stay with him," she informed the nurses.

"But…" One of them began to protest.

She stopped as the doctor said to Irene, "All right, but stay by the window until all the equipment has been removed."

When the rest of the family returned to the room, Irene was smoothing the sheets as she took her place next to her youngest son, holding his hand.

As the sun peeked a deep pink through the swirling mists, Marc opened his eyes briefly, looked lovingly at his family gathered in the room, smiled at his mother, and then he left them.

# CHAPTER 25

In the two years that followed, Veronique supported Kevin as he told his story and supported other men who had experienced the same abuse that Kevin had. Fortuno Laurio was convicted of vehicular homicide, among other things, as a variety of paraphernalia, including three loaded hand guns, were found in the limousine.

A year after Marc's death, Veronique and Kevin announced their wedding plans. Irene took Veronique to lunch the next day.

Veronique, who had taken Marc's death extremely hard, was much more low-key since the tragedy.

As mother and daughter sat in the Professor's Diner in Kings Park, Irene looked at her younger daughter and finally said, "Are you sure you're ready to get married?"

"I think so, Mom. I love him. He loves me. He's been through a terrible ordeal. So have I. I think we've come out stronger. We've been talking about everything—where we'll live, how many kid's we'll have, all that."

"How many kids?"

"We're going to adopt."

Irene looked distinctly relieved.

"I didn't think you'd take it this well," Veronique was surprised at her mother's response.

"Well, why not?"

"Right. That's what I think. I'm not really all that keen on being pregnant. Kevin thinks there are enough unwanted and abused kids in the world. We could give two of them a really good, loving home."

"That's true."

Veronique had expected a vigorous argument from her mother. Instead, she was getting support. "Mom, you're creeping me out. I thought you'd be upset if I wasn't having kids of my own."

Irene smiled at her gently. "If it's your decision not to, then I support you in that. Kevin agrees, so does it really matter what I think? No. I'll be happy with whatever children you bring into the family."

"Kevin had a vasectomy when he was in his early twenties."

"Oh. So he can't get you pregnant even if the birth control doesn't work?"

"That's right. At the time, he was making a statement about zero population growth."

"I like a man who has principles that he stands up for."

This was distinctly not what Veronique had expected from her mother, the devout Catholic who believed that the most sacred blessing in a marriage was children.

"Something's weird here, Mom. Are you sure there's nothing you want to tell me?"

"No, Ronnie, Honey. Everything's perfectly all right." She smiled brightly at her daughter before changing the subject. "Shall we share a dessert?"

❦ ❦ ❦

When Veronique had called her mother from the Dairy Barn two years earlier, Joe realized for the first time how serious Veronique was about Kevin. During his brief interruption to the phone conversation, Joe had indicated to Irene that something was amiss, but he would not say what it was. Pino had arrived home during the phone call, they had gone to the opera, and they had come home to Marc's accident. In the aftermath, the incident had been forgotten.

When Irene told Joe about Veronique's wedding, however, it surfaced again. They were sitting at Irene's kitchen table in the middle of the week having lunch.

"She's marrying Kevin?"

"Of course she's marrying Kevin. So far, they've bought two houses jointly, she supports him when he's being attacked by the people from his school, and he adores her. In most respects they're inseparable." Irene's own support of Kevin's speaking out against his abusers waffled between acceptance and rejection.

"Irene, you know where I was before I came to Kings Park, don't you?"

"Yes, the southwest."

"Right. But I was only there for two years. For ten years before that, I was in Toronto."

"So?"

"Do you know where Kevin grew up?"

"No." Irene's suspicions were mounting.

"Toronto. It was in a trade school outside Toronto that he says he was abused."

"Were you a teacher at that trade school?" Irene was almost afraid to hear the answer.

"No. I'm not part of the order of Brothers that ran those schools. I was already at Kings Park by the time Kevin was ten and in that school."

"Oh." Irene was momentarily relieved. "So, what are you trying to say?"

"There was a woman in Toronto..." Joe started, his eyes downcast.

It only took a second for Irene to ingest the information. "You're Kevin's father?"

"There's a possibility. It's ironic. It's almost the same thing that happened with..." Joe's voice trailed off. Then he resumed. "Kevin's mother, Mary, had a live-in boyfriend. He drank a lot, used to hit her. Anyway, she would never say whether I was the father or whether he was." He paused and looked at her. "I was a young priest, and I didn't have much of a say about where I was sent. I tried to keep an eye on Kevin, but he was wild, and he was unhappy. His mother died when he was ten. I tried to keep him in Jesuit schools, but he was known as a troublemaker. Eventually he got sent to St. Johns. I had already been sent back to the United States.

"I asked my colleagues to keep me informed of Kevin's whereabouts. When he decided to try the priesthood, I was overjoyed. He was happy to come to New York to study. Eventually, he became my TA. Then he brought those accusations against the Brothers and the Church. I'm disappointed that he would tell stories like that, but I think it's partly my fault."

"So, you're saying that there's a possibility that Ronnie's marrying her half brother." Irene was not interested in Joe's politics at the moment.

"There is also the possibility that I fathered only one of them, or neither of them."

"So how are you going to tell them?"

"I don't know. How do you feel about Veronique hearing about us?"

"Lousy. Rotten. What do you think?"

"Maybe I'll talk to Kevin first."

"That's just typical." Veronique stormed into the room.

"Ronnie," Irene was aghast. "How long have you been standing there?"

"Long enough to know that you two had a roll in the hay nine months before I was born and you," she advanced on Joe, "also had a roll in the hay with Kevin's mother nine months before he was born. That's just great. So Kevin and I may be half-siblings."

Joe took a breath to respond, but Veronique would not let him.

"No." She put up her hand. "Let me tell you something. You are not going to take this away from me. Even if the worst case scenario is true and you fathered both of us, we are getting married. I don't care what anyone says. We're not having children. We've been forewarned. That's fine. We didn't want children before I ever heard about this. Kevin can't get me pregnant. It's perfect. If either of you break your silence of twenty-five years, I'll never forgive you. Especially since so many people will be hurt and no one will be helped. Mom, you and Father are finally getting along. I have the man of my dreams, and I am getting married to him. Keep your past indiscretions to yourself. Kevin and I will take care of the rest." She paused. When she continued, her voice was low and decisive. "If you don't, I'll just go somewhere else and get married. You'll be left to explain to the rest of the family. It's your choice—keep your mouths shut like you have all these years, or open them and lose me."

She turned and walked out of the house without waiting for a reply.

❦   ❦   ❦

Kevin was not as sure as Veronique.

"There are reasons that siblings cannot get married. Maybe we should rethink this."

"It's not as though you grew up with me like Jon and…Marc." She still missed her brother.

Kevin was silent a moment before answering. "I know," he answered her gently, "but at the same time, siblings marrying each other is taboo. Look at Oedipus."

"That wasn't exactly siblings. And Antigone turned out fine," Veronique shot back.

"That's literature."

"Well, the first two humans to procreate had to be related."

He did not feel like arguing. "Let's at least take a DNA test and see if he is father to both of us."

"I tell you what. I really don't want to know. You take the test first. If he's your father, then I'll take the test. If he's not your father, I won't have to."

"Fair enough. I'll get it done this week."

❦   ❦   ❦

Veronique told Joe and Irene what she and Kevin had decided. Irene was pleased.

"Now you're going to have to speak to Kevin," Veronique told Joe. "You two had better start getting along again. I want you to do our wedding, but you can't do that if you're not speaking to the groom."

Joe sighed and nodded. "I'll have to be a part of the testing process, so I'll be waiting for Kevin's call to tell me how to proceed.".

Kevin got a home test from the internet, got Joe's blood sample and his own, and sent both samples back the same day he got the test kit. In the two weeks that followed, Veronique spent a lot of time thinking about what to do if the test came back positive.

The night before the results were due, she met Delfina and Jonathan at Jon's house. They sat quietly in front of Jonathan's fireplace for a long time, watching the flames. Finally, Veronique spoke.

"Listen, guys, I've got a problem. I don't know where else to turn."

Her siblings listened intently as she told them what she had overheard in their mother's kitchen and about Kevin's DNA test. Delfina did not seem at all surprised. Jonathan only raised his eyebrow.

"If that test comes back positive, I agreed to send in a sample," Veronique concluded her account. "If it's negative, the inquiry stops. It doesn't matter at that point who my father is. Honestly, I don't really want to know that Joe is my father any more than I want to know that, um…Pino is at this point."

Delfina and Jonathan laughed.

Veronique laughed with them, but sobered quickly. "I want to marry Kevin. I've been doing a lot of reading about this. From everything I can get, as long as we're not going to have any children, there doesn't really seem to be a reason not to get married, even if we are half siblings."

"What have you found?" Jonathan, always the teacher, insisted on reports.

Veronique knew this. She had come armed with the information she had found on the internet and from other sources.

"The only problems I can see are a religious one and a biological one. I'm not having children except by adoption. No way, no how. Kevin's been committed to not bringing more kids into the world since he was twenty. So that one's taken care of. As far as the religious one, who did Cain and Abel marry if their parents were Adam and Eve, the first people? Those tribes of David must have been marrying pretty close, too. In fact, I got the number of one psychotherapist in New York City who maintains that no species could survive without brother-sister love."

"Really?" Delfina was interested.

"Yeah. I called her and told her the story. She was really cool about the whole thing. She suggested that I read a book that tells the myth of Rhea. Basically, it says that the only taboo against brother-sister love is historical. She said that if I wanted to work with her, she'd be happy to. I'm thinking I'll probably want to get into therapy, but right now I have other things to think about."

"Myth or no myth, there is the social taboo," Jonathan pointed out.

"Yeah, but the social taboo only holds if the society knows. I'm not telling. I told Joe and Mom that if they tried to stop me, or if they opened their mouths on a twenty-five-year-old secret, lots of people would be hurt and no one would be helped. Mom and Father are getting along, I'm in love, and I'm marrying Kevin. Nobody else, other than you two and them two, can know that there's even a possibility that Kevin and I might be half siblings. So that's it on the social taboo."

"You know that I have to have a lot more than a social taboo to stand in my way of doing something," Delfina told her.

"If you really feel strongly about it, don't take the test," Jonathan suggested.

"Or I could take the test for you," Delfina offered, only half joking.

Veronique smiled, "Thanks, Del. I think I'm going to think long and hard about that one. But for now, I just wanted to know if you guys know of any reasons, other than the ones I've come up with, why two half-siblings who aren't going to have children shouldn't get married."

"Nope," Delfina said, without hesitating.

Jonathan just shook his head.

🍁　　　🍁　　　🍁

When the results came in, Kevin knew he could find Veronique at the beach. He walked slowly down to where she was sitting on a large yellow blanket. She could see him coming from the corner of her eye, and she knew by his pace that the results were positive: Joe was his father.

"Hi," he said, sitting down beside her.

"Hi," she kissed him on the cheek.

He sat, quietly watching the waves play gently around the jetty. The tide was low, and the water was calm.

"It was positive." She did not ask a question.

He nodded.

"I've been thinking about this for two weeks," she told him quietly. "I thought about cheating on the test, about all the worst things people could say if they knew, about everything. Kevin, you know what? I'd prefer not to know. We're not having biological children, ever. We both know that. The religious argument doesn't hold any weight with me. From what you've been saying, that doesn't seem to hold much weight for you either these days."

He nodded in agreement. His faith had been shattered in the wake of his accusations and the retaliation of the Church that had raised him.

"You know, it's weird. When Luca and I were fooling around, right here on this beach, I felt so...well, so reckless. I don't feel reckless about this, or about you. I'm not in this simply and solely for the thrill. I feel solid. This is right. It's the right thing to do."

He noticed that her voice sounded different, and he said so.

They sat together in silence for a while. Then she said, "Well, the only argument left is the incest one that we've heard at all those Survivors meetings. That's the 'power over' idea where one person is stronger and takes advantage of the weaker one. That's not happening here. We would have met with or without the Joe connection. I'm sure of it. If Joe hadn't said anything, we wouldn't be having this conversation today."

Kevin was quiet, listening to her.

She turned to face him, arms wrapped around her knees. "I thought seriously of having Del take the test for me, but I couldn't lie to you that way. I'm begging you now. Don't ask me to take that test. Our possible biological connection is a fluke. It's also something that no one has to know, not even us. If you're willing to live without knowing, just being with me, let's drop this. After everything else the Church has taken away from you, don't let its beliefs take this away from you, or from me." She got up. "Just think about it. Tell me later. Take as much time as you need."

She kissed the top of his head, and he took her hand.

"All I want is to spend the rest of my life making you happy. That's what'll make me happy. Forget the test."

He pulled her down onto the yellow blanket and held her close. They stayed wrapped in that blanket watching the sun go down. Then, under the stars, they made love on the deserted beach. When they were exhausted, they talked about their wedding plans.

❦   ❦   ❦

Veronique wanted a fall foliage wedding, but Kevin convinced her to wait until New Year's Eve 1999. Irene and Joe took Veronique at her word that she would marry Kevin with or without anyone's blessing. One afternoon, Irene tentatively broached the subject of the DNA test.

"Ronnie, did you ever get any information about Kevin and you, with…Joe?"

"I didn't get back a positive match," Veronique told her mother truthfully. "Has Joe finally agreed to do the mass, or do we get married at Town Hall?"

"Oh, no. He's doing it," Irene replied. Veronique skillfully redirected her mother's attention to the myriad of wedding plans left to be done.

❦   ❦   ❦

A day earlier, Irene had a frank talk with Joe.

"Look. If for no other reason, you should do the ceremony as a good Christian. Let Kevin's battle with the Church authorities be the Church's battle, not your personal battle. I remember a time when you told me that you kept your world in order so that you could offer solace and comfort to those whose lives were in chaos. Remember that? Remember that discipline you were so proud of? I think you called it a gift that you bring to the people you serve. Keep that discipline here. Don't fight a political battle with Ronnie's husband-to-be."

Joe sat, his eyes downcast, listening to her. Finally, he raised his eyes to meet hers. "I also remember telling you that there's another aspect of myself that I owe to the people I serve—an unflagging sense of faith in God and an unerring knowledge of what is right and wrong in the eyes of God.

"I remember that. I also remember you telling me that you're compelled to be a living example of goodness as defined by the Catholic faith." She paused. "It's obvious that you've had your ups and down on that score. But here you have a way to be a living example of forgiveness and compassion. Don't take sides. Just be a counselor and friend. Make up with Kevin. Jesus opened his arms to Judas. What Kevin did is hardly that type of betrayal. And *Kevin* didn't betray *you*."

As Irene spoke passionately about all the reasons he should do the service, Joe remembered the pact with God that he had made before he returned to

Kings Park after his retreat to Canada. He had vowed that he would be in Veronique's life as a significant factor. He remembered emerging from the cold chapel that day, returning to Kings Park and seeing Veronique for the first time. Joe realized that by embracing both Veronique and Kevin in this marriage, he could also become a more significant part of Kevin's life.

"Okay. You convinced me," he said simply.

Irene smiled gratefully.

❧   ❧   ❧

Both Kevin and Veronique had emphatically stated that they did not want a wedding shower, or bachelor/bachelorette parties, either individually or combined. Delfina and Jonathan wanted to do something special for their sister. With the help of their cousins and Kevin, they devised a type of roast for Veronique.

"It'll be the night before the wedding. Everyone'll be in town anyway for the big event," Jonathan said enthusiastically. "I can get the Landing Country Club and a really good DJ who can also emcee."

"I think I can convince some of her old teachers from the Academy to show up," Delfina smiled evilly.

"And her favorite guidance counselor from the high school, Juliet Stanton" Jonathan added, thinking to himself that Miss Stanton might actually be of interest to his older sister.

"There's also Dawn and Richie, I think," Delfina was making a list now.

"And you can't forget the Slope girls," Jonathan was playing off his sister now.

She raised her eyebrows and smiled. "Now *that* will make for an interesting roast."

And it did. When Veronique finally made her thank you speech at the end, she was giddy with enthusiasm, excited at seeing all the people she had met along her way, and looking forward to her wedding the next day.

"Let's dance. Practice for the big day. It's tomorrow! I can't believe it," said Veronique with a whoop. And she, Kevin and her family and friends danced until the wee hours of the morning.

❦   ❦   ❦

The next day, Veronique, alone in a white stretch limousine, took the long way from her house to St. Joseph's Church. She passed by the Old Dock Restaurant, and whispered a blessing to Marc. Then she circled around the entrance to Sunken Meadow State Park and blew a silent kiss to Luca. Next, the limousine headed up the road past the high school she had attended with Renee. She sent her friend a final blessing. Finally, it was on to the Church.

She stepped inside the back vestibule and readied herself on the red carpet that had been rolled out for her. Kevin and Veronique both wanted a very simple wedding, and so other than Joe who was officiating, the only ones in attendance at the altar were Dawn and Jonathan. Delfina had suggested Dawn to be the Maid of Honor. Veronique understood her sister's reticence at standing up for a wedding ceremony, any wedding ceremony, and agreed.

Half way up the center aisle, Irene and Pino waited for her. She had wanted both of them to walk her up the aisle, but she had also wanted to walk up by herself. This was the compromise she had reached. The wedding march started, and the leather-covered doors opened. She looked at the crowded church and was aware that all her relations were there. In the front, standing next to Joe, was Kevin. She smiled brilliantly as she looked at him.

As the cameras flashed, perhaps it was a trick of the light, but for a moment, she imagined that she saw an old man standing between and behind Joe and Kevin. But when she looked again, all she saw was the back entrance to the vestibule.

"Yes, everyone's here," she thought to herself, satisfied.

# CHAPTER 26

❀

Kevin asked Veronique if it would be okay to go to Fire Island for their honeymoon.

"Sure. I love it there, but it'll be New Years'. Pretty cold and desolate, don't you think?"

"If you don't mind, I'll make sure you're warm and happy. I'll tell you why when we get there."

After the wedding reception, they made the trip to Fire Island in the Land Rover that Veronique had bought Kevin as her wedding present to him. A private boat waited to take them over. The night was warm, and as the boat passed the midway point, its lights began to show mist on the calm water before the prow. The mist got thicker as they got nearer to the shore. As Kevin led Veronique to their honeymoon suite, the sparsely lit walkways of Fire Island itself were also shrouded in fog.

Kevin had a surprise for Veronique. It was a beautiful house, just steps from the water. By the time they reached it, the fog had gotten so thick that Veronique could not see the whole of it. When they got inside, however, she could see that it was completely furnished and a fire was roaring in the fireplace.

Veronique dropped her bags and ran around the house, exclaiming at the furnishings, the fireplace, the ready-to-use kitchen. "And from the sound of that fog horn, I'll bet the views will be spectacular."

"Thank you for marrying me." Kevin kissed her cheek as she looked out the window. Thick droplets of fog played around the deck lights. Even the deck railing was hidden from their view. "This is my wedding present to you. Our new home. Now let me tell you why I wanted to come here for our honeymoon."

They sat down on a plush rug in front of the fireplace.

"It was because of the fireplace, right?" She could not resist teasing him.

He smiled, but stayed on his thought. "I bought the house here after I realized that this would be the only place I could imagine our honeymoon to be. You see, this is where I fell in love with you, for real. The night of the explosion, I realized that you're the only thing I really ever wanted in my life. I could lose everything else. They could take it all away. As long as I had you, my life would be worthwhile.

She kissed him deeply, feeling her heart in a way she had never felt it before.

"And no one in the whole world knows we're here."

"No one?"

"Not your brother. Or sister. Or cousins." He punctuated each with a kiss.

"Now I have two things for you." She took a small book from her purse and read:

> "'Awake, O north wind; and come, thou south; blow upon my garden, that the spices thereof may flow out. Let my beloved come into his garden, and eat his pleasant fruits.'"

"That's the Song of Solomon," Kevin exclaimed, taking the book from her and reading aloud,

> "'I am come into my garden, my sister my spouse: I have eaten my honeycomb with my honey; I have drunk my wine with my milk...yea, drink abundantly, O beloved...'"

As he was reading, she took a CD from her purse and went to the stereo. Kevin stopped reading and Bob Dylan's voice came through the speakers.

> "'Oh, sister, when I come to lie in your arms/You should not treat me like a stranger...'"

Kevin looked at her in wonder.

"I've gotten to be a Dylan fan," she said, suddenly shy.

With Dylan singing *Oh, Sister* in the background, they undressed each other, slowly, thoughtfully in front of the fireplace.

Kevin had one final surprise for her. She turned to arrange her gown on a couch away from the fire. When she turned back, all he was wearing was one of his old Roman collars.

Seeing it, Veronique felt a surge of passion. She moved closer to him.

"Wow. I can't believe how turned on I am," she whispered in his ear.

He looked at her, surprised at how much she was feeling.

"What can I say?" she murmured, fingering the collar. "It must be in the blood…"

※   ※   ※

In the kitchen, volume low, the one telephone in the house was ringing.

0-595-28257-1